MORE ACCLAIM...

TITLES BY BRENDA JOYCE

Deadly Love
Deadly Pleasure
Deadly Affairs
Deadly Desire
Deadly Caress
The Chase
House of Dreams
The Third Heiress
The Rival
Splendor
The Finer Things
Captive
Beyond Scandal
The Game
After Innocence
Promise of the Rose
Secrets
Scandalous Love
The Fires of Paradise
Dark Fires
The Conqueror
The Darkest Heart
Lovers and Liars
Violent Fire
Firestorm
Innocent Fire

NOVELLAS BY BRENDA JOYCE

Perfect Secrets
Scandalous Weddings
Outlaw Love
Heart of the Home
A Gift of Joy

AVAILABLE FROM
ST. MARTIN'S PAPERBACKS

DEADLY PROMISE

BRENDA JOYCE

11-03
2074

St. Martin's Paperbacks

DEADLY PROMISE

ISBN: 0-312-98987-3

Printed in the United States of America

St. Martin's Paperbacks edition / November 2003

St. Martin's Paperbacks are published by St. Martin's Press, 175 Fifth Avenue, New York, NY 10010.

10 9 8 7 6 5 4 3 2 1

For my shining star—Adam.

CHAPTER ONE

FRANCESCA CAHILL MAY HAVE been born into society, in fact, she was an heiress of a very marriageable age, but recently she had become the city's most famous (and infamous) amateur sleuth. Having spent her entire life flouting both the spoken and unspoken rules of convention, being well-read, highly educated and an active reformer, she was already considered both unmarriageable and an eccentric. Her behavior of the past three months had not aided her flailing personal reputation. For she had helped the police commissioner, Rick Bragg, solve several ghastly crimes—even making the headlines of some of the city's most reputable dailies. All this while further scandalizing a good portion of society—not to mention her own family.

Her reputation was currently in shreds, not that she cared. However, it might very well take a stunning turn for the better. For Francesca had somehow become secretly engaged to one of the city's wealthiest and most notorious bachelors, Calder Hart. She still did not know whether to regret it or not. But if their engagement survived all that she had thus far done—and she winced thinking about it— a public announcement would take her from ugly duckling to swan.

But she seriously doubted Hart would even speak with her now—much less continue their engagement.

There was relief and there was regret.

"Francesca Cahill! You *disappeared* for an entire month! And I am dying to know why!" the former Connie Cahill, now Lady Montrose, cried. She had just barged into Francesca's bedroom.

Francesca cringed, but only inwardly, as she faced her always fashionably and terribly elegant older sister. It was ironic that much of the city thought of her as a hero, she mused. It wasn't true. She was, in fact, a coward, never mind the many dangerous and murdering hooks and crooks she had single-handedly faced and apprehended. She was a coward, because only a coward ran away from the man she was supposed to marry. She was a coward when it came to the darkly disturbing Calder Hart.

Connie faced her after closing the door to Francesca's beautifully appointed bedroom—a room she had had no say in decorating, as the decor had been chosen by her mother, Julia, and sister. Francesca hadn't cared then, just as she did not care now. Decor—and fashion, shopping, and teas— was hardly important to her. She forced a smile and hurried forward clad only in her corset and drawers and embraced her sister. "It's so nice to see you, too," she whispered, but she meant it. Connie was not just her sister; she was also her very best friend.

"Do not think to dissemble with me," Connie said, her hands on her slim hips. She was clad in a gorgeous dark blue evening gown, with sapphires around her throat and wrists, atop the white sateen gloves that ended at her elbows. "I know why you disappeared!" Her blue eyes flashed.

Francesca tensed. Connie could not know. Before leaving town to visit an old and ailing and very fictitious school chum, she had left Hart a brief note, one that hardly explained anything but did request that their engagement remain a private affair until she returned to New York City. Wisely, Francesca hadn't left a forwarding address; she had left the city to think about her life and her impulsive decision to accept Hart's proposal. "What is it that you think you know?"

Connie sighed then. "There is no Elizabeth Jane Seymour, Fran. I would recall a best friend by that name! You chose to leave the city because you could no longer handle the little predicament you have found yourself to be in." Connie, who was a platinum blonde generally considered to be a great beauty, eyed Francesca with some smug satisfaction now.

Francesca sighed in return. She hated deceiving anyone, much less her sister. And Connie was right. Marriage had never been a part of her agenda! What *was* she doing? Her agenda had been to become a journalist, to expose the world's ills to society, so those with means could engender badly needed reforms and humanitarian aid. That agenda had included a higher education at a renowned women's institution, Barnard College. However, her agenda—and her life—had begun to unravel some time ago: last January, to be exact. She had fallen in love while solving a terrible crime, and nothing had been—or would ever be—the same again.

And to make matters worse, it hadn't been Calder Hart whom she had fallen in love with.

Perhaps Connie hadn't learned about her engagement— which meant that neither had her mother. And it was Julia Van Wyck Cahill's dearest desire to see Francesca suitably wed—immediately, before she solved another crime and garnered another headline. Julia was a very powerful woman who always got her way. "Yes, I found the heat too much to bear," she said warily.

Connie met her gaze. "The heat? You sound like that little hoodlum you are so fond of. Joel Kennedy."

"I suppose his ways are rubbing off on me," Francesca murmured, as she had come to rely on the eleven-year-old heavily in her sleuthing. He knew the city's worst wards intimately. He was her guide, and more.

"Oh, Fran. They will both be at the Wainscot ball tonight." Connie's gaze moved to the bed behind Francesca, where a vivid and dark red ball gown lay. "Mama said you would attend. And I see you are wearing the red." A knowing look came to her eyes and she smiled.

"It's not what you think!" Francesca cried. Both Rick Bragg, the city's police commissioner, and his notorious and wealthy half brother, Calder Hart, would be at the Wainscot ball tonight. Out of the frying pan and into the fire, she thought. Oh, God, what should she do? Was she doing the right thing? And how could one marry a man one didn't love—even if that man's mere look could enflame her entire body? And could two half brothers be more unalike—and more bitterly jealous of each other? If only they weren't such rivals.

"Then tell me what to think," Connie said, moving to Francesca and placing her arm around her. Both sisters were considered almost as identical as twins, although Francesca's hair was the color of rich honey and her skin was tinged with tones of peach and gold. Francesca knew that was not true. Her sister was beautiful, while she, Francesca, was on the ordinary side of pretty. Connie always stood out in a crowd, but Francesca had been a wallflower (and a bookworm) for most of her life.

Until recently.

Francesca sat down beside her and they clasped hands. "I have been worried about me, too," she said softly.

"Oh, Fran, didn't a month away clear your head?"

"Yes . . . and no," Francesca whispered.

"You are still torn between Bragg and Hart?" Connie wasn't smiling now. She was concerned.

Francesca nodded, wishing she knew what to do—then slowly pulled a chain out of her bodice. On the end dangled a huge pear-shaped diamond ring, one worth quite the fortune. Her heart beat harder as she dangled the huge engagement ring.

Connie's eyes widened. "Oh my."

"Yes, oh my."

Connie blinked and met Fran's gaze. "You are engaged?"

"We were. Briefly. Secretly," she added. "I have no idea if we still are—and if we aren't, why, then it is for the best. Marriage is not for me and we both know it." But her words rang false and hollow.

Connie shot to her feet. "What nonsense is this? You fool! To run away and sabotage the best thing that could happen to you! I pray you are wrong and that you haven't single-handedly destroyed this opportunity, Fran."

Francesca swallowed. A part of her desperately wished that she had not run away—and that she had not sabotaged her secret engagement, too. "Can I ride over to the ball with you and Neil? I am really not in the mood for Mama's lectures tonight."

Connie nodded. "Of course." But she was staring intently now. "Still, you have been wearing his ring around your neck. Did you take it off even once?" She did not wait for Francesca to answer. "I daresay you did not. And you are wearing the dress. The dress he likes. I do think I am underestimating you."

"I am a fool, Connie, to think I am special, because every single woman he has had has thought the exact same thing!" Francesca cried. And it was the truth.

Connie gripped her shoulders. "But you *are* special! Good God, you are the bravest and most clever—and most stubborn—woman I know. You have spent your entire life since you were a child defending the rights of the poor and the helpless and fighting for those rights! You attend college, Fran, *college*; how many women do that? And need I add that you have become the city's most famous sleuth in the past three months? You have made the *news,* Fran. You have brought terrible criminals to justice."

Francesca blinked. "Well, when you say it that way, I do seem rather eccentric."

"No, not eccentric, original and brave and beautiful and *special!*" Connie cried.

Francesca hugged her hard. "You are the best sister a girl could ever have," she whispered.

"I wish you could see yourself the way that the rest of the world does—the way that I do."

Francesca smiled. "I'd better dress. I am quite late."

"Yes, you *are* late." Connie smiled back as warmly. "Do you need help? Should I call Bette?"

"I'm fine," Francesca said, turning to gather up the provocative red dress. But it was a lie. She wasn't fine.

She was terrified.

Francesca handed off her wrap. She was wearing the daring red, with black gloves that ended past her elbows, and she was clutching a ruby red beaded reticule—in which she carried the ring. Her hair had been tonged and swept up, and Connie had insisted she wear a delicate diamond necklace and small pearl-and-diamond earbobs. As Connie handed off her sable stole, Francesca glanced from the front hall into a large reception room with pale marble floors, a huge crystal chandelier, and white plaster walls. As they were very late, a crowd had gathered already, the ladies in glittering jewels and sleeveless silks and taffetas and chiffons, the men in black tuxedos. White-coated waiters were passing trays containing flutes of champagne. A band was playing in the adjoining ballroom. Francesca saw her brother, Evan, standing beside the flamboyantly beautiful countess, Bartolla Benevente, and then saw Rick Bragg.

Her heart skidded to a stop.

But he had already seen her, even from this distance, and he was staring, his eyes wide with surprise. He took a step toward her and Francesca tensed, now seeing the beautiful and petite woman at his side. Leigh Anne was tiny, her skin porcelain, her eyes emerald green, her hair raven black. She looked like a perfect little doll. Francesca's heart sank.

Bragg walked toward Francesca, his strides lengthening, leaving his wife standing there with a group of people Francesca did not know.

"You had better come to your senses and soon, Fran," Connie whispered. "I have seen them out and about constantly since you were gone. She is on his arm every time I see him at a function. She is well liked. She has joined several organizations, including the Ladies Club of Fifty and the Committee of Fifteen," Connie said, referring to several political organizations dedicated to the good-government reform movement. "And the other day, she invited me to a luncheon."

Francesca froze. For a moment, it was impossible to breathe. Leigh Anne was taking up reform? It hardly seemed fair! "You declined."

Connie was grim. "I accepted. The luncheon is tomorrow. The agenda is public education. I do believe the merits of fund-raising for more schools will be discussed."

Public education in the city was a disaster. Thousands of children did not attend school because there were simply not enough schools and not enough teachers. The city's recently elected mayor, Seth Low, had been elected on a very progressive platform, which included good government—government to ultimately benefit the people. And that included education.

As Connie had said, Francesca had been a reformer since she was a child, first selling cookies to raise money for orphans. She belonged to six societies, including the Citizen's Union Ladies Club, and was active in them all. Education for everyone was at the top of her agenda—and Connie knew that. Now, Francesca was torn between anger and admiration for a woman she so wanted to despise. Leigh Anne was beyond beautiful—but surely she was not a reformer at heart. Surely it was a ploy to capture Rick Bragg's heart.

"Why don't you join me?" Connie asked. "She has invited thirty of the city's wealthiest women. She probably intends to ask each and every one of us for a handsome donation. These are ladies you should know, Fran."

Sourly Francesca said, "Private money cannot fix the public education system in this city." But Connie was right. She should go and meet these women, perhaps enlisting some of them to her causes. She would have to attend Leigh Anne's luncheon no matter how she dreaded doing so.

"You are a mule, Fran, an utter mule, at times like these." Connie almost stomped her foot. She watched Bragg approach, as did Francesca.

He was so handsome. He had the tawny complexion and sun-streaked hair that many of the Bragg men were renowned for. His eyes were topaz, his cheekbones very high, and he was broad-shouldered and small of hip. Francesca wished that things could be different somehow. Then she caught herself and closed her eyes.

Wishing for the impossible was frivolous and a waste of time. She had come to grips with the ugly reality of his being unhappily married some time ago.

"Neil and I will mingle. Good luck, Fran," Connie whispered, then sailed off on her husband's arm.

Fran's eyes flew open and she watched Bragg take the last few steps to her side. He seemed incredibly purposeful now. He paused, and she tried to smile and failed.

"Are you all right?"

Her heart tightened. His first concern would always be her welfare. "Yes, I am fine. And you?" Her gaze crept past him and to Leigh Anne, who hadn't moved and who watched them very carefully now.

He shrugged. Then, "You left town without a word. You've been gone for four weeks. I heard something about an ailing friend. Francesca?" His gaze was serious and intent.

She swallowed and began to flush. "I had to get away. There was no ailing friend."

"I see." His jaw tightened and his golden eyes darkened. A silence reigned.

Francesca did not know what to say.

"I chased you away," he said darkly. "I am so sorry, Francesca."

"Do not blame yourself. I chose to leave," she said, omitting the real reason she had run away. She glanced again at Leigh Anne. In spite of her neutral expression, she was radiant and aglow. "How is your wife?" And after all of this time, it was still hard to utter those two terrible words that had ruined her life—*your wife.*

He stiffened visibly. "Nothing has changed," he ground out with a flash of anger. "Our agreement to divorce in six months remains."

Francesca smiled tightly, felt her heart break a little, and knew it would not be. Leigh Anne had left Bragg four years ago and had spent all of the ensuing time in Europe. Recently she had returned to reclaim her place at his side. Francesca felt certain that Leigh Anne would win her battle over their marriage. Bragg was too angry at his wife every time the subject even came up for him not to harbor intensely passionate feelings about her.

Francesca hadn't known he was married when they had first met—when she had fallen head over heels in love with him at first sight.

He said suddenly, lowering his voice, "I have missed you."

Francesca began to smile, because he was her best friend and she had missed him, too—and then she saw Calder Hart.

Her smile vanished; her heart lurched; her gaze slammed to a halt. He stood across the room with a group of five others, and a buxom blonde was hanging on to his arm. His back was toward her.

In fact, he was so engrossed with the blonde and his friends that he hadn't even noticed her—and did not look her way even once.

She began to tremble, unable to control it, as if the temperature in the room had violently dropped. *He hadn't looked at her even once—and she was wearing the eye-*

catching red dress. She was ill. He no longer liked her; he no longer found her at all interesting or alluring; he had a new paramour—he no longer wished to marry her.

"What is it?" Bragg asked sharply, but she could not tear her stare from Hart and the voluptuous blonde. Bragg shifted and grimaced. "He has seduced you after all, hasn't he?" he asked bitterly.

For one more moment, Francesca could not speak. "No. Of course not," she said, and it was the truth. No one had been nobler than the city's worst womanizer. In fact, he had made it clear he would not take her to bed until their wedding night, no matter how she wished otherwise.

But that night would never happen now. She was certain of it.

"I meant emotionally," Bragg said tersely. "You are upset. God!"

She faced him, forcing a sickly smile. "I'm not upset," she lied. The ring in her clutch now burned her hand, impossibly, through the velvet and beads. "I'm fine." She swallowed hard and wondered if she could retch if she went to the ladies' room. "Your wife is now standing alone."

He turned and saw that Leigh Anne stood apart from the rest of the crowd, the group she had been with having dispersed. She remained small and angelic—the most beautiful woman in the room. Then he faced Francesca again. "I am worried about you. First this disappearance, and now your reaction to Hart."

"You have no cause to worry about me," she said, her gaze having found Hart again of its own volition. He was nodding at something someone had said. The blonde, who was perhaps thirty, was laughing prettily—coyly. Hart had not looked Francesca's way even once.

He hadn't noticed her.

Because he didn't care. Not at all. It was over, then.

But that was what she wanted—wasn't it?

Bragg gripped her gloved wrist. "I will always worry about you," he said.

She faced him swiftly. "I am fine. Really."

"You are too pale. Except for those crimson patches on your cheeks. Are you feverish?"

She wondered if he was right, if extreme anxiety had caused her to become truly ill. "I think I will not stay long," she whispered, and suddenly she felt close to tears. Because Connie was right.

She had worn the red dress because Calder Hart liked it.

And she hadn't removed his ring from the chain around her neck in an entire month, not even once.

"I think that's a good idea," Bragg said. He glanced grimly at Hart, then said, "That is Mrs. Davies, and I have seen them together several times recently."

Now she would truly retch. He had promised her fidelity. But then, if they were no longer engaged, the promise did not count. "She is quite alluring."

"She's a widow," Bragg said sharply. "She and Hart are of the same nature."

Francesca felt herself bristle. "So you know her?"

"She has a reputation."

She should not defend him. Not now, not ever again. "He may be notorious, Bragg, but he has always been a perfect gentleman with me," she said. And that was the truth—until the moment they had become engaged.

Bragg was exasperated. "You adore defending him!"

"Hardly," she said, feeling waspish as well as ill.

"I have to go," he said abruptly. But he made no move to return to his wife. "When can we speak? Truly? It's been too long, Francesca," he said.

She softened but kept Hart in the line of vision from the corner of her eye. "Tomorrow?"

"I would like that," he said. He nodded and hesitated, then picked up her gloved hand. "Do not tax yourself tonight—and not over him." He kissed her hand, surprising her, and turned away.

Francesca tore her gaze from Hart, who remained oblivious to her presence in the room, somehow, and watched Bragg join Leigh Anne. The stunning, petite brunette smiled up at him, placing her small hand on his arm, and Francesca could feel how worried she was, even if her expression remained calm and composed. Then Francesca took another glance at Hart—who now had his back completely to her—and she could stand it no more. She fled through the closest door and into the nearest hallway.

There she collapsed against a plain white wall, refusing to cry but aware of the extent of how crushed she was. Servants moved past her—the hall led to the kitchens. The clatter of pots and pans loud in the background, Francesca had one desire now; she had to escape the ball—and Hart. She had to go home.

It was really over.

She hugged herself, turning from the wall, knowing that somehow she must regroup if she was to exit the party in a decorous manner.

"Did you really think to run away from me?"

She froze as his soft drawl washed seductively over the nape of her neck, and then her heart thundered with alarm and fear. Slowly she turned to face him.

She had forgotten how much he overwhelmed her. Francesca inhaled sharply as their gazes clashed and locked. He was darkly, disturbingly handsome, but not in any classical way. His undeniably virile good looks came from how dangerously seductive he was. It had nothing to do with his eyes, navy flecked with brown and gold, or his strong, straight nose, or his dark skin and midnight hair, or the muscular body that was hidden by his clothes. It had everything to do with the smoking sensuality his entire being exuded, that and the aura of power he forever wore.

He had been born a bastard on the Lower East Side. His mother, once a whore, had died when he was a small child. Now Hart was one of the city's wealthiest and most successful businessmen, a world-renowned collector of art, a man who had risen from the ashes of nothing to acquire almost everything.

He was smiling at her. But it was a fixed smile that did not reach his cool eyes.

Francesca inhaled again. He stood mere inches from her and she remembered every moment she had spent in his powerful arms. More memories assailed her, rapidly, one after another. She recalled the first time she had ever glimpsed him, in Rick Bragg's office, a darkly disturbing and enigmatic figure; his handing her a very generous donation for one of her societies in the restaurant of the Plaza, where he had been briefly pursuing her sister; her first sip of fine Scotch whiskey, shared with him. She had been a fool to run away, she thought instantly. There was something about this man that she could not quite put her finger on—something different, unique. And his presence—as always, powerful and overwhelming—had turned her brain to useless mush and her body to soft putty. But she owed him an explanation and an apology—if he would even listen.

"And when were you going to tell me that you had come back?" he asked darkly.

She opened her mouth to tell him that she had had no choice but to succor an old friend, that she hadn't run away, that she had returned that day—and then she stopped. She had only lied to him once, in that stupid note, and she would never do so again. "I knew you'd be here tonight. I'm sorry," she added helplessly, her tone sounding tremulous to her own ears.

If only she could breathe. If only she could think. If only she could recall why she had decided to flee the city for her heart, her soul, her life.

Their gazes held. He said finally, grimly, "You provoke me as no woman ever has."

Foolishly she whispered, "I don't mean to."

For one more moment they stared. And then he seized her wrist and held up her left hand. They both stared at her fourth finger now, Francesca as if hypnotized. No ring adorned it, neither on top of the glove nor beneath it.

Francesca wanted to tug her gloved hand free, but her muscles had lost their ability to function. She knew that she had to explain the fact that she did not wear his ring and the reason she had really left town. Now was the perfect and appropriate time. But the blood was rushing in her veins, pounding in her ears, causing her to become exceedingly dim of wit. *What should she do?*

"So this is your decision," he said tersely.

Francesca gasped in real surprise, their gazes clashing, hers startled, his hot. She suddenly realized what he was assuming—that she was ending their engagement—but he was wrong. The notion had been debated in these past four weeks, of course, but she hated that very idea. She simply did not know what to do—but before she could protest, he tilted up her chin. "And when were you going to tell me? Or did you think to run away and hide like a frightened child?" He demanded. "You cannot hide from me. Did you enjoy your stay at the Monument Inn, darling?"

She gasped, stunned. "How did you know where I was?"

His jaw flexed hard. "I made it my business to know. Money buys anything, Francesca."

"No," she managed, trembling. "It doesn't buy loyalty—it doesn't buy love." Only one person had known where she was going—her friend Sarah Channing. He had clearly forced the information from her.

He made a derisive sound. "Like hell it doesn't."

She found it hard to breathe; he seemed trembling and breathless as well. "Hart, this isn't what you are thinking."

"No?" He was incredulous. "Do tell me what I am thinking, Francesca, please do! And it's Calder, damn it."

His anger always unnerved her. And when she was nervous, she always called him Hart. She took a deep breath for composure and even courage. "First of all, what I did was perhaps thoughtless, but I didn't mean to hurt you," she began worriedly, trying to think of what to say and how precisely to say it.

"Hurt me?" His dark brows slashed upwards again. He laughed. "You hardly hurt me, Francesca. Do you really think my feelings so fragile?"

Of course she hadn't hurt him. The man was an island

unto himself—he needed no one. She stiffened. "I am sorry I *inconvenienced* you, then."

His eyes darkened. "You did not inconvenience me, either," he said grimly. "You are your own woman, an exceedingly independent one, and if you wish to travel, it is your right." Suddenly he gripped her left wrist and held her gloved hand between them. *"When were you going to tell me?"*

He did not give her a chance to speak. "I thought we had more than a passing attraction to one another, Francesca, no, I know we have more than that. We are friends, or have you forgotten? Has fear—has Rick—so addled your brain that you have forgotten why we are so fond of one another in the first place? That we began as friends and that, no matter what does happen, we shall end as friends?"

And she felt despair. "We are friends," she whispered, meaning it. "I could not bear to ever lose your friendship, Calder. Do not talk of endings!"

He started, his expression changing, almost appearing taken aback.

She swallowed and tried to find the right words. "I went away to think. It's been so hard. Things are moving so quickly. I—" She faltered.

"You what?" he asked, not letting her off the hook.

"Marriage is forever. I do not want to make a terrible mistake."

"And marrying me would be a terrible mistake?" he asked softly.

"I did not say that!" she cried. "Do not dare put words in my mouth!"

"Then what are you saying, my dear? And do not become an incoherent lackwit now!" His gaze hardened.

But she was. Her mind spun. She simply could not give up this man, and she knew instinctively that if she backed off from the engagement, she would. If she rejected him, how could they remain friends—even if she wanted to? She met his dark, smoldering gaze and smiled a little, a smile he did not return. He was frighteningly intense now.

She wrung her hands. "You have made this so very complicated by wishing to marry me. A part of me wishes we could go back to the way things were a month ago!"

"A month ago Rick's wife hadn't returned and you were denying all the passion you feel for me. Poor Francesca." He was only half-mocking. "Torn between tawdry lust and true love."

She trembled. "That isn't fair," she tried.

"Life is rarely fair. And do you deny it is Rick that you love? Do you? I am the man you merely wish to bed." He stared, waiting for her response, his eyes as hard as obsidian.

He was wrong—in a way. Rick Bragg was no longer attainable, and yes, she had fallen in love with Bragg and he would have made the perfect husband, but so much had happened since then. And while she could admit how much she wanted to share Calder Hart's bed, their being friends made it so much more than lust. But did that mean they should really marry? He had complicated their good friendship by his proposal—and she had accepted so very hastily, without any real reflection. But a month of reflection hadn't solved anything, not really—she was scared to lose Calder Hart, but she wished the speeding locomotive she had leapt aboard would simply slow down. "I don't deny the passion I feel." And the frustration made her reckless. "We would not be in this dilemma if you had done the deed and taken me to your bed!"

He made a sound, one of sudden amusement, perhaps, and suddenly stroked her cheek. "The only way you will ever get me in bed is on our wedding night. How many times do I have to make myself clear? You I will not ruin."

"For a notorious womanizer, one the world thinks to have not one shred of morality, you do know how to frustratingly play the saint."

"I would never even try to play the saint, my dear."

She shuddered. "Everyone claims I am stubborn. But you are truly the stubborn one. And if you want the truth,

I still cannot comprehend why you really want to marry . . . me."

"Why are we rehashing that subject? You know you are my one and only friend, and that seems to me the perfect basis for our marriage. And darling, I am hardly the stubborn one in this pair. You have decided that you will love my esteemed half brother until the end of time, never mind that his little vixen of a wife is in his home and in his bed. And because of that damnable fantasy—a script you have written for an audience of one—you would ruin what could truly be a very enjoyable union. We suit, Francesca, very well, and neither one of us would ever become old, bored, or staid in the other's company." He was grim. "You may keep the ring. Cash it in. Donate the money to your charities. Call it a farewell from me."

Tears came, making it hard to see. He was the most generous man she had ever met. "No."

"What?" He started.

"I never said I am ending our engagement."

He was a master at controlling his emotion; his face did not change, but she saw the spark of surprise alight in his eyes.

She swallowed hard. "In fact, the ring is in my purse, and I wore it on a chain against my bosom the entire time I was away. I truly needed some time away—without pursuit—without pressure—from anyone." In truth, Hart had been so honorable with her it had become frustrating, but his determination that she would one day be his wife, and Bragg's fervent belief that his half-brother was only using her, had become pressure she could not bear.

He seized her and pulled her right into his arms. "So nothing has changed?" he asked softly.

Her mind began to spin into jumbled thoughts, the effect of being in his arms, her bosom against his impossibly hard chest.

"Do not bother to reply," he murmured, his tone as seductive as the drape of silk. "If this is a game you are playing, you are adept, Francesca," he breathed. "As adept as a courtesan tease. Frankly, I have had enough."

She looked into a pair of smoldering eyes, truly alarmed. "I am not trying to tease. You know I do not play games. I am genuinely afraid." She did not add, "of you."

But he knew. "How many times do I have to tell you that I will never hurt you? I intend to take care of you, Francesca," he murmured. "I intend to show you the finer things in life . . . and some of the more controversial, the shocking, and the prurient, as well."

She stilled, except for her heart, which beat like mad, firing her blood.

His hands slid from her shoulders down her nearly bare back, large, warm, strong. He held her firmly but did not pull her closer. "My clever little sleuth," he whispered, "what am I to do with you?"

She opened her mouth to tell him that she was quite capable of taking care of herself, but all speech was lost, finally, and not just because of his sensuous touch—but because he smiled at her and it reached his eyes.

He wasn't angry with her. Not anymore.

Her heart turned over hard. "Kiss me?" she suggested, her gaze moving to his firm, mobile mouth. She could taste his lips just from the sheer memory of them.

"I am thinking about it," he said, with some humor. "It has been a very long month."

She leaned against him, her hands finding the lapels of his tuxedo. Instantly, sensation burned a heated course through her entire body. "Calder . . ."

He leaned closer. "It's Calder, now, is it? What am I going to do with you?" His mouth brushed hers. "Perhaps I need to marry you sooner rather than later," he said, brushing her lips lightly again. "Never run from me, Francesca. Promise me," he demanded then, his mouth hovering against her lips.

She really didn't hear. His lips caused a terrible pressure to quickly build, both between her thighs and in the tips of her breasts. She tried to move closer and was stunned by the hard, insistent pressure of his arousal. Abruptly, his hands tightened. "Promise," he demanded again.

"I promise," she muttered, not quite sure what she was promising.

Hart smiled and claimed her mouth.

Francesca was always surprised by his consummate kisses, his skilled touch. He knew how to play with her lips, her tongue; he knew how to stroke and fondle her body and arouse her to weeping desire. He covered her mouth, opened it, using his tongue to caress the corners, and as she moved more deeply into his arms—against the ridge of quivering male muscle against her hip—his mouth moved to a spot between her jaw and the lobe of her ear. His tongue wreaked havoc there. She clung, her knees seeming to vanish into thin air. She ran her fingers through the short hair at his nape, over his strong neck, down his shoulder blades, his back. His wicked mouth moved down her throat, causing her to moan and gasp, causing her nipples to harden and hurt. His hands splayed low on the sides of her hips— and the thin layer of silk between his fingertips and the flesh just inches from her groin ignited. She whimpered, trying to pull him even closer, into her, as he found her mouth with his, as their tongues sparred and their bodies rocked. Her back became wedged between him and the wall. His thighs, his chest, all rock-hard, immobilized her there.

Suddenly he broke the kiss, turning his cheek to the wall. Francesca cried out in protest, dizzy and dazed. Hart's heavy breathing filled the hall.

And Francesca's first coherent thought was that she had managed to thoroughly arouse this man, a master of self-control. He lifted his head and looked at her, and their gazes locked.

Francesca saw the smoking ash-gray desire first, but beyond that, there was keen intelligence and dark, deep reflection. She fought for coherent thought—some plot was being hatched there in his mind—she could feel his clever wheels turning.

He tilted her face upwards so that their eyes met. "I *have* had enough, Francesca," he said softly, warningly.

Her eyes widened with surprise. And sanity had returned. Pots and pans were clanging in the background,
servants were actually passing them by, and their conversation in the kitchens, punctuated with song, could be
clearly heard. They had just made a terrible public display
and servants loved to gossip. But more importantly, what,
exactly, did Hart mean?

"Come with me, Francesca," he said flatly, taking her
hand.

"What?" She inhaled, trying to still her trembling, trying
to think.

He gave her a long, dark look. "I have had enough of
our silly, sophomoric game. Haven't you?"

She did not understand. She was afraid to understand.
But he was already guiding her down the hall and toward
the door that led into the front hall, his hold uncompro-
mising, his strides hard and long.

It crossed her dazed mind that she must be extremely
disheveled. Had her hair come down? She touched it and
was relieved to find her coiffure in place. As she ran after
him, she glanced down, but her dress seemed to be, mirac-
ulously, in order and where it belonged. "Calder, perhaps I
should repair to the ladies' room."

He gripped her hand more tightly, quite dragging her,
through the fatal doorway. "It is time to end this nonsense."

She began to understand as he pulled her swiftly through
the crowd, and her heart leaped with excitement, over-
coming any lingering fear, any remnants of dread. He was
right. This was nonsense. She must make up her mind and
go through with the marriage, and if it did not work out,
well, so be it! She was hardly a romantic fool, or she had
never been one until recently. She was strong—she had
already proven that. If she married him and she could remain aloof, guarding her heart with care, then he would not
be able to ever hurt her and they would do very well indeed.

Ladies and gentlemen were stepping back to let them

pass. Hart seemed to have become a man with a mission, and no one dared stand in his way. Francesca saw her brother and the countess as she passed, but they were a blur. She saw Mrs. Davies, who appeared annoyed and far less of a blur. She reminded herself to ask him about that. Then she saw her parents.

Julia Van Wyck Cahill was a stunning blonde who had clearly passed her striking looks on to her daughters. She did a double take when she saw Francesca with Hart, and then she began to smile. Julia adored Hart and had been scheming for some time to match him up with her younger daughter.

Andrew Cahill had made his fortune in Chicago in meat-packing. He was short and stout, with a characteristic look of benevolence upon his whiskered cheeks. He also took a second look upon seeing Francesca towed along by Calder Hart, but then began to turn darkly red. Unlike his wife, he was not impressed by Hart's accomplishments and knew of his reputation as a ruthless womanizer.

Hart paused, whipping an empty flute from a passing tray. He tapped his nail upon it. "Ladies and gentlemen. Ladies and gentlemen, may I have your attention please?"

The conversation dimmed and died in the hall. Everyone turned their way.

Francesca now stood by his side, feeling faint, thinking, *This is it, oh, dear God*, but given the fatal attraction she felt for this man, that and his charisma, there was simply no other choice.

"Miss Cahill has done me the great honor of agreeing to become my wife," he announced loudly to the crowd gathered around them. "But in fact, the honor is all mine."

There was one brief moment of surprised silence, and then the applause began—followed by some male shouts of congratulations and a few hurrahs.

Francesca trembled. She blinked and saw Julia beaming in delight, then glimpsed Mrs. Davies, looking shocked. She glanced around and saw that every single lady in the room wished to throw a dagger in her heart.

Hart chuckled, murmuring, "Yes, if looks could kill, you would be dead now, my darling," and he took Francesca's purse from her, extracting the ring. Francesca forgot all about the crowd. Everyone in the room seemed to vanish into thin air, every voice disappeared, and she was alone with Calder Hart. Their eyes met. His dark gaze was beyond tender. So much so that it was a blow to her heart. Francesca could not look away. What did that oddly gentle look mean? That, coupled with his soft smile, was enough to win any woman's heart, much less hers.

"Tonight calls for champagne," he said softly. "A celebration, the two of us, alone."

She inhaled, knowing what being alone with him would mean. He smiled and slid the eight-carat diamond onto her gloved finger. Francesca stared down at it, feeling blinded, but whether by the dazzling diamond or the magical moment, she did not know. Her heart was trying to tell her something, and she felt a tear leaking down her cheek.

"I won't hurt you," he said softly in her ear, and he kissed her cheek.

Francesca was somewhat blinded now as she looked up and met his gaze. "Is that a promise?"

"It is far more. It is a vow," he said. Then he turned her around and held up her hand.

The ladies exclaimed loudly. There were gasps of awe and admiration, male cheers, more hurrahs. Someone exclaimed at Hart that he had finally gone and done it. Hart agreed, and the men laughed. Francesca felt even more faint as the feeling in her breast intensified. It was as if a huge balloon were inflating inside of her chest. And she knew she could not manage it. Her knees began to give way.

He knew and put his arm around her, holding her up. "Do you need a glass of water?" he asked with concern.

She decided she would not faint, as she had never done so before, and certainly not upon the announcement of her engagement. And as she murmured, "No, I am fine," she saw her parents approaching.

Julia was clapping her hands in excitement and delight.

Francesca's father, however, was clearly furious.

"Are you certain you are fine?" Hart asked, a whisper in her ear, solicitous and concerned.

Francesca was about to affirm that she was when she saw Rick Bragg.

He was as pale as a ghost. He stared, disbelieving and incredulous.

She started forward instantly, forgetting about Hart. *She had to explain.*

Hart gripped her hand, yanking her back. "I'll be damned if I let you chase after him now! When we have just announced our engagement!" he said low and darkly.

He was right—he was also wrong. Francesca was miserable as she watched Bragg mutter something to his wife, turn on his heel, and stride with stiff, set shoulders from the reception room. He was clearly leaving the ball. And Francesca desperately needed to speak with him now. He must not accuse her of treachery; after all, his wife had returned to his life and, as Hart had said, even to his bed.

Francesca closed her eyes, anguished. Then she opened them and saw Leigh Anne staring at them—at her. Their gazes met. She seemed as surprised as everyone else, but if she was pleased, she hid it well. Then Leigh Anne hurried after Bragg, who was waiting for her at the front door.

"Mr. Cahill, sir," Hart was saying.

Francesca was pulled into her mother's embrace. "My darling girl, this is a dream come true!" Julia cried. "I am so happy for you!"

"Thank you, Mama," Francesca managed, glancing at Hart and her father. They were having a terse exchange, and she gathered Hart was to present himself the next day to discuss the matter of an engagement. Then she caught her sister's eye.

Connie grinned at her widely, like a happy and well-fed Cheshire cat.

Francesca gave in and smiled back. She was engaged to the man who had been the city's most eligible bachelor, but the magic of the moment had vanished, leaving something sordid and worrisome in its place. Then she saw young Joel Kennedy stepping past the departing Braggs into the front hall.

Her eyes widened in surprise. Joel was far more than a downtown street urchin—until recently he had been a cut-purse and a thief, or rather, he had resorted to such desperate measures to aid in the support of his fatherless family. He was a small boy with jet-black hair in an ill-fitting and shabby wool coat, a felt cap atop his head. Patches were on the knees of his corduroy pants. His hands were jammed in his pockets. He looked terribly uncomfortable and out of place. And when their gazes met, he signaled at her urgently, mouthing something at her. She thought it might be, *Trouble,* and her body stiffened with alarm and keen interest.

She had recently hired him as an assistant, and now she wondered if he had a new case.

"Kennedy?" Hart intoned with mild surprise. Then he said wryly, "Well, I suppose I should have anticipated this moment, although hardly so soon."

"I'll be right back," Francesca said, not hearing him at all. Only something dire would bring Joel into a society function. And whatever that something was, it clearly involved her—or needed her attention. Francesca hurried across the room. "Joel! It's so good to see you!" she cried, embracing him.

"Miz Cahill! Thank the lord you are back!" he said in return, appearing stricken.

She clasped his shoulder warmly. "What has happened?"

"Me mom's friend's daughter been missing fer three whole days," he said urgently. "Poor Mrs. O'Hare been over every day, cryin' like a storm. We all been prayin' you would come home!"

Francesca stared, every single concern, worry, and aspect of her personal life vanishing from her mind. This was frightful news indeed. "A child is missing? She has been missing for three entire days?" she asked briskly, her mind racing.

Joel nodded grimly. "Little Emily O'Hare. I known her me entire life," he added.

This was dire. Francesca did not have a good feeling about the child's fate, not if she had been missing for three entire days. "We must interview the child's parents immediately," she decided. "It's still early. I doubt it is past nine o'clock. We can do so right now," she added impulsively.

"I'll go flag down a cab!" Joel cried, rushing away.

"So you are on another case?" Hart breathed from behind her.

She whirled, barely meeting his inquiring gaze, as she needed her coat. Then, to a passing servant, "My red cloak, please." And to Hart, "I am afraid so. A young girl has been missing for three days. Time is of the essence, Hart, so do not argue with me. The night is young—I wish to interview the child's family tonight." Impatience ruled— she had to get downtown immediately.

Hart sighed, shook his head, and said to another valet, "Sir. My coat and gloves, please."

Francesca started. "What are you doing?"

"Do you really think I would allow you to sleuth about the city tonight, in that dress, undoubtedly in some very unsavory wards, with only Kennedy for protection?"

She felt herself blink and it took her a moment to understand. "You don't mean—what are you saying?"

"I am coming with you, my dear." He smiled at her.

She was amazed. "You are accompanying me on my investigation?"

"Indeed, it appears that I am."

She was thrilled. There was simply no denying it. Hart would sleuth with her tonight. He would accompany her on a new adventure. But very nonchalantly she shrugged. "Very well, if you really think it is necessary. I do think I have proven that I can take care of myself." She accepted her red cloak from the valet.

"I do think it is necessary, so humor me, my dear." He accepted and shrugged on his black coat.

"There is one thing," Francesca said as they went to the door.

"Pray tell."

"You are an amateur when it comes to criminal investigative work, and you must keep out of my way." She knew she was being very tart, but there was a line in the sand, and he must keep to his side of it.

"Whatever you say, darling," he said contritely.

He was far too meek, but she would worry about it later.

They followed Kennedy outside, into the chill and moonless night.

CHAPTER
TWO

HART'S COACH WAS A lavish affair, a six-in-hand with elegant velvet and leather appointments. As the carriage sped through the night-darkened city, Francesca began asking Joel about Emily O'Hare: "Do you know anything about her disappearance?"

Joel shook his head, a negative. He sat beside her in the forward-facing seat, Hart having settled on the opposite squabs where he lounged far too comfortably. Francesca kept her regard where it belonged. "Only that she went out on Monday with a nickel for a fresh loaf. An' she ain't niver come back."

Joel had already given Francesca the missing child's home address—the O'Hares lived in the same tenement as his own family, on Avenue A and 10th Street. It was a grim neighborhood, where gangs of kids ran wild amidst a strong criminal element. However, hard-working and honest folk such as Joel's mother, Maggie Kennedy, also lived there, doing their very best to raise their children in the most genteel manner possible. Francesca sighed. "Does Mrs. O'Hare have any clues whatsoever?"

"Don't think so. Didn't know what to ask her, Miz Cahill, with you bein' gone and all," Joel said.

"Has she gone to the police?" Hart interjected calmly.

Joel nodded. "Them flies told her people disappear in this city all the time, that's what they said."

Francesca simmered with anger. Thank God she had come home. She finally looked at Hart, whose presence in the coach was actually a distraction. They shared a knowing glance. Had little Emily's home address been Fifth Avenue, her disappearance would have been attended to within hours. Francesca knew this for a fact, having worked on a child abduction case before.

Abruptly she looked away from him, recalling the many times she and Bragg had worked so closely together. They had been far more than a professional investigative team. She finally wrapped her arms across her chest, suddenly saddened. It was odd, Hart being with her now.

She stared outside at the passing buildings. Winter was abandoning the city. When she had last been home, dirty ice had covered the streets, muddy snow patches on the sidewalks. Now the gaslight cast by the tall wrought-iron street lamps revealed clear walks and cobbled streets marred only by an occasional puddle. The coach had turned off Fifth Avenue and was passing Madison Square—where Bragg let a pleasant older house. A homeless man in a potato sack had decided to spend the night on an iron park bench. She glanced past the square, at Bragg's Victorian brick house. The lights were on in the upstairs window, which she knew from her own experience was the master bedroom. Was he making love to Leigh Anne?

"Perhaps you should solicit my brother's help on this case," Hart cut into her brooding.

She jerked and saw he had been watching her and knew where she had been gazing. She opened her mouth to tell him that she had been considering just that, but then she refused to lie, even whitely, to him. She faced him grimly. "He will certainly assign a detective to the case."

"Yes, he will," Hart agreed. "As he would never refuse you."

She shifted uneasily, then tried a smile out on him.

He did not smile back.

"He would never refuse to pursue justice, Hart," she said softly.

Hart made a sound. "Of course not."

Francesca glanced aside. The one thing Bragg was, was a man of the most honorable inclinations. A reformer at heart, just as she was, he had been appointed to carry out the unpleasant task of reforming the city's notoriously corrupt police department, an on-again and off-again affair—dependent upon which party was in power. Bragg's brick home was left behind as the coach bumped down Broadway, passing an electric trolley that was empty. Hart remarked, "The police are right; people disappear every single day in this city. Even children."

"I know."

"Three days is a long time. Do not get your hopes up, Francesca."

"It isn't me whom we must worry about. It is Emily—and her family."

"I will always worry about you, even if you can take care of yourself."

She felt her pulse leap in response to his words, as she was more than pleased, but she did not smile. "Most missing children are runaways, I think."

"I am inclined to agree."

She glanced out the carriage window and saw 14th Street ahead. Three hansoms were in the intersection, and Raoul, Hart's driver, slowed the coach. She faced Joel. "How old is Emily, Joel?"

"Thirteen. Her birthday was last week," he said promptly.

"Did she attend school?"

He gave her an incredulous look. "No. She worked with

me mom and Mrs. O'Hare, sewing at Moe Levy's."

"Was she a happy child?" Francesca promptly asked. Working at such an age was common, never mind the education laws. And the Moe Levy sewing factory was actually a large room, not airy but not airless, the conditions quite bearable. Francesca had been there several months ago and had seen the premises for herself.

"I think so," Joel said, his brow screwing up. "Why d'you ask, Miz Cahill?"

"Do you think she has run away?"

He was startled. "No, I don't. She fought a bit with her mom, but why would she run away? Where would she go?"

Francesca had no idea, but Hart coolly said, "Was she pretty, Joel?"

Francesca whirled to look at him.

Joel nodded. "Real pretty. White skin an' black hair, all curly and long, and real blue eyes—like Miz Cahill."

Francesca stared at Hart, wanting to know what terrible thoughts he was having, but she refused to ask in front of Joel. Hart said, "Was there a young gentleman that she liked?"

Her heart sank. She looked at Joel.

"A gent? I dunno." He flushed now. "Gents were always lookin' at her when she walked down the street, Mr. Hart. An' the roughs would suggest things, if you know what I mean."

"Indeed I do," he said quietly.

"We are almost there!" Francesca cried, determined to stop the conversation.

"You don't think she ran off with one of them rowdies, do you?" Joel asked sharply.

"No, I don't," Hart said calmly.

Francesca wondered just what he did think. She could barely refrain from asking but did not want poor Joel further alarmed. He, however, asked shrewdly, "You think she been pimped by some fine dandy like yourself?"

Hart shrugged. "Perhaps a *gentleman* offered her something she had no wish to refuse."

Joel was blushing. "Mr. Hart, sir! I didn't mean no disrespect!"

"I know you didn't," he said, smiling finally, slightly.

"Hart! What do you mean, precisely?" Francesca demanded, no longer able to stand it.

He settled his gaze on her. "There are a sort out there, Francesca, who are on the prowl for young, beautiful, innocent girls. She may have been offered money, clothes, an apartment. If she was very pretty, that is my first guess as to the cause of her disappearance."

Francesca could not breathe. The coach had stopped. Raoul's weight above them shifted the chassis as he stepped down to the sidewalk. "She is a child. A child just turned thirteen."

"I am not condoning this kind of behavior," he said. "But it is a fact of life."

She stared.

He did not look away, not even as Raoul opened the door, not even as Hart said, "Thank you, Raoul."

A tug on her sleeve ensued. "He's right; he is, Miz Cahill. I heard of Tammie Browne. She used to live down the block. She was real pretty, with dark red hair and big blue eyes, an' when she was fifteen, she went away to live uptown with a gent. Her father disowned her, he did. He was only a butcher, but he was real honest, the godly sort, you know, an' t' this day, he cries whenever he hears her name."

Francesca briefly closed her eyes. It remained shocking, she thought, to step out of her glittering and lavish world into this other one, a world of darkness, despair, of hopelessness, a world people like Connie and Julia didn't even know existed—a world that made women such as Tammie Browne choose a life of depravity in order to survive.

He touched her elbow. "If you want to find Emily O'Hare, we should go up and interview her parents," Hart said.

Her gaze flew open. He had leaned close and his knees

bumped hers. "I hope you are wrong, Calder. I desperately do."

He hesitated. "There are worse fates."

Her alarm skyrocketed. "Such as?"

"Please." He gestured with only a slight nod toward the street. His gaze never left hers.

Francesca stepped out with Raoul's aid, thanking the swarthy, short driver, whom she had always suspected was actually a bodyguard. A moment later she and Hart were following Joel into a dark and soiled brick building and up two flights of narrow, dark stairs. He knocked on Apartment Seven, and the door was instantly opened by a bleary-eyed older man whom Francesca assumed to be Emily's father.

He was in overalls and a tattered sweater. "Joel?" The man appeared to have been sleeping. However, he did smell of beer.

"Mr. O'Hare, sir. I brought you Miz Cahill, a very famous crime-solver."

O'Hare blinked. He had dark hair and long sideburns and a very big belly.

"To find Emily," Joel added urgently.

Francesca swiftly pressed her calling card into his hand. It read:

> *Francesca Cahill, Crime-Solver Extraordinaire*
> *No. 810 Fifth Avenue, New York City*
> *All Cases Accepted, No Crime Too Small*

He blinked at it. "What's this?"

From somewhere in the flat a woman called out, eagerly asking who was there, hope in her tone.

"Mr. O'Hare, sir. My name is Francesca Cahill, and I am a sleuth. I am here to ask you some questions about Emily's disappearance," Francesca said firmly.

The sleepy look left his eyes, which began to fill with tears. "Is this a prank, boy?" he demanded of Joel. "You may not have a daddy, but I don't mind givin' you a good whipping!"

Francesca shoved Joel behind her skirts. "Mr. O'Hare. May I come in? I do wish to speak with you and your wife—if you want to find your daughter."

"Brian!" A chubby woman with strikingly black hair and vivid blue eyes hurried forward, and instantly her gaze locked with Francesca's. Never looking away, she said to her husband, "Maggie told me about Miss Cahill. She is a sleuth, Brian. She finds murderers, scoundrels, every kind of crook. Even missing children. Please, let her in!"

Brian started while Francesca stared at Emily's mother with real despair. If Emily looked like her mother, then she was more than pretty, she was beautiful, and Hart was probably, terribly, right.

"I lost my manners," Brian said gruffly, stepping aside and opening the door. "I truly lost my manners. I am sorry, Miss Cahill."

Francesca gripped his arm. "You are frightened and in grief. Do not apologize." She looked back at Hart, smiling, as she stepped swiftly into a small but neat apartment. On one wall was a sink and stove; on another, a bed where two small children peeped at her from beneath their covers. A curtain cordoned off another section of the room, where Francesca assumed Emily's parents slept. In the kitchen area was a large wooden table with five chairs. Another area contained a washtub. "Mr. O'Hare, this is my friend Mr. Hart."

O'Hare nodded at Hart. "Come in, do sit down. Kathy, see if we got something to offer our guests."

Kathy smiled grimly and did not move.

Hart said smoothly, "We have just eaten, Mr. O'Hare. But a glass of water would be welcome."

Kathy looked relieved, and she turned to the sink to comply.

Francesca was oddly proud of Hart as they sat down at the pine table. She smiled her thanks at Kathy for her glass of water, then leaned toward O'Hare, who had sat at the table's head.

"When was Emily last seen, Mr. O'Hare, and by whom?"

Brian O'Hare opened his mouth to speak, but no words came out. His face turned red, as did his eyes and nose, and he began to cry. He covered his face with his hands while Kathy ran around to stand beside him, her hand on his broad shoulder. "I'll tell you," she said, ashen. "On Monday she came home from the factory, as happy as can be. I was going to go out to buy a loaf of bread, but I was so very tired, and she said she'd go for me." Her face crumbled. "She went out and never came back. I remember looking at the clock in the window across the street and wondering where she was. It was five then. At six I began to really worry. At seven Brian came home and went looking for her." Tears trickled down her face.

Francesca said, "What time do you think she left the house?"

"Four, maybe half past," Kathy whispered, stricken.

"Did she go into the grocery?"

Kathy shook her head. "The grocer is Will Schmitt. He never saw her."

Francesca was silent for a moment, but she looked at Hart as she thought, in case he had anything to add. He understood and said, "Has she ever disappeared for a day or two—or even a few hours—before last Monday?"

"Never!" It was Brian who now spoke. "My daughter is a good girl, and she knows her duty, she does."

"Mr. Hart meant no harm," Francesca said, reaching out to cover his hand with her own. "But there are many questions we must ask, some of which are personal."

Brian nodded grimly. "Go on, then."

"Do you think she ran away?" Francesca asked.

Brian snorted. "No."

Francesca looked at Kathy, who shook her head. "No," she whispered. "I am certain of it, Miss Cahill."

Francesca glanced at Hart. He inclined his head imperceptibly toward her, and she knew he wished for her to continue. "Did she have a boyfriend?"

"No!" Brian shot to his feet, trembling. "Just what are you trying to say?"

Francesca also stood. "I am trying to make certain she did not run off with a handsome young man whom we might easily find."

"Emily wasn't that way," Kathy said tremulously. "She's very young for her age and she's shy where the lads are concerned."

Francesca was at a loss. "Where is Schmitt's Grocery? I'll have to speak with him first thing tomorrow."

"It's on the corner of Eleventh Street," Kathy said.

"What can you learn from him? He knows nothing!" Brian cried.

"Every investigation has to start somewhere. After I speak with Schmitt, I may interview every person who lives and works on this block. Someone saw something," Francesca said firmly, meaning it.

"God, we got nothing, not even a single clue," Brian said, his nose turning red again.

Francesca stood. "No, Mr. O'Hare, we have more than nothing. Your daughter left here between four and half past four last Monday. She did not make it to the grocery store. It takes mere minutes to walk a single block. So sometime between four and four-thirty she disappeared—on this very block, between your door and that of Schmitt's. That is hardly nothing. There is a witness out there who saw what happened to Emily. Of that I assure you."

Hart also stood.

Kathy looked at her eagerly, hope flaring in her eyes. "You think so?"

"I know so," Francesca said, and she added, as the idea occurred to her, "We shall post a reward for information. Joel, I'll make some flyers by hand tonight. You can post them first thing tomorrow, the rest I'll print up, and we'll post them in a four-block square by tomorrow evening.

That," she added with satisfaction, "should bring us a result or two."

Brian blinked at her, and for the first time that evening a light appeared in his eyes. "That's a grand idea," he said in wonder. "Why didn't we think of it?"

"Do not fret," Francesca said. "I have one more question. Joel said you went to the police. Was any investigation undertaken?"

Brian cursed the police roundly, then said, "No. If the Democrats had won the election, we wouldn't be in this mess. Tammany takes care of its own, it does."

Francesca bristled. "If you are so certain of that, why don't you go ask Boss Croker for his help?"

Brian stood, flushing.

Hart took her arm. "I think we have learned all that we can tonight. Mr. O'Hare, Mrs. O'Hare, Miss Cahill is a clever sleuth, and if anyone can locate your daughter, it is she. She is your best hope."

The O'Hares walked them to the door, Brian grim, Kathy anxious. Once there, Kathy gripped her hand. "Please find her, Miss Cahill. Please find my darling girl."

"I will," Francesca said. "I will do my best and I shall not let you down."

Kathy nodded, then said, "You will return tomorrow? Post the rewards?"

"Not only that, I shall keep you informed of the status of the investigation," Francesca said. Then, impulsively, she hugged the other woman. "Do not lose hope," she said.

She and Hart followed Joel down the narrow, dark stairs in thoughtful silence. On the first level they paused before the Kennedy flat. "I will see you first thing tomorrow," Francesca said to Joel.

"How early?" he asked.

"Half past seven," she returned.

He beamed at her. "I'll be there, Miz Cahill." Then he turned to Hart. "G'night, sir."

Hart chucked his jaw. "Get some sleep. I can see you shall have a busy day tomorrow."

They waited as Joel knocked lightly on his door. A moment later Maggie Kennedy opened it, clad in a flannel wrapper, her red hair in a long braid. Her blue eyes widened when she saw Francesca and Hart. "Miss Cahill! I mean, Francesca! This is a surprise."

Francesca smiled warmly at her. "Maggie, we wanted to see Joel safely home. We have taken on the Emily O'Hare case," she added.

"Thank the lord," Maggie whispered, her gaze tearing. "I am so glad, for I know you shall find her safe and sound."

Francesca wasn't certain of that last part, not at all, but she smiled anyway. Hart nodded politely and then went out to the waiting coach. As he handed her in, he murmured, "I am impressed."

His hand was large and warm on her bare elbow as she carried her coat. She was thrilled, and she smiled at him as she took her seat. "That was hardly an unusual interview," she said, trying to appear indifferent to his praise. It occurred to her that they were now alone and it was a long ride uptown.

He settled down beside her and Raoul slammed the carriage door shut behind them. "You gave them hope." He leaned back against the plush squabs, rather indolently. Only Hart could make such a simple position seem utterly decadent.

She tried not to think about his virility and said, with worry, "And I do hope it wasn't wrong of me to do so. I do hope it wasn't false hope that I gave them."

"I have little doubt you will locate Emily, Francesca." His gaze was warm, enough so to melt a frigid block of ice.

She started, surprised by the extent of his confidence but very pleased indeed.

"You may grin like a sated fat cat," he chuckled.

She beamed. "You will give me a very big swollen head, Hart, if you keep on flattering me so. And somehow, I do not think you would find a vain woman attractive."

He laughed. "I know you are not vain enough, my dear, and I find confidence in you charming." His smile faded. He gave her a long and thoughtful look.

It went right through her heart to her loins. Francesca sat up.

"I find you charming, Francesca, and I suppose the fact that you are unpredictable will keep me on my toes," he added, more to himself than to her.

"I am so sorry about that ridiculous note," Francesca said, then, in a rush, "Calder, I didn't know what to write! I should have spoken with you before leaving."

"Please don't ever lie to me again," he said simply. "I have never lied to you, and I expect to be repaid in kind."

She nodded, somehow undone and very flustered now.

He smiled a little at her and turned away. They were traveling up Fourth Avenue now, alongside the excavation for a new railroad tunnel. She seized the opportunity to stare at him, enjoying his strong profile. And finally, the events of the entire evening washed over her. Her arrival at the ball, her brief exchange with Bragg, her encounter with Hart in the servants' hall, and his ensuing announcement of their engagement. Tension stabbed her. An image of Bragg's shocked expression assailed her mind. All sense of well-being vanished.

She had hurt him. She hadn't meant to. How could they have made the announcement in such an untimely manner?

He continued to gaze out at the passing buildings. Traffic on the avenue was less than light—a lone hansom accompanied them, the bay's hooves clopping loudly in unison with Hart's team in the night. He was more than dangerously seductive—he was dangerous, period. Hart had been the one to make the announcement. It had been his decision—the timing had been his and his alone.

He glanced languidly at her. "I would be careful with those reward posters."

She felt ill now. "Why?"

"Every Tom, Dick, and Harry will claim to have seen

something. You will have a hundred supposed witnesses to Emily's disappearance, I think."

She hadn't considered that possibility. "You are right. Well, we will have to carefully winnow through all the false claims. I really believe that someone had to have seen what happened to Emily. Someone is out there with information that I need."

"You are probably right. What's wrong?"

She looked up and met his midnight gaze. "What we have just done has finally sunk in."

"And that is?" He watched her carefully now, like a hawk.

She held up her hand. Even in the cab, the big diamond glittered, catching the light. "I think our timing might have been better."

His jaw seemed to flex. The interior of the coach was softly lit, so it was hard to say. "Let me guess. You are worried about my poor half brother's feelings."

"Yes, I am." She sat up straighter, defensively. "It wasn't right. I saw his face. He was disbelieving. And he was hurt."

Hart leaned toward her, his eyes black now. "He has no right to be hurt, Francesca, and we both know it—only you will never admit it."

She inhaled, mentally preparing for an unpleasant battle. "Calder, I know he is married. I know he loves Leigh Anne, even if he refuses to admit it to anyone and not even to himself. But he is very fond of me. And you know that! His feelings are genuine, and he has every right to be hurt."

"Not in my opinion. In my opinion, he only seeks to keep you from allowing yourself to care genuinely for me."

"That is nonsense!" she cried, flushing.

"If he truly wanted you, Francesca, he would have slammed his front door—and his bedroom door—in little Leigh Anne's face."

How cruel he could be. She turned blindly away, trying not to think about Bragg and Leigh Anne sharing a bed together. And while she knew Hart was right, she said, "I encouraged him to stay with her. I begged him not to throw away his political future. With Leigh Anne at his side, I feel certain he will one day win the Senate seat. But if he were divorced, no such outcome is assured."

A dark silence greeted her words.

She dared to look his way.

His smile was twisted. "Darling, has it ever occurred to you that you encouraged him to continue his marriage for the sake of politics, when really you had another, ulterior, motive?"

She knew his blow was about to come. "What other motive could I possibly have?"

"His marriage has allowed you to be where you desperately yearn to be—in my arms . . . and soon . . . in my bed."

Had he been closer, she would have struck him. She wrenched at the ring to throw it back at him. He seized her hand. "I apologize. That was uncalled for."

"That was cruel," Francesca said breathlessly. "You asked me to be honest with you, as you are honest with me. I have never been anything but kind to you, and I ask you to treat me the same way!"

He was silent, and he did not release her hand. Then, "Did it never occur to you that your departure last month, with only that frivolous note for comfort, was an act of cruelty?"

"What?!"

He leaned close, his grip tightening. "Did it ever occur to you that the way you speak about him—to me—is cruelty?"

She stared into his eyes, then at his mouth, which was provocatively close. "But you don't love me."

"I don't believe in love, but I am damnably fond of you, and you know how I treasure you, Francesca," he said tersely. "And there are times—like now—when I feel like killing off Leigh Anne myself and tossing you and him together to be done with it all, at last!"

"Please, don't speak that way," she begged.

He released her hand, moving back into the space he

had previously occupied. "I am sorry if my emotions are not always noble ones. I am sorry I am not the epitome of virtue as he is."

"You are very virtuous," she whispered weakly, "when you wish to be. When you forget about competing with Bragg, when you forget about shocking pleasant company."

He made a rough sound, and it might have been one of acquiescence.

Francesca hugged herself. "What possessed you, Hart, to make that announcement tonight?"

"It is Calder, Francesca, not Hart, damn it."

"Please."

Hart stared without comment.

"We should have never made it public that way," Francesca whispered. "But I forgot he was there, my mind was so addled from lovemaking." When he remained silent, she added urgently, "Please, tell me you had also forgotten he was there."

He met her gaze. "I knew he was there."

She inhaled.

"But that doesn't mean I made the announcement to spite him, which is what you are thinking."

She wasn't sure whether to believe him or not. She hugged herself.

"I made that announcement to end your indecision, Francesca. I made that announcement because you accepted my proposal a month ago, and proved to me in the hall tonight that you had not changed your mind. Yes, my decision was a selfish one. But frankly, one of the reasons I am who I am today is because when I want something, I do what I have to in order to get it."

She swallowed. "I am not a painting." Hart was a world-renowned collector of art. "Nor am I a collectible."

"And I have always been opposed to marriage, in theory and in fact. But since meeting you, I have decided to undertake matrimony—with you as my wife. No, you are not a thing, Francesca, far from it. You are a unique—no, an amazing—creation of contradictions, wit, and will, not to mention beauty. I need not defend my desire to marry you. I probably should have discussed making the announcement tonight." He suddenly hesitated. "I am used to doing what I want, when I want, Francesca. Most bachelors are. In my case, I fear I am worse that way than most. However, you did run away in a very unseemly manner—the trigger for my behavior tonight. All of it," he added with a rueful look.

Francesca was having trouble getting past his statement that she was an amazing creation of contradictions, wit, will, and beauty. She shook her head to clear it. "Are you apologizing to me for announcing our engagement?"

"Yes, I am. However," he held up a hand to forestall he surprised comment, "if I had the entire night to do over, while I would not have behaved like a beast in the hall, I would still make that announcement."

She sat back against the squabs, wide-eyed and staring. "Hart," she finally said, "you are a very difficult man."

He smiled. "I know."

She began to smile, as well, then was struck with an image of the voluptuous Mrs. Davies on his arm. She hesitated. This was a subject she need not bring up—he had promised her fidelity, but she had run away and he had thought the engagement to be off. Still, she despised the other woman without knowing her and could not stand the thought of her with Hart.

"Is something on your mind, Francesca?"

She jerked, told herself to say "No," and instead said "Yes."

He seemed amused. "Do tell."

"I didn't have a chance to meet your friend . . . Mrs. Davies," she said carefully.

He didn't seem to understand what she was really saying. "She is an old friend," he said dismissively. "I doubt you would enjoy meeting her—" He stopped and stared. "Francesca, I made you a promise."

"But I left the town—and you thought our engagement was over," she said tersely.

His eyes widened, riveted on hers. "Surely you know I am a man of my word?"

She could barely believe her ears. Was it possible that he hadn't rushed into another woman's bed?

He took her hand. "I promised to be faithful, and if a man like myself cannot play a waiting game when the stakes are this high, then he is hardly a man."

She could only stare, thrilled and simply breathless now. "Calder? Isn't this the moment when you pull me into your arms?"

He didn't bat an eye. "No."

"No?" She was more than surprised.

"In case you didn't notice, we somehow survived our little indiscretion in the servants' hall tonight and your father is less than pleased with our decision. I am meeting him at your house tomorrow afternoon, Francesca. I intend to win the battle I must wage for your hand, at all costs, and therefore, I am delivering you intact and untouched to your door in the next fifteen minutes."

"Papa will come round. Because Mama always gets her way and she adores you, and you know it."

"Bless Julia," he said with a warm smile.

Her heart turned over. He was so unbearably handsome. And at times, he was also unbearable. But she didn't mind. She knew she could, in the end, outwit him. The real problem was, he did not believe in love and he never would.

She quickly looked away, aghast with herself, because it was suddenly so clear that everything might be different if he were espousing undying love for her, as Bragg had done. But Hart was never going to be in love with her. He would be a warm friend and a wonderful lover, but that was as much as he would ever give to her.

Hart cut into her thoughts. "We will be at your door in five minutes, Francesca."

She started, flushed, and barely met his eyes. "I am actually very tired," she said.

"And now you are once more running away from me?

Why?" He reached for her hand, finding it even though she had no wish for him to hold it.

"It has been a long and unusual day," she said, not looking him in the eye.

"Yes, it has. Did you know I would be at the ball, tonight?"

She finally met his gaze. "Yes."

"And did you wear that red dress for me?"

She lifted her brows. "What red dress?"

He laughed. "The one I shall tear off as soon as you wear it for me when we are married," he said.

She went still. Then, "It was very expensive—"

"Oh, I mean it."

She stared, images rioting through her, images she did not want, not now.

He smiled a little and said, "I am still waiting for the portrait you promised me. Sarah and I have discussed it at length."

She wet her lips, her pulse racing uncomfortably. "I will make an appointment to sit with Sarah immediately," she said. Sarah Channing was a brilliant artist and a good friend. Hart had commissioned Francesca's portrait well over a month ago, the very first time he had seen her in the gown, stipulating that she must be portrayed wearing it.

"Good." He leaned toward her. "I have changed my mind about one thing, however."

"That is?" she asked warily.

"I want you to pose nude."

She stared, speechless.

"We will probably be wed, my dear, by the time I get my portrait."

She melted in a heap. "I don't mind. You won't hang it . . ."

"Publicly? Of course not. I intend to hang it in my private rooms." He smiled at her in a way that made her skin begin to burn.

The coach jounced wildly and Francesca realized they

had turned into the driveway in front of the Cahill mansion. The grounds sweeping up to the limestone house were now muddy instead of snow-laden, and lights flickered in the two lower stories of the twenty-room house. Francesca looked back at Hart, flushing wildly. "I am flattered," she managed.

He grinned. "I am sure that you are. Other ladies would be insulted. You do realize that?"

"I do." She hesitated, aware of how pleased she was that he wished to admire her portrait at any time of night or day. Then, "I am not voluptuous, Calder."

He laughed as the coach halted in front of the wide steps leading up to the front door. "I know exactly what you are, Francesca; have no fear of that." His grin was a wicked one.

He helped her to alight from the coach and he walked her to her door. There they paused. Francesca trembled and moved closer, but he gripped her elbows and did not pull her into his arms. His gaze was oddly speculative now.

"My parents can't possibly be home," she said huskily. "It's far too early, Calder."

"Anything is possible," he said. Then he added, "And tomorrow? Will you enlist the aid of the police?"

She hesitated. Hurting Rick Bragg was the last thing that she ever wished to do. And she thought he would also be very angry. Facing him tomorrow would be terrible. She did not know if she could do it.

But she had no choice. She needed his help; of that she had little doubt. Because time was of the essence and in order to find a real lead they had to move swiftly now.

She tensed. "Yes."

"You should," Hart said dispassionately. "If you intend to canvass the entire neighborhood, you will need the help of his men. You also need the additional manpower to get a timely clue."

She asked warily, "You don't mind?"

"I hardly said that."

"After tonight, he may not be inclined to help my investigation," she said tersely.

"I wouldn't," Hart said. "But we both know he will. Remember, he would never let an injustice go unattended, and that is a major difference between us."

"You sell yourself short," she said swiftly. "I think you are more concerned with injustice and suffering than you let on."

"And you remain hopelessly naive and romantic. Another aspect of your charm," he said, and he kissed the top of her head as if she were a child. "Good night, Francesca."

"I am not as naive as you think," she protested.

Hart knocked and the Cahill doorman opened the door. "Well, let us put it this way—you are not as naive as you were several months ago."

She blushed.

He smiled and turned away, striding swiftly back to his coach. Francesca did not move, watching as the elegant barouche swept around the circular drive and finally exited back onto Fifth Avenue. Then, finally, she shivered.

A nude portrait. She would be the talk of the town if anyone ever found out.

She smiled.

Perhaps she would sit for Sarah tomorrow.

CHAPTER THREE

IN ORDER TO LEAVE the city—and when Francesca had left in late February she hadn't had any idea of how long she would be gone—she had finally given in to what now seemed inevitable. She had sent the dean of students at Barnard College a letter advising her of her immediate withdrawal. She had worked very hard to secretly enroll in the exclusive women's college, and her sister had helped her with the tuition. The enrollment had been kept secret because Julia never would have allowed it had she known—as she already rued Francesca's previous reputations, as a bluestocking, an eccentric, and a reformer. However, Francesca had decided that withdrawal was for the best; since embarking upon her new calling as a sleuth, there had been no time to study, and she had repeatedly missed classes.

Today was Friday, and had she not withdrawn, she would have been at a political studies class, her favorite, undoubtedly engaged in heated debate. Francesca smiled now at Joel as they paused before the grocery on the corner of 11th Street. "Why don't you post those reward posters up and down this block and the next one as well?"

The poster read:

WANTED:
INFORMATION ON THE DISAPPEARANCE OF EMILY O'HARE
LAST SEEN IN THE VICINITY OF AVE. A AND 10TH
MONDAY, MARCH 24, AROUND 4 P.M.
THIRTEEN YRS, DARK HAIR, BLUE EYES, PRETTY
POSTED: $100 REWARD
HONEST WITNESSES ONLY NEED COME FORTH

Joel was holding a dozen handwritten pages, a hammer, and a tub of nails. "Right away," he said with a grin.

Francesca watched him dash off happily, and then she faced the door of the grocery. A sign hanging inside the window said: OPEN. Through the clear glass she saw a heavyset man fussing with some items on a long oak counter. She smiled grimly and entered the shop.

Inside, it was neat and clean, the rough planked floors swept bare of any dust or dirt, the counters scrubbed and gleaming with wax. Big sacks of flour and sugar were lined up alongside the counter, while on top of it were loaves of fresh bread and platters of smoked meats. Tins of lard and butter were also present. Several aisles contained other dried food items, soaps and candles, and even some spices. The grocery was a very small shop, as much merchandise as possible crammed into its confines.

"Mr. Schmitt?" Francesca asked, approaching him as a young woman came out from the back.

"Can I help you, miss?" Schmitt smiled. He had a thick German accent.

Francesca took another glance at the young woman, realizing that she was far younger than she appeared—and Francesca now guessed she was probably about fifteen. The girl, who was quite plain and unremarkable, met her gaze and smiled. Francesca returned the friendly gesture and turned back to the grocer. "I do hope so." She handed him her card, waited while he read it, and said, "I am working on the Emily O'Hare investigation."

Schmitt looked up, silent, his gaze impossible to read.

Francesca was puzzled. "You do know that the O'Hares sent Emily here to your store, last Monday, around four, but she not only never bought the bread she was sent for, she was never seen again."

"I know. Beth, please go and start unpacking the dried fruit that just came in."

Something was amiss. Francesca turned and saw Beth, now very flushed, staring at her. She instantly rushed behind the counter and into a back room.

Schmitt smiled proudly. "That's my daughter," he said. "I'm really sorry about little Emily. "But I told Brian, I never saw her that afternoon; she never came in."

"Can you think about who your customers were that day? Particularly that afternoon?" Francesca asked. "Perhaps one of them saw something."

He started. "Young lady, I have a booming business. To try to remember who was in my store on a particular afternoon—that's impossible!"

"You won't even try?" Francesca asked. But she was getting another impression. This man did not want to speak to her, but she did not know why.

His jowls shook. "You make it seem as though I do not want to find Emily. Of course I do. Very well." He scowled and folded brawny arms across his thick chest. "Monday afternoons I have some regular customers. Mrs. Sarnoff, Mrs. Polaski, and Mrs. O'Brien. They come in every Monday afternoon for a week's supply of potatoes, flour, and sugar." His look seemed to suggest that it was time for Francesca to leave.

"Where do they live?" Francesca asked, taking a small notepad and a pencil out of her purse. In it she also carried several other useful tools of her trade. She had learned the hard way to always carry matches, a candle, a small knife, and a gun.

Schmitt practically sighed. Then he reached into a drawer for a notebook, and Francesca copied the addresses down. "Thank you. If there is anything else you think of, please, get in touch with Joel Kennedy, Maggie's son. He lives right up the block."

"I don't know anything more," Schmitt said, turning his back to her.

Francesca left the store, unsettled. Why would this man be so unhelpful? Was he withholding information from her? Did he associate her with the police? Or perhaps her stature as a wealthy young lady made him resentful or even anxious. Still, Francesca could not justify the treatment she had just received.

The sun was warming the morning outside. It looked as if spring would come early to the city that year—several of the apartments in the buildings up and down the block had flower boxes, and Francesca saw dandelions and daffodils just breaking the soil. Above her, the sky was surprisingly clear and blue. She unbuttoned her navy blue coat and was rewarded with a draft of pleasant air.

But she did not smile. As soon as Joel was finished posting her reward notices, they would go a few blocks uptown to 300 Mulberry Street. That is, she would go to police headquarters and seek aid from Rick Bragg.

If he was still speaking to her, that is.

Police headquarters was housed in a five-story brownstone building just around the corner from one of the city's worst slums—Mulberry Bend. As Francesca paid the cabbie, she saw Bragg's handsome motorcar parked on the street, a roundsman in his blue serge and leather helmet discreetly watching it. Other roundsmen were leaving the building; a police wagon was coming down the block. Her heart tightened. She hated the moment of confrontation that must surely come. If only last night could be undone.

Then she let herself think about Calder Hart and her heart tightened even more, in a different way, and her skin tingled and she blushed. She forced herself to concentrate on the investigation at hand. "Will you come up?" she asked Joel, who, given up his recent occupation as a "kid"—a child pickpocket—despised and distrusted the city's finest with a passion.

"Don't think so," Joel said, scowling. "I bet we could find Emily on our own, Miz Cahill. We really don't need any coppers on our tails."

"I disagree, and you *do* work for me," Francesca said, patting his shoulder. "If you need me, I will be upstairs in the commissioner's office."

Joel nodded, walking over to a sickly elm tree, which he leaned against, and began whistling tunelessly.

Francesca hurried into the reception room. There, a long counter faced her, behind which were several officers, all of whom she now knew quite well. An officer was on her side of the counter with an elderly lady, apparently discussing a complaint that involved the theft of her purse. Two men in ill-fitting suits and bowler hats were seated on benches, in handcuffs. To the far right there was an empty holding cell. And in the background there was the ever-constant pinging of telegraphs, the pounding of typewriters, and the ringing of telephones. The noise was more than familiar to Francesca; she realized with a pang that she had come to enjoy the intrusive sounds. In fact, she thought, smiling, she had missed not just the sounds of the precinct, but being there on an active investigation as well.

Captain Shea was the first officer on duty to remark her. He stopped what he was doing, smiling. "Miss Cahill! It has been a long time. How are you?" he asked.

She smiled, coming quickly forward then. "Hello, Captain," she said. "I'm afraid I had to go out of town."

"Yes, we heard," Shea returned, adjusting his horn-rimmed glasses.

Sergeant O'Malley, a stout fellow, approached. "Headquarters hasn't been the same without you, Miss Cahill," he said.

"I missed it, too," she said, suddenly happy. This was

where she belonged, in the midst of a criminal investigation, among these good, honest men.

"Are you on a case?" Shea asked.

"Yes, actually, I am. Is the commissioner in?"

"He's upstairs," Shea said, glancing oddly at O'Malley. "I'll go up and ask if he will see you."

Francesca was surprised. Shea walked out from behind the wood counter, going upstairs on foot, ignoring the iron cage of the elevator. She was accustomed to coming and going in police headquarters as she pleased; she had been going up to Bragg's office without any formalities for months now.

"It ain't you," O'Malley said, low. "The c'mish is in a mood, he is. No one's ever seen him like this before."

Francesca stiffened. "A bad mood?"

"Like a thunderstorm," O'Malley said with a nod.

Oh, dear. She certainly knew why he was in such a foul humor—she knew it was because of her engagement to his half brother.

"And look at what the spring breeze blew in."

The tone was just barely hostile and just barely mocking. Nevertheless, as always, the sound of Brendan Farr's voice curled the hair on her body, and even her toes. Francesca slowly turned to face the city's recently appointed chief of police. She still did not know why he disliked her so, but their enmity had become mutual. "Hello, Chief." She was terse.

"Long time no see," he said flatly. He was a very tall man, perhaps six-foot-four or even more, with steel-colored hair and steely eyes. He was smiling politely. Francesca had never, not even once, seen a smile in his eyes.

"I have been out of town," she said stiffly.

"Really? Business or pleasure?" His smile remained.

"Neither," she said, smiling as coolly in return. She knew he wanted information, and she would never give it to him.

"And what brings you to headquarters? Oh, let me guess. The commissioner—or is it another investigation?"

The less this man knew about her affairs, the better. "I wish a word with the commissioner. I shall go up. Thank you, Sergeant. Good day, Chief." Francesca did not wait to be told that she could go up. She quickly hurried past the two men, passed the holding cell, and went up the single flight of stairs.

Captain Shea was approaching in the hallway; behind him, the door to Bragg's office was open. He nodded at her. "He'll see you—not that I had any doubt."

Francesca thanked him as Bragg appeared in the doorway of his office, staring. Her strides faltered.

He was more than grim; he seemed tired and unkempt. Francesca saw circles beneath his eyes and lines around his mouth. Their gazes met.

Her heart beat hard. Could she really marry his half brother? For Rick Bragg, married or not, would always be a dark shadow standing between them.

He didn't nod and he didn't greet her. He turned and walked back into his office. Francesca followed.

Nothing had changed. His desk was a huge affair, covered with files and folder. A rattan-backed chair was behind it, a window overlooking Mulberry Street behind that. On the mantel above the fireplace were numerous family photographs, as well as other, more impressive ones, including one of Bragg with both the mayor and Theodore Roosevelt. Francesca searched for a photograph of Bragg's wife, but she was not to be found amid the ones of his father and adopted mother, his half brothers and sisters, his cousins, nieces, and nephews.

And there was no photograph of Calder Hart, either. But Francesca hadn't expected there to be one.

Francesca removed her coat, hanging it carefully on a wall hook by Bragg's greatcoat, while he went behind his desk, where he sat. She turned with dread. He had steepled his hands and bridged his nose upon them, not looking at her.

"I'm sorry."

He made a disparaging sound.

"Can we speak? Please?" she asked. And she had forgotten now about Emily. All she could think about was how unhappy this man was and that she was the cause.

And he didn't deserve unhappiness or pain. No one deserved a life of joy more than he. Bragg had earned it by a lifetime spent helping others.

He stood, went to the door, and closed it. Then he faced her. "Do you love him?"

She stiffened. And she could not find an answer to his question.

"Well? If you are marrying him, you must love him!" Bragg was angry now.

"I don't know if I love him. I only know that my world was turned upside down the day you told me that you were married!" she cried, and it was the truth. "Nothing has been the same since."

"So your marrying him is my fault."

"I hardly said that." She couldn't believe they had come to this—it was as if they were foes and in the midst of a bitter battle.

"It is my fault and we both know it. Because a month ago you were in my arms, Francesca, vowing eternal love to me, and now you are engaged to him!"

She backed up. Because he was right. "A month ago Leigh Anne was in Europe, a wicked witch of a woman whom you despised, a woman with lovers, a woman who was never coming back!"

"You know I wish she never came back," he said almost viciously. "You know I despise her!"

For one moment she could not speak. "I know no such thing."

"You also know that I don't lie," he said harshly. "Or has your plan to marry him led you to doubt my word, my integrity?"

"I would never doubt your word or your integrity, and that wasn't fair!" she cried, shaken.

"And is your marrying Hart *fair*?" he asked bitterly.

She fought for composure and could not find it. "You

are with Leigh Anne. I have every right to marry someone else."

"But it is temporary!"

"Is it? And don't jump on me and say I am doubting you."

"If you are not doubting me, then what are you doing?" he demanded.

She took a breath. "I think," she said carefully, "that you have very complicated feelings for your wife, and you refuse to be honest with yourself. I know you'd never lie to me deliberately, Bragg."

He stared. "Why are you doing this?" he finally asked. And it was a plea.

His tone held anguish, and Francesca started forward, about to rush to him—to comfort him was automatic. But she stopped herself. "I am genuinely fond of Hart," she heard herself say. "I enjoy being with him. He wants to marry me. I cannot seem to resist." She didn't add that she no longer wanted to resist.

Bragg laughed, the sound harsh and unpleasant. "He hates me. He has hated me for as long as I can remember—and I remember the day our mother died, the day I tried to hold him in my arms and comfort him. He was only a small frightened and angry boy of ten. I had just turned twelve and I was every bit as frightened as he. Of course, I dared not reveal how I really felt. He pushed me away then and has done so ever since—and worse. He only wants you, Francesca, because I do. He only wants you to get at me."

She hugged herself. "That is not true. He is as genuinely fond of me."

Bragg rolled his eyes and stalked away, his back stiff with anger. Then he whirled. "You didn't find the timing of his announcement a bit odd?"

She became uncomfortable. "Yes, I did, actually. I'm sorry. I'm sorry you had to learn the way that you did. I wish I had told you privately, first."

"How can you even be thinking of marrying him?" he cried. "If you are in love with him, he will break your heart—immediately, I believe. What are you doing? Are you, in some way that you do not realize, trying to punish me for allowing Leigh Anne to move into my home? How often must I repeat the fact that it is only temporary? You know we have agreed to divorce in six months—five, actually, now."

"I am not trying not punish you," she gasped. "How can you say that? And will you stop sleeping with her, too, in five months' time?"

He jerked, eyes wide.

She wished she had not uttered what was really on her mind. She knew the blow was a cruel one—just as she suspected he would sleep with his wife time and again, should the opportunity present itself.

He flushed. "It's not what you are thinking."

"You still love her. Why can't you admit it?"

"I despise her. And Francesca, you are worldly enough to know that a man can sleep with a woman and it has nothing to do with love."

She did know that, at least intellectually, but after seeing Leigh Anne—and seeing Bragg with her—it was different. Francesca could not believe that he slept with her and no love was involved.

Francesca turned away, recomposed herself, and faced him again. "I know I promised you my heart, and Rick—you still have it. But my feelings for you have nothing to do with my feelings for Calder."

Suddenly he crossed the room and gripped her shoulders. "Francesca, how can you say that? You deserve a wonderful husband—I want you to be happy. But I am afraid! This really isn't about me. I love you and I do not want to see you destroyed by him. Please. Rethink what you are about to do. Please."

Being in his arms was awkward—and Calder Hart was the one who had made it so. She eased away, and in spite of herself, he had managed to feed her small, niggling doubts about Hart. "I am a grown woman, and I can think for myself—just as I am quite good at taking care of myself," she said briskly, to hide how she was really feeling.

"And what will you do when you find him in bed with a lover? Take a fry pan to his head?" Bragg asked sharply.

She stiffened, for he had just verbalized her worst and most secret fears. "I will cross that bridge when I get to it," she said. She would not tell him Calder had promised fidelity. He would laugh at her—he wouldn't believe it.

And a part of her refused to believe it—or trust Hart—either.

And what kind of marriage was that?

"So that's it? You are blindly allowing him to lead you to the altar? You will go through with this? I am in shock!"

A part of her was ready to throw in the towel, to back out and end the engagement. "We are hardly at the altar, yet," she said through stiff lips. "We intend to marry in six months." It suddenly occurred to her that now their wedding would take place in five months, as that date had been set a month ago when she had accepted Hart's proposal.

And Bragg kept insisting that he and Leigh Anne would be divorced in five months, as well. What if he meant it?

Francesca closed her eyes, fighting for air, the office suddenly claustrophobic. *She didn't believe he would ever walk away from Leigh Anne. There was simply too much there, between them.*

Did that make Hart a second choice?

It did.

But was that so terrible? He already knew it and didn't care. She also knew it and didn't care.

Whom was she fooling? Hart might not love her, but he cared very much that she had first chosen Bragg and that he was second fiddle. And she cared, too.

"You look about to faint. I'm sorry." His arm slid around her waist, and her eyes flew open. How familiar his touch was. "I'm sorry that I still care so much, and I'm sorry I ever put you in this position in the first place." His gaze met and held hers. "But I will always care where you are concerned, Francesca."

"I know you will," she whispered, turning to face him,

and suddenly, briefly, she found herself in the circle of his arms. Her bosom met his chest. His thighs were hard against hers. She glanced at his mouth. She knew what he tasted like. She knew how his tongue felt in her mouth. Instantly, quickly, she lifted her gaze and met his yet again. His arms tightened around her. His golden eyes warmed impossibly.

The air seemed to disappear from the room.

He leaned toward her, his mouth parting. A fraction of an inch separated their lips. She smelled coffee and cologne, a blend of the woods and the earth.

An image of Hart's sardonic face quickly came to mind, followed by an image of Leigh Anne, tiny and gorgeous.

Francesca pushed him away. "Don't." She leaped out of his embrace, shaking.

He flushed. "I'm sorry. It just happened. Or it almost did. I can't think clearly now, it seems!"

"Nothing happened," she said, her heart pounding like a drum in her chest. But it was a lie. For one moment, one single, small moment, the desire had returned and the future had beckoned, an impossible dream once more.

But she thought she had burned the bridge to that dream; she thought she had buried it and left it far behind. She wet her lips. "I am on a case, Bragg, and that is why I came here to speak with you today," she said briskly. "I need your help."

He stared for a long moment, then turned and slowly walked behind his desk. There he opened the window, then faced her. He was flushed. "I will always help you, Francesca, in any way, be it as police commissioner or as friend."

She smiled a little, because she knew he meant his every word. "A child is missing," she said.

"Tell me what I can do."

CHAPTER
FOUR

"JULIA!" ANDREW CAHILL LOOKED up in real surprise at his wife. She stood in the doorway of his study, fully and fashionably dressed in a fitted ensemble in hunter green. While Julia arose every morning at eight, she never left her suite until noon, as she was busy with household management and her social correspondence. His wife was a very beautiful woman, with rich blond hair and bright blue eyes, her figure still pleasingly trim in spite of her middle years. Andrew both respected and admired her. Now, however, he knew why she was in his den, and his knowledge had nothing to do with her serious expression and everything to do with how well he knew his wife.

"Good morning, Andrew. May I come in?" Julia smiled briefly.

"Please do," he said, standing.

She swept forward and came to stand before the large mahogany desk where he worked. He had been born the son of an honest, hard-working, and generally poor farmer and had not risen to the top ranks of society by luck. Sheer fortitude coupled with organization and discipline had made him a millionaire. His desk was clean of clutter, several business files stacked neatly in the top left corner, his business correspondence in the right top corner, personal correspondence below that.

"May I assume you have come down at this unusual hour to discuss my afternoon appointment with Calder Hart?"

She planted herself firmly in front of his desk. "I want Francesca to marry Calder Hart, Andrew," she said warningly.

He did not want to battle with her—they had fought too often of late, mostly over their son, Evan, whom Andrew had threatened to disown, but hadn't been able to go through with it. Not that it mattered. His errant son had quit the firm, moved out of the house, broken off his engagement to Miss Sarah Channing, and continued to gamble and incur monstrous debt. Worse, every time Andrew heard of him he was told that the scandalous Countess Benevente was on his arm. "Julia, please sit down," Andrew said evenly.

"He will be here at any moment!" Her tone rose. She did not sit. "He is the best thing that has ever happened to Francesca! A man like that! Andrew, he is one of the wealthiest men in this city, and the most eligible bachelor as well."

"The man keeps company with divorcées and widows, and you know as well as I do that they are his lovers, Julia. He keeps a mistress. He has no social grace. He mocks social rules. For example, it was absolutely unacceptable for him to announce an engagement to Francesca! I have not approved and you know as well as I do that he should have spoken with me first. We would have held an affair and made the announcement then. And did I forget to mention his art collection? Everyone knows he has a shocking life-size nude sculpture in his front hall and some frankly anti-Christian paintings."

Julia folded her arms across his chest. "I think he adores our daughter, Andrew. I have seen it in his eyes. As for his behavior, well, I do believe his wealth allows him to do as he pleases."

"And you condone his behavior?"

"I like him, Andrew," she warned again.

"I do not. You say he adores Francesca. He may—for a moment. But what about a year from now? Or two, or three? One does not teach an old dog new tricks. Do excuse me, Julia, but this man is oversexed. He changes lovers the way you change your gowns. He will never remain faithful to Francesca, and while she may act like a sensible blue-stocking, these past few weeks have proven her to be a passionate and hopeless romantic. Besides, she is in love with Rick Bragg."

Julia threw both hands into the air. "That is a foolish infatuation—and he is married! And Andrew, every rake has his day."

They stared at each other. Julia was the first to speak. "Do not refuse him, Andrew, please."

He said softly, "Is it Francesca's welfare you are thinking of, or how the rest of society will applaud you for attaining such a groom for your daughter?"

She gasped. "It is Francesca I am thinking of!" she cried, but she had paled. And it crossed her mind that she had been thinking about the ladies she would have lunch with that day. She knew the only topic of conversation would be that the notorious Calder Hart wished to marry her daughter. Julia had been anticipating that luncheon all morning.

"Andrew," Julia said slowly. "I really do think Calder is smitten with Francesca, but . . . what if I am wrong and you are right? I have been enjoying every moment someone has come to me and congratulated me on an outstanding match. I have so wanted to see Francesca suitably wed and I never dreamed it would be to a man like Calder Hart."

He left his desk and embraced her. "I know. And I did not mean to imply that you were only thinking of yourself, because no one knows better than I how much you love our children. I don't think Francesca can manage Hart, Julia. I really don't. For all her intellect, she is so naive. And she only sees the good, even in the face of the bad. I don't want her unhappy and I don't want her hurt."

Suddenly Julia's confidence in the match collapsed. "I don't want her hurt and unhappy, either, Andrew. But what if? What if Calder Hart proves to be a wonderful husband? It does happen, you know."

"Yes, it does happen. But the fact that he chose to indifferently announce an engagement without our approval first speaks volumes. I do not like or trust him, Julia."

"And I so like him," she whispered. "Oddly, I also trust him."

He smiled a little. "That is because you are a woman, my dear. Let me interview him and we will take it from there."

She nodded, praying Calder would prove himself the man she wished him to be. "Very well," she said.

At the front desk, Bragg asked Captain Shea for the month's list of missing persons reports. Francesca stood beside him, having told him everything she had learned about Emily's disappearance, including how odd Will Schmitt had been. A moment later, Shea returned with a thin sheaf of papers. He handed it to Bragg, who thanked him.

It was a relief to no longer be in Bragg's office alone with him. Yet it felt good to have him at her side on another investigation. There was no one she trusted more while on a case, and no one she would rather work a case with. Would it really be possible for them to continue to work together when they were both so torn? "And why did you suggest we look at these reports?" she asked him with a small smile.

He smiled back, and suddenly it was as if the intense and terrible exchange a few moments ago had never taken place. "There may be something in the report that the O'Hares forgot to mention."

Francesca glanced at the top page—the missing person was a woman in her thirties. She started through the pile, remarking, "I never did ask the O'Hares if they filed a report, but if they went to the police, I assume that they did."

"And if they did not, they shall, as this is now an official police matter," Bragg said.

She paused, facing him, their gazes meeting. "Thank you, Rick," she said softly.

His gaze, which was topaz, moved slowly over her features, as if he enjoyed looking at her. He said, "Things will never be the same, will they? When you call me Rick, it is all I can think of."

Francesca glanced at Shea, but he had moved aside and was looking at a document just handed him by a clerk. If he had heard, he gave no sign. "I don't know why I called you Rick. It just slipped out."

"I know." His gaze slipped to her mouth, then jerked back to her eyes. "I will ask Farr to assign a detective to the case."

"That would be wonderful," Francesca returned, not meaning it. She hardly wished to have a partner who would be reporting directly to Farr. Did this also mean Bragg had no intention of teaming up with her? And that saddened her no end. God, was she making a huge mistake in accepting Hart's proposal? She flipped through four more reports. "Here it is!" Excitement filled her. "Emily O'Hare listed as missing this last Monday." Then her excitement vanished as quickly as it had risen. "Bragg, there is absolutely nothing in this report that we do not already know. Who is in charge of this bureau?"

"It's hardly a bureau," Bragg said. "Cases are passed along. In fact, most of these missing persons cases are runaways—children who decide to leave home and spouses who decide to abandon their marriage or their families. The worst cases turn out to be homicides. A murder will become linked when it is solved with a missing person, so Homicide ends up solving a good portion of the real missing persons cases."

"This report doesn't say who took it. No one has signed it, Bragg."

He took the page from her, scanned it, and said, "That must be an oversight. Captain Shea? Is Newman at his desk?" Bragg asked.

Shea turned back to them. "No, sir. He's in the field. A murdered gent, sir. His body was found around dawn this morning in some old lady's basement."

"Have Newman come to my office when he returns." Bragg faced Francesca. "What is your next move?"

"I think I shall go back to the neighborhood and start knocking on doors, asking questions. Someone had to have seen something. I also wish to speak with Mrs. Sarnoff, Mrs. Polaski, and Mrs. O'Brien."

He smiled. "Schmitt's three regular Monday customers. Canvassing an entire neighborhood could take some time. I have an important meeting at noon, but I could help you if you wish, for an hour or so."

She was surprised—and then she was delighted. It would be like old times—almost. Smiling, she said softly, "I'd love your help. I would never refuse such an offer."

He smiled back at her. A real, genuine smile, one that excluded the present and the past. "I'll round up a few men to help us. Shea, get me some eager rookies—say, a half-dozen men."

Shea hurried off.

Francesca pushed the pile of reports away, then paused. An idea tried to form in her head but failed. She stared at the reports. There was nothing new or significant in Emily's report, was there? Unsure of why she was doing it, she pulled the pile of reports back across the counter.

"What is it?" Bragg asked.

"I don't know," she said, the hairs on her nape tingling. She found Emily's report and read it over again, but this time slowly and word for word. No, there was nothing there. Oddly consternated, she stared at the pile. There was really no reason to go through these reports, none at all. But the urge to do so was strong, never mind that she had no idea of what she was looking for. And as she began to go over them, she said, "Emily was very beautiful. Hart thinks Emily may have been offered an unsavory position by some rich and depraved gentleman."

Tersely, Bragg said, "I am not surprised Hart would reach such a conclusion."

His comment was rude, but Francesca did not respond. She went through the reports one by one, rejecting case after case involving women and men, and then froze. Her heart leaped. "Bragg."

"What did you find?"

"Listen to this!" she cried. "Deborah Smith *disappeared* March second while on her way home from school. The disappearance was on Fourteenth Street, just a few blocks from where Emily disappeared. She is twelve years old, blond and blue-eyed, and according to this report, unusually pretty. The case is open. A Detective Moynihan has signed this." Francesca looked at him, wide-eyed. And now, even the fine hairs on her arms stood up.

"There is no reason to suspect a link between Deborah Smith's disappearance and Emily O'Hare's. There is a public school on Fourteenth between Second and Third Avenues."

Francesca trembled. "Yes, there is really no reason to suspect a link, but both girls were about the same age, both were very pretty, and they both simply vanished."

He stared. "Of course," he finally said, "we should leave no stone unturned. Where do the Smiths live?"

"On Fifteenth and Second," Francesca said with a smile, as they always did think alike. She quickly checked the last two reports, but one was an older man and the other a boy of eighteen, and the detective who had worked the latter case had scrawled "runaway" on the page.

Shea returned with several blue-coated policemen. "Here's Keene, Livingston, O'Dell, and O'Donnell, sir."

Francesca looked at the officers, all so baby-faced that she doubted any one shaved, and she smiled. They looked her own age or even younger. But they were as bright of eye as beavers, and they would probably bend over backward to help.

"Let's retire to the conference room, gentlemen," Bragg said with a gesture. He was also hiding a smile, and the first officer, who had pale skin and carrot-red hair, was so flushed he looked like he might faint. "I am assigning you to a missing child's case and I will brief you there."

The tenement was no different from any other. Francesca removed her driving goggles, which were coated with spots of mud and dirt, as Bragg turned off the engine to the Daimler. He removed his goggles as well, and they both climbed out of the once gleaming and now rather dirty roadster. As they were on 14th Street, a major thoroughfare crossing town, traffic was heavy around them, and noisy as well. Omnibuses, trolleys, hansoms, private carriages, and drays jockeyed for position, passing them by. Pedestrian traffic was heavy as well. Francesca skirted several muddy puddles and made it safely to the sidewalk.

"I am sorry, we should have taken a cab," Bragg said.

She glanced at her navy blue coat, which was spotted with mud. "It's actually a beautiful spring day—the mud notwithstanding."

"It wasn't that bad this morning. The puddles were still frozen over from last night."

"If I don't care about my coat, you shouldn't, either," Francesca said as they approached the building where the Smiths lived. "Bragg, how are the girls?" she asked, referring to Katie and Dot. Their mother had been murdered, and the children were being fostered at Bragg's until the right adoptive family could be found.

He smiled. "They're doing very well, although they both have asked for you repeatedly. Katie has the appetite of a horse. Dot's little mistakes are fewer and farther between.

Of course, that nanny your mother found has been a true blessing."

Francesca hesitated. She missed the children terribly, but in order to visit them, she would have to enter a home where Leigh Anne now reigned as lady of the house. "May I visit them?" she asked.

"Of course!" he cried, as if shocked. "Any time, Francesca."

She avoided his gaze as they entered the building. Inside, it was dark and dank. She smelled rotting potatoes and, unfortunately, urine. "I do not want to intrude."

He gripped her arm. "You could *never* intrude!" he said vehemently.

She met his fervent gaze. "It will be awkward," she heard herself say.

"Do you want me to arrange a time when Leigh Anne is not there?"

In that instant, Francesca remembered that his wife was having her luncheon that day. Dread filled her—she really did not want to go. But her many good causes were far more important than her own personal feelings, and she would also be able to see the girls. "I forgot," she said quietly. "Connie told me about Leigh Anne's luncheon. I intend to go. If I can, I hope to recruit any number of the women present at some future time for some of my charities."

He simply stared.

"You do not think it a good idea?"

"Not really," he said rather tersely.

"Why?"

He hesitated. "I just don't like you being around her. She is clever, Francesca, so promise me that anything she says, you will not heed."

How odd his comment was. And Francesca no longer believed Leigh Anne to be the scheming witch he made her out to be. In fact, she wasn't sure just how bad—or good—his wife really was. "I'll try," she said. Then, "How does she feel about the children being in your home?"

He hesitated, looked away. Then, "Oddly, they do get on."

Francesca was surprised—and dismayed. But she quickly told herself that her dismay was extremely selfish—for if they got on, it was wonderful for the children. "Are there any prospective adoptive homes for them, Bragg?"

He was grim. "Yes." Then, "I have become very fond of them, Francesca. I just don't know if I can let them go. But of course, I must."

She took his hand. "You are a wonderful father."

"I am not their father."

"You are wonderful with them," she said, and her eyes suddenly teared. She dared to recall a time when she had dreamed of having his children, and when she had seen him with the girls, she had even dreamed of the four of them becoming a family.

She dropped his hand, lifted her skirts, and started up the stairs. "Apartment Three, is it not?"

"Yes," he said, following her after a pause.

Her knock was answered by a bare opening of the door after the removal of a bolt. Francesca met a single blue eye. "Hello. I am Francesca Cahill, a sleuth, and I was wondering if I could ask you some questions about Deborah Smith?"

The crack widened slightly and Francesca met two wide blue eyes, a small nose, and pale brows. A voice bellowed from the back of the flat, "Who is it?"

The door was now ajar by several feet. Francesca smiled at the woman, who did not smile back. She seemed frightened. "It is a sleuth, Tom," she said. "A lady who wishes to ask us about Deborah."

"Tell her to get the fuck out of this house!" he cried, and a large man in an undershirt and patched trousers came into view.

"I only wish to help," Francesca said quickly, placatingly.

"Shut the door, Eliza," her husband ordered.

Bragg stepped forward, pushing the door open. "Excuse

me," he said to Eliza Smith. And he stepped inside the flat.

"I said get out," Tom Smith said, and he seemed very angry indeed. He also seemed drunk.

"I am the police commissioner," Bragg said. "And we have some questions to ask you and your wife, so sit down."

Tom froze.

Eliza shrank against the wall.

Tom turned to his wife. "You went to the police?" His tone was disbelieving—and furious.

She nodded, just barely, cringing even more.

"It is hardly unusual to go to the police when a relative is missing," Bragg said.

"She ain't missing, an' my wife's a fool! She went to her aunt's, she did, so she could work uptown in some fancy house for some fancy lady." He looked at his wife again, with murder in his eyes.

"I'm sorry," Eliza whispered to Tom. "I made a mistake." She faced Bragg. "I made a mistake, sir. I truly did."

Francesca knew that something was terribly wrong. Tom was a drunken lout; his wife was terrified of him, and Francesca's every instinct told her that Deborah Smith had not gone uptown to work as a lady's maid. "And where does her aunt live, Mr. Smith?" she asked, careful to appear neutral.

"Ain't none of your damned business," Tom sneered.

"She lives on Twenty-second Street, between First and Second Avenue," Eliza whispered desperately.

Tom moved so quickly that it was impossible to stop him. "Stupid bitch!" he roared, striking his wife across the face.

The slap was resounding. Eliza crumbled against the wall and Francesca caught her before she could fall to the floor. Francesca felt how fragile she was. Her entire body was shaking. The woman turned to meet her gaze. Blood trickled from her nose. And her eyes spoke as loudly as if she had uttered the words: *Please help*.

Bragg struck as quickly. Before Tom could react, his

neck was in a chokehold and he was against an opposite wall. "Apparently no one has ever told you that men do not strike ladies," he said.

Tom managed, his eyes bulging, "She ain't a lady, asshole, and we both know it."

Bragg increased his hold. "You are under arrest," he said.

Tom tried to speak and began choking.

Eliza cried out, in protest.

Bragg released Tom, who was quite larger than he, and threw him to the floor. He landed on his hands and knees—Bragg stepped on his lower back, hard. Tom coughed. "You can't arrest me. I did nothing wrong!"

"Assault is a felony, my man, and so is battery."

Tom began cursing so profusely and graphically that Francesca felt her cheeks turn red. She looked at Eliza. "Let's get some ice on that nose."

"It's not broken," Eliza whispered, beginning to cry, but without a sound. "I'm fine, really." She held her fist to her nose to stop the bleeding.

"Let me get some ice," Francesca said kindly. She could not imagine how this woman survived, living with such a man.

"No," Eliza said sharply, surprising Francesca. Then Eliza looked pleadingly at Bragg. "He didn't hurt me, sir. He really didn't. Please. Don't arrest him. He's a good man, he is. It's just the whiskey. Please."

Francesca closed her eyes, anguished. She understood all too well what was happening. Bragg could easily arrest Tom Smith, but for how long? And when he came home, she felt certain Tom would take his arrest out on his wife.

Bragg looked from Eliza to Francesca. She silently urged him to agree. Appearing very grim, he released his foot from Tom's back. The man moaned and made no move to get up.

Bragg knelt. "If you strike your wife again, I am locking you up in the Tombs and throwing away the key. Did you hear me?" he said very softly.

Tom nodded.

Bragg straightened. "We are paying a visit to Deborah Smith's aunt. Is she your sister?" he asked Eliza.

Eliza nodded, pale and fearful.

"What's her name?"

Eliza didn't speak.

Tom heaved himself to his feet. He looked at Bragg with hatred.

Bragg calmly returned the look. "The aunt's name?"

"Charlotte Favianno." It was Tom who spoke or, rather, spat. "She married a wop, she did."

"Thank you," Bragg said. He leaned close. "If Deborah isn't there, you will be hauled downtown in a paddy wagon. Lying to the police is a crime. It is officially called obstruction of justice."

Tom sneered but didn't speak.

"Francesca?"

Francesca faced Eliza, who looked terrified now. Francesca did not want to leave her alone with her husband, but was there any choice? An idea occurred to her. "Why don't you come with us?"

"I can't," Eliza breathed.

Francesca pressed several cards into her hand—in case Tom took one of them. "Call on me if you need me, Mrs. Smith. Please. I want to help."

Eliza hesitated, glanced worriedly at Tom, and said, "You are so kind."

Bragg and Francesca left.

And one hour later they learned that not only wasn't Deborah at her aunt's, but Charlotte Favianno hadn't seen her niece or sister in at least ten years.

CHAPTER
FIVE

FRANCESCA THANKED HER CABBIE, and as the hansom
rolled away, she turned to face Number 11 Madison Square.
A dozen handsome coaches were lined up along the block
in front of Bragg's town home, many of them double-
parked. Liveried drivers stood on the sidewalk in clusters
of two and three, chatting amiably while awaiting their mistresses. Traffic passing around Madison Park was therefore
congested, resulting in the frequent blaring of horns and
even a few curses. Francesca knew there would be no traffic
summonses today. Not when the wife of the police commissioner was having a luncheon.

Francesca trembled, foolishly afraid to go up to his dark
green door and use the knocker. And her fear had nothing
to do with being late.

How could a portion of her heart remain exclusively
Bragg's? She was about to marry Calder Hart, who had
been the most eligible and seductive bachelor in the city—a

man she was dangerously, overwhelmingly attracted to. She was also genuinely fond of him—more than fond, in truth. She knew she anticipated the next time he walked through the door of the same room she was in, just as she knew she eagerly awaited his embrace, his kisses, his touch. He fascinated her, he confused her, and he infused her with lust. And just about every single lady in the city would give her right hand to be in Francesca's shoes.

But she and Bragg had just parted company thirty minutes ago after their brief interview with Deborah Smith's aunt. Neither one of them had been very surprised by Charlotte Favianno's admission, or the fact that Tom Smith had lied. As always, they had been thinking along the exact same lines.

Bragg had gone back to headquarters to issue a warrant for Smith's arrest while she had gone uptown to attend his wife's luncheon.

Francesca closed her eyes briefly. Working so closely with Bragg again had been more than enjoyable—it had been familiar, comfortable, reassuring, and even right. They made, as always, the perfect investigative team. But this past morning had proven even more—it had reminded her that there was no one she admired and respected more than Rick Bragg. He put the welfare of others and the pursuit of justice first—always. He was, in fact, a real-life hero.

Francesca knew it was over with Rick Bragg; her every instinct told her that—she was certain Bragg would never divorce his wife. But the terrible truth was it would never really be over, not as long as he continued to be the man that he was. A very strong bond remained between them and she had become acutely aware of it while working with him that morning. That man would always have a piece of her heart and it was as simple as that.

The challenge was in their remaining real friends—given that he had Leigh Anne and she was now marrying Calder Hart.

She could not linger on the sidewalk—several of the drivers were eyeing her with curiosity now. She inhaled for courage and strode determinedly to the front door. Peter, Bragg's man, answered her knock immediately. He was huge, six-foot-four, with blue eyes and blond hair. Francesca knew from firsthand experience that he was a jack-of-all-trades; at various times he had been Bragg's butler, his valet, his household manager, his driver, and even his bodyguard. And until her mother had hired Mrs. Flowers to take care of the girls, he had also been their nanny.

If he was surprised to see her, he gave no sign. Impassive, he inclined his head and stepped aside so she could enter. Ahead, on Francesca's right, was the dining room. But no sounds emitted from it and she knew it was too small to host a luncheon for thirty ladies. Still, the sounds of animated conversation and laughter drifted to her. "They are in the salon?" she asked nervously.

He nodded. "And his study," he said. "Mrs. Bragg has made a buffet."

She winced, handing him her navy blue coat, which remained a mud-splotched mess. Then she wished she had thought to wear a dress that day—not that she had any pleasant day dresses. As always, Francesca wore a simple navy blue skirt and a white shirtwaist. It was her daytime uniform, so to speak. She also wore Hart's ring as she had promised she would.

She twisted it nervously. And she had to face the fact that it always bothered her to see Leigh Anne.

"Follow me," he said.

She gripped his arm impulsively. "Are the girls upstairs? I would so love to see them for a moment, first."

His eyes flickered. "Yes. Shall I show you up?"

She flushed, as he knew she did know the way. "I'm fine, thank you, Peter." She quickly started up the narrow staircase that was before her in the front hall.

His next words made her pause. "It is good to have you back, Miss Cahill."

Surprised by his declaration, she turned and smiled, but felt how anxious her expression must remain. "It is good to *be* back," she said, but in truth, she doubted the veracity of her own words now.

He was about to leave. Francesca could not help herself. "Peter?"

He hesitated.

"How are the girls? I mean, how have they fared with Mrs. Bragg in residence?" She began to blush. The question was highly inappropriate.

"They adore her," he said.

Francesca had to grip the smooth wood banister to keep from falling. "What?" Then she caught herself. "How wonderful," she said, feeling ill.

She turned and hurried up the stairs, almost devastated. But Peter was a man of few or no words. She had learned that if he did bother to speak, his every word was an honest one.

The girls adored Leigh Anne. She should be thrilled—she wanted to be thrilled—but she was upset, terribly so. Leigh Anne was beyond gorgeous—Bragg clearly thought so, never mind his protestations that he despised her—and she was holding a charitable luncheon, the girls adored her, and damn it all, she would make such a perfect senator's wife.

You have Calder Hart now, she told herself grimly. And her heart tightened as his image came to mind.

She did, and if anything, she felt even firmer in her resolve to go through with the engagement and marriage, even if their attraction was based on lust and not love. But that did not make being in Leigh Anne's house now any easier.

She had reached the top of the stairs. The children's room was on her right, but she turned to her left. The door there was ajar. It was the master bedroom and Francesca knew it.

It was wrong, but extreme curiosity propelled her now and there was simply no denying what she must do. She opened the door and stepped inside.

Francesca inhaled, hard. Leigh Anne had changed the

simple and stark decor. The room was painted a rich golden hue, gold-and-red-striped brocade drapes hung from the window, the bed was covered with red paisley bedding, and a gold Chinese rug with a floral design was underfoot. She trembled wildly. She could even smell Leigh Anne's perfume. It enveloped her, heady, sensual, and strong.

Her glance wandered to the dressing room, which had no door. A red Oriental rug was there, along with a red velvet stool. The vanity remained the original one, the wood old and scarred, but Francesca gazed upon perfume bottles, a pretty silver box she suspected contained powder, and several jars of cheek and lip rouge. Her gaze caught something else.

A long scrap of nude-colored silk was hanging on a peg beside the vanity.

Don't, she told herself.

She grimaced and hurried forward and lifted up the garment. It was a transparent nightgown, and the bodice was nothing but black lace.

Francesca dropped the sensuous and clearly revealing gown as if it had burned her hand, which it had not. But it did seem to burn her heart.

Upset, she hurried from the bedroom, and as she crossed the short hall, she told herself that she had gotten what she deserved for snooping so unconscionably. His private life with his wife was just that, private, and none of her affair.

"Frack!"

Francesca blinked at the familiar little screech, and then saw a blond blur racing toward her just before Dot hugged her around the knees, screaming, "Frack! Frack!"

It was simply too much—Francesca felt tears rising, fast and hard, as she bent to embrace and lift up the two-year-old. "Hello, darling," she murmured, hugging her hard.

Dot beamed at her, an angelic child with a head of blond curls and big blue eyes.

Francesca smiled back, wishing she had a free hand so she could wipe away all traces of the tears trickling down her face. "I missed you, baby girl," she whispered.

"Dot hap," Dot said, dimpling with laughter. "Hap hap!"

"That means she's happy."

Francesca looked past Dot and saw Katie, dark and unsmiling, standing in the doorway of the children's room, her skinny arms hugging her chest tightly. "Katie, how are you?" Francesca cried eagerly.

Katie simply stared accusingly at her, then turned and disappeared back into the children's bedroom.

Francesca's heart lurched. Katie remained sullen and hostile, at least with her, and she had a very good idea why. "Hello, Mrs. Flowers," she said to the tall, bespectacled woman who had come out of the room. As she spoke, she was aware of Dot playing with her hair. Her weight had become uncomfortable, so Francesca shifted her in her arms, ignoring Dot's grip on her hair. She was expecting a friendly reply to her greeting but not the one that she received. For Mrs. Flowers never spoke—as she did not have the chance.

"Hello, Francesca," Leigh Anne said from behind her.

Francesca whirled.

Leigh Anne was smiling slightly at her. As always, she was more than stunning and she made Francesca feel like a clod. The first thing one saw was her breathtaking face—pale skin, black lashes, emerald-green eyes, a tiny nose, and full lips. Her long jet-black hair was neatly swept up, a startling yet perfect contrast to her fair complexion. She wore a pale green silk dress that was extremely plain and on other women would have appeared drab, but on her it was perfection. The gown revealed every single perfect curve: her tiny waist, her full bosom, her lush hips. Francesca instantly saw her in that scrap of a negligee she had espied in the boudoir, and she was sickened.

Of course Bragg was smitten with this woman. Why wouldn't he be?

"I heard the doorbell and Peter said you had come up to see the girls," Leigh Anne said. Her gaze moved over Francesca's face slowly.

Francesca suddenly realized that Leigh Anne had noticed her tears. She was horrified. "Yes, I hope you do not mind." To make matters worse, her tone was thick.

"Of course not. Dot, do stop playing with Miss Cahill's hair," Leigh Anne said in a firm tone, but it was too late. Francesca's hair spilled free from its pins, landing wildly about her shoulders, a mass of honey-hued waves.

"Dot, that wasn't nice," Leigh Anne said, quickly taking Dot from Francesca before she could react and protest.

But Dot beamed at Leigh Anne. "Momma play," she demanded. "Momma play!"

Francesca felt the floor tilting beneath her feet.

"No, Dot, I have guests, but if you are a good girl, Mrs. Flowers will bring you and Katie down and you may have dessert with us." Leigh Anne spoke softly and firmly, but then she kissed the toddler hard on the cheek, her eyes closing as she did so.

Francesca stared, forgetting to wipe the tears from her cheeks. She was stunned. *Leigh Anne loved Dot. And Dot was calling her Momma. . . .*

"Mrs. Flowers? We will be serving dessert in a half an hour. I'd love for the children to come down," Leigh Anne said, slipping Dot gracefully to her feet.

"Of course," Mrs. Flowers said.

Dot clung to Leigh Anne's hand. "Frack! Desert! Frack come desert!"

Francesca could not speak.

"Dot, darling, it's *dessert*. Katie?" Leigh Anne called, walking to the doorway, still holding the grinning Dot's hand. "Have you said hello to Miss Cahill?"

Francesca now wiped her face with her fingertips and turned so she could see into the bedroom. Katie had been standing rigidly with her back to the door. She turned stiffly. "Yes," she said, unsmiling.

"Katie! What is wrong?" Leigh Anne asked, releasing Dot and rushing to the six-year-old. She slid her arm around her. "What has happened?"

Katie looked up at her and said, "I don't want her coming here."

"What?" Leigh Anne stroked her hair. "Dear, what are you talking about?"

Katie cast a baleful look at Francesca, who became horrified. "Tell her to leave."

Leigh Anne was startled, and she straightened, glancing at Francesca. Then she swiftly turned back to Katie. "Katie, a lady always minds her manners. That was beyond rude. Please apologize to Miss Cahill. And have you forgotten how kind Miss Cahill has been to you? Please apologize."

Katie bit her lip, cast an angry glance at Francesca, and said, "Sorry," clearly not meaning it.

Leigh Anne stared at the child and Francesca knew she was debating whether to take Katie to task now or later. Then Leigh Anne said, clasping Katie's thin shoulder, "I know how much you have been through in the past two months. We'll talk about this later, after the ladies have left."

Katie nodded, suddenly looking close to tears, and to Francesca's shock, she suddenly threw her arms around Leigh Anne, hugging her hard, sobbing.

Leigh Anne rocked her, murmuring, "There, there, darling, there, there."

Francesca backed away, realizing that this was all her fault. Katie had felt abandoned even before her mother had been murdered, due to Mary's hectic work schedule, and then her death had escalated those feelings. Francesca realized that Katie felt abandoned by her now, as well, as she had disappeared for an entire month. "Katie, I'm sorry," Francesca heard herself say. "I had to go out of town, and I am so sorry."

Katie stopped crying, sniffling now and wiping her eyes. She ignored Francesca.

"Do you feel better?" Leigh Anne asked, her arm still around her.

Katie nodded.

"You don't have to join the ladies and me for dessert if you do not want to."

Katie hesitated. "Did Peter buy those chocolate éclairs?"

Leigh Anne smiled. "Yes, he did."

Katie smiled back. "I'll come."

"Good." Leigh Anne kissed the top of her head, told Dot to be a good girl, and joined Francesca in the hall. Their gazes met and held, both women pausing.

Francesca stared into her unusually dark green eyes, thinking that any woman who cared for two orphans this way was a good person.

"Shall we?" Leigh Anne asked, staring back at Francesca as intently.

Francesca realized then that Leigh Anne was also thinking about her, not that she had a clue as to what the other woman's thoughts or real feelings about her were. She nodded grimly, but before either one of them moved, Leigh Anne's gaze dropped to Francesca's hands. A silence ensued; then Leigh Anne looked up and said frankly, "That ring is simply stunning."

An image of Hart, smiling and confident, flashed through Francesca's mind. In spite of the terribly uncomfortable encounter with Katie and Leigh Anne, his presence seemed to touch her and it was vastly reassuring. "Thank you. It's far too much for me, however."

"No, it's not." Leigh Anne smiled a little then.

Francesca thought about the way Leigh Anne had been with the girls and then thought about the extremely daring negligee in her boudoir. "You are truly fond of the children."

Leigh Anne pinkened slightly. "I always wanted children. But when Rick and I separated, I assumed it would never be."

Francesca hadn't known that. "Did he know?"

"Of course. When he was courting me we discussed our dreams and made so many plans." She became somber. "It feels like a bad but fading dream. How can two people fall in love, share so much—and then have it all vanish almost overnight?"

"I don't know," Francesca said hoarsely, because that

was exactly how her brief and unrequited love affair with Bragg could be described.

Leigh Anne glanced again at Francesca's hand. "You and Calder make a stunning couple."

"Do we?" Francesca didn't believe it, and she was almost certain Leigh Anne was being polite.

"Yes, you do. He's so strikingly dark, you're so golden, it's almost magical," she said.

Francesca looked her in the eye. "You didn't seem surprised when he announced our engagement." What she really wanted to say was, *You didn't seem pleased.*

"I was surprised. Every single person in that room was surprised." Leigh Anne then smiled. "There are a hundred women in this city who are green with jealousy, Francesca."

Francesca shrugged. "I truly doubt anyone is jealous of me."

"Hart is a catch. You know, it's almost incredible that he is in love, that he wants to marry. The man I met four years ago was a sworn bachelor."

Francesca wasn't about to tell her that love was not involved.

Now Leigh Anne appeared ever so slightly anxious. "May I ask you something? It's personal and impertinent."

"At least you are honest." She hesitated. "Only if I may ask you something in return."

Leigh Anne smiled genuinely then. "A barter. Very well."

"You first?" Francesca also smiled.

Leigh Anne nodded. "Do you love Calder Hart?"

"That is personal." She hesitated, knowing she did not have to answer. "I enjoy being with him. Very much so. And . . ." She stopped. "Marrying him seems like the right thing to do." She did not add, *Given the circumstances I now find myself in.*

"But you were in love with Rick, not so long ago."

Francesca tensed.

When Leigh Anne had first come to the city in February,

she had confronted Francesca immediately, making it clear
that she would not abandon her husband after all. The interview had been terribly unpleasant. To this day, Francesca
was not certain how Leigh Anne had learned of her romantic entanglement with Bragg. But they had been seen
together frequently, in the most public places, and the world
knew how closely they were working on the various cases
they had solved. Once, at the theater, a friend of Julia had
been observing them quite closely. Celia Thornton resided
in Boston, as did Leigh Anne's family, and Francesca felt
certain that it was Mrs. Thornton who had alerted Leigh
Anne to the romance. "I fell in love with him before I even
knew he was married. The day I found that out, why, it
changed my life forever."

Leigh Anne nodded. "I understand why you love him.
You are so much alike. But you know the old saying—
opposites attract. I am very different from Rick—and that,
I believe, is why he is so greatly attracted to me. I see the
same thing with you and Calder."

Francesca tried not to think about the scrap of a negligee. "Do you love him?"

Leigh Anne smiled softly. "Very much," she said.

She seemed so sincere. "Then why did you stay away
for four years?"

She raised her brows but spoke with great calm. "Now
that is impertinent. And frankly, that is my business—and
Rick's."

Francesca wasn't surprised by her answer. They started
downstairs. Leigh Anne said, "Have you set a wedding date
yet?"

"We are thinking of August."

Leigh Anne nodded. "It will be hot. June would be better."

Francesca stared, thinking about the divorce Bragg insisted he would have that August. Was the woman a mas-
terful poker player? Did she manipulate and scheme, as
Bragg claimed? Or was she simply the graceful and genteel
woman that she always appeared to be? Francesca finally

said, as they went downstairs, "Calder insists on five months. And my parents haven't agreed to anything."

"Your mother seems ecstatic—and I can't blame her." Leigh Anne smiled.

"There you are!" a familiar female voice exclaimed.

Francesca saw Bartolla Benevente, the flamboyant auburn-haired countess, coming gracefully toward them. She smiled. As usual, Bartolla flaunted convention, wearing a daring royal blue gown more suited for a dinner party than a luncheon. Much of her voluptuous bosom was revealed; her slim arms were bare. She wore numerous sapphires and diamonds. She embraced Francesca warmly. "Connie said you would be here, but I didn't think you would really join us," she said, her dark eyes warm. Still, her innuendo was clear—after all, it was Bartolla who had found Francesca in Bragg's arms on a sofa at a party two months ago.

But that had been before his wife had returned to him and their marriage.

"How could I pass up such a cause? The disgraceful state of public education is one of the issues I am most passionate about," Francesca said. She noted that Bartolla, always a head turner, was more radiant than ever. In fact, she almost looked as if she had very recently been in bed with a man.

Francesca knew that her brother was half in love with Bartolla. Evan was a bit of a rake, and he had always gravitated toward frankly sensual and stunning women. He had been overcome from the moment he had first met the widowed countess. But at the time he had been engaged to Sarah Channing, against his will. Francesca knew he had broken off the engagement several weeks ago. He had also quit the family firm and moved out of the house that had been built for him when the Cahill mansion had been constructed. He now resided at the Fifth Avenue Hotel.

It was hard to say who had disowned whom, Evan or her father.

"It is a very important cause," Bartolla agreed.

"Thousands of children are denied the education that is their right, due to a lack of teachers and schools," Leigh Anne said.

Francesca stared at the petite brunette. "Some would say that education is a privilege, not a right," she remarked, testing her.

Leigh Anne lifted her brows. "But certainly not you."

Francesca wished to draw her into a debate—to see if she was genuinely a reformist at heart. "I believe in our Constitution," she said, refusing to say why.

"As do I." Leigh Anne smiled.

Francesca stared, refusing to expound upon the Bill of Rights and wondering if Leigh Anne had a clue as to what she was talking about.

"We all believe in freedom and equality," Bartolla said with a sigh. "Let me see that ring, Francesca," she added slyly. And before Francesca could react, Bartolla lifted her hand, exclaiming over the huge stone. Francesca felt herself blush.

"I am certain that is from Asprey! Francesca, are you tickled pink? Imagine, bringing Calder Hart to heel like that!" Bartolla laughed heartily. "You, a blue-skirted blue-stocking, a sleuth, dear God, have brought down the city's worst womanizer! You do know that a hundred ladies are conspiring even as we speak to bring about your untimely demise?" She laughed again, as if truly enjoying herself.

"I doubt that," Francesca murmured, feeling herself blush.

"He must be smitten. And I can imagine why! You are the first woman to say no, are you not?" She grinned widely then.

"I beg your pardon?" Francesca said, her ears now burning. If only Bartolla knew that Hart was the one saying no, refusing to heed Francesca's pleas to the contrary.

"I think it is wonderful," Leigh Anne said.

"So who will be his best man?" Bartolla asked slyly. "Let me guess—Rick Bragg?"

Francesca almost gasped, looking directly into Bartolla's laughing eyes.

"Well, they are brothers," Bartolla said, clearly enjoying herself.

Francesca could not think of a word to say.

Calmly Leigh Anne said, "You know very well that they do not get along. I feel certain Calder will invite Rathe to be his best man." Rathe Bragg, Rick's biological father, had taken both Calder and Rick in when their mother had died. Calder had been ten, Rick twelve. Rathe had raised the boys with his other children.

"And you must be thrilled!" Bartolla cried, hugging Leigh Anne. "Things have certainly changed since you first arrived in town, haven't they? And when did you arrive, my dear? It was early February, was it not?"

"I arrived on the fifteenth," Leigh Anne said with a composed smile. "I must get back to my guests. Ladies?" And she swept past them, inviting them to join her.

But neither Francesca nor Bartolla moved. They stared after Leigh Anne until she had disappeared into the salon or at the end of the hall where the ladies were dining. Bartolla sighed. "Now, I am utterly bored with this insipid little luncheon. I am meeting your brother for tea, and he is taking me shopping. Do you wish to join us?"

Francesca shook her head. "I must mingle. How is Evan?"

Bartolla's eyes glinted. "Dashing, handsome, irresistible," she laughed.

Francesca had to smile. She was relieved at the change of topic. "I heard he finally broke it off with Sarah. How is she?"

Sarah and Bartolla were cousins. "Happier than ever. Painting like mad. She has started on your portrait, Francesca; I've seen some preliminary sketches. I am truly impressed. Calder will be thrilled." She grinned.

Francesca winced. She had promised Hart last night that she would speak with Sarah today and reminded herself now that she must do so before going home. "Tell Evan I adore him—and that I miss him."

Bartolla's smile vanished. "He will come to his senses soon. Trust me. I am certain of it."

Francesca did not think so. Her brother was furious with their father, and she had never seen Evan take such a stand before. "Papa blackmailed him into that engagement, Bartolla. I do not think he will return home or to the company anytime soon."

"He is being a child," she said with a shrug. "An angry child. And did you hear he has taken a pitiful job as some lawyer's clerk? Trust me. I will make sure he does the right thing." And she smiled.

Francesca wasn't sure she favored Evan returning home. She was very proud of him for doing what he wanted to do with his life instead of doing as their father wished.

Bartolla asked Peter for her coat. Then she smiled at Francesca. "I did not mean to be rude before. I am so excited for you! But things have truly changed, haven't they? How strange life can be. Do you love Hart? Has he seduced you?"

"Bartolla," Francesca tried.

"You can tell me!" she exclaimed. "I saw this coming months ago! Hart was so jealous of your sleuthing with Bragg. But he is irresistible, isn't he? And frankly, darling, there is *no one* better in bed."

Francesca trembled. She already knew that years ago Hart and Bartolla had had a brief affair. Now, done with each other, they had mutual feelings that bordered on mild dislike for each other. Still, Francesca did not need to be reminded of his long ago affair now.

But Bartolla knew she had discomfited Francesca. "Darling, with a man like Hart, you will be faced with his previous paramours constantly. In fact, when you walk into a room, you will always wonder who he has slept with and who he has not."

Francesca stared. Suddenly she was stricken. But it was true. Hart had been with so many women—suddenly she was ill. How would she ever bear it? She and Hart would attend an affair and there would always be a woman present who knew him intimately. In that moment, Francesca knew she could not bear it. It would kill her, not knowing who his ex-lovers were—and knowing would be even worse.

Bartolla thanked Peter and took her coat. "And how is Bragg taking the news? He certainly seemed upset last night."

Francesca flinched, unable to stop thinking about all of Hart's ex-lovers. "He is very happy with Leigh Anne," she lied.

"Oh, please. He can hardly bear to be around her—it's so painfully obvious—although I suspect they are a good match in bed." She shrugged on her gray brocade coat, trimmed with chinchilla. "He still loves you, Francesca. That is painfully obvious, too."

She froze. With Bragg, she would never have to worry about ex-lovers and his eventually breaking her heart. "He does? You think he still loves me . . . that way?"

"How could you not see what everyone else sees?" Bartolla asked with surprise, drawing on her gloves.

Francesca inhaled. Hart had warned her not to trust this woman, but they were friends and Bartolla was such a worldly woman. "I am confused," she whispered unsteadily. "I am very confused, Bartolla."

Bartolla took her hand. "Tell me about it. Although I am sure I already know. You are torn, aren't you?"

Francesca nodded, suddenly miserable. "But I do adore Hart," she whispered.

"You adore his bed," Bartolla said, her eyes big and sincere. "We both know that if Bragg were single, you'd never look twice at a rake like Hart."

She shook her head, wanting to deny it, but she was afraid that Bartolla had hit the truth. "No. Hart and I have become real friends. It simply happened."

"Hart doesn't have friends," Bartolla said.

"I am his first," Francesca whispered.

Bartolla raised her dark brows, clearly disbelieving. But

that was the one thing Francesca was sure of—that Hart was really her friend. He had proven it too many times to count.

"Have you slept with him?" Bartolla asked.

Francesca flushed. "Bartolla . . ."

"I won't tell." She smiled.

Francesca hesitated. "Hart insists that we wait for our wedding night."

"Really?" Both dark brows lifted. "How odd."

"He is not a predictable man," Francesca said.

"No, he is hardly predictable. And I daresay he will be a difficult husband, too."

Francesca hoped not.

Bartolla shrugged. "Not that it matters. You will do as you choose, for you are a headstrong woman, which is one of the reasons I so like you. And marriage isn't the end of the world, really. If you did get bored, or decided that Hart was too much of a tyrant—or became bothered by his affairs—why, you could always have an affair, as well."

"I'm not that way," Francesca said, shocked.

"But you are so bohemian!"

"I am actually, foolishly, rather romantic."

"Oh, dear. Then you had better think twice about marrying Calder Hart, as he will break your heart quicker than I can utter these words."

Francesca turned away. She already knew this, and now her fear and panic were surging forth. She must be mad, to be marrying Calder Hart, because he would do more than break her heart; he would rip it into useless little shreds. She knew it—and Bartolla knew it, too.

"At least Rick will always be waiting in the wings to pick up the pieces," Bartolla remarked.

Francesca inhaled, hard. Bartolla was so perceptive. Because that was what would happen, wasn't it? She would eventually find Hart with another woman, she would be broken into pieces, and Bragg would be there, to hold her, comfort her, and tell her it was all right. And she knew he would never say, "I told you so." Francesca closed her eyes, overwhelmed with the reality of her dilemma.

But would he still be with Leigh Anne?

"I didn't mean to upset you so!" Bartolla exclaimed, taking her hand again.

Francesca forced herself to smile. "I am not upset. And fortunately, I am not in love with Hart. I am fond of him and I look forward to sharing his bed." She could not believe she had been so nonsensical, so matter-of-fact. To add to the effect, she shrugged as if she had not a care in the world.

"Well spoken." Bartolla grinned. "And I am off. Good luck then."

Before joining the company, Francesca watched her leave. She was grim. Worse, she was afraid again, the way she had been a month ago when she had run away from Hart. How could she even think of marrying him? She was simply too fond of him!

"Francesca? Are you joining us? Oh, dear, what is wrong?" Leigh Anne asked, a silver tray containing pastries in her hands.

Francesca blinked. "I am fine," she managed.

Leigh Anne stared. "Whatever Bartolla said to you, I would not think too much about it."

Francesca felt herself send Leigh Anne another sickly smile. "Really."

"Bartolla adores causing conflict."

Francesca looked away. She wasn't about to tell Leigh Anne that in this instance the conflict already existed and Bartolla had merely been confirming Francesca's worst fears.

"She is the one who wrote to me in Boston, urging me to come back immediately—she is the one who told me that my husband was in love with you," Leigh Anne said.

Francesca gasped. *"It was Bartolla?"*

Leigh Anne nodded gravely.

Before Francesca could assimilate the extent of such treachery, the front door opened and Bragg walked in. He halted upon seeing both women.

"Rick?" Leigh Anne gasped in surprise. She gave Francesca an odd look and hurried to him, still holding the dessert tray. "What brings you home in the middle of the day? I am hosting that luncheon I told you about."

"I know." He looked at his wife for one more moment and then looked past her at Francesca. "I came to speak with Francesca."

Francesca already assumed this. Tension overcame her.

"To speak with Francesca?" Leigh Anne set the tray down on the small entry table, beneath a wall mirror, looking from her husband to Francesca and back again. "But how did you know she would be here?"

"We are working on a case," he said, not looking at Leigh Anne now.

Francesca came forward. "What has happened?"

"I sent my men to arrest Tom Smith. He is dead, Francesca."

CHAPTER
SIX

FRANCESCA GRABBED BRAGG'S COAT sleeve. "What? He is dead? Do you mean murdered?"

"He was found by a resident of the area in an alley that cuts between Tenth and Eleventh Streets. His throat was slit."

Francesca knew she gaped. Her mind raced.

Leigh Anne said, "Would you both like to retire to the dining room? You can have some privacy there."

Bragg never took his eyes off Francesca as he nodded. She somehow followed him into the dining room, where Leigh Anne closed the single oak door solidly behind them. Francesca said, "There is simply no reason to think that his murder has anything to do with the disappearance of his daughter, or of Emily. We do not even know that Emily's and Deborah's disappearances are linked."

"I agree. The Daimler is outside and still running. Unless

you truly must attend this luncheon, I suggest you get your coat."

Francesca smiled grimly. "The school?"

"I think so," he said, finally smiling in return.

Francesca rushed into the hall. "Peter! May I have my coat, please—the one covered in mud?"

He nodded and went to the closet.

Leigh Anne stepped out of the salon, coming slowly down the hall, looking from Francesca to Bragg. There was the barest hint of anxiety in her eyes. "I take it this is an emergency?" she asked Bragg.

He finally looked at her. His eyes narrowed as he did so. "Murder is usually an emergency," he said.

"I am only asking. We are supposed to dine at Ron Harris's tonight." Harris was the city's treasurer. "Mayor Low will be there. And so will Robert Fulton Cutting."

Bragg nodded grimly. "What time?"

"Seven."

"I'll meet you there," he said.

"Will you be late?"

"I'll try not to be."

Francesca had put on her coat, and watching them, she felt terribly sorry for them both. She also felt like kicking Bragg in the shins. His wife was being proper and polite, not to mention very generous about the investigation he was on—and who he was on it with. But Bragg was being a real boor. She came forward, unfortunately aware of how disastrous her appearance was compared to Leigh Anne's. "I will make certain he arrives at seven precisely," she said, meaning it.

Leigh Anne turned to her and smiled in relief. "It is a very important dinner, Francesca. It's an honor that Rick was invited."

Francesca had no doubt that some serious political bargaining would take place after supper tonight. "He will be there, on time and fully dressed." She gave Bragg a look, because he could not attend such an affair in his current clothing. He would have to go home to change.

But he smiled at her, understanding. "I have a set of dress clothes in the office. I'll have an officer bring them to me when the time is right."

"Then let's go," Francesca said lightly, excitement now joining her determination. Because no matter what she had said, she suspected that Tom Smith's murder had something to do with his missing daughter. After all, he had lied about sending his daughter to her aunt's, and he had been murdered immediately after speaking to the police.

The public school was just a few minutes south of Madison Square, and as they were traveling downtown, with most of the city traveling uptown to home and hearth, they arrived within fifteen minutes. School, of course, had been let out. As they approached the limestone building, which badly needed a wash, Francesca realized it was an elementary school, from first to sixth grade. Deborah Smith had obviously been in the graduating class.

They entered the building, where some faculty were in the halls, along with a janitor who was mopping the granite floors. Bragg stopped a plump middle-aged woman who was clearly on her way home. "Excuse me, ma'am. Could you direct us to the principal's office?"

"Right down the hall," she said, giving them a curious look. "Is this about poor Deborah Smith?"

Francesca almost fell down. "Yes. Why do you ask?"

"He's a policeman by the look of it, and she was in my class. I am Mrs. Hopper," she said, smiling briefly. Then her smile vanished. "So was Rachael Wirkler. I just don't understand how two such beautiful girls could simply disappear."

"Rachael Wirkler?" Francesca echoed.

"There is another missing child?" Bragg asked.

"Yes. Rachael has been missing since February. Her parents are beyond distraught."

Francesca glanced at Bragg. She said, "How did she vanish?"

"I don't know. She was here one day, and they say she never went home. It was February tenth. The same with

Debbie, but that was only a few weeks ago. I so adored those girls, so sweet and kind they were. Two of my best students."

Francesca stared at Bragg. He stared back. "We now have one child—a pretty girl of thirteen—who disappeared on her way to the grocer's after work. And we have two more children, both girls of—how old was Rachael, Mrs. Hopper?"

"Rachael was fourteen. She started school two years late."

"And we have a twelve-year-old and a fourteen-year-old girl who both left school one day, never to arrive home."

"Were they attractive children?" Bragg asked.

"Deborah was pretty, with a laughter like tinkling bells. But Rachael was so beautiful, sir. She stopped men in their tracks."

"What are you thinking?" Francesca asked Bragg tersely.

"Have any other children, male or female, disappeared that you know of?" Bragg asked the teacher.

"Yes, about the same time Rachael vanished, one of Linda Wellington's students also vanished, but apparently on her way to school. Her name was Bonnie Cooper. We are having an epidemic of missing students, sir, and I am glad that the police are finally involved."

Bragg said, "I am very surprised the police were not called in sooner."

"You would have to ask the parents about that—or Principal Matthews." She was frowning now and clearly disapproving.

"Has anyone seen anything? Perhaps one of the students knows what happened to either Rachael, Deborah, or Bonnie?" Francesca asked.

"We did make a general announcement asking any student with information to come forward, but no one did. I also spoke at length with my own class, hoping one of my children knew something, but no one did."

"How many children are in your class, Mrs. Hopper?" Bragg asked.

"Forty-two—it was forty-four."

Francesca winced. How large and unwieldy the class was. "And there is one other sixth grade?"

"Yes, Linda Wellington's. She has about forty-five students, I believe."

Francesca glanced at Bragg. "Leigh Anne should have more luncheons," she said.

He ignored that. "I may need to ask you more questions, Mrs. Hopper. If so, I will have one of my men bring you downtown to police headquarters."

Mrs. Hopper's eyes widened. "Police headquarters?"

"I am the police commissioner," Bragg said. "And this is Miss Cahill, a sleuth. She is working for another family who have a missing daughter."

Francesca handed Mrs. Hopper her card. "If you remember any detail that you think may be significant, please get in touch with either me, Commissioner Bragg, or Inspector Newman."

Mrs. Hopper nodded but said, "I wish I had more to add, but I don't. I just want those two sweet girls back."

They left her and hurried down the hall. "These are too many disappearances, Bragg. They must be linked. But why?" Dread was creeping over her now.

He glanced at her, his expression severe. "Perhaps the children are being forced into a sweatshop, Francesca."

She was relieved. For she had begun to dread another possibility—one she dearly did not want to think about. "I read about immigrants being forced into labor in the worst conditions in Jacob Riis's book," she said quickly. "But I never expected to encounter the situation in reality. I never thought to uncover such an elaborate plan to find workers and then abduct them into the workplace." She had become outraged. "And children at that!"

"Every now and then a ring of white slavers is broken up. We will find the perpetrators of these crimes."

Francesca was silent as they paused before Principal Matthews's door, thinking about the fact that all four girls were missing now. The plot had certainly and quickly thickened. She glanced at Bragg. He hadn't even remarked on her worst fear. And he was so terribly grim, so terribly concerned. He must ache for the girls, as she did—how frightened and despondent they must be. How could this be happening in the twentieth century, in the greatest and most modern city in the world? Very easily, she thought, as the schism between rich and poor, between the haves and have-nots, was so terribly vast.

Matthews called out for them to enter, breaking into her dark thoughts. He was a portly man with heavy side-whiskers, and he was at once surprised and oddly pleased to see them. "Do come in," he said. "I feel certain you are not parents of any of our students?" It was a question.

Bragg shook his hand. "I am Police Commissioner Bragg, Principal, and this is Miss Cahill, a sleuth employed by the O'Hares. We are here in regard to the students missing from your school."

Matthews's face fell. "Do sit down," he said somberly. "It has been so odd, first Rachael Wirkler, then Bonnie Cooper and Deborah Smith."

"Were the police called in?"

"That was a decision I left to the parents. When Bonnie disappeared, her father refused to seek the help of the police. He is a rather disreputable sort, and I gathered he disliked the police. I encouraged him to ask for help, but he never did."

"He has a criminal record?"

"I think he was in jail, yes."

Francesca had taken out her notepad, and she made a few quick notes. "What was his name?"

"I am not sure. Perhaps it was John. Yes, it may have been John Cooper."

Francesca glanced at Bragg. "Can you have one of your men go over the mug book?" she asked, referring to the book of sketches and photographs that was otherwise known as the Rogues' Gallery, as it contained almost every known criminal in the city.

Bragg nodded. "Principal, what is the Coopers' home address?"

Matthews said, "My secretary has left for the day. I'm afraid I do not understand the filing system, but I can get you the home addresses of all the missing students Monday, if you wish."

"Monday is too late," Bragg said. "Why don't *you* try to find the records we need?" He smiled politely now.

Matthews stood. "Of course. I'll be right back," he said, walking into the adjacent front room, where several small desks were.

Francesca turned to watch him go to some filing cabinets. "It is odd that he did not summon the police, Bragg."

"Yes, it is."

"And what was that nonsense about not knowing how to file?"

"I am not sure." They shared a glance.

Bragg walked into the next room, Francesca following. Matthews was bent over the file drawer. "And the Wirklers? Is there a reason they did not file a police report?"

"I think they did. At least, I seem to recall them telling me that they would." He looked up and smiled at them.

Francesca could not help herself. "I find it odd that you would not be certain about the police being asked to investigate when a student of yours has disappeared. I also find it odd that you did not summon the police yourself. After all, the children here are in your care and they are your responsibility."

He visibly stiffened but continued to smile. "I have eight hundred children in this school. I cannot begin to tell you the work involved in administering it all. If the Coopers felt that the police should not be involved, I felt it was their decision to make. As for Rachael Wirkler, I do believe but cannot recall clearly that the police were asked in." Matthews continued to smile. "This is a trying job. I do the best that I can."

Francesca thought him negligent in both his duty toward and responsibility for his students.

"Has any student volunteered information regarding the disappearances?" Bragg asked calmly.

Matthews softened. "No. No one seems to know anything. We had a general assembly a month ago, requesting help. No one came forth."

"Children do not disappear into thin air," Francesca said tersely. "Surely someone in this vast school saw strange suspicious men lurking about."

"You are suggesting foul play?" Matthews was surprised, his dark eyes wide.

"I most certainly am."

"You do know that children at the adolescent age these three girls were at often run away, sometimes with a lover."

"Yes, I do. But Deborah Smith was not that kind of girl, and I have no doubt that if I speak with the Coopers and Wirklers I will learn the very same thing about their daughters," Francesca said, now firmly disliking the principal.

"Francesca, you are leaping to assumptions," Bragg murmured, touching her elbow.

"I feel very strongly about this, Bragg," she warned. "Principal Matthews, have you found any records?"

"No." Matthews hesitated. "They seem to be missing, Miss Cahill. There is no Wirkler in the 'Ws,' no Cooper in the 'Cs.' I will try 'Smith' now."

Bragg quickly stepped past the principal. "May I?"

"Please." Matthews stepped back, looking quite uncomfortable now.

A moment later Bragg straightened and met Francesca's regard. "Well, well," he said. "It appears there are three missing files."

She stared. "Perhaps they are misfiled?"

He gave her a doubtful look. "Perhaps."

"I am certain my secretary can solve this matter on Monday," Matthews said.

Francesca doubted it. The files had been removed—or even destroyed. She smiled grimly at him. "You may be sure I will find out what happened to the three girls, Principal Matthews."

"And I look forward to your findings, Miss Cahill." He walked them to the hall. "Are you the infamous sleuth who caught the Randall Killer with a fry pan?"

"Yes, I am," she said, unsmiling. She not only disliked the man, but he had a strong body odor that was offensive as well.

Once in the hallway, with the principal's door closed behind them, Francesca faced Bragg in disbelief. "You were very hard on him," he said softly.

"I don't like him. He should be dismissed instantly for negligence of duty. He should have called in the police the very day Bonnie Cooper did not come back to school!"

Bragg smiled and clasped her shoulder. "I happen to agree, but we will get more from him with honey than vinegar."

She softened. "You are right. Bragg, someone has removed those files, obviously to cover any trail leading to what really happened to those girls!"

"That may be the case. Or there may be another explanation."

"I don't see how there could possibly be another explanation!" she cried. "I am beginning to think that Matthews is involved himself, somehow."

"That is a huge conclusion to draw. Francesca, you are getting very emotional and that is not a good way to get to the bottom of this case."

She hesitated, because he was right. With more girls missing, with the possibility of foul play now a near certainty, she was angry. She could not bear the idea of sweet, innocent girls being forced into slave labor—or, God forbid, something worse. But to successfully conduct an investigation, she needed her wits about her. "I want those children safely home, Bragg."

He held her shoulder for one more instant, his grip reassuring and warm. "I know you do," he said. "And so do I."

Their eyes met and she softened and they smiled at each other in understanding. It crossed her mind that no one understood her the way that Bragg did, not even Hart. She pulled away then. He gave her a look, as if understanding her still, and they started down the hall.

"What's next?" Francesca asked. "It's already half past four. I'd like to speak to Will Schmitt again, but I fear that will have to wait until tomorrow. I promised Calder I would speak with Sarah today and get that portrait started." The moment she spoke, she regretted her words and wished she had not mentioned Hart's name. She did not want to argue now. It had already been a long and eventful day.

He didn't speak as they walked out of the building.

Francesca winced, trying to make out his expression, but it was engraved in stone.

Then he said, "I will have my men canvass the neighborhood until we locate the Wirklers and Coopers. I can give you a ride, if you wish. I have a meeting at the Fifth Avenue Hotel at five, so I have the time."

"That would be nice," she said.

His Daimler was parked ahead. He said, "Are you seeing him tonight?"

She faced him squarely and declared, "I don't think so. We made no plans. Bragg, you will be out and about with your wife tonight, so even if I am with Calder, it should not bother you so much."

"Well, it does."

She seized his arm as he started past her, halting him. "The girls adore her. And she adores them."

He stared, looking annoyed now, dangerously so. "They do adore her. I admit to being more than surprised. But it is the one light in my life right now."

"The one? She is determined that you be at a very important political dinner tonight, one which benefits your future, not hers. I think you are behaving terribly toward her, Bragg, I really do." There, she had said what was on her mind and eating at her all afternoon.

"The dinner affair tonight only benefits my future? I beg

to differ, Francesca. Leigh Anne covets the glory that she will have should the day come when she is a senator's wife! She is already thrilled at being Mrs. Police Commissioner. And yes, she allows people to address her that way."

"That is not an uncommon way for a commissioner's wife to be addressed!"

"Why are you defending my wife? You know as well as I do that she returned only because of you—and only because I am in some degree of position and power, now. Damn it, Francesca, the woman slept her way through Europe."

"Did she? And even if she did, so what? Were you celibate the four years you were separated? Will you never forgive her and give her another chance? She seems a wonderful mother, Rick. She seems a devoted wife. I have never met a more graceful woman, if you want to know the truth." Unfortunately, it was true. She hesitated and then added, "She reminds me of Connie, in a way. At once elegant and gracious and always composed."

"She has bewitched you, too, for that is what she does best." His eyes glittered with anger now.

Francesca stiffened. "You can be a dolt at times."

"No, but I know better than to go by appearances, Francesca, for I know the woman far better than you do."

"Do you? Oddly, I really don't think so."

He stared, flushed with anger, and she stared coolly back.

"Why not give her a real chance? She is your wife. If you are right and she is the terrible woman you think her to be, the truth will eventually tell. And you can separate or divorce then. But why not see, first, if there is some goodness and love left? What do you have to lose?"

"You."

She recoiled.

He stared, the anger fading until only frustration was left in his eyes. "Why are you doing this? So you can continue on with Hart with little or no guilt?"

She was relieved to be attacked and she bristled. "This

isn't about Calder, damn it. This is about you—and it is about a woman I can't help but like no matter how hard I try not to. And that's the real problem. I feel you are being terribly unfair with her, when you are more than fair with every stranger on the street."

His eyes blazed. "That is enough! I refuse to allow you to butt into the state of my marriage."

She cried out.

He realized what he had said and reached for her, but she jerked away. "Don't!" she cried.

"I am sorry. I didn't mean that."

She stared, shaken to the core, and said, "But you did. You more than meant it, and not for the first time. However, you are right." She inhaled harshly, trembling. "I have been concerned with your private life, and it is not my affair. Because you are married and we are merely friends."

"Francesca."

She turned her back on him and got into his motorcar.

Sarah Channing lived with her mother, a wealthy widow, on the city's West Side, commonly referred to as the Dakotas, because that part of town was so far away from the rest of the city and was both so bleak and desolate. The rather Gothic mansion, recently built, was huge, and the only building evident for several blocks. All the surrounding lots were vacant or had rough lean-to structures upon them where homeless squatters lived. Francesca always felt that she was entering a foreign country when going to the West Side.

The Channing doorman swiftly answered Francesca's knock and she found herself standing in a dark entry hall that was a tower with high ceilings and gleaming oak floors. Some animal heads adorned the walls, as Sarah's father, Richard Wyeth Channing, had been keen on hunting and had assembled a collection of animal trophies from all of his various hunting trips in Africa, India, Russia, and Europe. As she waited for Sarah, she tried to forget about

Bragg, and her thoughts quickly turned to Hart. By now, or very shortly, he would be facing her father in the interview that would ultimately decide her fate.

Her heart lurched, but before she could analyze why, Sarah appeared at the far end of a hall, a tiny figure in a huge and drab gray dress that was splotched with old dried paint in various colors. Sarah was beaming, and it lit up her tiny face. Francesca knew most people thought Sarah plain, with her mousy brown hair, dark eyes, and unremarkable figure, but Francesca was finding her prettier and prettier the more she got to know her. And now, with Sarah filled with excitement, her long, curly hair coming down about her face, in spite of the ugly dress, she was truly beautiful. In fact, no spirit seemed freer.

"Francesca!" Sarah broke into a run and the two women embraced. "Hart sent me a note telling me that you returned. I have been so worried about you!"

Francesca noted some ocher and rust tones of paint on Sarah's face. "I am fine. But how are you?"

"I am wonderful," she said, with a grin. "You do know that Evan broke it off about two weeks ago?"

Francesca saw that Sarah was simply thrilled. "I heard the moment I came home."

"Please, don't be angry with me that I am so happy. But I don't want to ever marry and you know it. Besides, we both know Evan is smitten with Bartolla."

Francesca had to hug her. "I know it was a terrible mismatch. Has he been with Bartolla as often as she led me to believe earlier when I saw her at a luncheon?"

"They have become lovers, it's obvious. I think she is with him every night." Sarah smiled happily. "Perhaps another engagement is in the air?"

Francesca thought that might well be the case, too. "How is your mother taking the news?" she asked.

"Not well! Try telling Mother that we were the worst possible match! She took to her rooms for an entire week, weeping and sulking in turns. Now, if the Cahill name comes up, she leaves the room. She refuses to listen to me when I explain that I am married already—to my art. And Bartolla and I agreed not to let her know that Evan is courting her."

Sarah was in many ways a kindred spirit, and Francesca laughed as Sarah took her hand and hurried her down the hall. Her studio was in the back of the house on the ground floor. "That would be like my telling Mama that I am a professional investigator with no time for a husband."

"Yes, it would." Sarah lifted Francesca's hand and beamed at her ring. "How wonderful! I saw this coming a mile away!"

"You did?" Francesca paused before the open door of Sarah's studio, which was artificially lit now due to the late time of day. Sarah favored portraits of women and children, and her walls were lined with her work, some in progress, the others finished. She had several standing easels, and two had canvases upon them. Francesca thought Sarah's work brilliant. She had clearly been influenced by the impressionists, but her work remained classic.

"Oh, Francesca, when a man insists upon your portrait, the writing is clear upon the wall."

Francesca was delighted, even if she didn't want to be. "Hart only insisted on my portrait to annoy me because we were fighting at the time."

Sarah gave her a look of disbelief. "Please. So why did you leave the city? Did you really have an ailing friend?"

"I needed to think," Francesca said.

"I thought so." Sarah squeezed her hand. "But you are back now and I am so glad, and not just because of the portrait."

"I am actually glad to be back, as well," Francesca said, and now she meant it. It was good to be back; and thank God she was back, otherwise she would not be on this new investigation, with so many children's fates upon the line. "I am also glad to see that you have fully recovered from the last investigation," she said, referring to Sarah having been a killer's target.

Sarah's eyes widened. "I am fully recovered. Thank God

that terrible time in my life is over. In fact, I hardly ever think about it!" Her tone was a bit high now.

And something in her eyes alarmed Francesca—she felt certain that Sarah wasn't quite over the trauma of almost being murdered. Francesca took her arm. "Is Rourke still in town?" she asked, referring to Rourke Bragg, Rick's younger brother. He was a medical student in Philadelphia, but he had been helpful in the last investigation.

"Rourke left a month ago. I haven't heard from him," Sarah said briskly, looking away as if avoiding Francesca's gaze.

Francesca stared. Rourke resembled his brother and father almost exactly. He was terribly handsome, with dark brows and golden eyes, hair a dark tawny shade that was almost brown, and dimples that never quit when he was smiling. Sometimes he looked so much like Bragg he could be his twin, which he was not, as they were half brothers. He had been gentle and kind with Sarah during the last investigation and had, in fact, saved the day when she had been brutally attacked in this very house. Francesca had felt certain she had seen some attraction to Sarah on Rourke's part. "I am sure you will hear from him the next time he is in town," she said.

Sarah shrugged with indifference. "And why would I? He isn't a doctor yet, and he is not my physician."

"Is he not your friend?"

Sarah faced her, flushing. "I hardly know what he is, Francesca. Why did you even bring him up? To upset me? We have work to do! Do you have time to pose now?"

Francesca hesitated, stunned by Sarah's almost angry and very strong reaction to a simple conversation about Rourke Bragg. "I'm not trying to upset you, Sarah," she said softly.

"I know you're not," Sarah said, still flushed. "I'm sorry. It's not you, it's him. I know I was very ill and he spent the night nursing me through that fever, I know he saved me from a brutal attack, but I did thank him, and that is that. I don't like him, Francesca, and let's just leave it at that. Do you have some time to pose for a sketch?" She smiled firmly, clearly closing the door on the subject of Rourke.

Francesca knew a fire was smoldering, as she had just seen the smoke, and she smiled, letting Sarah think as she chose. Posing required disrobing, and to both disrobe and re-dress would take a good forty minutes or so. However, it was the end of the day and tomorrow promised to be as eventful as that day had been. "You know, I think I can . . ." She stopped. She had wandered farther into the studio but now glimpsed one of the canvases on an easel. It was clearly an unfinished portrait of Calder Hart.

And looking at his likeness was like looking at him—it took her breath away and she felt his presence envelop her, as if he had actually joined them in the room.

Sarah came to stand behind her. "I could not help myself. He is my mentor, and it simply seemed right. I have been so inspired, it's almost done. Do you like it? I had so much trouble with his expression, with his eyes. He is so smug and confident, but there is a vulnerability within that I have found almost impossible to capture. It's not quite right yet, is it?"

Francesca hugged herself. Was she falling in love with the man? And was Sarah infatuated, too? The portrait had captured the Hart whom society knew and so often rejected. The Hart who could walk into a room and upset everyone present while laughing about it. The Hart who cared not one whit for society and its rules. Sarah had caught Hart's renegade spirit perfectly, his confidence, his attitude of "I don't give a damn," his aura of power and wealth. But she had missed the vulnerability that was an essential part of him. Francesca knew few ever glimpsed or were even aware of that fragile side, but she was not surprised that Sarah had seen it and understood it so well. "No, it's not right. It's almost right, though. Has he seen this?"

"Oh, no! I am terribly afraid to show it to him. I doubt I ever will!" she cried nervously.

Francesca clasped her shoulder. "It is spectacular, Sarah.

And I do think you should show it to him when you are ready. You have captured his magnetism, his sardonic side, and his power perfectly."

"But he has a soft gentle side, a frightened side, that is missing. I will give it to him as a gift one day." Sarah smiled, but nervously, as if afraid her gift would be rejected or scorned. Then she said, "Did Hart speak to you at all about the portrait?" Suddenly she flushed. "Oh, Francesca, I apologize. I am so excited to finally have you here sitting for me that I have not even congratulated you on your engagement. I am so happy for you!"

"Thank you."

"I think it is a wonderful match." Sarah looked closely at her now. "Don't you?"

She didn't hesitate. "Sarah, I hardly know what I am doing when I am around Hart. I still have strong feelings for Bragg. And Bragg and I are alike—in every way. Hart and I are so different. Still . . . I seem to be on a speeding train, one I cannot leap off." She smiled grimly.

Sarah took her hand. "Bragg is with his wife. I'm not sure I understand their relationship, but it appears a volatile and passionate one. I do not mean to hurt you by saying that, Francesca. It's just that while I know how close you and Bragg are, I don't think you are the one."

"I know that, too," Francesca said grimly. "A month ago your words would have hurt. Now, they do not. I am merely frightened since this thing with Hart is gaining so much momentum. It is like traveling at top speed when what one really wants is to apply the carriage brakes."

"I think Hart adores you, and frankly, the fact that he wants to marry you instead of seduce you says it all, doesn't it?" She smiled. "Now, did he speak at all with you about the portrait?"

Francesca patted her back. "I am more than happy to pose nude."

Sarah cried out in pleasure. "I haven't done a nude since art class in Paris. I am beyond excited. Francesca, this will be so beautiful, and I promise you, we will conceal every-thing that needs to be concealed."

Francesca grinned and crossed one thigh over the other, held her arm over her breasts, and said, "Shall I dangle a scarf or a mink stole?"

Sarah laughed as well. "That would be obvious, don't you think? You can disrobe behind the screen. You can use that dressing gown."

Francesca did as she was told, aware of her excitement taking on a sensual edge. She was posing nude for Hart. Now was not the time to feel desire stirring, but she did. As she stripped down to her corset and drawers, she said, "Should I take my hair down? And Sarah, I am not modest, so do not worry about that!"

Sarah laughed. "I didn't think you would be modest, my dear. And no, I don't think so. In fact, I have thought about it and I think your hair should remain up. I'd also like to see you in a choker. Perhaps pearls and diamonds. My mother has one which we could borrow when the time is right."

"Whatever you think," Francesca said, slipping the silk jacquard kimono on. It caressed her naked flesh, sending tingles up and down her legs, her spine. She stepped out from behind the screen.

"Every painting tells a story, Francesca, and in this story, you have come home from a ball and are waiting for your new husband," Sarah said, ushering her to an emerald-green damask daybed, with pillows piled about its head.

Francesca felt her body tighten even more. "And who is telling this particular story, Sarah, you or Hart?"

"I am, as I am the painter," Sarah said with a grin. "Don't disrobe yet. Try to find a comfortable position, first. I think on your side, facing me, with your thighs crossed as you did earlier while standing."

Francesca slid onto the sofa, leaned into the pillows, and posed herself to the best of her ability. By crossing her thighs and crossing her upper arm over her breasts, she felt that the right amount of concealment had been attained. But Sarah frowned.

She shook her head. "That pose is beyond classic—it's common. We must do better. Francesca, sit up, with your back partly toward me."

Francesca obeyed, glancing curiously over her shoulder at Sarah.

Sarah grinned. "Turn a bit more to the right. I would like to see a profile of your breast. Yes, that's right. Now place one leg completely over the side of the bed. Oh, I like this! Can you curl your right leg up under you? Will that be too uncomfortable?"

"I don't know," Francesca said, amused by Sarah's excitement, but then, her own excitement remained high. This was, in fact and surprisingly, the perfect ending to a very interesting day. And she could not wait to present Hart with the portrait when it was done.

"That may be it. Don't move—let me help you off with that robe!" Sarah cried. She rushed forward and the robe was removed while Sarah kept chiding Francesca to "Freeze, don't even blink, there!"

Francesca had little idea of what the pose would really look like in a portrait, as it was mostly of her back and backside, with her glancing at Sarah from over her shoulder. "Is this really all right?"

"It's spectacular—a bit more daring than what I imagined, but you have such a lovely body, and Hart will adore this portrait, so if you do not mind, I'd like to try it. If you object, we can start over tomorrow," Sarah said, all the while sketching rapidly.

Francesca smiled at her. She was already becoming uncomfortable in the position she was instructed to remain in.

"Can you pretend you are looking at Hart instead of at me?" Sarah asked, her strokes upon the canvas long and bold.

Francesca blinked. "Of course. Sarah, don't you start on paper?"

"Yes, but all the preliminary sketches I did were of you

reclining on your side, and that is simply too boring. Worse, I do not know when I will get you back! I think it best to skip that stage. Think about Hart, Francesca. Pretend he has just walked into the room."

Francesca started, an image of Hart appearing behind Sarah coming to mind. Her heart skipped and her body tightened. Why hadn't they made plans for the evening? Hadn't he promised her a private celebration, just the two of them, with champagne? She knew where such a celebration would lead, and she smiled.

"Thank you," Sarah breathed.

An hour later Sarah told her she could get up. Francesca slipped on the robe and did so, asking, "Can I see?"

"Only if you promise not to shout at me. We can modify the pose," Sarah said, breathless and flushed.

Francesca was very curious now. She hurried over to the easel and gasped.

She sat on the bed, her back to the viewer, but partially turned. Her shoulders were square and elegant, her back and waist long, her buttocks lush and full and completely revealed. One long leg was also fully revealed, and so was her left breast. Sarah hadn't hidden anything, and her nipple was erect and peeking out from her forearm.

But what really caught Francesca's attention was her expression. She was staring at the viewer with such a frankly provocative expression. Her eyes were smoldering and sensual—a stunning contrast to the upswept hair and pearl choker.

"I am going to paint that red gown in a heap on the floor by your foot," Sarah breathed. "Do you like it? It's daring and sensual, but Francesca, you are stunning and I love it!"

"I like it," Francesca whispered, staring at herself. "Am I so voluptuous? And did I really look like that? My eyes, I mean?"

Sarah bit her lip. "For a while, and whatever you were thinking, it was perfect."

Francesca knew what she had been thinking. She had been thinking about celebrating alone with Hart—she had been thinking about being in his arms and, eventually, in his bed. "Hart will never be able to show this painting to anyone," she mused breathlessly.

"Never is a long time, and Mrs. Huntington has a Courbet she hides in her closet," Sarah said. "Many collectors have certain works that general society is simply not ready for."

Francesca nodded, aware of her cheeks being quite hot. "Well, I think it unusual and I do not object."

Sarah took her hand. "Francesca, the beauty of a painting is, one can always change it. Shall we go forward then, this way? Down the road, if you object, I can easily move your arm to hide your breast, and add a pillow to hide your buttocks. But I do feel this pose is the right one."

Francesca smiled at her. "You are the artist," she said.

"I cannot wait to finish this and show Hart," Sarah breathed.

Silently Francesca agreed.

Night had settled over the city as Francesca left the Channings' in the Channing coach, having promised Sarah to return the next day around the same time to continue work on the portrait. Although it had been a very long day, Francesca was too exhilarated to feel any fatigue. She had hated the idea of a portrait initially, and now she was very pleased. Of course, she felt certain that the sensual and beautiful woman in the sketch was a romanticized version of herself. She knew, in reality, she hardly looked like that sketch! But if Sarah wished to portray her that way, she did not mind.

The drive across town, through Central Park, was a quick one, and during that time Francesca tried to imagine how the interview had gone with Calder and her father. By now, it had surely been concluded, so when she saw Hart's lavish and elegant six-in-hand parked in front of her house, she was astonished. She thanked the Channings' driver and started toward the house, wondering if it was a good or bad sign that the meeting had gone on for so long.

Francesca was about to take the first step up the wide stone steps leading to the front door when someone spoke to her from behind. "Miss Cahill?"

Her first thought was that it was that sneaky news reporter Arthur Kurland, who would do anything for a scoop. He had accosted her at her front door before. She halted and turned. But she saw no one standing by the hedges lining the drive, and beyond that it was too dark to see anything. Had the sound of someone speaking her name been a figment of her imagination? "Hello?" she tried.

There was no immediate answer. She became a bit uneasy and very curious, straining to see. The house was fully illuminated within from behind, but there were no lights on the grounds until the avenue, where there were two gas lamps at the gated entrance to their property. She thought she saw a movement behind the hedges, by several large elm trees. "Kurland? Is that you?" She opened her clutch and slid the small derringer into her palm.

"Yes."

She blinked. "Come out, then. I don't bite."

"I need a private word," he said.

This was more than strange, it was simply intriguing, and Francesca left the first stone step, putting the tiny gun away. She started toward the hedge and elms where he was hiding. What could be going on? Kurland was dangerous, but only in that he seemed to know the extent of her relationship with Bragg and, if he wished, he could cause a scandal and hurt Bragg's career, both present and future. Francesca's mind raced with possibilities now as she stepped across the graveled drive. Perhaps this time Kurland could prove to be a useful ally in her latest cause. Her case was newsworthy. He could write a feature about it and flush information her way. He might know something himself. Newsmen often had information about life on the street.

She liked the idea of his writing about the missing children very much. Could he make tomorrow's morning papers? "Kurland, why are you lurking about in my bushes?" she asked, stepping over to the hedges.

He seized her suddenly, without warning, pulling her behind the bushes, pressing something sharp and cold to her throat. *It was a knife.*

"Because I ain't Kurland," he said.

CHAPTER
SEVEN

ODDLY, HE WAS SOMEWHAT nervous, and that did not make any sense.

But then, this was a new game, one he'd never played before. The stakes were Francesca Cahill.

Hart smiled grimly to himself as he removed his coat. If he did not know better, he would almost think himself to be infatuated or in love. But he knew without a doubt that love was for hypocrites and romantic fools; he knew it was an illusion meant to sweep away the tawdry urges of lust. And he hadn't been infatuated with a woman since he was a boy of sixteen.

He removed his black coat, handing it to the Cahills' butler, thanking him with a nod. He calmly reminded himself that as high as the stakes were, he was prepared for battle and would undoubtedly win. In fact, he had spent an hour or two last night making notes in preparation for the war of wits and wills to come. He frequently engaged in such battles in the course of conducting his many and various business affairs—he owned the city's largest shipping company, an equally large insurance company, and a fledgling transportation company, not to mention major shares in several railroads and utilities. But he was never nervous, not in the least, when confronting an adversary or even an enemy; in fact, he relished each and every battle. He usually won.

In fact, he could not recall the last time he had lost.

Still, he also had to consider that very possibility. He analyzed every business dealing in such a manner, and so he would analyze this. If Andrew remained against this marriage, he could marry Francesca anyway, as he was certainly wealthy enough and powerful enough to defy her father and do so. Or he could stand back—as he knew in his own heart that he wasn't good enough for her. He could stand back and lose her sooner or later to another man.

A real gentleman would take the latter course. But he wasn't a gentleman and he would never be one and his choice should Cahill refuse him was outstandingly clear. In fact, there was no choice. Francesca had entered his life very much like a brutal thunderstorm—his life had been black before the storm, but now, in the storm's wake, there was rebirth: new blades of grass, the budding of dandelions, the shimmer of a rainbow, the smile of the sun. Every day was a new one.

He told himself he was turning into a romantic fool, but one fact had become inescapable in the past month when she had been gone—he needed her. He preferred the green of springtime to the black despair of winter, and that had also become terribly clear. Francesca was a breath of fresh air.

Hart refused to reflect anymore. Julia was hurrying toward him, smiling. She grasped his hands tightly, but he felt certain that she wished to throw herself into his arms. He was amused. The emotion was a welcome one. "It is so good to see you, Calder," she said.

"And I am more than pleased to be here," he returned smoothly and actually meaning it.

"Andrew is in the study," Julia said as they went down the hall. "I cannot tell you how surprised I was last night when you announced your intentions toward Francesca."

He felt like murmuring that her surprise had undoubtedly equaled his own surprise when he had first realized he had no recourse but to marry her. "I made my intentions clear to Francesca quite some time ago."

That stopped Julia in her tracks. "Really?" Her blue eyes were wide with complete surprise.

"Yes." He smiled at her. "She did not wish me to approach her father. She wanted to consider my proposal first."

Julia made a sound. "That sounds exactly like my foolishly independent daughter! I must confess, Calder, Andrew is very taken aback by you not coming to him, first. And now I see this is entirely Francesca's fault. But why should I be surprised when she is—" She halted in midsentence, beginning to flush.

He took her arm. "But I encouraged Francesca to think about it, as marriage is a very serious step," he smoothly lied, not wanting Francesca to be blamed. Instantly Julia's face relaxed. "My dearest Julia," he added, "I admire your daughter for her independent and headstrong ways, and have no fear, there is little you can say that will dissuade me from my plans. She may be a handful, but it is an intriguing handful, after all."

Julia sighed with relief. "Which is why you are so perfect for her. Most men would be terrified of such a wife!"

"Francesca would run roughshod over most men."

"We are in agreement, then," Julia said, leading the way down the hall once again. She gave him a significant look. It warned him to succeed in the upcoming interview. "We agree that this match is a perfect one."

"Have no fear," he murmured. "I have analyzed this match from every conceivable angle, and I have no doubt that we suit. Andrew will soon agree with me."

"I do hope so," Julia said with visible worry. "I fear for the ensuing hour. It shall be a battle of the titans! Do reassure him, please." She met his gaze.

Hart understood. "That is why I am here," he murmured. Then he glanced inside. The door to Andrew Cahill's study was open. A fire roared in the hearth beneath a gleaming mahogany mantel, and with the moss-green fabric walls, the wood paneling below, and stained-glass windows, the effect was cheerful and inviting. Andrew was on the emerald-green leather sofa with the day's *New York Times*. Upon seeing Hart and his wife, he dropped the paper upon the small table beside the couch and stood. He was in a paisley and velvet-trimmed smoking jacket, his trousers, and monogrammed black velvet slippers.

"Good evening, Hart," Andrew said. Then, a dismissal, "Thank you, Julia."

Julia smiled grimly and stepped out, closing the solid door behind her.

"Drink?" Andrew asked.

"Please," Hart said. He was more than aware of how much this man distrusted him and knew that he also disliked him. But then, most men did not like him, simply because women were so attracted to him. His job that day was not just to convince Andrew Cahill of his sincerity when it came to Francesca, but to begin the task of melting the man's dislike as well. Otherwise, given Francesca's attachment to her family, their marriage would be reduced to strife and conflict, and frankly, he did not need the aggravation.

"Scotch?"

"Yes."

Andrew went to a handsome glass-and-brass bar cart, pouring two scotches from a decanter and adding ice from the sterling ice bucket there. He handed Hart his drink. Hart sipped and was pleasantly surprised by a well-aged, superbly smooth scotch. He thought about how Francesca now enjoyed his favorite beverage, and he reminded himself to tell her what her father kept in his study.

"Shall we get to business, then?" Andrew asked, not sitting.

"By all means." Hart smiled, watching his opponent carefully.

"I am very disturbed by the announcement you made last night."

"I cannot think clearly where your daughter is concerned," Hart said smoothly, and it was a glib reply but not quite a lie.

"A man of your accomplishments? I hardly think so."

Hart smiled. He knew that Andrew referred to his notorious reputation with women. "My *accomplishments* are in the past," he said.

"Really?" Andrew raised both brows. "I find that impossible to believe."

Hart set his glass down. "Has it ever occurred to you that I have changed since meeting your daughter?"

"Unlike others in society, no, it has not," Andrew said.

Touché, Hart thought grimly, silently liking Cahill's frank manner. "I was a confirmed bachelor until I met your daughter. It is public knowledge that I mocked marriage and that my intention was to never wed. Surely you are as aware of that as the rest of society?"

Andrew nodded gruffly. "My wife has assured me that was the case. So has my eldest daughter. They have both come out strongly in favor of this match."

Hart was pleased. "It is also a matter of record that I have never, not once in my entire life, courted an available and innocent young lady. As every mother in society knows, I have avoided young ladies like Francesca like the plague."

"Yes, instead, you have carried on with divorcées and widows, not to mention actresses and opera singers," Andrew said.

"That is correct," Hart said flatly. "I made myself from nothing, Andrew; in fact, I do believe we have that in common. I am now a wealthy man. Wealthy enough to do as I please and not give a damn what anyone thinks about it.

You are more than correct. Until a month or so ago, I lived very much like a hedonist. However, that has all changed."

Andrew stared. "Do you really think I would believe such a claim? Last night you had Mrs. Davies on your arm."

Hart smiled. "I did. And once, years ago, we were lovers. She is a friend, Andrew, nothing more. Although she has made it clear repeatedly that she would like far more."

"I do not trust you. I find you glib," Andrew stated.

"Sir, haven't you wondered why, a man like myself, a man who could have any woman he wants, a man sworn to forever avoid marriage, would so suddenly about-face?" he asked casually.

Andrew seemed taken aback. "Are you going to tell me that you have somehow fallen in love with my daughter? Because I find it very difficult to understand how my daughter, an intellectual, a reformer, and yes, a sleuth, could captivate you. Francesca may be beautiful, but she is a crusader, Hart. The women you are seen with are, frankly, a different type."

Hart smiled. "No one is like Francesca." The words slipped out, his first spontaneous utterance of the evening. Then he recovered. "I am not going to lie to you and tell you that I am madly in love."

"Then this conversation is over."

"I'm afraid not. Because I am determined to marry your daughter, and I beg you to consider the question I previously posed."

"As to why you have had this change of heart? Frankly, I cannot begin to comprehend it. Francesca is very eccentric. Why have you set your cap on her? She would hardly suit you, surely you can see that!" He had become flushed.

Hart knew when the enemy was unraveling. Calmly he raised both brows. "I beg to differ. She suits me very well, as I am as unconventional."

Andrew started, his eyes widening, and Hart knew he had finally scored.

"Do you really see Francesca in a state of matrimony

like her sister or your wife? Can you see her married to some gentleman, a lawyer or a doctor, or even a senator or judge? Is Francesca's lot in life to be hosting teas for the wives of her husband's associates, shopping the Ladies' Mile, supervising the household, bearing and raising children?"

Andrew's color was very high now. "She will settle down with the right man," he muttered.

"You know as well as I do that Francesca is unique, and that she would die of unhappiness in a conventional union. For you love her for her eccentric ways, sir. Andrew, I can offer her a life of perpetual education. I can offer her a life in which she will never become bored or complacent. If she wishes to gaze upon the pyramids in Egypt, I can take her there. If she wishes to adventure in China, to view the Great Wall, we can go. Not only can we go, we can bring a retinue of servants with us—as well as the children."

Andrew stared. A long silence ensued, in which Hart refused to smile. But he smelled victory; it was that near. "Other wealthy men can also show her the world."

"Yes, they can. But other men will seek to clip her wings and control her."

"She needs control."

"I beg to differ. She needs someone standing beside her to make sure that she, in her desire to help others, doesn't wind up jeopardizing herself. But she does not need to be controlled. Horses are controlled. Dogs are controlled. Francesca is a woman meant to fly."

Andrew stared, becoming thoughtful. "Your case is a good one, Hart. I'll hand that to you."

Hart finally smiled when Andrew said, "Have you seduced her?"

"No!" He felt the anger rise up, swift and hard, and he tamped it back down, but with a great effort. And now he could not smile smoothly. "If your daughter were a merry widow, I can guarantee that by now she would have been in my bed. I have never, and will never, seduce fragile innocence."

"So you have some morals after all," Andrew started.

"Hardly," he said coolly, still angry in spite of his efforts to be otherwise. "My motives are purely selfish ones. I have no wish to be bothered by the consequences of such a seduction."

Andrew made a harsh sound. "And this is why you do not suit my daughter, sir! No woman is more noble of mind than she."

"Of mind and heart. And yes, I do agree. In this one area, we are opposite, as I could not care less about nobility."

"Then you are not for my daughter, and this conversation is over."

He paused, regrouping, and smiled slightly—tightly. And when he spoke, he was calm, composed—in control. "I do not care about nobility, but I do care about your daughter. I have never met anyone, man or woman, that I admire and respect more."

Andrew had been turning away; he now whirled to face Hart, wide-eyed with surprise.

He was direct. "I also treasure her friendship. And we both know that friendship, admiration, and respect are a far better foundation for a marriage than love, a passing romantic illusion, or lust." This was his premeditated coup de grâce.

"I happen to agree with you," Andrew said, flushing again and looking very grim. Hart knew he was on the verge of capitulation then. But his adversary had one last move to make, the one Hart had been waiting for—the one that would give Hart victory. "Do you wish to know what my real objection to this union is?"

"Please." But he already knew.

"Francesca may be a bluestocking, but she is also a romantic. Clearly she is in love with you, and as clearly, you will break her heart one day."

He didn't smile now. "I have no intention of straying from my wife's bed. I am a very disciplined man, Andrew. And furthermore, I do not see the point of marrying if I am

going to be living as I have been my entire life, flitting
from lover to lover. Why shackle myself with a wife if I
wish to live as a rake? No, those days are over, and it is
good riddance."

Andrew started to speak, but Hart forestalled him by
raising his hand, knowing he would win this battle here and
now. "Besides," he said. "Francesca isn't in love with me."

"But . . . she has accepted your suit!"

"I am her second choice. Or have you forgotten?" His
smile was cool and mocking. "She is in love with a married
man—she is in love with Rick Bragg."

It was a knife that he held to her throat. She felt the sharp
metal stinging as it cut her skin, and fear paralyzed her.
Was he going to slit her throat? And if this wasn't Arthur
Kurland, then who was it?

Was this the prelude to an act of thievery? Or was this
something more?

"You forget about the little girls, bitch," he hissed in her
ear. And the knife went deeper.

As pain stabbed through her throat, as fear became terror, blinding her, she had the answer to her question, and
she had one single horrifying thought. *First Tom Smith—
and now, she would be next.*

She cried out, her hands finding his hand as it held the
knife. His grip tightened and she felt moisture trickling
down her neck. She was panting uselessly—for she could
no longer breathe, as if the earth no longer had an atmo-
sphere of air.

"Next time you're dead, you got that?" he sneered in
her ear. His breath was hot on her neck, and it stank.

Francesca did not move. She could not. She wanted to
beg him to spare her life. But she couldn't speak, she didn't
dare, for fear that the blade would sever her artery if she
did.

"Forget the girls," he warned. "They ain't none of your

concern." And suddenly the knife was gone—and the man had vanished.

Francesca fell to the ground the moment he let her go, gasping for air and choking upon it—or her sobs. Her fingers dug deep into cold earth and mud. She dug up pebbles, rocks. She felt the world spinning around her, wildly, precariously.

Dear, dear God. She had just been in the hands of Tom Smith's killer.

The land continued to tilt up and down beneath her hands and knees. Her pulse was madly racing, alarming her with its speed and strength, and she tried to slow her breathing, to compose herself, so she would not pass out, not now. And finally the odd rotations of the ground began to slow and then subside, just as her breathing evened. She sank back on her haunches, gasping now, and was met by a sky filled with stars and a crescent moon. How normal it was.

She began to think.

This man had cut her throat, but she was fine, wasn't she? She started to inspect her neck, but her gloves were filthy, so she tore them off. When she touched the wound, she felt the blood, and when she tried to look at her fingers, she saw the dark moisture there. She was alive, she told herself, trying to be rational now. If he had wanted it, she would be dead.

Like Tom Smith.

Whoever was responsible for the abduction of the children had committed murder to conceal the crimes.

And how badly was she hurt? Surely—and it was a prayer—the cut was superficial, skin-deep.

She heard a door and she shifted and gazed at the house. How could she go inside, now, like this? And then a shadow detached itself from the house, going down the front steps—a form she instantly recognized. Relief flooded her, and with it, utter, sheer gladness. "Calder!"

Her cry was a croak. She somehow managed to get to her feet, stumbling, but realized he had heard her, because he had paused and was looking her way. As she was in the shadows by the hedges, she doubted he could see her. "Calder!" Her voice was louder now, her strength returning. She started forward at a run.

He heard her and hurried toward her. "Francesca?" Lights from the house illuminated him from behind, and while she would be clearly visible, he remained in some shadow. Still, he faltered and she saw his eyes widen in shock.

"I'm fine," she said, suddenly exhausted and unable to take another step. She halted, and her body seemed to sag.

He rushed to her and she was in his arms.

"How bad is it?" he demanded, ripping off his tie.

"I think it's just a cut," she said as he wrapped the silk tie swiftly about her wound, making a bandage from it.

He lifted her into his arms. "What happened?"

In his arms, she felt a huge tremor course through him. "Someone assaulted me near these hedges, just after I was dropped off at the house. Calder, I'm fine."

"Rourke is home for the weekend," he said, striding to his coach. "Raoul!"

But Raoul was already at the door to the barouche, and he opened it for them. Hart set Francesca on the backseat as gently as if she were a newborn baby, then climbed in beside her, saying, "I want to be at the house in two minutes. And I mean two minutes."

Raoul grunted, slamming the door closed.

Francesca took one look at Hart and could not help herself. She moved deep into his embrace. The look on his face—anger and anguish—was one she was never going to forget.

He held her tight, kissing her cheek. Francesca closed her eyes. She was safe now, and it felt so right.

His embrace briefly tightened. "Did you get a look at the assailant?"

"No." She met his dark gaze and saw how worried he was. "I am fine. My throat hurts, but it's only a cut."

"We shall let Rourke decide that."

Francesca realized that going to his house, only a few blocks uptown, was a far better idea than going to her own home. "There are more missing children, Calder. My investigation into Emily O'Hare's disappearance led me to a nearby school, where three other girls vanished, two on their way home, one on her way to classes. One of the children's fathers, Tom Smith, told us that he had sent his daughter to her aunt, but it was a lie. He was murdered this afternoon." She looked up at Hart.

"What is it that you're not telling me?" he asked grimly.

"His throat was slit," she said. "And I have no doubt that I was just in the killer's grasp."

Hart's jaw flexed. His temples seemed to throb.

"Bragg feels certain we have uncovered a white slaver, Calder," she said.

He made a sound.

"They are abducting these innocent children and forcing them into a sweatshop. They have to be stopped!" Suddenly the burden of having to free the children became too much for her. She leaned against him, her cheek to his cashmere coat. "Those poor children need to go home," she whispered.

He took her hand and pressed it to her lips, silencing her and causing her to look up at him. "Calm down. There is nothing more that you can do tonight."

She analyzed that. Bragg was, by now, at the supper affair he had promised he would attend. And her neck was throbbing—she needed medical attention. She didn't want to alarm Hart, but she was afraid she might need stitches.

"Tell me about the other missing girls," he said quietly, cutting into her thoughts. He was stroking the hair at her nape, just below her hat.

She inhaled, the sound loud and harsh in the confines of the coach. "Rachael Wirkler disappeared more than a month ago. Bonnie Cooper was the next to vanish, and then Deborah Smith March second. They were all in the sixth grade."

"So they were all twelve or thirteen years old?"

"Rachael was fourteen, I think," Francesca said, uncertain only because she had amassed so many facts she could not get them all straight now without the use of her notes. Her purse was somewhere on the Cahill grounds, she realized, and in it were not just her notes but also her gun. She moaned.

"What is it?" he cried, moving closer to her.

"I dropped my purse. Someone will find it. Mama will know it's mine! If she sees my gun, I am finished!"

"God, Francesca, you frightened me," he said, gripping her hand. "I thought you were in pain."

She was in pain, but she decided not to tell him that. "It's better now," she lied.

He gave her an odd look—as if he knew exactly what she was up to. Then, "Were the girls half as pretty as Emily appears to be?"

"Yes, just as pretty, I think."

He gazed up at the ceiling of the coach, his expression grim. He did not let go of her hand.

"What is it?"

He met her gaze. "Bragg is being less than honest with you."

"What?" She was incredulous—then she began to bristle. But before she could protest, he lifted his hand.

"We are dealing with white slavery, Francesca, of that I have little doubt."

"Then what are you talking about?" she demanded as they turned into Hart's long driveway.

"Child prostitution," he said.

CHAPTER
EIGHT

BRAGG WAS LATE. HE followed the butler down a short hall, across gleaming parquet floors, toward a salon at its far end. The two mahogany doors were wide open, and not only could he see the assembly gathered inside, but he also could hear Leigh Anne's soft voice as she responded to a query. He stiffened.

By now, Francesca was at home, and he imagined her dining with her family, as she had mentioned she intended to do that evening. He envied her quiet evening spent at home; he remembered the last evening spent that way, because he had firmly decided that Sundays would be spent at home, no matter the invitation. And given his position, invitations were many, far more numerous than he could possibly accept. Recently he had let Leigh Anne decide which affairs they would attend. She had surprised him—she was only accepting the most politically and socially significant. They'd yet to waste an evening on an event not worth his while.

Bragg's gaze never left the salon. He was tired from the events of the day—and he hadn't slept at all last night, not after his half brother had so smugly announced his engagement to Francesca. Bragg was very worried about what he suspected was really happening to the missing children, and while he did not like misleading Francesca, he knew she would take their plight to heart and he hoped to spare her that. The police department had a history of being linked to prostitution and gambling—in one of his predecessor's terms, a study had estimated that the police took in about $4 million a year from such establishments. He also knew children were often used as lookouts or to hand out a brothel's business cards; was it possible that the girls were merely being used in that far less despicable manner? He did not think so.

And what should he do about Francesca? She had every right to marry, he knew that, and while a part of him clung to a dream of her in his home, he knew it was only that, a foolish dream, with no more substance than vapor. He also knew Hart was using her—the man had done what he did best, seducing her to his will.

He paused on the threshold of the room and for one moment stood there unobserved. Leigh Anne was listening to the Reverend Parkhurst, a smile on her face, her gaze so intent it was as if she were mesmerized by the minister's speech. But of course, she was not. She was just so clever that one would think so. It was the same with that little luncheon she had hosted today. Bragg knew she couldn't care less about public education or any other charity, for that matter.

But he stared. She was wearing a mint-green satin gown that bared her small ivory shoulders and some of her décolletage. She was such a small woman, almost fragile, her waist tiny enough for him to touch fingers when he closed his hands around it, yet she was surprisingly voluptuous, surprisingly lush, and he couldn't prevent a torrid image from the night before quickly rising in his mind—Leigh Anne astride him, her small body slick with sweat, her long hair wildly down to her waist, streaming past her breasts, over them, around them, her face beautiful and strained as she climaxed violently around him.

He closed his eyes and swore he would not touch her again. But it did not matter that he knew her game, nor did it matter that he knew she was a scheming seductress and that he was her target; he could not seem to keep the vows he made to himself. When the moon was high, the house silent, the city streets empty, the city asleep, his vows vanished as if they had never been conceived, much less made.

He met her gaze. Her smile changed almost imperceptibly, warmth coming to her eyes, a greeting silent and unformed there. He hardened against her, willing it. Never mind that the other women in the room were older, plump, their faces lined. Never mind that she stood out in their midst like a beautiful hummingbird among fat, clucking hens. Not for the first time, he wished she were different— that she had aged, that she was less attractive, that something had happened to mar her physical perfection.

He looked away now, as if he had not even seen her. Her face fell. Briefly he thought he had seen saw confusion and hurt in her eyes. He was glad—he would not feel for her now!—even as he knew he was being a miserable cad for taunting her that way. Surely, as Francesca had pointed out, it was time to forgive and bury the past. The gentleman in him knew that. The savage simply refused to do so.

It was a secret that only Leigh Anne knew. He wasn't half the moral man that everyone thought him to be. With her, his morals vanished and he was nothing but a beast.

Which was the real reason he could never remain married to her. He hated the man he was when she was present. He hated the man he had become—the man she had turned him into.

Robert Fulton Cutting seized his arm. "Rick! Finally! Good to see you, my boy; I am so glad you could make it."

Bragg smiled. Cutting came from an old and wealthy family, and the man was one of the driving forces behind the Citizen's Union party and the good-government reform movement. "Sir, the pleasure is all mine."

Ron Harris, his host, now pumped his hand. An appointee of Low's, he was a middle-class Protestant Yankee like the majority of Low's supporters. "We were just discussing the fact that you might run late. The missus was going to hold up supper."

"That won't be necessary," Bragg said, smiling at Mrs. Harris, who looked sixty to Harris's forty-five.

Parkhurst hurried over. "Your pretty little wife was just making your excuses. A busy police commissioner is a good police commissioner. How are you, sir?" He smiled, but his gaze was dark and sharp.

Bragg shook his hand, fully aware that the reverend's political agenda was at times at odds with the department's. Parkhurst had formed the Society for the Prevention of Crime, and he had hundreds of fervent followers. At times, members of his society had raided various establishments, including brothels, making citizens' arrests. Parkhurst was also vehemently opposed to the saloons' being open on Sundays and expected a strict enforcement of the Blue Laws. Bragg fully expected a debate that night, as the policy that had evolved, under his auspices and in conjunction with the mayor's political needs, was one of selective enforcement of the law. The worst and most flagrant violators were closed. The rest of the saloons were left alone. The decision was a political one—Low could not afford to alienate the working masses.

Herman Ridder, leader of the German Reform Movement, gripped his hand. "Good to see you, Rick. I've been hoping we could catch up."

Bragg smiled, knowing that what Ridder really meant was to encourage him to even more selectively enforce the Blue Laws. The majority of the city's German population were adamantly against any infringement on their right to drink on the Sabbath. "Good to see you, Herman." And Bragg finally looked at his wife.

She smiled at him. He saw the anxiety in her eyes. It was like looking at a dog that eagerly awaited his master's return but then expected to be kicked.

He hated himself. He leaned toward her and kissed her cheek. His lips did not touch her skin.

Their gazes met. "Hello," she said softly, a sweet, seductive caress.

He nodded and turned back to the assembled company.

"So what have you planned for this Sunday?" Parkhurst asked. He smiled at Bragg, but it did not reach his eyes.

Aware of his tiny wife standing close beside him, he said, "I'm afraid I cannot give away police policy, Doctor."

"Am I to understand that this Sunday will be like last Sunday—a general apathy to the acts of sacrilege performed on the Sabbath?"

Before Bragg could answer, Cutting said smoothly, "The commissioner just walked into the door. It's been a long day. I'm sure he could use a drink."

"Thank you, a scotch would do nicely," Bragg said. But he faced Parkhurst. "Doctor, could we have a brief word?"

Parkhurst started, looking uneasy, but nodded. They stepped a few feet from the assembly. "Rick, you know I am only doing my duty," the reverend began.

"I know. I am not here to debate police policy today."

Parkhurst was intrigued. "Then what is on your mind?"

"Children," he said. "Children being abducted and sold into brothels."

Parkhurst blanched.

"Have you come across any children in any of the raids your society has held?"

Parkhurst hesitated.

"This is off-the-record, Doctor," Bragg said firmly, as they both knew any act of vigilantism was illegal and criminal.

"Not to my knowledge," he said. "But I have not been

on every raid, and frankly, since you took office, there have only been two."

Bragg knew why. The Society was giving him a chance to reform the police department, which was why he had been appointed in the first place. Two months ago he had shaken up the entire department by demoting the detectives and officers in charge of the wards, then reassigning just about every single man. In that way, he had broken the chain of graft and bribery, as each ward had its own system in place. By now, there were surely some payoffs taking place between the brothels and the police. It was like shifting the moving sands of a desert. For a while, a hole would be there—eventually, it would fill up again.

"Can you put the word out among your people to see if there are any children being used in any brothels? Four young girls are missing, Reverend, since the New Year, all between the ages of twelve and fourteen."

Parkhurst now flushed with anger. "I will call a special meeting first thing tomorrow," he said. "Good God, the depravity of it!"

Bragg placed a restraining hand upon his shoulder. "No vigilante raids, Doctor, please."

They returned to the assembly to see that the mayor and his wife had arrived. Low was shaking his head, amused. "We are already debating the Raines Law? But I have not been in the room for two minutes!"

Everyone laughed, including Bragg, but then Ridder said, "A study has shown that the Raines Law has actually increased crime by encouraging brothels and gambling halls! The sooner these useless laws are done away with, the sooner we can all enjoy our personal freedoms again. Am I not right, Mayor?"

Low sighed. "You all know I believe morality cannot be legislated," he said.

Bragg tensed as his wife came up to him. "You look very tired, Rick. Should I get you another drink?"

"I am fine," he said abruptly.

"Katie has a slight cough. I don't think it is serious, but

I spoke to Rourke, and he said he'd take a look at her tonight."

He met her gaze. "You're worried. How bad is it?"

"It's very slight." She hesitated. "I can't help it—a tiny cough and I am thinking about tuberculosis! I'm sure she's fine," she added, her smile uncertain.

He had wondered over and over again whether her concern for the children was a ploy. "When is Rourke stopping by the house?"

"I suspect he's there now. I know." Her smile was fragile. "I wish we were at home, too."

Their gazes met. He flinched and looked away. She said, "How is your case going?"

When he looked at her again he couldn't help himself. He glanced at the white swath of skin that was her upper chest, then at the hint of a valley just barely revealed by her gown. "The case involves missing children, and it is not going well."

"Missing children?"

"Girls. Girls between the ages of twelve and fourteen." He was terse. His body was far worse than terse. It was responding to her in the way he simply hated. An urgency was rippling through him. . . .

"Thank God Katie is only six," she whispered.

"Katie isn't pretty enough for these monsters," he said stiffly.

"She's beautiful!" she flashed angrily.

He started, refusing to be drawn into the debate. "I have company to attend," he said.

She didn't follow him toward the assembly. But he heard her say, "I can't believe you don't think Katie is beautiful," in utter disbelief.

She had misunderstood. Katie was pretty, of course she was, but not like Emily O'Hare and the others.

"Rick, what do you think?" Cutting asked. "Surely you saw that ridiculous article in the *Sun* today."

He was calm. "The editorial surmising that Platt will abandon Odell?" But as they began to discuss the absurd notion that the master of the Republican machine was falling out with the state's governor, he was aware of Leigh Anne's gaze upon his back. It was accusing.

And he had the terrible urge to explain.

Francesca refused to let him carry her into his house, where his foster parents, Rathe and Grace Bragg, and their son Rourke were in residence. The Braggs had returned to New York City two months ago and were building a new mansion not far from Hart's place. But as she walked in with Hart firmly holding her arm—as if he thought she might faint at any moment—Alfred appeared. He took one look at her and paled. "Miss Cahill!" the bald English butler cried. "Whatever has happened?"

"I am fine, Alfred, a slight incident with a thug, that is all," she said, over her shoulder now, as Hart was propelling her into the closest salon.

His home was as large as a museum, monstrously so—it was less than a year old—and the salon was the size of a small ballroom. He ordered her onto the first sofa they came to, and there were a dozen seating arrangements in the room. "Get Rourke, his medical bag, and two Scotch whiskeys," he said. "Is Rourke in?" he demanded, turning to Alfred.

"Yes, sir, he is." Alfred left instantly, almost at a run. It was the first time Francesca had ever seen him without his composure.

"This can't be happening." She turned to Hart, facing her worst fear. "Children as prostitutes?! The thought had occurred to me, but Bragg feels certain this is about sweatshops." She was trembling now.

"Do not get up," Hart warned. "My saintly brother has been lying to you."

"But why?" she demanded—but she knew.

"To protect your fragile sensibilities," he said flatly, "and to prevent you from worrying so."

Francesca hugged herself. She had already suspected the

truth. Why else would all the missing girls be so beautiful? She was ill, facing it now. What ordeals were those poor children going through? "We have to find these children, before it is too late. We have to save them, Calder."

He didn't speak. He began to pace the room, not looking at her, removing his jacket and tossing it carelessly at a chair. He missed and it fell to the floor. He never missed a long, hard stride. He was as restless as the tiger Francesca had once seen caged at the Bronx Zoo.

Francesca had to admire him, nevertheless. She knew he was extremely upset because of her injury, yet he remained calm and in control—enough so to be the commander of an army on a battlefield. In moments like these, Hart was every bit as heroic as Bragg, she thought, her heart tightening oddly. The biggest difference between them was that Hart never put a sugar coating on anything.

Hart had stripped off his tie, having used it to bandage her neck; now he unbuttoned his collar, facing her. His face was carved in stone. It was an angry, determined expression, and it did nothing to detract from the man's dangerous and oh-so-seductive appeal.

She wet her lips. "Is there any chance you are wrong?" she whispered. "Is there any chance Bragg is right and these girls have been forced into a sweatshop?"

Hart halted, staring down at her, his stance a terribly offensive one. "I doubt I am wrong. They would abduct younger children for a sweatshop, as they would be far easier to control. Besides, I overheard a stranger a few nights ago mentioning something to his friend about a new brothel, one that offers purity and innocence." He never took his gaze from her face. "I do believe those were his exact words—'purity and innocence.'"

The girls were enslaved in a brothel. It was too terrible to even contemplate. She felt the tears rising then, blinding her.

She could not fail them.

And he was on his knees, at her side. "Darling, don't

cry. You cannot save the entire world," he whispered, lifting her chin in his hand.

Her mouth was trembling wildly as their eyes met. And she didn't want to cry. She stared into his navy blue gaze, flecked with amber and gold, and whispered, "But I can try."

"Yes, you can try—but perhaps with a bit less passion?" He smiled a little then, but his gaze was searching.

"Calder, the plight of those children . . ." She could not continue and she moved into his arms, her cheek upon his chest, somehow kneeling on the floor with him.

He unpinned her hat, threw it aside, and stroked her hair. "I know, darling, I know." He kissed her cheekbone, and suddenly his mouth, against her skin, stilled.

And Francesca felt the beast the moment it arose. His mouth remained unmoving, pressed against her cheek. In that second, Hart's sudden desire slammed over her, as hard as any physical blow. In that moment her heart lurched wildly, and when it began beating again it was to fill her veins with hot blood. And there was simply no doubt about the need that had so swiftly arisen.

He pulled back and their gazes locked.

"Calder." His name sounded like a seductive caress, even to her own ears, in the still of the huge room.

His jaw flexed. He tilted her face up, his fingers long and strong. "Maybe if I keep you in my bed, we can avoid the dangerous episodes that you constantly find yourself in."

"Maybe," she breathed.

Hart stared, his gaze smoldering, and he lowered his face toward hers.

"What's happened?" Rourke's voice sounded from the threshold of the room, at once doctorlike and calm.

Hart gracefully stood, bringing Francesca to her feet with him. Then he turned away, but she saw his lids lower, shielding his eyes and the urgency evident in them. It was a moment before he looked up at his brother and Grace, who was at Rourke's side. In that moment, Francesca tried to breathe naturally and hoped her cheeks were not too red. "Francesca was assaulted with a knife. Hopefully the cut on her throat is a superficial one." How calm he sounded then.

Rourke had his black medical bag in hand, and instantly he faced his mother. "Please bring me a bowl of warm water, clean rags, lye soap, and any linens you may find for a bandage."

"Of course." Grace gave Francesca one wide-eyed look and raced from the room, past Alfred, who was entering with a tray containing two whiskeys.

Rourke smiled at Francesca. "We must stop meeting this way. Could you sit down, please?"

Once, it had disturbed her to look at him, as he could be Rick Bragg's twin. But that was no longer the case—he was very different from his older brother, and not just because he wished to be a doctor. She sat down on the edge of the sofa. "Yes, we must. It is nice to see you, Rourke."

He smiled, a smile always accompanied by two dimples, as he gently untied the tie Hart had used as a bandage. "But I do wish it were under better circumstances," he said. "How are you feeling?"

She almost told him that she was quite ill, but that had everything to do with the missing girls and nothing to do with her neck. "I was very dizzy at first, but I couldn't breathe when he assaulted me. I am fine now."

Rourke paused. "I need warm water to remove this. I am going to take your pulse and listen to your heart."

Francesca nodded. As he lifted her wrist, she glanced at Hart, who stood behind Rourke with Alfred, a scotch in hand. Hart never removed his gaze from her, and he seemed terribly grim. She thought about what would have happened if Rourke and Grace hadn't entered the salon when they had, and she looked away.

"Pulse is normal," Rourke said cheerfully, taking a stethoscope from his bag. He did not glance behind but said to Hart, "Could you step out, please?"

"She is my fiancée," he growled.

"Congratulations. Now step out. Grace may come in when she returns," he said amiably.

Francesca glanced at Hart, who quaffed half the whiskey and then marched out with Alfred, closing the double doors behind him. She unbuttoned her shirtwaist, uncomfortable now and aware of blushing.

"That's enough," Rourke said mildly after she had undone three buttons, and not even looking at her, he laid the stethoscope against her bare skin, listening to her heart beating. As he moved it around, never glancing at her, she felt her cheeks cool. He was very professional, she thought. And she dared to study him.

He had the Bragg cheekbones, high and sharp, the golden skin, the amber eyes. He was about Bragg's height, six feet, but not as lean. His hair was more brown than gold, but there were sun-bleached tips around his face. His brows were startlingly dark.

She thought about him and Sarah Channing. Rourke was a catch, and undoubtedly many beautiful women chased him. Sarah was both a bohemian and an artist, at once skinny and some would say plain. But Rourke had been so interested in everything she had to say that night at supper at the Waldorf. Perhaps he had only been playing the part of a perfect gentleman.

Still, when Sarah had fainted, he had taken her home and nursed her through a raging fever. But he was in medical school; he would one day be a doctor.

"I am going to listen to your lungs," he said, sliding the icy cold stethoscope beneath her shirtwaist and down her back.

"How is Philadelphia?" Francesca asked.

"Hush."

A moment later he removed the stethoscope. "Your pulse, heart, and lungs are normal. Now we need to remove that tie and look at the wound."

"How is Philadelphia?" Francesca tried again.

His dark brows lifted. "I did very well on my midterms," he said.

"You must study very hard."

He seemed amused. "Yes, I do. We all do."

"All work and no play, how boring." She grinned.

He began to appear slightly suspicious. "One must always find the time to enjoy oneself, Francesca. By the way, is it true? You and Calder are engaged?"

She flushed and held up her hand, showing him the ring.

He was suitably impressed. "My, things have swiftly changed since I was last here." He gave her an odd look.

She knew he referred to Bragg. She shrugged. "Yes, they have. So what do you do when you are not studying?" she asked lightly.

He studied her. "I have friends. I do what most gentlemen do. Supper, the occasional affair, a club."

She simply had to know. "And who is she?" She grinned but was breathless now, praying for the right answer.

"I beg your pardon?"

"Who is the lady who holds your heart?"

He looked at her for a moment and then shook his head with a small laugh. "If you are asking me if I am seeing someone, the answer is no. At least, not in the way that you mean."

Her mind raced even as she was exultant—for he wasn't involved and that gave Sarah a chance! Then she blinked. "You have a mistress?"

"Francesca," he had begun sternly when Grace suddenly came into the room. "Ah, the troops have arrived—just in time."

"Dear, how are you?" Grace asked, setting the tray down on a small side table. She was a tall, willowy redhead in her middle years, still very attractive, even with the horn-rimmed spectacles she wore. She had also been one of the nation's first suffragettes. Today she was considered a leader of the women's movement.

"I believe I am fine."

"Are you on another case?" Grace asked.

"Yes, and it involves missing children—all young, attractive, and female."

Grace grimaced. "Oh, dear. May I help?"

Francesca started as Rourke began to sponge down the tie. "That is a wonderful offer. I am sure I can use some help."

Rourke shook his head, gently prying the tie from her skin. "Mother, Francesca attracts danger the way honey attracts bees. I don't think your involvement is a good idea."

"Do not dare treat me as an elderly individual," Grace warned. And she smiled at Francesca, sending her a wink.

Rourke sighed as Hart paced into the room, demanding, "Well?"

"A moment, please," Rourke said, peeling off the tie.

"Where is my scotch?" Francesca asked, wincing.

Hart came to her and handed her his half a glass.

She gulped it down.

"Sorry," Rourke murmured.

Grace was staring. Francesca realized she had seen the ring, and she began to flush uncomfortably now. Hart said, "They heard this morning. I told them the news."

Francesca didn't know what to say as Grace looked up from the ring. Their gazes held. And while Grace wasn't Rick's or Calder's natural mother, she and Rathe had taken both boys in upon the death of Lily, their mother. Francesca knew she considered both Rick and Calder her sons.

And she was no fool. She had seen right through everyone's charade the moment she had met Francesca—Grace knew both Rick and Calder vied for Francesca's attentions, and it had worried her enough for her to speak sharply to Francesca about it. Francesca remained uncertain of how Grace felt about the entire situation. She had made it clear she did not want to see Rick and Calder fighting over any woman. She had also made it clear that Rick remained married. Her last words to Francesca had been about the fact that Calder was not.

"Is this official?" Grace asked quietly.

In that moment, as Rourke finally got the tie free from

Francesca's wound, Francesca realized she had no idea of the outcome of Hart's interview with her father. She gasped, meeting his gaze. "Calder! What happened when you met with Papa?"

He smiled at her. "We are official, my dear. But your father insists upon a year-long engagement."

Francesca wasn't surprised that Hart had won this battle. He seemed undefeatable, at least to her. "A year?" And real dismay overcame her. They would have to wait an entire year to wed?

"A small price to pay for his consent, don't you think?" Hart smiled. But his eyes were glinting and he knew where Francesca's thoughts lay.

"Well, this is good news indeed," Rourke said. "The wound is superficial. A mere cut. No stitches are necessary, my biggest fear." He smiled at her. "I will clean this up and you shall be healed in no time."

"Will she scar?" Grace asked.

"No. But I'd suggest you put an ointment on it just to make sure. It's called Doctor Bill's Vitamin and Mineral Miracle Salve." He finished cleaning the wound with lye soap. "How about some bed rest, Francesca? The human body heals faster with rest, as it gives the cells time to repair."

Francesca nodded. "I will try." Suddenly she realized that not only did she have a huge cut on her throat, but her shirt was stained with blood also. She turned to Hart, alarmed. "I can't go home like this! If Julia or anyone sees this cut, I will never be allowed out of the house, at least not unless I am on someone's leash."

Hart turned to Grace. "Do you have a fresh shirtwaist?"

"Of course." Grace smiled at Francesca. "I have a high-necked blouse that should do nicely."

"Thank you," Francesca breathed.

"I would also like a moment alone with my bride," Hart said.

Rourke raised a brow; Grace hesitated.

"I will hardly ravage her a year before the wedding," Hart murmured.

Grace said, "Francesca, I would like to have lunch with you. Do you have time tomorrow?"

Francesca went on alert. She knew what this was about—it was to be an interview in which she would be tested, and the subject would be her marrying Calder Hart. "I am on a case," she began, knowing her day would be full indeed. Then she gave up. She had to meet Grace Bragg, because she was determined to have her approval. Yet she dreaded the intimate and very personal confrontation that would ensue. "I can meet you tomorrow." She so admired Grace Bragg—yet the woman also intimidated her.

"Do you want to dine out? I assume you will be busy downtown, so perhaps the Fifth Avenue Hotel will do?"

Francesca nodded.

"One o' clock?"

"That's fine," she said.

"And I would like a chance to see you tomorrow afternoon," Rourke said.

An idea came to Francesca. Trying to appear very innocent, she said, "I will be at Sarah's around half past four or five."

Rourke was clearly indifferent, because he nodded and his expression did not change. "That's fine. I'll come by about five, then. Good night." He smiled at her and went out, followed by his mother.

Hart did not close the doors. He sat down beside Francesca, taking her palms in his. She stirred. His gaze was dark and steady, holding hers. "I am very relieved that you are all right."

She smiled. "I know," she said softly. "Calder—we must wait an entire year?"

He smiled fondly and then kissed the tip of her nose. "I believe your mother is already planning the wedding. I doubt we will have to wait a year." His gaze turned teasing.

"I doubt I could withstand your seductive onslaught for an entire year, darling."

Only he could kiss her nose so chastely and bring to mind images of his muscular naked body. "Of course you could. You are the strongest person I know."

His brows lifted. "I see I am finally beginning to impress you." He cupped her cheek. "I like the flattery, Francesca, when it comes from you."

She had the oddest inkling then that he yearned for more of her praise. But he was also one of the most confident men she knew, so she doubted he needed her approval. Teasingly she said, "You were very heroic tonight, Calder."

He laughed. "You are on a high roll. Keep rolling, darling." He pulled her close and touched her mouth with his. "You scared the hell out of me tonight," he murmured, his mouth brushing hers. "Will our entire marriage be one of my forever worrying about your welfare?"

She trembled as his mouth dipped, kissing her skin just below the bandage. Her loins filled instantly. "I am afraid so," she breathed, tugging his hand toward her breast.

But he didn't allow her to place it as she wished; instead, he moved apart. She opened her eyes and found him staring at her. And he was so serious that she stiffened. "What is it?"

"I have a plan."

"A plan?" For one moment, she did not know what he could be talking about—and she assumed it was a plan regarding their wedding. "There is a club renowned for all kinds of deviations. I have never been there, obviously, but it is infamous, and I would be surprised if it did not traffic in children. I think it is time that I venture into the establishment in question," he said.

Francesca was on her feet. "That is brilliant," she said. "Will they let you in?" She imagined the door policy to such a sordid place was quite severe.

He also stood, but he wasn't smiling. "There is a saying, Francesca, and it is 'Money talks.'"

"What?" she breathed. "What is wrong? Calder, your plan is perfect! You will enter as the most jaded and dissolute sort and sniff out the children—or word of them!"

"Let's just hope that your father never hears that I am on the prowl," he said.

CHAPTER NINE

LEIGH ANNE RACED AHEAD of him up the walk, to the house. He followed more slowly, while Peter put the motorcar away in the carriage house. She hurried inside, and when Bragg finally entered, she was calling breathlessly for the nurse. "Mrs. Flowers!" She dropped her chinchilla fur upon a stool; it slipped to the floor.

Leigh Anne did not notice; she was clinging to the banister and peering up the stairs.

Bragg picked up the coat, hanging it in the entry's closet.

"Hush, madam, you will wake the children," Mrs. Flowers said, coming down the stairs. "Good evening, sir." She smiled briskly at Bragg.

Leigh Anne was halfway up the stairs, meeting her there. "Did Rourke come by? What did he say about Katie's cough?"

"Mr. Rourke was here, and he said it is a bit of a cold and nothing to worry about."

Leigh Anne smiled widely, in obvious relief, and without even a single backward glance, flew up the stairs, past the nanny. "I promise not to wake them!" she cried softly.

Bragg stared after his wife for a moment, terribly aroused. He reminded himself of his vow. He turned then and said to the nanny, "Thank you. Good night."

"Oh! Sir, an envelope came for you a short while ago. It is on the table," Mrs. Flowers said as she went downstairs. There was one small bedroom behind the kitchen, where she slept. Peter had taken up residence in the apartment over the carriage house.

Bragg about-faced. He found the envelope on the entry table in the silver tray reserved for mail and calling cards. He turned it over and his abdomen clenched. It was from Hart.

What the hell did he want?

There was a letter opener in the table's single shallow drawer, and he used it to slit the envelope.

> *Rick,*
> *Francesca was assaulted tonight outside of her parents' home. Other than a minor cut, she is fine. She suspects the assailant to be Tom Smith's killer.*
>
> *Calder*

There was a single chair beside the table and he sank down on it. *Francesca had been attacked.* He quickly reminded himself that she was fine. The one thing he trusted Hart to do was accurately report any situation involving Francesca's welfare.

He stood, his mind spinning. Tom Smith had been murdered. Francesca had been attacked. Why? Had they intended to murder her, too, or had it been a warning? And why had Tom Smith been killed? That answer, at least, was clear: he knew something; he was somehow involved. And Francesca suspected her assailant to be the same person who had murdered Smith. Why?

He was in his evening clothes, so he had not worn his greatcoat. He hesitated, thinking about the woman upstairs, and then felt a feral sense of triumph—tonight he would live up to his vow. He took the stairs two at a time.

She sat in bed with the children, still in her mint-green evening gown. Dot was curled up against her hip, Katie snuggled to her other side. Both children were sound asleep. Dot looked like a little angel; Katie looked like a thin, homeless waif. Leigh Anne looked up when she realized he was standing there. She smiled. "Rourke said it's nothing."

"I have to go out."

She started and for one moment he thought he saw dismay in her eyes, but he could not be sure. Then she nodded. "Is it police business?" Her tone was carefully neutral.

He took pleasure in his reply: "Francesca was attacked tonight."

Her eyes widened.

He strode out and did not see her face fall. And had he turned, he would have seen Leigh Anne hugging herself, tears shimmering in her eyes.

He thought she called softly, "I hope she is fine," but he could not be sure.

"This is hardly a surprise," Hart drawled as he opened the front door himself and found his half brother standing there.

Bragg looked angry, and he stepped into the house without a word.

Hart noted his evening clothes. He half-turned. "Go to bed, Alfred. Good night."

"Are you sure you won't be needing anything, sir?" Alfred said, standing a few steps behind Hart and not moving to go.

Hart eyed Bragg with amusement. "Actually, my brother looks like he could use a stiff drink." He could not help himself: he loved the fact that Bragg was so enraged, and he knew exactly why. He hadn't been there that evening to protect the woman of his dreams. How frantic he must be.

Worse, it was Hart who had been there to rescue her. Hart hid a smile. Not that Francesca had needed rescuing. It was easy, now, to be amused. He hadn't felt that way several hours ago when he had seen all that blood—all her blood.

Bragg nodded at Alfred. "I do not need a thing."

"Very well then, sirs. Good night." Alfred inclined his head and left.

"Do come in," Hart said.

"You are smirking," Bragg returned evenly. "But then, you *would* find enjoyment in your fiancée being in a killer's hands."

Now Hart was annoyed. "I am enjoying the fact that you are out of the loop, Rick, and do not dare to presume what I think where Francesca is involved."

"I don't presume. I *know*," Bragg said simply.

"You think you know—when you are nothing but a fool," Hart said. He turned and stalked through his huge house, past priceless paintings and sculptures, including some works so provocative that his guests had been offended by their public display. The doors to his library were open. Hart strode to the bar set in the granite counter, above which was nothing but rare books. He poured his favorite scotch. "I am surprised I managed to rouse you out of bed," he remarked coolly.

"I sense a barb but cannot imagine what it might be."

Hart turned, smiling. "Leaving the lush little woman all alone tonight? My, I applaud your discipline, Rick, I really do."

Bragg strode to him and knocked the glass right from his hand. It fell to the floor, onto an old and faded Persian rug, breaking into pieces, proof that the crystal was fine. "You are the last man on earth to talk about discipline when the subject is women," he said.

Hart felt like telling him the truth—he had plenty of discipline when the circumstances warranted it—and that he'd been faithful to Francesca for the entire month of their secret engagement. But he did not. It was not his brother's affair. "Why deprive oneself?" He shrugged. "We are men, after all, and society makes too much of what is nothing more than primitive and basic physical needs."

"I cannot fathom how you seduced Francesca to your will," Bragg said harshly. "Doesn't she care that you keep Daisy downtown? Doesn't she care that you have been keeping company with Mrs. Davies while she is gone? Has she forgotten your alibi on the night Randall was murdered? Has she forgotten you were sharing a bed with two women?"

He shrugged. "Perhaps she is fascinated by my darker side," he purred. "Perhaps you do not know Francesca as well as you think you do."

And for one moment, as Bragg darkened, Hart thought he would strike him, and he was pleased, his own fist curling closed in real anticipation, in savage satisfaction. But Bragg did have discipline, which he damn well knew, and his brother merely stood there, fighting himself when he so clearly wanted to deliver a blow. "Bravo," Hart breathed, turning and calmly pouring another scotch. "Are you certain you do not want one?"

"How pleased you must have been last night, announcing your engagement, shocking everyone present—shocking me."

Hart turned and saluted him with the glass. "It is definitely a memory I will cherish." He smiled.

"You bastard. I won't let you destroy her."

He stopped smiling, setting the glass down behind him. "I am genuinely fond of Francesca. I have no intention of destroying her."

"She deserves love, an emotion you are incapable of."

Hart stiffened, even though he knew Bragg was right—he was incapable of love, and Francesca deserved a man foolish and romantic enough to love her. He said, "The kind of love you wish to give her? Oh, wait, or the kind of love you give to your wife?"

Bragg struck.

Hart ducked and Bragg's fist only grazed his cheek. He came up quickly, seizing Bragg's wrist. The two men strained against each other, inches apart. "I am going to make sure Francesca learns the truth about you," Bragg said, breathing hard.

"She already knows the truth about me. Perhaps she should learn the truth about you," he said softly, meaning it. He was so sick of the way she idolized his brother. Bragg might sincerely wish to save the world, but when it came to his wife, he was nothing but a hypocrite. And they both knew it.

"I know you hate me," Bragg said, shaking Hart off. "But maybe you should consider this question: Do you really hate me enough to use Francesca this way? Now I am asking you for one single favor," he said. "Leave her out of this. She deserves more. And you know it."

Hart stared, and inwardly his heart lurched. She did deserve more. He had always known he wasn't good enough for her, and if he were at all noble, if he had even a single fiber of real character, real morality, he would send her on her way, so she could find the true love she secretly yearned for. "Of course I'm not good enough for her," he said quietly. "But oddly, Rick, I can't bear the notion of losing her to another man."

Bragg started, staring with wide eyes. A long pause ensued. He finally said, "That is a performance worthy of a dozen awards. You almost had me fooled."

Hart felt his jaw tighten and he walked away. He would never reveal anything to his brother again.

"What happened tonight?" Bragg asked, staring after him.

Hart shrugged, not turning. "Francesca came home in a Channing vehicle. When she got out, someone called to her. She thought it was Arthur Kurland, that nuisance from the *Sun*."

"And?" Bragg was terse.

Hart turned. "You know Francesca. Curiosity killed the

cat. Fortunately, it has nine lives. I calculate she's got six or seven left."

"Go on."

"She went over to investigate, was seized from behind, a knife to her throat." He watched his brother pale. There had never been any question in Hart's mind that Rick truly loved Francesca. It was just a more cerebral affair than a sensual one. Because she was a crusader whom he admired with all of his heart—because she was, in a way, a reflection of his own dreams and desires. Unfortunately, Hart also knew they would have made a successful match had Rick been available. It was very obvious.

"How badly was she hurt?" Bragg asked, utterly pale now.

"Her throat was scratched. It won't scar," he added, relieved that it would not. "He warned her to drop the case she is on."

"What did he say—specifically?" Bragg asked sharply.

Hart did hand it to him: his brother was a fine investigator—and an even better police commissioner. He sighed. "Something to the effect of 'Forget about the children.' You'll have to ask Francesca."

"Where is she?"

"Home." He was mildly surprised. "I took her home some time ago. And, Rick—she is not about to reveal what happened to anyone in her family. She would appreciate it if you did not make a fuss in front of Andrew or Julia."

Bragg paced over to him, staring. "And just why are you so involved in this case, Calder? Do you think to truly win Francesca's heart if you help her solve this latest crime?"

He was angry—he hid it behind annoyance. "I don't like her being in danger any more than you do."

A silence fell. "Did she get a look at him?"

"No."

"Can she identify the weapon?"

He was surprised—he had overlooked this question. "I don't know. I would imagine so."

"And the wound is superficial?"

He nodded. "Yes."

"At what time did the attack take place?"

"Around seven. A bit before."

"And how is it, if the attack was outside of her house, that her parents do not know about it? She came here, to you?" He stared.

"Is that a personal question?"

"Just answer it," he said coldly.

He sighed. "I was leaving the house. The timing was pure coincidence. She saw me and called out." He was grim, remembering. "It was rather terrifying, actually. She was wearing a white shirtwaist beneath her suit and coat, and there was blood all over it."

Bragg stared.

Hart looked up. He smiled grimly. "But you know Francesca. She cannot be on a case without attracting the worst criminal elements."

"I am glad you were there," Bragg said.

Hart blinked.

Bragg nodded. "I mean it. All right, then. I will speak with Francesca first thing in the morning. If you happen to recall anything else, even the most minor and insignificant detail, let me know. You know where to reach me," he added with mockery.

Hart sipped his drink, debated a mocking response, and decided not to bait him any further.

Bragg left.

The house was dark, except for the single lamp burning on the table in the entry hall. The unpleasant interview with Hart had rankled the entire way home, as had the fact that it had been Hart with Francesca in her time of need, not him. Now Hart's image receded. Francesca's faded. He turned off the light, starting slowly up the stairs, pulling off his bow tie.

An image of Leigh Anne assailed him.

He refused to entertain it. He thought about the attacker.

He had used a knife, had held it to Francesca's throat. That was undoubtedly why Francesca assumed it to be Tom Smith's killer. The other links were obvious—Smith was somehow involved, as he had lied about his missing daughter, and the assailant had warned Francesca off the case. Bragg entered the master bedroom.

She had left one small lamp on, in a far corner of the room, on her secretaire. From the corner of the eye he saw the bed—he saw her small, sleeping form. He ignored it, her. He walked into the dressing room, stripping off his clothes, his movements hard now, angry.

If only he had taken Francesca home that night. But he had instead attended Harris's political affair. And Hart had been there to rescue her. He seized his nightshirt from a hanger, suddenly furious. How had his life come to this?

Leigh Anne's image came to mind, naked, lush, her eyes seductive and glazing over as they did when she climaxed. He cursed. He threw aside the nightshirt. He went and stood on the threshold of the bedroom, staring at the bed.

The covers hid her from view.

He looked up at the night-darkened ceiling. Francesca was engaged to Hart. It was unbelievable.

Was she somehow thinking to punish him?

No, he thought rigidly, she was falling under Hart's spell; he had seen it himself.

He looked at the bed. And it was all because of Leigh Anne. If she hadn't decided to return to New York, to their marriage, to their life, perhaps things would have stayed the way they were. And now he refused to think of how impossible that had been, as well.

Leigh Anne shifted in her sleep.

He froze, afraid she would wake up—a part of him wanting her to. And he stiffened—he would not give up. He turned, shrugged on the nightshirt, and allowed himself to recognize how exhausted he was. If he let the anger go, he could probably be asleep in minutes.

He went to the bed, refusing to look at her, but her breathing was soft and deep. He slid under the covers, keeping a good distance between them. He rolled over, his back to her.

Exhaustion vanished. His manhood taunted him, as stiff as a baseball bat. Francesca had undoubtedly been in Hart's arms tonight. If Hart had his way, she would become his wife, sooner or later.

Why hadn't Leigh Anne stayed in Europe? Why had she returned? Why did she have to be so seductive? So utterly sensual in bed? So loving with the children? So dutiful as a wife? God, he hated her! He had hated her for four years, and now she stood between him and Francesca; worse, because of her, Francesca was running to Hart.

He turned over abruptly, his arousal brushing her buttocks. It was like being struck by lightning. No, it was worse.

He moved closer. The nightshirt just covered his thighs, was entangled, in the way; he lifted it aside.

She was wearing a scrap of sheer silk he instantly recognized, by feel, not sight. He closed his eyes, moved closer, down the cleft of her buttocks, prodding her silk-covered thighs. She sighed.

The red haze of lust consumed him. He lifted her nightgown, briefly caressed her soft behind, knew the moment she was awake. He pushed between her thighs, silently coaxing her to open for him. She did not breathe. Nor did she spread her legs.

Annoyed, his body racked with a terrible urgency, he nipped her neck.

She whimpered—the bite had been a dangerously real one.

"Open for me," he said roughly, prodding harder now. He reached down and found her sex. He touched the small nub there with his finger and then began to stroke.

"Rick," she began—a protest.

He palmed her hard, then began to rotate her entire mound, nuzzling her neck now. He couldn't breathe—he heard himself panting. He felt insane—insane with desire, with lust. She opened her thighs, reaching behind, for him, touching his mouth. He sucked down her fingertip.

And from behind, through her thighs, he slowly began rubbing himself over her vagina, up against her lips.

She made a sound—sheer sexual capitulation.

And she hooked her calf over his, the invitation unmistakable.

He laughed in her ear, triumph spilling over him the way her wetness was spilling over his hand. "Come for me," he said, a command. He tongued her ear.

"Hurry," she gasped.

He thrust hard and deep, all the way into her.

She cried out.

CHAPTER
TEN

BRIDGET O'NEIL WISHED THEY hadn't come to America. Trembling, afraid, she stared at the carts and wagons moving past her on the street and then at the pedestrians swarming every which way on the sidewalk. She could hear the roar of one of those funny trains, the kind that traveled high up in the air, and, unlike in County Clare, the air was thick and stinking and gray. She missed home, dear Lord, she did.

"Bridget O'Neil! Get that sack o' pots, me girl, gawkin' won't move us in!"

Bridget started at the sound of her mother's scolding voice. She rushed to the wagon that was stopped in front of the building that was to be their new home. Fortunately, the wharves had been so busy that morning and Mama had hired the carter to bring their belongings first thing upon disembarking from the ship that had brought them all the way across the Atlantic Ocean to this odd and frightening new land.

Bridget petted the donkey hitched to the cart, grateful that at least one thing was familiar. God, the building where they had a small flat was enormous, like the castles kept by Lord Randolph, the English earl who until recently had been their landlord and Bridget's mother's employer. But something terrible had happened at the big house, and Mama wouldn't speak of it. She and Papa had fought until she cried and he stormed out, not even coming home in the wee hours. And then the handsome young earl had stopped by with a present for Mama, the prettiest glass Bridget had ever seen. Someone had shaped it into a pretty fawn, and Mama had been about to hide it when Papa returned. A terrible argument had ensued, with Mama crying some more and Papa breaking the fawn, all the while shouting how he'd kill the handsome earl. The next time Lord Randolph had come calling, Bridget had met him at the door and told him that Mama was ill.

Now Papa was in jail, charged with the terrible crime of trying to murder an English aristocrat, and Mama and Papa were not speaking. Papa hadn't even tried to ask Mama not to leave the country. In fact, he had told her to go, as if he hated her. And Mama had spent the whole voyage staring at a newspaper clipping, one that had a pencil sketch of the earl, his likeness so real it was as if he were smiling at Mama.

It was all the earl's fault. Bridget hated him; she hated the English and she hated this new land.

"Bridget! We need to get settled and you're gawkin' still!" her mother cried, pausing beside her, a small box filled with their valuables in her hands. Everyone said Mama was a beautiful woman, and Bridget thought so, too. She had dark red-brown hair that curled wildly when let down and stunning green eyes with long black lashes. She was only twenty-six, and she always reminded Bridget to be a good girl or she'd have a baby at fifteen, too. Bridget knew she meant it, but she was only eleven even if she did look a lot older, so she didn't really have to worry about boys yet. But she would always nod solemnly and swear

to behave. Mama liked to worry. She worried about everything, constantly, and Bridget knew she still worried about
the handsome earl—but not about Papa.

"I'm sorry," Bridget breathed, swinging her long dark
red braid out of the way and hefting up the heavy sack. As
she straightened, a gent paused before her and sent her a
wink.

She blinked, meeting the pale blue gaze of a middle-
aged man who was dressed the way Lord Randolph
dressed, which meant he had riches and estates. He was
short, though, and very thin, his skin as white as a baby's.
His stare made her uncomfortable, and flushing, she turned
and hurried away.

Mama was standing in the doorway of the building
where their flat was, and she had seen. She gripped
Bridget's shoulder, staring at the street. Bridget turned and
saw the rich gentleman stepping into a fancy coach. "You
don't speak to anybody, you hear?" Mama said. "Especially
not strange men!"

"He didn't say anything," Bridget said. "Not even
hello."

"You're too pretty for your own good, and you look
fifteen, not eleven. That's what got me into trouble, and I
want to spare you that."

Bridget looked up at her beautiful mother and saw how
worried she was. "I won't get into trouble, Mama. I promise."

Gwen O'Neil bent and hugged her daughter, never mind
the small box poking them both. "Still, you are the best
thing that ever happened to me." She straightened and
smiled. "Now let's go up and get unpacked so we can do
some grocery shopping."

Francesca said, "How many?!"

Joel was equally dismayed. "Forty-one, Miz Cahill. I got
forty-one here on my list say they know what happened to
Emily O'Hare."

Francesca and Joel stood on the street in front of Schmitt's Grocery, her first stop of the morning. She took the list from Joel. He had made each man—and woman—sign his or her name, and as many of those who had responded to her reward poster were illiterate, a good many signatures consisted of slashes and Xs. "Oh, dear," she said. "Calder was right. Every unscrupulous lout seeking easy money has come forward to claim the reward. But maybe, Joel, just maybe, one of these informants really has seen something."

"I didn't know what to do, so I said you'd be here on the corner tomorrow at noon and that everyone should come back then."

Francesca was pleased. "That is an excellent idea! I'll bring a small table and a chair and interview everyone on the spot!"

Joel beamed. "Yeah, it is a good idea, ain't it?"

She patted his shoulder when she saw his gaze wander and fixate on an object behind her. His cheeks colored, so she turned and saw a tall, striking auburn-haired woman with a small cardboard box in her arms standing outside of the building where the Kennedys lived. "What is it?" she asked, now noticing the equally striking girl standing beside the woman. Clearly, the child was her daughter.

Joel shrugged, his cheeks pink. "New folk. They're taking the flat above ours. Guess they just come over from Ireland."

Francesca looked at him and had a suspicion. "The girl is very pretty."

Joel shrugged, beet-red now. "She is? Didn't notice. All look the same to me."

Francesca hid her smile. "I have a job for you while I go interview Mr. Schmitt again—as I am convinced he knows something he is not telling us. See if anyone knows where the Wirklers or the Coopers live. We must speak with Rachael Wirkler's and Bonnie Cooper's parents, and their school records are missing, so we don't know where they live."

"Okay, I'll try, see what I can learn," Joel said, turning, his hands now in the pockets of his wool coat. He glanced toward his building, but the mother and daughter were gone.

Francesca patted his back again and turned and pushed open the door to the grocery. The bell tinkled as she did so. Schmitt was at the counter, ringing up a sale for an elderly woman and her daughter, the latter being about Francesca's age. His daughter was stocking items on a shelf in another corner of the store. Beth glanced her way and froze upon her stepping stool, her cheeks turning red. Then she turned quickly back to the task at hand.

Francesca knew a suspicious reaction when she saw one. She approached the counter, Schmitt not having looked up. He finally said, "That's two dollars and twenty-three cents, Mrs. Polaski." Then he saw Francesca.

Displeasure covered his features.

But Francesca had heard, and she hurried forward as the younger woman counted out the sum for Schmitt. "Mrs. Polaski?"

The elderly woman turned, leaning heavily on her cane. "Yes? Do I know you?" She blinked at Francesca through the thick lenses of her spectacles.

"I am Francesca Cahill, a sleuth," she said, handing the woman her calling card. Upon returning home from Hart's, she had retrieved her purse last night, outside where she had been assaulted. It had been intact. Her small gun was now fully loaded—in case her assailant decided to strike again.

"A sleuth?" The woman cackled. "Since when do uptown ladies sleuth downtown?"

Francesca smiled firmly. "I was wondering if you might help me on a case," she said.

The old woman brightened. "You want my help? I would love to help!"

Francesca glanced at Schmitt. He seemed angry. He turned his back to her, saying, "Beth, please check that shipment out back that just came in."

Alarm bells went off. Francesca recalled very clearly that the last time she had been in the store, he had sent his flustered daughter away as well. "Mr. Schmitt says you are in the store every Monday afternoon."

Mrs. Polaski nodded. "And every Friday, too."

"Did you know Emily O'Hare? A small, pretty child of thirteen with fair skin and extremely dark hair?"

"Emily O'Hare. Of course I know her—I see her on the block all the time. Sweet girl. Sweet mother. Don't like the father, though, a mean drunken lout."

Schmitt turned abruptly. "This is a place of business, Miss Cahill, not a gossip parlor."

She lost her temper. "And just what are you hiding, Mr. Schmitt? Did you know that withholding information from the authorities is a federal crime?"

He stared. "I'm not withholding anything." He walked into the back.

"William is angry," Mrs. Polaski remarked. "Isn't he, Olga?"

The younger woman nodded. "I am Olga Rubicoff, Mrs. Polaski's daughter-in-law," she said with a smile.

"Why is William angry? And why are you asking me about little Emily?" Mrs. Polaski demanded.

"Emily disappeared on her way to this grocery last Monday between four and four-thirty in the afternoon. I was wondering if you had seen her that day or, more precisely, if you had seen what happened to her."

"Emily has disappeared?" Olga gasped.

Mrs. Polaski was equally shocked. "That's terrible! How does a child disappear?"

"I don't know. I was hoping you might be able to tell me."

"I haven't seen her in a while," Mrs. Polaski said. "Have I, Olga?"

"I was with my mother-in-law on Monday. I usually help her with the shopping. We didn't see Emily, Miss Cahill. I am so sorry," she said.

"Well, thank you anyway," Francesca said, dismayed.

As the women gathered up their bags, Francesca dared to unlatch the counter door and step behind it. A curtain separated the front of the store from the room in back, and she stepped through.

Instantly she saw Schmitt and his daughter in a tête-à-tête and Beth was crying. The room was small and filled with boxes and sacks of merchandise. Schmitt saw Francesca and stiffened. "No customer is allowed back here!"

Francesca was as rigid. "Beth, it is a crime to withhold information from the police—and this is an official police investigation. If you know something, you must come forward," Francesca said earnestly.

"Get out." Schmitt started toward her, looking angry enough to strike.

Francesca felt her gun slip into her hand before she even thought about what she was doing. She blinked at the tiny pistol—but it stopped Schmitt in his tracks. "I am very nervous today," she said, meeting Schmitt's wide, watchful gaze as she trained the gun vaguely in his direction. "Because last night someone assaulted me with a knife. He held the knife to my throat. He warned me to forget this investigation. Something criminal is going on. And I will find out what. Beth? If we learn that you have been hiding information from us, charges will be pressed. The charge will be obstruction of justice and it carries a prison sentence. You will go to jail," Francesca said.

Of course, the threat was only that, as she had no intention of ever sending Beth to jail. But it worked, because Beth turned white and cried, "I saw two men grab her right outside of the store. Two thugs, from the look of it, one short and fat, the other big and bald! Emily struggled but didn't have a chance. They threw a sack over her head and tossed her in the back of a wagon and took off."

"Why didn't you tell the police?" Francesca cried.

Beth hugged herself. "Because they saw me watching, and before they took off, the fat one grabbed my hand and almost broke it. He said if I told anyone what happened, I'd be next!"

Schmitt made a despairing sound and sank down onto a box, his body slumped, his shoulders hunched.

Francesca put the gun away and went over to Beth, putting her arm around her. "You have done the right thing, telling me what you saw. The police will protect you," she added.

Beth nodded, in tears.

"Like hell they will!" Schmitt cried.

"I will protect you," Francesca said firmly, then. "But first, we are going to have to go to headquarters."

"Headquarters?" Beth trembled.

"Police headquarters. They have a book of photographs and sketches of known criminals and crooks, Beth. Perhaps you will be able to identify the two men who abducted Emily."

Beth wiped her eyes with the edge of her apron. "I want to help. I've always wanted to help. Father refused to let me." She looked terrified now.

"I don't want you hurt," Schmitt said, heaving himself to his feet. "You're my only child," he added passionately.

Francesca knew the importance of an eyewitness. She made a decision. "Beth can stay with me until the case is solved," she said. "She will be safe in my home, Mr. Schmitt."

He blinked. "Your home?"

Beth also blinked. "I am going to your home?"

"Yes. We have plenty of guest rooms. First we will go to police headquarters, and then you can stop back here to pick up a few things." She smiled at them both. "She will be safe uptown, Mr. Schmitt."

He seemed truly confused. "Why are you doing this? What do you care about my daughter—or even Emily?" he demanded.

"I do care," Francesca said firmly. "I care very much, in fact." She took Beth's elbow and guided her from the back room and out of the store.

"Don't blame Father," Beth said. "He is afraid. He was only trying to protect me."

"I understand that," Francesca said. "But he was going about it the wrong way." She halted abruptly, as a police officer on a bay horse was coming down the street. A mounted officer in this vicinity was an unusual sight. He suddenly veered toward her.

Francesca quickly assumed that he was looking for her. Did Bragg wish to speak with her? She hadn't told him about last night yet, so maybe there was another development on the case. And as the mounted officer trotted swiftly her way, she glimpsed a familiar figure on the opposite sidewalk—Eliza Smith, Deborah Smith's mother and Tom Smith's widow.

"Miss Cahill," the officer said.

Francesca vaguely recognized him as he dismounted. "Yes?"

"You are needed at headquarters. I've been told to find you and instruct you to go directly there," he said.

Curiosity reared. She prayed there was a good, hard lead. "We were on our way there, actually," she said. "I have a coach. We'll take that." She was using the family brougham that day, and her driver, Jennings, was waiting patiently down the block.

"Very well, miss," he said, saluting her politely before turning his gelding and loping off.

Francesca smiled at Beth and said, "I must speak with Eliza Smith. Wait here. Don't move."

Beth nodded and Francesca dashed across the avenue, weaving past various drays and carts. "Mrs. Smith! Mrs. Smith?"

Eliza had seen her and had halted, waiting for Francesca on the corner, her face pale and pinched. "Is there any news?" she whispered. Her eyes and nose were red—she had been weeping. Had she been weeping for her murdered husband? Francesca wondered.

Francesca took her hand. "I will find Deborah. I have a witness to her abduction. We will find the thugs who did this."

Eliza nodded, clearly unable to speak, clearly about to weep.

"I am sorry about your husband," Francesca added.

"I'm not!" Eliza cried. Then she gasped, covering her mouth with her hand. "God forgive me, I'm not mourning, Miss Cahill. Not at all."

"I understand," Francesca whispered. "Do you have any idea why he was murdered? Do you have any idea who killed him?"

She wet her lips. "He lied about Deborah. I knew it was a lie right from the start—I knew he'd never send her to Charlotte. He hated Charlotte!"

Francesca took her hand. "Do you know who killed him?"

Eliza shook her head.

Francesca sighed. Then, "Do you know the Wirklers? Or the Coopers?"

Eliza hesitated. "Do you mean John Cooper's family?"

Francesca gripped her hand. "Yes."

"John used to drink with Tom. They were friends. I didn't know them well. I seem to recall they had a lovely daughter, a bit younger than Deborah."

Francesca sensed the connection now. "Where do they live?"

"Around the corner. But I haven't seen them in some time." She added, "So maybe they moved."

"Which building?" Francesca asked with excitement.

"The tan one with the blue shutters," Eliza said. "Why? Why are you asking me about the Coopers?"

"Because their daughter is missing, too."

The precinct was very busy that morning. The moment she and Beth entered, Francesca saw a number of civilians gathered at the reception desk, with a very harassed and red-faced Sergeant O'Malley. The holding pen was also full—a half a dozen scruffy men were in it, two sleeping curled up on the floor. It was also louder than usual, and not just because of the chorus of raised voices coming from the half-dozen complaining gentlemen at the desk. The telegraph was pinging constantly, and several phones were ringing as well.

Francesca saw that Captain Shea was also busy. He was at a desk behind the reception counter, with two officers and an inspector, and they were going over some paperwork. She decided to forgo any formalities. She knew Bragg had sent for her, anyway.

"I'll put you in the conference room upstairs," she told Beth, who continued to tremble and was wide-eyed now. "You can go over the mug book at your leisure then."

Beth seemed speechless; she nodded.

They were about to hurry to the stairs when Francesca saw a familiar form detach itself from all of the gentlemen gathered at the front desk. He was slim and dapper with a small mustache, dark-haired and in his thirties. She halted. He smiled at her, approaching.

"Kurland," she said. "You are just the man I have been looking for!" She was brisk, as she so disliked this newsman.

"Really? And how are you, Miss Cahill?" His gaze slid to the high collar of her shirtwaist, as if he knew she'd had a knife to her throat the other night.

But that was impossible. Francesca fingered her collar. "I am fine. I am on a new case."

"And you are eager to spill the beans?" His eyes laughed at her.

"More than eager, Kurland. For once, I do think we can help one another."

Kurland eyed Beth. "Really."

"My case is headline news," she said with a smile.

His brows lifted and he did not seem impressed. "Do go on."

Francesca felt her temper flare. "Four children are missing, Kurland, all very pretty girls between the ages of twelve and fourteen. We fear a white slaver—we fear the girls are being forced into prostitution."

"We?"

"Bragg and myself," she said with impatience.

His brows lifted again. "Really, I thought 'we' might refer to you and Calder Hart—now that you are engaged. Oh, by the way, congratulations."

She stiffened. "Thank you."

"Odd, how a short time ago you were such a frequent guest at the commissioner's home. Oh, but I forgot, his wife was not in residence then, was she?"

Francesca was furious. "Kurland, Bragg and I are friends. We will always be friends, and you know we also work closely together! I am giving you a scoop. Are you interested or not?"

"I am interested in everything about you, Miss Cahill, seeing as you are such an unusual woman." He smiled.

"Their names are Bonnie Cooper, Rachael Wirkler, Deborah Smith, and Emily O'Hare. The first three girls all went to school on Fourteenth Street between Second and Third Avenue. Emily worked at Moe Levy's with her mother. She was the last to disappear, just this last Monday. I've yet to speak with the Wirklers or Coopers, and for some odd reason, the principal of that school did not go to the police. All school records pertaining to the girls are missing. Oh. I forgot. Deborah Smith's father, Tom Smith, was murdered yesterday." She glared. "Let's go, Beth."

"Thank you, Miss Cahill, for the scoop. Oh, by the way, when is the wedding?"

But Francesca had taken Beth's hand and was already hurrying up the stairs. How that newsman infuriated her. And he knew the truth. He knew she had been carrying on with Bragg before his wife had come to town. What he did not know was that their affair had never been consummated, that it had come to nothing. Francesca felt ill. She felt as if a time bomb were ticking and Kurland was the one who would light the fuse.

Francesca forced herself to calm, showing Beth into the conference room and asking her to wait there. Shutting the door behind her, she faced Bragg's frosted glass door. She squared her shoulders and inhaled. Kurland had the knack of being able to shake her composure as no one else could. But then, she sensed he enjoyed discomfiting her.

She knocked.

"Come in."

Francesca stepped into Bragg's office and instantly saw him seated at his desk, his face on his bridged hands. He seemed grim, unhappy, and deeply lost in thought. "Rick?"

He looked up. His expression changed as he stood swiftly. "Good. I am glad you are here." He moved swiftly to her side, helping her off with her coat. "Are you all right, Francesca?"

She blinked, meeting his gaze. "You know?"

"Calder told me. Damn it, he told me, Francesca." His gaze darkened.

She understood. Once upon a time, she would have run directly to him, had she been assaulted the way she had been last night. "I'm fine. But it had to be Tom Smith's killer. He held a knife to my throat and told me to forget the girls, Bragg."

He tilted up her chin, unbuttoned the two highest buttons on her collar, and grimaced when he saw the fine dark red line on her throat. "Smith is dead. I want you off this investigation."

"Never!" she cried, backing away.

His hand dropped.

"How can you even suggest such a thing? And I do have the means to protect myself. I am carrying my gun and it is loaded."

He folded his arms across his chest. He had an odd look now, one dangerously annoyed. "I am not burying you on this case."

"No, you are not," she said.

"And Hart will allow you to continue on?"

"Hart doesn't allow or disallow anything," she shot back.

"Then you do not know the man you think to marry," he said softly—unpleasantly.

She stared. "You are in a foul mood today. Do not take it out on me."

"Why not? My mood is worse because you were threatened last night, you went to him—and I was not there to help."

"Yes, I was with Hart last night. Just the way you were with Leigh Anne."

He flushed, which she did not understand.

"I had thought you sent for me because there was a new lead."

"No."

"No? Well, I have one. In fact, she is here. Schmitt's daughter is an eyewitness to Emily's abduction, Bragg, and I want to get her started on the mug book. I also want to see if we can find John Cooper in there."

"Beth Schmitt saw the abduction?" Bragg asked, diverted now.

Francesca nodded. "There were two men. One short and fat, the other big and bald. The short one threatened to come back for her, too, if she said a word." Francesca stared. "Calder thinks this is about child prostitution."

He grimaced. "Calder would."

"I think so, too."

He stared. "So now you both think alike?"

And she lost her temper. "Hardly! But we are in agreement, and if we are right, this is a ghastly crime!"

He reached for her. "Calm down. Shouting will not solve either the crime or anything else."

She pulled away. "What do you really think?" Her heart hammered hard.

"I happen to agree," he said flatly. "I wanted to spare you the worry you are now so clearly afflicted with."

"By lying to me?" she asked, incredulous and dismayed. "By misleading me on such an important investigation?"

"I was trying to protect you," he said sharply.

"Maybe it is your wife you should be protecting," she said without thinking.

He snapped back, as if struck.

"I'm sorry," she whispered, aghast at making such a cutting remark.

"Let's get Beth Schmitt started on those photographs and sketches," he said.

Francesca watched him walk to the door. Dismay immobilized her. How had they been reduced to such straits?

Bragg turned. "He is winning, you know. Because this is exactly what he wants, to drive us apart, in every way, even as genuine friends."

Their gazes locked. "You are wrong."

He made a sound of disgust.

But she was afraid. Afraid that he was right.

An hour later, Beth had failed to identify the thugs who had abducted Emily, leading Francesca to believe that both men were rowdies and little else. Clearly they were the brawn for the brain behind the child prostitution ring. However, they did find John Cooper in the mug book.

He had done time. Two years, to be exact. His crime? An odd con involving his daughter, whom he had claimed to be someone else's child, missing since birth. The ecstatic parents had paid him several thousand dollars for the return of their supposed daughter, and had Bonnie not been recognized by chance on the street, the con would have never been revealed. She had been three at the time.

Nine years ago, the man had sold his own daughter, and here was the proof.

"He did it again," Francesca whispered.

Bragg had avoided looking at her for the past hour. Now their gazes met. "I shall enjoy interrogating this man," he said.

Francesca was a bundle of nerves as she entered the grand entrance of the Fifth Avenue Hotel. Now, with John Cooper on her mind, she wished very much that she had put off Grace Bragg. But it was already a quarter past one and it was too late to send her a note canceling their luncheon.

She entered the lobby where oak floors gleamed underfoot and paneled wood columns met a vaulted ceiling with a huge crystal chandelier. The lobby was filled with hushed conversation coming from the clusters of gentlemen, all in their business attire. Clerks in dark suits graciously registered new guests. Francesca saw Grace instantly, as she was the only woman in the entire lobby. She was seated on a coach in the central lounge area, and two distinguished-looking gentlemen had paused to speak with her.

Francesca inhaled for courage, smiled firmly, and started toward the woman who would be, in a way, her mother-in-law. Grace saw her and stood.

Francesca smiled, because Grace was wearing a very severe gray suit, as plain and drab as Francesca's navy blue one. However, the gray color did wonderful things to her fair complexion and brilliant red hair, which was tightly pinned back beneath a matching gray hat trimmed with black soutache. Her spectacles were hanging on a chain around her neck.

"Hello," Francesca said as they embraced. "I am sorry I am late."

"I understand. The case?"

Francesca brightened. "We have several new leads today, and I am extremely hopeful," she said.

"That is wonderful," Grace said, clearly meaning it.

"Mrs. Bragg, good day."

Francesca turned as a slim and dapper gentleman about Grace's age paused to greet her. He was exceedingly well dressed, his complexion very fair, his eyes pale blue.

Grace hesitated and Francesca thought she was trying to recall the gentleman's name. "Mr. Murphy," she smiled firmly, and Francesca realized she was wrong—Grace knew this gentleman and did not like him.

"Yes, Tim Murphy. We met at a function in Washington, I believe." He smiled at her. "I had heard you and your husband were back in the city and I wanted to say, 'Welcome.' "

Grace's smile was cool. "How nice of you. May I introduce Miss Cahill?"

Murphy turned and leveled his pale eyes on Francesca, smiling. "Any relation to Andrew Cahill?"

She smiled politely. "He is my father," she said.

"Well, I am pleased to meet you then," he said, taking her hand and politely lifting it. "Are you here for lunch?" he asked, his gaze now riveted on hers.

"Yes."

"Do enjoy. Chef Tomás is wonderful." He excused himself and left.

Francesca glanced at Grace and saw her expression, clearly one of distaste. "Who was that?"

"A Tammany rat," she said calmly. "He is a good friend of Croker's. I do believe he was in Van Wyck's administration. Shall we go in?"

Van Wyck had had one of the most corrupt administrations in the city's history, and that on the heels of the reform administration of the previous mayor, Strong. Fortunately, Julia was not related to those Van Wycks. Francesca had been present at inauguration day to witness the happy event of Seth Low becoming the city's mayor and great good-government white hope. Van Wyck had not dared stay for the ceremony, he was so unpopular and so disliked. He had slunk away without a word the moment he had handed over the ceremonial keys to the city. And it had been good riddance, too.

They were ushered into an elegant dining room filled with gentlemen—the only women present. Grace clearly did not care and she accepted many greetings as they were led to their table. As they sat, she asked Francesca if she would like a glass of wine with lunch.

"No thank you," Francesca said. "I have far too much work to do this afternoon."

Grace asked the maître d' to bring them tea, and when

he had left, she smiled at Francesca. "I am very pleased that you could have lunch with me."

Francesca smiled grimly. "I feel as if I am on the executioner's block." The moment the words were out, she wished she hadn't spoken so frankly.

"Oh, dear." Grace reached across the table for her hand. "I am very impressed by your intelligence and determination, Francesca. I like you very much."

Francesca managed to smile. The unspoken word was *but.*

"How much thought have you given to your engagement with Calder?" she asked.

"More than you can ever know," Francesca said ruefully. She hesitated. "I accepted his proposal a month ago, Grace."

She was surprised. "A month ago? And then you left town. Tell me, Francesca, why did you accept Calder's proposal? Are you in love with him?"

She tensed. "I am very fond of him."

"That is hardly love."

"No."

"Are you in love with Rick?"

Francesca could not speak. She could only stare. Was she in love with Bragg? Hadn't she promised him her heart, forever, no matter what?

"Have you asked yourself this question? I hardly think it fair to Calder if you marry him when you have given your heart to someone else."

Francesca wished the afternoon would evaporate. "Calder doesn't love me, Grace. He doesn't even believe in love. But he is as fond of me as I am of him, and he wishes to marry me. Upon reflection, I think it will be a very interesting union." She felt herself begin to flush. She was so erudite, and that was the best she could do.

"Calder is a complicated man," Grace said. "He seems smug and confident—I find him terribly fragile. You have clearly turned his head, otherwise he would not wish to marry you. I think he may very well be in love with you, my dear. But I don't think he is capable of admitting it, not now, perhaps not ever."

Francesca stared, for one moment reeling, and then she recovered, because she knew Grace was wrong. "What are you really saying?"

"I am very fond of you," Grace said. "But I don't want either of my sons hurt."

Francesca stiffened, because Grace could not have been clearer. She did not want Francesca marrying Hart because of Francesca's remaining feelings for Bragg.

Grace smiled, but it was firm and hardly reassuring. "I do not think you known what you want. The last I heard, you were very in love with Rick."

Francesca knew she was supposed to respond, but she did not know how. "There is no one I admire more," she managed hoarsely. "But I support his marriage."

"Do you have a choice?" Grace bluntly asked.

"No," Francesca admitted, flushing. "But I truly support his marriage. I have encouraged Rick to forgive his wife, to give her a real chance."

Grace stared. Then, "The fact that you and he would even have such a conversation speaks volumes. I support his marriage as well, Francesca."

Francesca swallowed uneasily.

Grace continued, "Leigh Anne was an immature young woman with stars in her eyes and many foolish romantic notions in her head when she met my son. He was as foolish—and as romantic. Both were naive when it came to relationships. Neither one knew the other, and the courtship was brief. An impulsive, somewhat selfish, and angry girl left my son four years ago. A mature and, I believe a very different woman has returned to his side. Leigh Anne has changed—and the change seems to be for the better. I want them to have a real marriage, Francesca. But first, they need a real chance."

"Why are you telling me this?" she asked, dismayed. But she already knew what Grace's answer would be.

"Because the bond between you and Rick remains—and it doesn't help his marriage at all."

Francesca flushed. Carefully she said, "Then why aren't you encouraging me to marry Calder?"

"Because you don't love him. Because it upsets me to see my sons fighting one another—over you." She toyed with her glass, then said, "I don't like it. I don't like this entire scenario. Not one bit."

Francesca felt ill. "So you are asking me to break it off with Calder?"

"I would never do such a thing. I am asking you to think carefully about what you are doing—and why. It is your decision to marry. Just be certain you are marrying for the right reasons. Not because you are hurt and cannot have the man you really want."

Francesca felt real despair. She had been excited, she realized, about her engagement, and now she felt hurt and even, oddly, crushed. Francesca stared at the linen tablecloth. What should she do? ·

Could she break it off with Hart?

She couldn't breathe. The thought of breaking up with Hart made her ill, almost violently so. But she didn't love him, did she? She had briefly found true love with Rick Bragg, but what she felt now for Hart was so very different. It was wild and frightening and dangerous.

She simply couldn't imagine being with Hart in a house filled with their children, a white picket fence about the yard. And it had been so easy to see herself with Rick Bragg that way.

The only thing she could envision when it came to Calder was being in his bed. And that, dear God, was hardly love.

Maybe Grace was right. Maybe she should break it off before it was too late. Maybe she was marrying him for all the wrong reasons.

"Francesca? I hope I haven't been too brutal in my honesty."

Francesca managed to meet her gaze and somehow managed to smile. "I appreciate your honesty," she said. "You are right. I am marrying for all the wrong reasons." She smiled, but she felt deathly ill.

Grace smiled back. "I know you will do the right thing."

Francesca could not speak. If she did the right thing, she was going to have to break if off with Calder Hart.

It was a beautiful spring day, but her heart was so heavy that the skies seemed gray, not cornflower blue. Leigh Anne walked slowly down Broadway, so immersed in her thoughts that she had forgotten to open her umbrella. She was so fair that she burned easily.

Images of last night came to mind, hot and torrid. But along with the tingle of need there was hurt and despair. He was punishing her, she knew, by refusing to give her a chance to have their child.

If only she could hate him. When she had returned after their long separation, she hadn't known what she would really feel. The anger had faded long ago, leaving an odd wistfulness, a strange nostalgia, in its stead. Those old-fashioned dreams of true love, children, a happy home and handsome husband seemed quaint and as if they had belonged to another woman. Leigh Anne couldn't even identify with the spoiled and selfish child who had walked out on her husband that long ago and oh-so-fateful day.

She paused before a window filled with beautiful hats and bonnets, not seeing a single one. Tears rapidly filled her eyes.

She fought them, but she knew that the day that loomed ahead was a long one and this was her single chance to cry, and she quickly gave up. She wept, silently.

For how much longer could she go on this way? Being ignored by day, being ravaged by night? Yet even if she could leave him again, she could never leave the girls. She had been hoping to bring up the subject of their adoption with him, but every time they came face-to-face, she changed her mind, afraid of his reaction, knowing what it would be. He would accuse her of using the girls to reach him. He had become such a bastard, she thought, and that was the real crux of the matter. Once he had loved her, now he hated her, and it didn't seem as if there would ever be any going back, no matter how hard she tried to be a good wife.

She wiped her eyes. At least they had the nights. They would always have the raging, insatiable desire. Today it felt like a curse.

What should she do?

What *could* she do?

She had come back because Bartolla had told her he was in love with another woman. She had left him four years ago certain he would never give his heart to anyone else— she had been so confident, so sure of it. When she had received the countess's letter, she hadn't really believed Bartolla's words. Yet when she had met Rick and Francesca at the train, when she had seen Francesca for that very first time, she had understood and she had been terrified.

He worshiped the other woman because she was selfless, noble, and good. He had set her on a pedestal, and Leigh Anne simply could not compete. Nor did she wish to do so—it felt far below her dignity. Besides, she also admired and respected Francesca Cahill. In fact, had the circumstances been different, Leigh Anne suspected they might have become friends.

Leigh Anne set her unopened parasol down and fumbled in her bag for a tissue. Feeling sorry for herself was utter idiocy. It solved nothing. The bottom line was, she had her marriage back and she wasn't giving it up. She wasn't giving Rick up—and that was that.

She needed to be strong.

Unfortunately, just then it felt as if the last reserves of her strength were waning dangerously low. For how much longer could she last? Where would she find the strength to renew herself?

Then she thought about Katie and Dot and warmed. The girls needed her. He might not need her outside of the dark hours of the night, but the children needed her—just as she needed them.

She reached for her parasol, opened it, and stepped out onto the sidewalk. And someone screamed.

"Look out!" a man shouted at her.

And she heard the hooves on the cobblestones, dangerously close; she heard the splintering of wood, the shrieking of carriage wheels, the grating of pressure brakes. And the snorting. . . .

Leigh Anne turned.

The coach was out of control. The horses were on the sidewalk, galloping directly toward her. The frightened driver was a blur. He screamed at her. Leigh Anne felt sheer terror then, and as she stared into the whites of the horse's eyes she knew the end was near.

She was going to die.

Leigh Anne somehow moved. Screaming, she leaped aside, but too late.

Iron-shod hooves caught her left leg and she went down.

Time stopped.

She knew she had to roll aside, but the pain was blinding, paralyzing, and she could see more hooves coming, directly at her, and the single, terrifying wheel. . . .

Sobbing, Leigh Anne tried to pull herself out of the way.

She failed.

CHAPTER
ELEVEN

SATURDAY, MARCH 29, 1902 — 3:00 P.M.

BRAGG WAS WAITING FOR her on the street in front of the brown building with the blue shutters where they hoped the Coopers currently lived. They had made plans to meet before her luncheon with Grace. He smiled slightly as she approached. "How was your lunch?"

Francesca tried not to wince. "I had a fabulous piece of cod," she said. It was a lie. She'd barely been able to eat.

He started, his gaze piercing, sensing something was amiss, but she hurried past him to the building's front door. She was more upset now than she had been before, because Grace Bragg was right. She was marrying Calder Hart for all the wrong reasons, and it wasn't fair—not to anyone, not even to herself. She did not want to talk about it, especially not with Bragg. But could she really break up with Hart?

She must not think about it now. There was work to do and not much time in which to do it. She had promised

Sarah she would sit for her at half past four.

Bragg said from behind her, "They're here. I checked with some neighbors. Flat Number Four."

Francesca nodded. "Let's go up."

He seized her arm. "You are distraught. What happened?"

"I'm fine." She smiled too brightly at him.

He studied her. "Grace can be too honest sometimes. But she means well. She is one of the kindest women I know."

"I know all that. Let's see if John Cooper is at home. We have missing children to find, Bragg." She pulled free and hurried into the entry, a small, narrow windowless square. The fourth flat was on the second floor. Francesca did not hear a sound from within it and she was dismayed as she knocked sharply upon the battered wood door.

There was simply no answer.

She faced Bragg after knocking twice more. "No one is home."

He gave her a look. "Let's go in anyway."

She was startled. He smiled at her and tried the door—but it was firmly locked. Bragg took a small knife from his breast pocket and began fooling with the lock. It clicked. He smiled at her and tried the door, and this time the door swung open.

"Very nice," Francesca breathed. "Have you been taking lessons from Joel?"

He chuckled as they stepped inside, closing the door behind them.

The flat was one room. It was not partitioned into separate sleeping areas. Francesca instantly became uneasy, glancing around. There was one bed on the far wall. "Where is Bonnie's bed?"

"I don't know. The neighbor told me they have been here for about six months."

"This is odd. I am worried." There were a series of wall pegs by the bed and she saw several garments, all clearly belonging to a grown man or an adult woman. In case she had missed something, Francesca went to them and inspected the clothing. "There's nothing here for a child."

"Bonnie was twelve. She might have been tall for her age—she might have worn the clothing of a small woman."

There was one rickety and stained bureau near the bed as well. Francesca went to it. She found some very nice linens, the kind that would have cost a fortune for the Coopers, and some other odds and ends. Then she saw the rag doll. She seized it. "Evidence that there was a child."

But Bragg was going through the set of shelves in the kitchen area. He held up two silver candlesticks. "Someone is up to his old tricks," he said, "unless I miss my guess."

Francesca clutched the doll. "Where are her clothes? Where is her bed? Why does this flat seem to belong to a childless couple?"

"Perhaps Mrs. Cooper's way of grieving was to get rid of all signs of her daughter."

"I smell a rat," Francesca said grimly.

Suddenly they heard footsteps in the hall. Francesca tensed as a man with a barrel chest and a heavy growth of beard appeared in the doorway. "What the hell are you doing in here?" he shouted angrily.

Bragg stepped forward in a such a manner that he shielded Francesca from the intruder. "John Cooper?"

"Jesus! You a copper?" the man demanded.

"I'm afraid so," Bragg said calmly. "Are you John Cooper?"

He stared sullenly and then nodded. "You got a warrant for bein' in here?" he asked.

"No, but I can have one, appropriately dated, anytime I choose."

Francesca winced.

"What the hell do you want?"

Francesca stepped past Bragg. "We want to know where Bonnie is," she said.

"Bonnie?" His gaze narrowed. "She's dead."

Francesca almost cried out. Bragg restrained her. "What happened?" he asked.

His nostrils flared. "She was beaten up by some rough, out on the street. She didn't make it."

Francesca inhaled, her mind spinning. Was this man telling the truth? It would certainly explain why none of Bonnie's belongings were in the flat. "But the school doesn't know."

"I guess I never got down there to tell 'em what happened. Now get out."

Bragg strode past Francesca. "You're going to have to come with me," he said.

"With you?" he cried.

"I'm afraid so. Your daughter was murdered. Those responsible need to be apprehended and brought to justice," he said. "I'll need a statement from you and your wife."

"We don't know who did it," he growled. "I didn't see it and neither did my wife. We were told about it. It was some rowdy, giving her a hard time. By the time we got there, she was dead."

Francesca glanced at Bragg, and they shared a look. He was also skeptical. She said, "I'm so sorry."

Cooper stared at her, an ugly look in his eyes.

"You will still have to come with me and make an official statement," Bragg said.

Cooper cursed, his way, Francesca supposed, of agreeing. "Where is she buried?" Francesca asked.

He eyed her. "St. James Cemetery," he said.

"Sarah, I am sorry I am late!" Francesca said breathlessly, shrugging off her coat. A valet took it away for her.

"I am happy you could come at all," Sarah said, smiling, her eyes alight. "I can tell you are hugely busy with your latest case."

"I am," Francesca said, instantly grim. Was Bonnie Cooper dead? Or was this a convenient way to excuse her disappearance? But that would imply that Cooper was involved. Yet hadn't he once pawned off his own daughter as an impostor for that ransomed child, in the hopes of collecting the reward? He was a despicable and foul man. Francesca shuddered, wishing she'd had the opportunity to interview his wife.

"You seem very preoccupied," Sarah said as they went down the hall to her studio.

"I *am* preoccupied," Francesca admitted, suddenly thinking of her luncheon with Grace Bragg. Today Sarah was very conservatively dressed in a navy blue dress. Splotches of paint marred the fabric, and her chignon was falling down. She looked very bohemian, Francesca thought. "Do you think I am marrying Calder for all the wrong reasons?" she asked very quietly.

Sarah halted in her tracks. "Only you can answer that, Francesca," she said quietly. Then, "I do think he adores you. And you seem very fond of him. I like the match." She shrugged, but there was a question in her eyes.

Francesca sighed. "Grace doesn't." She felt like telling her everything. Her spirits felt impossibly low.

Sarah started and then firmly pushed open the studio door. "She actually said that?"

"Yes, she did."

"Oh my," Sarah said softly. "How terrible for you. But Francesca, you must please yourself, not Hart's foster mother and not anyone else."

Francesca managed a small smile when it struck her that Rourke was to meet her there. She wondered if she might convince Sarah to let down her hair. "What time is it?"

"Almost five. Why?"

He should be there at any moment. "I had better disrobe," she said, hiding a real smile. "Sarah, your chignon is coming apart."

Sarah shrugged, clearly indifferent, but her eyes narrowed. "Is something going on that I should know about?"

"Of course not," Francesca said, stepping behind the lacquered screen. As she began to take off her clothes, she listened to Sarah moving about, arranging her palette and brushes, occasionally humming. Francesca had just slipped on the silk kimono when she heard a different set of footsteps—heavier, male. She tensed, but she was grinning.

"Sarah, good day. I do hope I am not intruding," Rourke's pleasant and smooth voice sounded.

There was silence.

Francesca stuck her head around the screen. Sarah looked stunned to see him, and now her cheeks were turning red. "Rourke . . . Bragg . . . " she stammered. "This is a surprise! I thought you were in Philadelphia." She sounded breathless, and now she was busily fussing with her brushes and avoiding his gaze.

"I am in town for the weekend. How are you?"

"Fine. And you?" Sarah glanced up and colored instantly again.

"I'm very well, actually, thank you. Is Francesca here? She asked me to meet her here. I need to look at her throat."

Sarah stared in surprise. "Is Francesca ill?"

Francesca decided she should come out. She stepped out from behind the screen, smiling. "Hello, Rourke. No, Sarah, I am not ill. But there was a slight incident last evening," she said.

Sarah looked at Francesca's throat, now exposed, and she gasped, paling. "What happened?!" she cried.

"I am fine, really," Francesca said.

"The wound is a superficial one," Rourke told Sarah. Then he glanced at Francesca, more precisely at her pale ivory kimono. "This should be an interesting portrait," he murmured. "Do I dare ask whose idea this was?"

Francesca felt herself blush. "I refuse to tell," she said lightly. "Do not breathe a word of this to anyone, Rourke. If my mother ever learns I am posing nude, well, I cannot even imagine what she will do."

Rourke bit back a smile. "Why would I tell? I guess I will never be able to view the finished portrait."

Francesca gave him a stern look.

Rourke laughed wickedly. "Lucky Calder," he said.

"That will be up to Mr. Hart," Sarah said firmly.

Francesca started. Surely Sarah did not think that Hart would someday publicly display her portrait?

Sarah stared back. "I think this will be the most amazing work I have ever done. I hate the idea that it will be hidden in Hart's closet."

"Sarah," Francesca began, flushing.

"I know. I am being selfish. But you are so beautiful and the painting will be breathtaking. I am determined, in fact."

"Sarah—showing my portrait would be scandalous."

She sighed. "I know." She glanced briefly at Rourke, who was listening with interest to their exchange. "Rourke, perhaps you should examine Francesca, so we can get started."

Rourke glanced at her, his face impossible to read, and then he tilted up Francesca's face. As he inspected the wound, Sarah fiddled with her brushes. "Everything is healing cleanly, and there is no infection," he said with a smile. "How do you feel?"

"I am fine," she said cheerfully.

"I think you are fine, too. Of course, you are a lucky lady," Rourke said. He faced Sarah, shoving his hands in the pockets of his suit jacket. "A group of us are going to the opera," he said casually. "Hart, myself, Francesca, and Nicholas D'Archand." The last was his cousin.

Francesca almost gasped. She had forgotten entirely about the opera that night. Hart had mentioned it to her on the drive home last night and she had accepted his invitation.

"It is supposedly the best production of *La Bohème* in years. We have a box. You're welcome to join us if you wish," he added nonchalantly.

Francesca's heart beat hard. Was Rourke being polite and companionable, or was he interested in Sarah? Francesca could not tell, as he was so poker-faced. But Sarah was flushing yet again.

"We can pick you up," he added, smiling.

How could Sarah refuse? The man had two deep dimples, twinkling amber eyes, a cleft chin, and the kind of

body any woman would love to become lost in. Francesca
smiled happily.

"I was planning to work tonight," Sarah said then, avoiding his gaze. "Francesca, we really must get started."

Francesca felt like kicking her. Was she a fool? "Sarah,
do come! I should die alone in the company of three such
rakes!" D'Archand, while only eighteen, was a superior ladies' man. "Please," she added.

Sarah met her gaze. She looked distressed. "I really must
work on your portrait," she said softly.

Francesca gave her an incredulous look.

Rourke said smoothly, "That's fine. I understand. And I
do agree—it will be an amazing work of art." He kissed
Francesca's cheek. "I will see you later, then."

Francesca looked him in the eye, but if he felt rebuffed
or rejected, it was impossible to tell.

He nodded at Sarah and walked out.

A silence fell.

Francesca turned to Sarah, actually angry with her—then
saw how miserable she appeared. "Are you all right?"

Sarah forced a smile. "I am fine. I was just surprised—to
see him here. I hadn't realized he was in town."

Francesca seized her arm before she could turn away.
"Change your mind. Come with us."

"I don't think that's a good idea."

"Don't you like Rourke? Isn't he gorgeous? And kind?"
she cried. "He will soon be a wonderful doctor, Sarah, and
while I know you are not interested in marriage, he is a
catch! He will not be available for long!"

Sarah jerked away, wide-eyed. "What are you trying to
do? And what do his looks have to do with anything? And
you are right—he will soon find the woman of his dreams,
of that I have no doubt."

"I think he likes you," Francesca said.

"That is absurd." Sarah was terse. "He is kind, just as
you said, and nothing more. And we are practically sisters,"
she added in a huff. "Which is why he is so polite. Francesca, he is a ladies' man. It is obvious. I am certain he

has left a string of broken hearts in Philadelphia."

"I don't think so," Francesca said urgently. "In fact, I happen to know for a fact that he is not in love with anyone!"

"You asked him?" Sarah was incredulous and dismayed.

"I did." Francesca grinned.

"Francesca, please, desist! I know you probably think you are doing me a good turn, but you are not! The only thing that interests me is my art. And I am not going to make a fool of myself running after a man like that. You're mad, Francesca, to think he even has noticed me as a woman. Now, may we please begin?"

Francesca knew a brick wall when she ran into one. She nodded but refused to give up. She began to plan.

He stood staring at his reflection in the mirror over the cherry wood vanity, tying his bow tie. From the dressing room he could hear Katie speaking in soft tones and Dot answering in happy giggles. The girls, he knew, were playing with two new dolls, dolls that Leigh Anne had bought for them recently.

He glanced out of the dressing room and at the bronze clock on the bureau. It was half past six.

Where was she?

They were joining Mayor Low and his wife, the Cuttings, and another couple at the opera that night. The opera curtain lifted at half past seven. By now, Leigh Anne should be beside him in the boudoir, applying makeup and getting dressed.

There was no gown hanging on the ironing rack, freshly pressed and waiting to be put on.

Where the hell was she?

Something sick and angry twisted deep inside of him. Was she late? Or had he finally succeeded in chasing her away?

Had she left him? Again?

He stepped quickly from the boudoir, suddenly finding

it airless inside the small dressing room. His heart raced. If she had left, he was pleased. It was what he wanted.

After all, why else had he been so miserable to her for the past month and a half?

Images filled his mind: Leigh Anne asleep in their bed, Leigh Anne reading the girls a bedtime story, Leigh Anne at her secretaire, bent over the desk in deep concentration. Leigh Anne in bed, beneath him, smiling and seductive, encouraging him to move deeper, harder, faster. . . .

He had known all along that it would come to this, hadn't he? He had known from the moment she had first reappeared in his life that she simply would not stay.

He was more than pleased. He was ecstatic, wasn't he?

He roared and struck out, smashing an expensive Oriental vase against the wall. It shattered loudly and he realized what he had done; worse, he realized that there was a tidal wave inside of him, rising up, one he refused to identify—one he did not want.

He was sick. And it was a sickness of the heart.

She wasn't coming back.

The sickness roiled, black, terrible, vast.

"Mr. Bragg?" Katie whispered from the doorway.

He whirled, horrified, and saw her standing there, looking skinny and afraid, holding Dot's hand. For once Dot wasn't beaming—she looked unhappy, in fact, and confused. Suddenly the toddler burst into shrieking sobs.

Bragg rushed forward. "It was just an accident!" he cried, stricken, quickly lifting the sobbing Dot into his arms. He tried to smile reassuringly at Katie and knew he failed. "The vase fell. It was an accident."

"Where's Mrs. Bragg?" she asked hoarsely, her huge eyes unwavering upon him.

He stared, his mind racing—and he could not come up with a single lie.

Katie hugged herself. "She said she was going out to tea, with that beautiful countess. She said she'd be home by five. It's not five, is it? It's way later than that."

Hatred surged—it was one thing to do this to him, but another to do it to the children. And because he knew Leigh Anne wasn't coming back, he struggled to find a plausible lie that would buy him some time so he could decide how to best tell the children the truth.

"Mrs. Bragg's father is very ill. He lives in another city, in Boston." That, so far, was the truth. "She decided to go visit her father," he added, trying to smile.

"But she didn't say good-bye," Katie said, looking stricken.

"It was an emergency," he said, his heart breaking into different parts, and this time it was for the children.

Katie stared, appearing as if she did not believe him. Then she said, "Our momma didn't say good-bye, either. She went out and never came back."

He inhaled, reaching for her with one hand, but Katie dodged, tears now forming in her dark eyes. He just couldn't tell her that this was different, that Leigh Anne was coming back, not when he didn't believe it. And he cursed her then, silently, for doing this to the children—for doing this to him.

Katie choked on a sob and raced from the master bedroom.

He ran after her. "Katie, wait! I need to speak to you."

Katie dived onto the bed she shared with her little sister and lay on her abdomen, her face buried in a pillow. At least Dot had stopped sobbing. He sat down beside Katie, gently placing Dot on the bed. Dot stared curiously at her sister. "Kat sad," she announced, looking worried.

He reached out and stroked Katie's thin back. It shuddered with her silent sobs.

"Katie? I just lied to you. I'm sorry."

The shudders wracking her thin body stopped.

"Can we discuss this?" he asked, feeling helpless and wishing he knew how to be a real father. But only instinct and love guided him now.

Katie nodded into the pillow.

"It would help if you sat up," he said softly, clasping her shoulder. "Please."

She slowly sat up, turning to face him, her eyes wide and anxious and riveted on his.

He wondered how it had happened—how and when he had fallen in love with these two children. "I'm so sorry," he said, and to his horror, his tone broke.

Katie's eyes widened.

He fought for control—grown men did not cry. And not over self-serving wives who were merely glorified whores.

Katie reached for his hand and held it.

That almost undid him. He struggled and finally found a degree of composure. He said, "I don't know where Mrs. Bragg is."

Katie gasped in dismay. "But she is coming home, isn't she?" she begged.

"I don't know," he said.

Katie whimpered. "Momma didn't come home because she couldn't. Momma didn't come home because she was dead."

Dot began to howl, the anguished sound of a wounded animal—as if she understood their conversation. Bragg pulled her into his arms. "I'm sure Mrs. Bragg is fine."

"Then why hasn't she come home?" Katie asked.

He hesitated. "It's hard to explain."

Katie looked ready to weep. "She's dead, isn't she?"

He gripped her hand. "She isn't coming home because of me, sweetheart. It's not because of you. It's because of me."

"I don't understand."

He hesitated, at a loss. "Sometimes, in a marriage, things change. Sometimes wives leave their husbands."

Katie stared. "But why?"

He felt his body stiffen. "Because she doesn't love me."

Katie stared, disbelieving. "No, Mr. Bragg, she does love you. And I thought she loved us, too." Tears fell.

He had no more words left. He pulled Katie close to his side and held the girls that way for a long time.

• • •

The pain was blinding.

"Pulse?"

"One-ten over fifty, Doctor."

Where was she? Oh, God, the pain, it was burning from her legs, burning through her entire body, she was in a fireball of pain, and she couldn't breathe; there was no air; she was going to suffocate! Oh, God, what had happened? Where was she? Panic began, and it was followed by terror.

There had been an accident, a terrible carriage accident.

She had been run over.

Oh, God. It all came back to her now, the clarity stunning—meeting the horse's eyes, inches from hers, going down, so slowly, hitting the concrete, twisting, turning, seeing those wagon wheels, coming toward her. . . .

She had been run over.

Was she going to die?

His image filled her mind, golden and handsome, and he was smiling, his eyes filled with warmth. It was followed by the girls, pretty and smiling at her.

"Anybody know who this lady is? Clamp."

The voice again, the one with authority, cutting through the brilliant pain, the fire, the ice, the blackness.

She was in a hospital—briefly she was relieved. But the doctor or doctors did not know who she was. She had to tell them! Because she needed Rick. . . .

"Suction, damn it, Brad."

She had to speak. She was Mrs. Rick Bragg. Where was Rick! She needed him now.

"We're working on it. There was a runaway coach. Chopped her right up on the sidewalk."

"No calling cards?"

"No, Doc. But she's a lady from the look of it. Did you see that face?"

"I don't have time to look at her face, Brad, get me that number-three scissor."

She swallowed, trying to speak. Mrs. Mrs. I am Mrs. Mrs. Mrs. Rick Bragg.

"Doctor, she's conscious." A woman now spoke, briskly, surprised. "She's trying to speak."

"Give her more laudanum. I want her out. Shit. Look at this."

A silence fell.

What was he looking at? The fear was explosive, begging to become terror. Everyone sounded so serious, so worried. How badly was she hurt? Surely she wasn't going to die!

But she had been run over by two carriage wheels. She remembered every moment, every detail. She remembered the incredible pain.

"Is she going to make it?"

Leigh Anne strained to hear.

"I don't know. She's in shock. She's got at least two broken ribs and I think a ruptured spleen. It's the spleen I'm worried about—Oh, Christ. I take that back."

"Oh, God," Brad said.

The pain was lessening slightly, becoming tolerable, and she was beginning to float. What were they talking about? What was happening? How badly was she hurt? Why did they sound so dismayed? She tried to listen, but it was so hard, because their voices were fading, because she was fading, quickly now.

The pain was almost gone. She was floating, comfortable now. Cocooned in fuzzy warmth, in blackness. Was she dying? Was this what dying was like? Because it was so peaceful. . . .

"Jesus, look at that leg. Jesus, Doc."

"Oh, Christ. I need an identification on this woman! I need it now, because from the look of it, this leg is coming off, and I'd really like to speak with her family first."

"What a goddamned shame."

What? What had he said? Were they amputating her leg? It was so hard to think now, so hard to feel, so hard to be. The sensation of floating increased, She was weight-

*less, drifting, high. God, she could even see the doctor and
his nurses; how odd. She was in a hospital room after all,
lying naked on the table, covered with a sheet. Blood was
everywhere. Then she saw the doctor adjusting the sheet
and she saw the bloody pulp that was her left leg and she
stared.*

"She's going into shock! We're losing her."

She closed her eyes.

Rick, please, come, please, Rick, please.

I want to say good-bye.

CHAPTER
TWELVE

"He's here," Julia announced, standing on the threshold of Francesca's bedroom. She was beaming.

Francesca felt ill. She couldn't stop thinking about her interview with Grace Bragg, and now there was no denying that marrying Calder Hart was very wrong. She slowly faced her mother, clad in a pale dove-gray gown that was high-necked and more appropriate for day than night. "I have such a headache, Mama."

Julia started. "What is this?! Don't tell me you are thinking of standing Calder up! He's downstairs, Francesca. And why are you wearing that dismal dress?"

Francesca was in despair, and worse, she was also miserable. She so wanted to fly downstairs and into Hart's arms. But it wasn't right. It wasn't fair. Not to him and not to herself.

"Francesca, you are not going to back out now," her mother said, as if reading her thoughts.

"What are you talking about?" Francesca feigned innocence. "Mama, I am on a terribly grim case. I am worried about the missing girls. Worse, I didn't have a chance to visit the cemetery where John Cooper claims Bonnie is buried. I am exhausted, really."

Julia always knew everything that went on in her household, and she clearly knew all about Francesca's latest investigation, because she did not blink. Instead, she came forward, seized Francesca's arm, and started her out the door. "I can see right through you, my dear. I know you are having second thoughts. Well, have them tomorrow! Besides"—she smiled as they went downstairs—"Andrew and I saw this production last week and it is magnificent. You will truly enjoy yourself."

Francesca doubted that. The reception room came into view, the entry hall beyond that. The floors were wide slabs of black and white marble, and plaster columns supported the ceiling. Francesca only saw Hart, clad in a black tuxedo, impossibly seductive, impossibly handsome. His back was to her—he was speaking with Andrew. Then he heard her and he turned.

Her heart turned over hard. He held a bouquet of red and white roses in his hand. He smiled slowly at her.

"My daughter, at long last. You will have to get used to it, Calder, but Francesca is so busy with her various affairs that she is always late."

"I don't mind," Hart said softly, his gaze never leaving Francesca. And briefly, the way he gazed at her was as if she was the most beautiful woman he had ever seen.

Which was absurd. "Are those for me?" she managed, tearing her gaze away.

"Yes."

"Red and white roses. They're lovely, thank you." She accepted the bouquet, still avoiding his eyes, terribly uneasy now as well as dismayed.

He murmured, "Red seemed terribly clichéd, if not appropriate. Passion and innocence. That's you, Francesca."

She had to look up.

He started, clearly seeing the despair in her eyes.

She turned away, handing the bouquet to her mother. "Can you put those in my rooms?"

"Of course." Julia smiled. "Are you going to have supper after the opera?"

"Yes," Hart said, before Francesca could answer. "But I will have her home around midnight."

Francesca accepted her coat from a valet.

"Enjoy yourself," Julia said happily.

Francesca nodded, kissed her father's cheek, and walked out with Hart. The moment the front door was closed behind them, he said, "What is wrong?"

Her heart lurched with dread. It was a moment before she could answer, and when she did so, it was as he helped her into his brougham. "Bonnie Cooper may be dead. That is what her father claims."

Hart settled on the seat beside her, reaching for her hand. Without thinking, Francesca pulled her palm away. She felt him stiffen; she turned to look at him. He stared, his expression impossible now to read.

"Where is Rourke?" she managed too brightly.

"He is meeting us at the opera. What is it, Francesca? Why are you behaving as if you are frightened of me?"

She swallowed. "I am not afraid of you, Hart. That is one thing I have never been where you are concerned."

"Really? Then why are you flustered, uneasy? You only call me Hart when you are upset."

"The case," she began.

"Don't lie to me," he said, hard.

She stiffened. "I'm sorry."

He studied her as the coach rolled off. "Something has happened. I want to know what."

She didn't want to lie to him. Lying to him felt wrong; it made her ill. "I've been thinking."

"Oh ho." His words were tight, his tone unpleasant. He sat back, watching her closely now. "Let me guess. You are having second thoughts about us?"

She nodded miserably.

"Now I wonder why," he said softly, dangerously.

She shrugged. "It's just wrong, I think, to marry simply so we can jump into bed. It's—"

"Stop the nonsense, Francesca," he warned.

She tensed, her gaze meeting his.

"First of all, you may be marrying so you can enjoy my favors, but that is not why I am marrying and you damn well know it." He was angry but controlling it. "Who has been whispering in your ear? Oh—let me guess. My dear half brother!"

"No." She shook her head, swallowing again, terribly nervous. "Grace."

He stiffened as if shot. "I beg your pardon?"

"We had lunch," she whispered, feeling close to tears.

"I do not believe this. Grace advised you not to marry me?"

"No! Calder, she is worried that we are marrying for all the wrong reasons and she said so. She made me think. She asked me to think about rushing into this!"

She saw him tremble. She became alarmed—he was livid. "Calder, this is not what you think! She has your—our—best interests at heart!"

"How dare she interfere in my personal life," he said dangerously.

Oh, God, she shouldn't have said anything. She reached for his arm—it was like touching a steel piston. "Calder, she loves you, it is so obvious, and—"

"She thinks you should be with Rick. Doesn't she?" he demanded.

"No! She thinks Rick and Leigh Anne should remain married. But she is worried that I will hurt you!" Francesca cried.

He stared, his eyes widening. It was a long moment before he moved, and then he looked away. "That is absurd."

"I think so, too. But what isn't absurd is that marriage should be securely based on a foundation of love."

He didn't answer, staring out the carriage window. They were traveling swiftly down Fifth Avenue now. Traffic was heavy, as it was a Saturday night. But it was moving at a handsome clip. Finally he looked at her. "I am hardly an expert on marriage, Francesca. But I have lived a good twenty-six years, and I have seen one or two good marriages in my entire life. A good marriage is based on many things, and from what I have seen, respect, friendship, and affection are far more important than 'love.' "

"I happen to disagree," she said softly.

"You are still wearing my ring," he said flatly.

She clutched her hand. It was impossible to speak; eternity seemed to pass. "I don't know what to do."

"Has it ever occurred to you that I am afraid, too?"

She was stunned. "But . . . you seem so certain!"

"I am certain . . . that I cannot lose you to another man. I am not letting you go, Francesca."

She thrilled, even though she did not want to. "I can't imagine life without you," she whispered. "The thought makes me sick. I don't want to lose you, either. But marriage . . ." She hesitated. "You see, Grace is right—but she is also wrong. You aren't the one who is going to be hurt." She felt a tear forming then. Her whisper became rough, hoarse. "I am the one who is going to care too much. I am the one who is going to be hurt."

Their gazes locked. A long and pregnant pause ensued. And then he was pulling her into his arms. "No."

She closed her eyes as her cheek touched his chest, as his arms gripped her tightly, as their bodies firmed, the one against the other. Pleasure warmed her. Being in his arms was like being in a safe and protected harbor, a harbor, though, surrounded by dangerously violent seas. As he held her, as she breathed deeply against his chest, she felt the new urgency begin, the new yet old desire.

He kissed the side of her head, near her temple. "I am not going to hurt you. I would hate myself too much," he said roughly.

"I'm afraid, afraid of what I might feel for you if I let myself," she heard herself whisper.

He hesitated, his embrace tightening. "Then let us stay

friends, good friends, and we will have a marriage of friendship and passion. What could be wrong with that?" He kissed her temple now.

Her body warmed, melting at the same time. Could she somehow keep her emotions at bay? If only he were not so fascinating. If only he did not have the ability to mesmerize her the way sorcerers might.

She looked up. "I don't know. I can never think clearly in your arms."

He smiled a little. "Have I ever told you that I find you adorable?"

Her heart turned over with joy. "No. I like that, Calder."

His gaze was turning gray, into smoke. "I like you," he said roughly.

She waited, yearning now.

He smiled a little again, then lowered his mouth to hers. The first touch of his lips was exquisite, hot and wet at once. She moaned softly, opening, but he merely brushed her lips teasingly, softly, repeatedly, until she could not stand it. Whimpering, she caught some short strands of hair at his nape, pulling, and he smiled against her mouth, murmuring her name. He tugged on her lower lip and, finally, claimed her fully for a kiss.

The carriage darkened into shadow and heat.

Francesca knew one thing. She wasn't ready to give this man up.

She just couldn't.

The intermission was spent by most of the opera-goers in the lobby, sipping champagne and sherry. Julia had been right, the production was fabulous, and Francesca had quickly been swept away into a story she knew by heart. Stepping into the lobby with Hart and Rourke was as odd as traveling through place and time. She shook her head to clear it as they paused in the midst of the glittering crowd.

Hart held her hand. His mouth brushed her ear. "Champagne?"

She scanned the faces surrounding them. "That would be nice."

"Who are you looking for, Francesca?" he asked.

She didn't look at him. "Sarah. I have been a terrible friend, Calder, as I told Mrs. Channing that we would be here and that Sarah intended to paint on all night instead of joining us." Francesca's heart skipped as she spotted Sarah and Mrs. Channing entering the lobby from another exit, clearly just leaving their box. Sarah was wearing a vivid red dress, one too gaudy for her tiny frame and small face, but Francesca didn't wince—she was used to Sarah being the victim of her mother's taste in fashion. "They're here." She waved.

"What are you up to?" he breathed, laughter in his tone.

"Go get champagne," she ordered, poking him with her elbow.

He bowed, his eyes oddly smoky, and he slipped off into the crowd.

"Sarah! Sarah! Mrs. Channing!" Francesca waved frantically.

Rourke, who stood behind her, came abreast. "The Channings are here," he said, not sounding surprised.

She glanced at him. He was amazingly handsome in his tuxedo, and a woman would have to be blind not to think so. "Isn't that a surprise?"

His amber gaze slid over her, and he smiled, clearly suspicious but not annoyed. "Truly." Then he added, "My brother is here."

Francesca started and followed his gaze. Instantly she saw Bragg standing with a group of gentlemen that included Mayor Low. She warmed a little, and as she studied Bragg, she wondered if she would always be happy to see him. Then she wondered where Leigh Anne was.

She looked again. He seemed grim. His smile was forced. Something was wrong.

"Francesca, dear, how are you?" Mrs. Channing appeared, a true vision in a pearl-encrusted ball gown that was terribly overdone. She dripped pearl and diamond jewelry as well and wore a large pearl-and-diamond tiara. "Dr. Rourke, how wonderful to see you!"

Rourke smiled, dimpling, and bowed over her hand. But even as he spoke, his gaze slipped to Sarah, who stood just behind her mother. She wasn't smiling. In fact, she looked very annoyed. "Have you been enjoying *La Bohème*?"

"Julia Montana is fabulous," Mrs. Channing said. "And to think she is an American!"

Rourke turned more fully to Sarah. "This is a pleasant surprise," he said, his gaze slipping over her figure. "You decided not to work tonight?"

Sarah smiled tightly. "Mother insisted we come." She gave Francesca a dark look.

Rourke followed it and his brows raised, a speculative look in his eyes.

Francesca clasped Sarah's hand. "But aren't you enjoying the opera?"

Sarah softened. "Yes, Francesca, I am." But then she gave her a plaintive look, one that clearly said she wished Francesca hadn't interfered and put her in the position she was in.

"Rourke? Rourke Bragg? Is that you?" a woman cried.

Francesca turned and saw a gorgeous brunette her own age embracing Rourke. She frowned, not liking this development at all.

"This is such a surprise!" the young woman exclaimed. Her sapphire gown was as stunning as she was. "What are you doing here?" She clearly was delighted to see Rourke, and she clung to his arm.

"I'm visiting family. I could ask you the same thing, Darlene."

Francesca glanced at Sarah, who stared at them unblinkingly. She tried to smile reassuringly, but Sarah was too rapt to see.

"Daddy decided to visit his sister this weekend, so we all came up."

Rourke turned. "Darlene's father is a doctor at the hos-

pital where I am doing my residency," he said. He made
formal introductions all around.

Darlene studied Francesca as he did so, glancing instantly at her hand, and when she saw the ring, she turned
to Sarah. As quickly, she turned back to Rourke, clearly
not bothering with a similar inspection. "I'll have to tell
Daddy you are here. Maybe you can join us for Sunday
dinner tomorrow."

"I think my family has other plans," Rourke said politely
as Francesca strained to watch their every gesture and expression. Was there something between them? Rourke was
impossible to read.

Hart returned, carrying three flutes of champagne. "I see
I am short several drinks," he said dryly.

Darlene's gaze riveted on him, wide with interest. Francesca took her flute, kissing his cheek, instantly despising
the other woman. "Thank you, darling," she said.

Hart had only given Darlene a mild glance, and he gazed
at Francesca, clearly amused. "Anytime . . . sweetheart," he
murmured.

"Darlene, this is my brother, Calder Hart. Calder, Darlene Fischer."

Hart nodded, appearing indifferent to the beauty standing in their midst.

"Have we met?" Darlene asked, stepping closer. "You
seem terribly familiar, Mr. Hart."

"I don't think so," he said. "Rourke, it's your turn to
make a run for more drinks."

"No problem," Rourke said mildly. "Sarah? Would you
mind joining me? I am terribly clumsy when it comes to
carrying delicate wineglasses."

Sarah started, flushed, and said, "Of course."

Francesca almost laughed. Rourke, clumsy? She didn't
think so. She watched them walk off, Rourke speaking to
Sarah and Sarah replying. She continued to stare, and when
Sarah finally laughed, she smiled. Her plan was working,
or so she hoped.

Then she realized that Darlene had taken a position on

Hart's other side and was saying, "So, are you an opera aficionado, Mr. Hart?"

Francesca turned in time to see a coy smile, bright eyes, and a posture that positively enhanced Darlene's already voluptuous breasts. Instantly she seethed.

Hart smiled. "I am an aficionado of any of the arts when done in a superior manner," he said. "I saw this production last week. I enjoyed it immensely and decided my fiancée must also see it." He turned and pulled Francesca close. "Are you enjoying yourself, darling?"

Francesca felt a dangerous emotion swirl within her chest. It felt terribly like love. She knew exactly what he was doing—he was making it clear to Darlene that he was not available. How could she not love him for it? "I am having a wonderful time," she said softly, meeting his dark eyes. "Thank you."

"Darling," he corrected, kissing the tip of her nose.

Francesca smiled, and when he released her, she had a chance to see Darlene watching closely. Instantly the other woman smiled. "When is the wedding?" she asked.

Hart didn't answer. Francesca said, "Soon. My mother is planning it, as I am too busy to do so."

"You are too busy to plan your wedding?" Darlene was mildly shocked.

Francesca nodded. "Yes."

"My little bride is a sleuth," Hart drawled. "She is on a case."

Darlene gaped.

Francesca found Hart's hand and squeezed it. Hart could be playful, and she hadn't realized before. It was a new side, one she was thoroughly enjoying.

Then, just past Darlene, she saw Rick Bragg walking by with Robert Fulton Cutting and his wife. Bragg was so immersed in his thoughts that he didn't see them standing there.

She was holding Hart's hand, so she felt him stiffen. Something was wrong. She had remarked it before. Unease assailed her.

"I'll be right back," she said, rushing off without even looking at Hart. "Rick!"

He didn't hear her. Mrs. Cutting was chatting away, her husband smiling, Bragg as preoccupied as before.

"Rick!" She seized his arm from behind.

He started. "Francesca."

"Hello." She smiled breathlessly at him, then smiled at the Cuttings. "How are you?"

"Francesca, hello. We are fine, thank you," Robert said. Then, "Would you excuse us? Rick, we will see you at the box."

Bragg nodded and they were alone in the crowd.

"I didn't know you would be here tonight."

He didn't smile. "I didn't know you would be here, either." His gaze moved past her.

She turned. Hart was observing them, but so was Darlene. Rourke and Sarah had rejoined the group, and they were listening to Mrs. Channing as she chattered away. Francesca knew Hart was displeased, but he would have to wait. "Are you all right? Is something wrong?" she asked quickly.

"I'm fine."

She plucked his sleeve. "You seem disturbed."

"It's been a long day, Francesca," he sighed.

She sensed that was true. "Where is Leigh Anne?"

He did not bat an eye. "She isn't joining me tonight."

Francesca stared. What did that mean? Was Leigh Anne ill? Or were they fighting? "It's a wonderful opera," she said lamely.

He made a sound. "I wouldn't know. I had better go back to the mayor's box," he said.

She took his hand. "If something is wrong, if I can help, please, you know I'd love to."

He softened. "Thank you. We'll speak tomorrow."

She nodded, not wanting to discuss the case now.

He slipped his hand free and walked away.

Francesca watched him for another moment, until he disappeared through an exit, and she returned to Hart's side.

His gaze slid over her, not quite pleasantly, and she tensed. But she smiled as she slid her hand into his. "Maybe we should return to our seats."

"You haven't drunk your champagne," Hart said.

She met his gaze.

He held it for one moment and then looked away. "So tell me, Darlene, how often do you visit our fair city?"

Francesca knew Hart was annoyed with her. He remained as courteous as ever, but there was no mistaking that he had tried to provoke her by spending ten minutes during the intermission in conversation with Darlene. Now he held her elbow, guiding her down the wide front steps of the opera house. A line of double- and triple-parked coaches and carriages lined Broadway in front of the theater. Rourke, Sarah, and Mrs. Channing were behind them— Mrs. Channing had eagerly accepted Rourke's invitation to join them for the second half of the performance in their box. The crowd was heavy on the street, but Francesca saw Darlene and her father climbing into a cab. She hoped to never see the gorgeous other woman again.

Then she saw Bragg with the Lows. They were parting company, and again she wondered why Leigh Anne had not shown.

"Shall we?" Hart intoned.

She glanced at him and saw that he had followed her gaze. She bristled, glanced back at the Channings and Rourke, and said, "I would like a word with you. Alone."

He inclined his head, his gaze narrow enough to make her uneasy. "Excuse us," he said. They were all having supper together that night.

Hart and Francesca walked away and faced each other, Hart releasing her arm. "Maybe you wish to court Darlene," Francesca said tersely, then could have kicked herself, as that was not what she wanted to say; in fact, she did not wish to discuss Darlene.

Hart smiled tightly. "I'm only interested in courting one

woman, Francesca. You." His gaze was black and very direct.

She could almost forgive him his utterly immature jealousy. "You have no right to be annoyed with me. You have known from the moment we met that Bragg is my best friend."

He folded his arms across his chest. "So now he is your *best* friend? That is news to me, Francesca."

She flushed. Things were awkward enough between her and Bragg, and it had been a slight exaggeration to call him her best friend. "You know what I mean."

"No. I don't."

"He will always be a dear friend, Hart, even after we are married. Your jealousy is inappropriate."

He stared.

She became uneasy. "Aren't you going to respond?"

"Very well. You wanted to marry him. You have spent several hours passionately in his arms—or so I believe. And my jealousy is inappropriate? I don't think so, Francesca. We are engaged. You are going to be my wife. I have no intention of looking the other way so you can run off to console your oh-so-noble star-crossed lover." His eyes glittered now.

She stepped back. "He is not my lover."

"But he was. Except that I talked you out it, didn't I? When you were rushing headlong into a very nasty affair, one which could only have tragic consequences, when I was a real friend to you, and not romantically inclined, I cared enough—as a friend—to beg you to think about the consequences of an affair with a married man."

She inhaled harshly. He was right. "Still, we will always be friends. You will have to accept it. And your flirting with that ugly woman was immature, Hart!"

He dared to smile. "Yes, it was. It was a knee-jerk reaction, and I find her distasteful, too."

She blinked. Her heart sped. "Can you ever respond the way I expect you to?"

He took her hand and reeled her in. "That would be boring, don't you think?"

She was in his arms. She made a slight effort to dislodge him, not really wanting to, because she loved being in his arms, against his chest. "You will have to trust me, Calder, when it comes to Rick."

"I do trust you," he said, "but I am insanely jealous when you rush off to him. And I do believe with just cause."

She could only stare breathlessly at him. *He was insanely jealous.* She tried to remind herself that Hart was jealous of his half-brother no matter the subject, just as Bragg was jealous of Calder. But it didn't work. She realized she was smiling. He was insanely jealous of her!

"Stop looking so pleased," he breathed, smiling now.

"I *am* pleased," she said, smiling even more. "You don't have to be jealous," she began, her instinct to reassure him. But in a flash then she thought about all she had shared with Bragg and she knew how false her words were. Calder had every reason to be jealous, because she shared a special bond with his brother that no one could sever, not ever, not even him.

He raised a brow, clearly skeptical.

"We are engaged," she said, touching his face. "And the one thing you must know is that I will be loyal to you."

"I know that," he said.

She hesitated, because clearly he had more on his mind. "What is it?"

"Your loyalty isn't enough."

She flinched. "What more can I give you? What else could you possibly want?"

He hesitated now, his jaw hard and tight, his eyes as black as the night.

"Your heart," he said.

Hart hesitated on the threshold of the very exclusive and private club, a club of which he was not a member. He had paid handsomely to get in—he had bribed the doorman with fifty dollars. "The Jewel" had a very sordid reputation—one of lechery, drunkenness, drugs. It was also well known that here a gentleman might find any type of pleasure that he wished—should he be able to afford his own exotic habits.

The Jewel was housed in a Fifth Avenue mansion that had once, half a century earlier, belonged to a Flemish merchant. From the spacious front hall where Hart stood, he could look into a salon and a dining room, all elegantly furnished, right to the original paintings hanging on the walls. Several young gentlemen gambled at poker; others dallied with young, lush prostitutes. The whores were all attractive and expensively dressed. In the dining room several patrons and their paramours were dining. Not far from where Hart stood, a pianist ripped out a jaunty tune on a grand piano. Beyond the pianist, a wide staircase led to the two upper floors of the house, where one could indulge in one's whims, both sexual and otherwise.

A woman approached. Hart instantly knew she was the madam of the house, but he did not know if she was the owner. She was in her thirties, blond, elegant, beautiful—the pale blue gown she wore was high-necked and had sleeves to the elbows; still, it could not disguise her superb figure. She wore several small rings—a sapphire and two diamonds, as well as a beautiful sapphire bracelet. Everything about her was understated. As elegant and modestly clothed and jeweled as she was, she could easily enter any genteel salon and fool everyone present into thinking she was a real lady. She was smiling as she paused before him, but he was a master at reading people, and he knew she was alarmed by his presence.

Why? The doorman had accepted the bribe but had then had to ask permission to allow him in. He had used his real name, considering it an asset in this particular instance, and while he was engaged to the woman investigating the missing girls, he highly doubted that news would have reached the ears of the management of this club. Not yet, anyway.

He smiled charmingly at the woman and took her hand. "Madame?" He spoke the word as the French did—he found the anglicized version too harsh and ugly. "I am Calder Hart, at your service." He bowed over her hand. Her gaze did not flicker. "Thank you for allowing me entrance into your establishment."

She inclined her head, the slight gesture quite regal. "Mr. Hart. I do believe your reputation precedes you. I am flattered to have you with us tonight." She smiled as charmingly back at him. "I am Solange Marceaux, and you may call me Madame Marceaux. Until we are better acquainted."

He knew her first words were false. Why? She should be thrilled to have a man of his wealth in her club. And what did that last statement mean? "The Jewel's reputation is quite well known as well." He smiled and glanced around. "I am impressed."

Her smile slipped easily back on. "That is difficult to believe; nevertheless, I am pleased. Would you like a drink? A cigar? A bite of supper, perhaps? Our chef is from Paris. He is superb and he is serving a wild duck in a peach brandy sauce tonight."

"I am afraid I have already dined, but a scotch would be nice."

She turned and a beautiful young woman of about eighteen appeared, her dark eyes sultry and inviting, a pleased smile on her lips. She had dark milky skin, suggesting some African-American heritage, and she wore a magenta gown that revealed a good portion of her small breasts.

"Linda, please get Mr. Hart a glass of our finest Scotch whiskey."

Linda smiled seductively at him and left to obey. As he turned back to his hostess, he caught a glimpse of a familiar face, and his heart skipped. He did not, however, look back again at Rose.

But as he calmed, he thought about the fact that his mistress's lover was present at the club. And while he had stopped seeing Daisy the moment he had become engaged to Francesca last month, he had allowed her to remain in the house he had bought for her until the end of the term they had agreed upon for their affair—which would be in another four and a half months. Hart had discovered Daisy on the street one day and had mistaken her for a lady. He had soon realized she was a prostitute, and, rather taken with her unusual beauty, he had gone to visit her at the brothel where she worked. There he had met her lover, Rose. One thing had led to another, and before long he was in bed with them both. The fact that Rose was present now was a problem. She had been furious with him for his setting Daisy up as his mistress. And undoubtedly Rose also knew about his engagement to Francesca, as Daisy had surely told her. She hated Hart with a vengeance and he did not trust her for an instant.

"So what brings you to the Jewel, Mr. Hart?"

"Boredom," he said with a smile.

Both of her pale brows lifted—she was hardly impressed. "I can hardly imagine a man like you being bored. But I am sure we can remedy that."

"I have little doubt. Which is why I am here," Hart said easily. He now felt eyes upon his back and knew Rose was staring at him.

"Shall we adjourn to my office? We can discuss the matter of your boredom there." Solange Marceaux smiled at him.

Hart agreed and followed her past the two salons and into a lavish sitting room. The door to the adjoining bedroom was open, and he glimpsed an elegant bedroom with gold wainscoting on the ceiling, jade-green fabric walls, and matching brocade draperies. The furniture in both rooms was antique.

He turned back to his hostess, who had been watching him, and took the seat she gestured at. "Your rooms are quite elegant."

She sat in a facing chair, the sofa and a small table between them. "I have heard the same about your home, Mr. Hart. Now, how may I help you?"

At that moment, there was a knock and Linda appeared with his scotch and another drink, which looked like ice water. She smiled at Hart as she handed him his drink, then looked inquiringly at Solange. "You may go," Solange said. "Please make certain that we have no interruptions."

When Linda was gone, Solange set her glass untouched on the table between them. "What is your pleasure, Mr. Hart?"

"I am looking for innocence," he said. "And beauty, of course."

She did not bat an eye. "And the age preference?"

"Fourteen perhaps. Thirteen might do. But no older than fourteen."

Solange smiled politely at him as she stood. She paced slowly to the fireplace behind where they sat and paused, one hand on the white marble mantel there. She faced Hart. "I am afraid you are in the wrong establishment. While we offer various types of entertainment for you patrons, we do not offer children."

Hart settled back in the chair, crossing his legs, taking a sip of his scotch. "This is excellent," he said.

"Yes, it is," she agreed. "Can we possibly amuse you with mere beauty? We have many beautiful young women here, Mr. Hart. I have a magnificent redhead who is only sixteen."

He shrugged with elaborate indifference. "My dear Madame Marceaux, I have had many mistresses of that age. I am looking for unspoiled innocence in the extreme. And I will pay handsomely to attain it."

She stared. Then, "I am afraid I cannot help you."

He stood. "Then you are right, I am in the wrong place tonight." But he smiled warmly at her.

She approached and touched him for the first time, her hand lying lightly on his forearm. "I hate for you to leave unsated tonight. It is late. Perhaps you might wish to briefly amuse yourself. It is on the house." She met his gaze.

Her eyes were pale gray and simply impossible to read. She did not remove her hand. He wondered if she was offering herself—he sensed that—yet she was undoubtedly a master of the game and could probably beat him in a poker game, or come damned close to it. If she was offering herself, it was very hard to say.

He thought about Rose. She hated him, but she had to be thrilled that he was no longer sleeping with Daisy. And he did not know whether Solange Marceaux was telling him the truth. If she did traffic in child whores, she probably wished to test him. Had he not been engaged to Francesca, it would be so very easy to bed her and get the information he wanted from her. However, he would have to find a different way to achieve his ends.

He smiled at her. "Perhaps you are right."

She held his gaze with her lovely yet remarkably cool gray eyes for one more moment and dropped his hand. She smiled, inclining her head.

"I saw a magnificent woman when I first walked in, dark skin, dark hair, sloe eyes. I know her from Madam Pinke's. Her name is Rose. Perhaps she is available?"

If Solange Marceaux was surprised, if she was disappointed, it was impossible to see. She did not even blink. "A good choice," she said. "Rose is magnificent, as you have said, and she is the kind of woman capable of sating a man like yourself. I believe she is free tonight. Excuse me," she said, and she smiled.

He was alarmed, as he had no wish for Rose and Solange Marceaux to speak about him with his not being there. Rose might say too much; in fact, he rather thought she would. "Madame Marceaux, excuse me, you did not let me finish," he said smoothly.

She turned back to him, and for the very first time that night, he thought, her expression changed—he thought he saw a flicker of surprise in her eyes. "I am sorry."

He smiled and said, "I do not want Rose for myself."

She seemed to stiffen. "Oh."

He had finally won, and he smiled even more, thrilling

now before the final blow. "I would like to amuse myself by watching Rose with another woman," he said.

She knew. Her smile was gone.

"And that woman would be you," he said.

CHAPTER
THIRTEEN

SUNDAY, MARCH 30, 1902 — 9:00 A.M.

FRANCESCA HAD BEEN TOLD she could use the carriage as long as she was home by noon. She had taken that to mean that her parents needed the coach back at noon, not herself, so she intended to send Jennings back with it after he dropped her off downtown. Now, having told him to wait, she paused before the rusted iron gate in front of the St. James Cemetery.

It was a dreary morning, cold and windy and threatening rain. Francesca wore a heavy wool coat, and as she stared through the iron bars at the small churchyard cemetery, a centuries-old stone church not far from where the coach was parked, she shivered, but not from the cold. It was an awful day to meander among the small, plain headstones and grave markers, looking for a twelve-year-old girl's grave. Nor did she look forward to setting up shop on the corner of 10th Street in order to interview the forty-one people claiming to have information about Emily O'Hare's disappearance.

She wondered what Hart had found out last night.

Francesca sighed and pushed open the gate, its hinges squeaking loudly. It must have rained in the night or dawn, as the grass underfoot was very damp, while the stone path in the center of the graveyard was mostly overgrown with weeds. Francesca vaguely disliked cemeteries and this one was no exception—it felt dismal, sad. She scanned the headstone at her right—the person buried there had died twenty years ago. She moved forward, past markers dated in the two previous decades. Her heart was not in this. She fervently hoped that John Cooper had lied and his daughter was alive and well. Claiming that she was dead was, after all, the perfect excuse to cover up her disappearance. Francesca dreaded finding out otherwise.

Francesca increased her pace. If Bonnie was dead, hers had to be the newest grave in the cemetery—or one of them. At the far end, she saw some stones that were brightly white and one had freshly turned-up earth beside it. She hurried down the overgrown path, slipping once on the slick stones.

The first white stone read: "Mark Johnson, May He Rest In Peace, 1858–1902." She was briefly relieved, and she turned to the even smaller marker beside it. She froze.

A bouquet of wildflowers lay beside it.

BONNIE COOPER
DEARLY BELOVED DAUGHTER OF JOHN AND RITA COOPER
MAY 1, 1889–FEBRUARY 27, 1902

Francesca inhaled, stunned. Bonnie Cooper was dead. Her father had been telling the truth.

Then she straightened.

But the date on the grave was wrong, wasn't it?

Francesca stared at the fresh grave. Bonnie Cooper had disappeared February 10—Mrs. Hopper had said so.

Today was the thirtieth of March. Meaning that Bonnie had died a month ago—approximately two full weeks after she had disappeared.

"Hey, mister, wait yer turn!" Joel snapped.

Francesca had erected a small card table on the corner, along with a folding chair. She had laid out her notebook and several pens and pencils. She was now interviewing her tenth would-be informant. The previous nine men, all rather disreputable in appearance, all thug types, had been absolutely worthless. Their stories had been absurd.

The long line of men and women from the ward began in front of her small table and continued to the end of the block—ending in front of Schmitt's Grocery. He had already come out of his shop three times to stare disapprovingly at her, his hands on his hips. The customers attempting to enter the grocery had to push their way through the crowd. Now the man Joel had just addressed, who looked as if he worked at the docks on Front Street, said angrily, "I been standing out here in the cold for an hour! I got better things to do on me day off than to freeze me arse out here waiting upon Her Highness!"

Francesca folded her hands in front of her and said calmly, "Then why don't you leave?"

"You want information or not, lady?" he sneered.

"Only if it is sincere. And even if it is, you still must wait your turn."

Maggie Kennedy appeared behind Francesca. "Mind your manners, Ralph Goodson."

Surprised, Francesca glanced up at Maggie, whose blue eyes flashed. "Thank you," she said.

Maggie smiled at her. "You are very brave, to be dealing with these roughs."

Francesca glanced at the striking woman with Maggie, recognizing her from the other day. "Do I have a choice if I want to find those missing girls? Hello." She smiled at the woman with the auburn hair whom she had seen moving into Maggie's building.

"Oh, Miss Cahill, this is Gwen O'Neil and her daughter, Bridget. They are my new neighbors," Maggie said.

Gwen O'Neil smiled, then told her daughter she would be going downtown to look for work. "Behave yourself," she said. "I'll be home by five."

"Yes, Mama," Bridget said, staring at Francesca with wide eyes.

"I am a sleuth," Francesca said with a smile, answering the child's unspoken question. Little Bridget was too good-looking for her own good. "I am working on an investigation."

Bridget, her green eyes huge, her dark red hair flowing to her waist, whispered, "What's a sleuth?" Her Irish brogue was delightful.

Joel stepped forward. His face was beet-red. "Miss Cahill is my boss. She solves crimes. Real dangerous ones. I'm her assistant."

Bridget gave him a scornful glance. "No, you're not. You're a boy!"

"Joel really is my assistant," Francesca said. "He has provided me invaluable service, time and again. He has helped me solve every single crime I have worked on, in fact." She smiled at the child. "How old are you, dear?"

"Eleven," she said, now gaping at Joel. "Blimey, you're not like the boys at home, then!"

Joel flushed even more. "No, I ain't."

Francesca was relieved. Bridget looked twelve or thirteen, but she was not—she was too young for the criminals forcing those young girls into a life of prostitution, if that was what was really happening.

"Hey, Miz Cahill! You goin' to talk to me, or not?" Ralph called out, spitting tobacco on the curb.

"Yeah, yeah, what's the deal?" a chorus of impatient voices sounded.

"One minute," Francesca said sternly. She already had

a headache from dealing with the monstrous claims of this riffraff. "How have you been, Maggie?"

"Very well," Maggie said, smiling softly. "Joel missed you while you were gone, Miss Cahill."

Francesca was pleased. "I missed him, as well." Suddenly she started, recognizing not one but two coaches coming down the block, approaching. One belonged to her brother; the other, extravagant, loud and lavish, belonged to Hart. Her heart did speed.

Maggie turned to follow her regard and her cheeks seemed to color. "Mr. Cahill is taking the children for a picnic in the park," she said. "It seems to have become a habit of his on the Sabbath."

Francesca knew how fond her brother was of Maggie's children. Still, he was, she had heard, so busy with Bartolla Benevente. "How wonderful," she said, meaning it, but now quite curious.

Evan's carriage halted first, the passenger door quickly opening. Maggie turned to watch him alight. Evan came strolling up the block, a handsome, dark-haired figure, tall and lean. His black greatcoat whipped about him, hanging carelessly open. He was whistling. He smiled at Francesca, shaking his head. "I am afraid, Fran, to ask you what in God's name you are doing."

Francesca smiled sweetly back. "I am on a case. I have posted a reward for information, and as you can see, I am interviewing everyone who lives in the ward."

He laughed and turned his bright blue eyes on Maggie. "Mrs. Kennedy, good day."

She glanced away. "Mr. Cahill. The children are ready. They are very excited. I'll go get them."

Evan had his hand on Joel's shoulder. "I'll come with you," he said, his glance moving over her. She, of course, did not see.

Maggie was already moving away, and she appeared flustered, at least as far as Francesca could tell. "No, that's fine. I will bring them down in a moment."

He smiled at Maggie. "Would you care to join us? That is, if you do not have other plans?"

She stumbled and faced him abruptly. *"What?"*

He approached her, smiling, intent. "Please join us, Mrs. Kennedy. I know it's a rotten day for a picnic, so I have arranged a surprise for the children. I think you'd enjoy it, too."

She blinked at him. "I couldn't possibly. . . ."

"Whyever not?"

"I . . . I do have other plans, I'm afraid," she said.

Evan continued to smile, but Francesca knew him very well, and he was disappointed. She saw it in his eyes, for they instantly sobered, darkening. And as for Maggie, well, she was definitely not telling the truth. That much was clear to Francesca.

She stared. This was not the first time she had witnessed an exchange between her brother and Maggie Kennedy, one that confounded her. Her brother was a gentleman. He would never casually dally with a good honest woman like Maggie Kennedy.

Besides, she was not his type. Not at all. He'd had a mistress, a famous stage actress, a beautiful and flamboyant woman. He preferred women of that type and nature— women like the widowed Countess Benevente.

And now he was head over heels in love with the countess. Wasn't he?

Maggie was quiet, sincere, pretty enough, but she was a widowed seamstress raising four children alone in poverty. She was simply not the kind of woman his brother was interested in, and even if he were, as he would never dally with her, he certainly would not bring her home. Even Francesca, a true liberal, knew that Evan could never bring a simple seamstress home.

On the other hand, he had disowned his home and his father, quitting the family business, taking employment in a middling lawyer's firm. And he had been disowned as well, in turn. She was very proud of her brother for doing what he felt he must do. But what *was* this? What *was* going on?

Francesca felt certain that something was afoot. She had witnessed one too many interesting interactions between her dashing brother and the oh-so-reticent and good-hearted Maggie Kennedy.

Evan had nodded, accepting Maggie's avowal that she was occupied that day, while she had disappeared like a frightened schoolgirl. "Evan?" Francesca began curiously.

But Evan had gripped Joel's shoulder. "I have taken over an exhibition at the Museum of Natural History. We shall have our picnic there. I think your mother would enjoy herself. What do you think?"

Joel smiled fiercely at him. "I'll get her to come," he said. And he looked questioningly at Francesca. "Miz Cahill?"

She smiled at him. "Go do your best," she said.

He ran off.

Francesca looked at Evan. "And what is the countess up to today?"

"She likes to sleep late," he said, unperturbed. "This is not what you are thinking."

"And what am I thinking?"

"Mrs. Kennedy is a noble woman, Fran. A noble, kind, and industrious woman. I adore her children. She could use an amusing day."

Francesca simply gaped. And then she saw Hart approaching. Her heart seemed to quicken. How glad she was to see him.

"Hello, darling," Calder Hart said. He was smiling, and he bent and kissed her cheek. "Good morning."

She smiled at him widely. "Thank God you are here! Bonnie Cooper is dead. I found her grave this morning."

His smile vanished. In fact, he looked very solemn indeed. "That is sober news," he said.

She studied him and felt a frisson of unease. "Is anything wrong?" she asked.

"We need to speak," he said, unsmiling. "Privately."

Francesca did not like the sound of that.

. . .

When they had settled in his coach, she on one seat, with him facing her, he smiled at her. "What is on your mind?" she asked warily. "You look odd."

He sighed. "Hold your temper, darling."

She blinked and stiffened. She could practically hear alarm bells shrieking. "What is it?"

"I went to a very disreputable establishment last night, as I said I would."

Francesca sat up straighter. "Which establishment?"

"You are the last person I would tell the name to," he said soberly. "As it is not a place you should ever set foot in."

Blurry half-formed images of some dim, dark smoky room filled her mind, and in them lush, half-naked, beautiful women pranced around. "What did you find out? What happened?" She had a bad feeling. She could not take her gaze from Hart.

But his attention was riveted on her, too. His brief smile was oddly derisive. "Usually I can read people, Francesca, like a book. The madam of this club, Solange Marceaux, is undoubtedly a master poker player. Madame Marceaux wasn't thrilled to have me in her place of business, which was odd; she also told me she could not fulfill my desires to be with a beautiful and innocent child of thirteen or fourteen."

"And?" she breathed, visualizing an orange-haired older woman with garish makeup as the brothel's keeper.

"Well," he said dryly, "I could not determine if she was being truthful or not. She may not have trusted me; she may have wished to test me. In any case, even if she does not traffic in children, I would be surprised if she could not direct me to a brothel that did. But her club has the strongest reputation for catering to the needs—any needs—of its patrons."

Francesca had crossed her arms over her chest. "What is it that you really wish to say, Calder?"

He grimaced. "She offered me more standard entertainment," he said.

She sat up as if shot with a bullet. "Oh, no!" And instantly she could see Calder, naked, powerful, aroused, in some faceless woman's bed.

He held up a hand. "Francesca, surely you don't think I spent an hour or so in bed with a whore? That isn't what I wish to tell you."

She relaxed, hugely relieved. "Go on."

"Rose was there."

Francesca gasped. Rose hated Calder passionately, as she was terribly in love with his mistress, Daisy. Calder was still keeping Daisy until the term they had agreed upon expired, even if he wasn't seeing her. Francesca knew both Daisy and Rose; in fact, she liked Daisy very much and sympathized with Rose's plight. But the fact that Rose had been at this club could not be good, oh no. "Did she expose you as my fiancé?"

"No." He sighed. "I was on the spot. I was hoping to get Rose aside, alone, to speak with her—as she was in the underworld, I thought she might know something. When Madame Marceaux offered me a woman, I told her I knew Rose and would accept her offer if Rose was free."

"What did Rose say?" Francesca cried, straining forward eagerly.

He reached for her hand and clasped it. "Madame Marceaux is very clever. She instructed me to wait while she went for Rose. I could not let that happen. I don't trust Rose and I did not want the two of them speaking privately about me. I had an instant in which to think of a way in which to circumvent a tête-à-tête."

Francesca did not like this. She tugged her hand free, staring. What was he about to tell her? Maybe sending Hart off into an illicit establishment hadn't been the best idea after all, and certainly not one that had women like the terribly seductive Rose. "What did you do?" she whispered.

"I told her that the entertainment I had in mind was to

watch Rose with another woman, with Madame Marceaux, in fact." He smiled slightly then, as if something had amused him, but he never took his watchful gaze from Francesca's face.

Alarm bells went off. Calder Hart was the most seductive man she knew—Francesca had never met a woman immune to his charm, his looks, his power. "While you have been telling me this story, I have been imagining a fat old woman with orange hair. But that isn't what Madame Marceaux is like, is it?" she cried.

"No." His brows raised in surprise. "She is rather an ice queen, Francesca, pale blond, regal, elegant."

"Wonderful," Francesca said, trembling. Hart had met a woman he could not read, a blond ice queen, a woman she just knew was beautiful, a rare woman who could outwit him at his game. How amused he must have been. How enthralled. Jealousy was a cloak shrouding her, and as it did, more images tumbled through her mind—Hart, aroused, intent, standing over a bed where two women, one pale, one dark, were passionately entwined. Her heart beat now like a drum. She should have accompanied him last night. She knew his dark past included Rose, but she also knew that was over—or so she had thought. But the thought of him now, sexually attracted to Solange Marceaux, sparring with her, drawn to her, was terribly hurtful. It was also terribly disturbing—in a shocking way.

"Last night, while I was sleeping, you were amusing yourself watching Rose and Madame Marceaux making love," she said huskily. And had he really been able to do nothing but watch? No one was more virile and sexual than Hart.

He started. "Madame Marceaux declined, as I knew she would. The request was an adversarial tactic, Francesca, a strike designed to shake her up and put her off balance, that is all. And it worked—for a moment."

She stared at him. The compartment had become airless, while those darkly seductive images continued to dance in her head.

"This was a test," he said softly, reaching for her hand again, and this time she did not—could not—pull it away, "and the only reason I had to pass it was because I am helping *you* solve *your* case."

"So you watched Rose and some woman in bed," she breathed.

He started again. "Yes, I did."

"Did you join them?" she asked, faint. Dear, dear God, she was so terribly attracted to Hart that the idea of his being with two women last night did not merely cause jealousy to consume her. It did not simply hurt her. Desire also trickled through her limbs, building, warming her blood.

"I did not," he said, aghast.

She believed him, as his reply was so instantaneous, so disbelieving, and she could only stare in real relief.

"Francesca, I gave you my word. Besides, you are the one on my mind now, not a pair of whores." He was incredulous.

She continued to stare, suddenly close to tears and afraid of herself far more than she was afraid of him. "But you love pleasure," she whispered. "I suspect you are addicted to it. And you like being with two women at once."

He took her hand firmly in his. "Darling, after this moment, I do not want to discuss my black past again. Because if you shall hold my past over my head, we will never do well together. Do you understand?"

She nodded, blinking back tears.

"Why are you crying?" he asked softly.

"I'm not," she lied.

He cupped her face in both hands. "You are the one I want to be with. A long time ago, the chase, the conquest, it all became terribly old—terribly boring—a mere game to play in the interminable hours of the night."

She wet her lips, aware of how close his lips were, needing his hot, wet kiss. "But you were with Daisy and Rose, together, in the past," she murmured, trembling.

He stared. And he knew. He recognized the beast immediately, as how could he not? It chose the oddest moments to arise, hot and huge, between them. "Don't cry," he whispered, their gazes locking. And he leaned forward and brushed her mouth with his.

She gasped; his tongue filled her; their lips mated wildly, quickly, urgently. As quickly, he broke the stunning kiss, staring into her eyes. He seemed surprised by what had just happened. "You are the one I want in my bed, Francesca."

She nodded, not able to speak, not quite yet.

"As for Daisy and Rose, it was simply another game to play for a man as jaded as myself. I won't deny that I like sex and that I need it." He lifted her chin. Her gaze was smoke and fire, but hard now, too. "I won't deny that my current state of self-imposed celibacy isn't physically annoying, because it is. Actually, at times it is rather painful, but there are ways to circumvent that." He smiled derisively then.

Francesca straightened, very curious as to what he meant.

He dropped his hand. "But adhering to the vow I made to you isn't difficult, Francesca, and why should it be? If I didn't want to marry you and change my life, I wouldn't. If I wanted to continue on, with whores and divorcées, I would. But I don't. I was in that club last night to find those missing girls. I have never been in that club before, as it is hardly elegant and I demand elegance in all that I do. If you wish, I will never go there again." He smiled briefly but stared intently into her eyes.

She shook her head, inhaling, shaking and shaken and urgently yearning for his embrace once more. It was another moment before she could speak. "Didn't you want to make love to them?" she whispered finally, the real question now.

"No, darling," he said, suddenly amused. "Oddly, it is you I want, and only you." He added, "Frankly, Francesca, I *was* bored."

She bit her lip, her heart continuing to strain against her breast now, her flesh even more alive, painfully so. "You are an enigma, Hart."

He shrugged. "Darling, voyeurism was never a game of mine. In this case, there was no choice. I stayed for maybe twenty minutes, announced I was bored, and left. As I did so, I gave Madame Marceaux my card, instructing her to find me what I truly desired. I was tested, and I believe my charade worked. Again, it was hard to read what Madame Marceaux was thinking when I left. If she knows where she can procure a child for me, I would be surprised if she does not do so, and shortly."

Francesca stared at his handsome face, her mind racing, sorting it all out. "I'm glad you did what you did. You are right, this is about the case—not you or I. Calder, what if I spoke with Daisy and asked her to ask Rose to work for us?"

He was intent. "We are thinking along the same lines, Francesca. But I can do that. After all, she is indebted to me."

Francesca reached for his hand. "She isn't happy that your arrangement with her is over before it has even begun. I think it might be better if I approached her as a woman and a friend, rather than you ordering her to help us."

He studied her and nodded. "She does like you. Very well. Do so."

"I will." Her smile was brief. "We need a real lead, Calder, and we need it now."

"Yes, we do, especially if Bonnie is really dead." He was grim.

She started. "Do you think the grave a ploy of sorts—a diversion?"

"I think we should dig it up," he said.

CHAPTER
FOURTEEN

FRANCESCA HAD TOLD THE would-be informants to return on the morrow at the same time. Then she and Hart had hurried the few blocks uptown to Mulberry Street. But Bragg had not been at police headquarters, where they had hoped to get a police order to dig up Bonnie Cooper's grave. He wasn't in a meeting, either; the sergeant at the front desk simply didn't know where he was. But Francesca hadn't had time to dwell on how odd that was. She did not want to go to Police Chief Farr, asking for his help on her investigation. Farr would only complicate matters, as he so despised her.

Now Hart's six-in-hand was parked outside of the cemetery, incredibly incongruous with the old stone church and small, dismal graveyard. Francesca watched him as he dug up Bonnie Cooper's grave with a shovel purchased from a saloon keeper. Raoul was with them—he and Hart had been taking turns digging, for the ground was hard and rocky.

She was glad it was mid-afternoon—had they been dese-
crating the grave during a mass, she felt certain they might
wind up in the midst of a riot.

And what they were doing was quite illegal. Francesca
was keeping one eye on the street, in case a policeman
happened to go by.

Hart's shovel hit something in the ground with a thud.
Francesca tensed. "Another rock?" she asked hopefully.

He poked it and glanced back at her. "I don't think so.
Not this time."

He had removed his black suit jacket and tie and had
rolled up his sleeves. It was very hard to be indifferent to
his body, as the muscles in his broad shoulders, arms, and
back rippled firmly beneath his close-fitting custom shirt
with every movement. He dug with more urgency now.
After several more moments, he stopped.

She simply knew, and she gave up her post as watchman
and stepped over to the edge of the hole he had dug. The
top of what was obviously a plain and simple coffin faced
them both. She glanced at Hart.

"We need to bring it up and open it."

"If she's in there, we are disturbing the dead," Francesca
said, suddenly terribly dismayed and uneasy.

He gave her an odd look. "Don't become cowardly
now."

She stiffened. "I am not afraid and I do not believe in
ghosts. It's just . . ." She stopped.

"What?" He stared, leaning on the shovel, his face shiny
with perspiration.

She tried to ignore the swath of broad, hard chest revealed by his open shirt, which was also damp and clinging
to his every muscle and tendon. "I have a bad feeling," she
said lamely.

"So do I." He began digging again.

Twenty minutes later, Raoul now with the shovel, Hart
said, "That's enough. Let's bring the coffin up."

Hart and Raoul got into the huge hole, each man taking
an end of the coffin. Hart said, "It's not empty."

Francesca felt ill, enough so to retch. "We had better make sure it's Bonnie. But on the other hand, how will we know?"

"Bonnie was twelve, blond, pretty. We need to see who is inside. Raoul, you get up top, I'll try to push it over the edge," Hart instructed.

"I should help," Francesca said, realizing that lowering a coffin was one thing and raising it by hand quite another.

"No."

The two men quickly lifted the coffin out of the tight hole and heaved it onto the level ground at Francesca's feet. Hart climbed out of the ground, covered with mud and dirt. "That was oddly heavy," he said, giving Francesca a sidelong look.

Francesca was on her knees, attempting the latch. It unclasped. And she hesitated.

Then she felt Hart cover her shoulder with her hand. He didn't speak.

She smiled slightly to herself, remaining incredibly grim. She opened the coffin and cried out.

It was filled with rocks.

The house Hart had bought for Daisy was on Fifth Avenue but downtown. The elegant Georgian mansion had a brick facade and was surrounded by lawns and gardens that would undoubtedly be striking in the summertime. Francesca was shown into the foyer by a butler, and there she paused, having been told to wait.

Being there again, in that house, under the current circumstances—as Hart's fiancée—felt surreal, like an odd dream. How many months ago had she been happy for Daisy upon visiting her here and learning of her new status as Hart's mistress? It felt like a lifetime ago, but it had only been in February.

"Hello, Francesca." Daisy approached. She was the most ethereal woman Francesca had ever met, her skin and hair strikingly pale, her eyes a clear blue. She had a slender, willowy figure and a small, breathless voice. She was beautiful in an unearthly way, and she always made Francesca feel tall, gauche, and even fat. "This is an unexpected surprise," Daisy said softly, but she wasn't smiling.

Francesca met her steady gaze and was taken aback. They had not spoken since Hart had told her he was ending the liaison. And had Daisy heard that their engagement was an official one? One thing was clear—Daisy wasn't smiling. She wasn't pleased to see Francesca, and their relationship had undeniably changed.

"I hope I am not intruding," Francesca began, about to say that Hart had said she could call. She swallowed those words. "How are you? You look lovely, Daisy, as always."

Daisy attempted a smile; it seemed more like a grimace of disbelief. "You are the one who is radiant, Francesca. But why should I be surprised? Apparently being engaged to Calder suits you. And to think I thought it was Rick Bragg you were after."

Instantly Francesca became tense. "I know things are awkward, now, between us, but is there any way we can remain friends? I like you very much, Daisy."

"Of course we remain friends," Daisy said. "Why wouldn't we? After all, I am no longer Hart's mistress, not in bed, at least, and as you do not seem to mind his keeping me here, with the appearance that he still sleeps here, there is no conflict of interest." Finally, Daisy smiled. It was razor sharp. Worse, her eyes were clearly unhappy.

But Francesca had a terrible thought—Hart was being true to his word to Daisy in supporting her until their six-month agreement expired. But what if Francesca's father learned that Daisy remained under Hart's roof? He would not listen to an explanation—he would never believe that Hart no longer visited Daisy—he would end their engagement faster than Francesca could take a single breath.

"You must be in heaven, I suspect. Can I offer you some tea, some pastries?" Daisy asked, leading Francesca into an elegant salon with several works of art upon the wall, all of which, Francesca knew, Hart had chosen for Daisy's home.

"Tea is fine," Francesca said absent-mindedly. She must speak to Hart, immediately. But how to do so without appearing as jealous as she had been earlier, as jealous as a shrew?

"Your ring is lovely," Daisy remarked after asking her butler for refreshments.

"Thank you. It is too lavish for my taste."

"Really? The saying is a diamond can never be big enough."

"Daisy, I can see you are upset. I am sorry!" Francesca finally cried. "I never meant to interfere with you and Hart. Everything just happened, somehow. I can't even begin to think of how we got to this place in time!"

Daisy folded her arms across her small breasts. "Hart decided to marry, and there you were—his brother's love interest."

How cruel Daisy was. "Hart and I became friends, and he realized he wished to marry me," she returned sharply.

"Yes, he suddenly came to his senses after all those years of avowing he would never wed. It must have been a *coup de foudre*—and to think you are the lucky one."

Francesca was ramrod-stiff. "As you must know, there is no predicting Hart."

"No, there is not. And he is noble after all; how odd. But can he really remain faithful to you, I wonder?" And she finally smiled.

Francesca stared. It was as if they were enemies now. She finally said, "I am choosing to take him at his word."

"One month is easy," Daisy remarked. "A lifetime of fidelity is quite another chore."

Francesca sat down, grimacing. If Daisy was trying to upset her, she was succeeding. "Hart is vastly misunderstood. I have seen his best side. There is good in him, as I am sure you have also learned."

"Francesca, there is something I must tell you," Daisy suddenly said, sitting down in a moss-green damask chair

beside her. She gripped her arm. "Hart was at a club called
the Jewel last night. It is a decadent place where men go
to satisfy their most eccentric sexual appetites. He was
there, I know, because Rose works there and she was with
him."

Francesca stiffened, holding her tongue, not about to tell
Daisy that she knew. Her heart beat hard. What was Daisy
about to tell her? "Really?"

"I'm sorry," Daisy said, very solemnly, "but I cannot let
you go on believing how noble Hart is. He was with Rose
and another woman. The three of them, Francesca. It was
a threesome, a ménage à trois." She sat back now, hands
clasped in her lap, watching Francesca carefully.

Francesca stood, refusing to doubt Hart. She would not
become a victim of Daisy's barbs. "Clearly, our friendship
is at an end," she said coldly. But she was trembling, for
Daisy's words contained a poison that she wasn't completely immune to.

"I am only the messenger," Daisy said, also standing. "I
like you, Francesca, and I see you are about to be hurt."

"Hart was at the Jewel because I sent him there," she
said stiffly.

Daisy's eyes widened.

"We are working on a case, together, Daisy. In fact, the
reason I am here is to ask you and Rose to help us."

Daisy's surprise vanished. Her face became expressionless. "How bohemian, how liberal, you are. I would have
never guessed. So you do not care what Hart does when
he is not with you. Still, the tower of his fidelity came down
quickly enough. But I am not surprised. Hart is not the kind
of man to deny himself his pleasure."

Francesca's face felt as brittle as a ceramic mask. *Hart
had told her he had done nothing, and she believed him.*
She knew what Daisy was doing. She wanted to create suspicion, doubt, mistrust. "I care. I care very much. And we
both know Hart did nothing with Rose and that other
woman except watch."

Daisy smiled tightly. "Is that what he said? How clever he is."

And Francesca collapsed. Doubt reared its monstrous head. It was an ugly blow, but the moment she became breathless with suspicion, wondering if Hart had lied to her, she also recalled his disbelief and how aghast he had been with just such accusations. She reminded herself that they really were friends. He had yet to lie to her, and as he had said, the only reason he had gone to that club was to help her in her investigation—to help find the missing girls. Besides, the ultimate platform of his logic was irrefutable— why marry if he wished to carry on as he had his entire adult life?

"I trust Calder," Francesca said, and she meant it. But getting the words out and meaning them were very hard. How vulnerable she was to the kind of attack Daisy had just inflicted.

"You could always ask Rose what happened. After all, she is here," Daisy said with another slight smile.

Francesca started and then the anger began. Being angry was a relief. "You wish to break us up. Rose loves you— I suppose she would do whatever you asked her to. Including lie. I didn't come here to investigate my fiancé, Daisy. I have come here asking for your help."

Daisy shrugged. "And if I refuse, Hart will order me to act otherwise, won't he?" It wasn't really a question.

"Yes." Francesca held her tongue. She was an instant away from telling Daisy that if she wished to be a free woman, she should not be living in this man's house, a bought and paid for whore.

Daisy shrugged. "Then I have no choice."

"Please ask Rose to join us," Francesca said, relieved to be in control of the situation once more. But she was perspiring. Facing Daisy—and her accusations against Hart— had been an ordeal. In fact, remaining there in her house, bought and paid for by Hart, remained an ordeal.

Rose stepped into the room. Francesca started as their gazes met, realizing Rose had been in the adjacent room, eavesdropping. And for one moment, as she stared at the tall, striking, olive-skinned woman, she thought about the fact that Hart had watched Rose making love to another woman last night. But that was all he had done. She was quite certain. Wasn't she?

Rose nodded. "Hello, Francesca. Congratulations."

"Thank you." Rose wasn't being hostile to her, but they had been rather friendly up until now. "How are you?"

Rose shrugged, coming forward to stand beside Daisy. "Other than having to entertain your fiancé last night?" Her eyes glittered with hatred then. "Fine."

Francesca understood the innuendo and worked hard to ignore it. "Four girls between the ages of twelve and fourteen are missing. They are all lovely, and we suspect they have been forced into prostitution. I know that you despise Hart, Rose, and Daisy, it is clear that you despise me, but these poor children have been torn out of their families and homes and forced into a horrible world of depravity and lust, and I beg you both to put personal differences aside. We must find the children. We must stop these deplorable creatures who are abducting the children and forcing them to be prostitutes. Can you please help us find them?"

Rose and Daisy stared at her and then looked at each other. Rose slid her arm around Daisy; Daisy closed her eyes for a moment. Then she looked at Francesca. "You're right. I'm sorry. I lied to you about Calder—Rose said he was pacing the room and drinking scotch and hardly paying attention to her and Linda. He never touched either one of them. I'm sorry."

"And I am sorry that you are hurt," Francesca said softly, flooded with relief. "I am sorry that you have fallen in love with him."

Daisy stared at her, not denying it, and a silence fell. It was hard and harsh. Rose stared at Daisy in disbelief, a wild accusation in her eyes. "You love me!" she cried.

Daisy looked small and fragile, lost and forlorn. "I do, but I love him, too. I am not ready to give him up." Tears filled her eyes and she hurried from the room.

Rose looked up at Francesca, a frightening light in her eyes. "He had better stay away from me," she warned. "And he had damn well better leave Daisy alone. I may kill him otherwise. You tell him that, Francesca."

Francesca inhaled, because Rose looked murderous at that moment. The threat did not seem idle; it felt real.

Rose rushed after Daisy.

Francesca didn't hesitate—the girls' lives were at stake. She raced after Rose, seizing her arm. "Rose, I need your help. I have to find those girls. Please, ask around, find out who is running a brothel with children. Please!"

Rose shook her off with a furious glance and left the room.

Francesca sank down in a chair. Her head hurt her now and she cradled it in despair. She had struck out—there would be no help from this quarter.

There was a fire burning in the hearth in his study. He was working at his desk, taking care of the paperwork he had not been able to get to at the department all week. Dot was seated on the floor halfway between his desk and the blaze, playing with her new doll, making soft sounds, and occasionally saying a genuine word, smiling and laughing. Katie sat cross-legged beside her, watching, her small narrow face taut with unhappiness.

Bragg realized he had been staring at the children instead of reading the report before him. He sighed and gave up, cradling his face in his hands. At least Dot was too young to understand that her new mother was gone, but Katie was very upset, and it hurt him.

How could she do it? Come so determinedly into their lives and, in the blink of an eye, walk out?

But she had done it once before. In almost the exact same way.

He stiffened as a real and physical pain arced through his chest. For one moment he wondered if he was having a heart attack, but the pain turned into something suspiciously like grief, and he realized he was not. *It was as if he was reliving the past, as if that terrible time four years ago had been reinvented and was happening all over again.*

But she had almost fooled him into thinking she had changed. She had almost fooled him into thinking she was kind, caring, selfless. In fact, he thought, hurting the way a bleeding man did, she had fooled him because deep in his heart he had believed she was the graceful, compassionate woman she had presented herself to be.

But it had only been that—a presentation. And a damned good one, too.

You damned fool. She did care, and you know it, deep inside, but bastard that you are, you tested her, one time too many, pushing at her, as hard as you could, until she left. This is your fault and no one else's. Damn you.

He stood abruptly, clutching the edge of his desk. He didn't care. It was better this way. He would get the best lawyer in the country and get a divorce even if it meant letting the world know she had abandoned him. And he would adopt the girls. It was better this way. He hated Leigh Anne—he always had and he always would.

He started, realizing Katie had come to stand beside him, gazing up at him anxiously. He forced a smile. "Tired of playing with your sister?"

Katie shook her head "no" and didn't speak.

It was impulsive; he pulled her close to his side, murmuring, "It's going to be all right."

"She's never coming back, is she? That's why you're so sad," Katie whispered.

He almost choked as he spoke. "No. She's not coming back."

Katie buried her face in the vicinity of his rib cage. He stroked her hair; his hands were shaking. "Is she dead?" Katie finally choked out.

"No," he said, inhaling hard. But maybe he should have told her yes. Maybe the lie would have been easier.

Katie looked up, her eyes glistening with tears. "Then why? Why did she go? I don't understand!"

He cupped her thin shoulders. "It's complicated," he whispered unsteadily. *Why? I chased her away and we are all better off. We are better off, God damn it.*

Katie looked at him, begging him for an explanation she could understand, with her big doe eyes.

He had to come up with something, he realized. But he was at a complete loss now, angry, hurting, resentful, confused. Francesca's image came to mind—she could help, he realized with real relief. If he told her the truth, she could come and help explain to the children what had happened—and why.

A knock sounded on his door. "Sir?" Peter intoned.

Bragg turned, one hand now on Katie's shoulder. "Yes?"

Peter looked at him gravely, and the worry was also reflected in his eyes. "Chief Farr is here, sir, and he wishes to speak to you."

Bragg nodded, too numb to be surprised, and he smiled at Katie, wondering if it was as strained as it felt. "I'll be right back."

Katie nodded, clearly trusting him.

And that she did warmed him from head to toe. He followed Peter into the hall and saw Farr at its end, standing there in the entry. Bragg approached. "Chief. What brings you here on a Sunday?" He heard how brisk his tone was, how professional. A police crisis was just what he needed, he realized.

Farr was in his Sunday best, and he twisted a fedora in his hands. "Sir," he began, his gaze skewer-sharp, "is Mrs. Bragg in residence?"

The question stabbed through Bragg like a blunt knife. *"What?"*

Farr actually looked uncomfortable. "I know the question is an odd one, but I need to ask you if Mrs. Bragg is here."

Some inkling began. "What is going on?" he asked sharply.

"Sir—"

"She's not here," he snapped. "Chief?"

Farr was grim. "There was a carriage accident—a runaway coach. Yesterday afternoon."

Bragg stared, the inkling becoming dread. The room grayed.

"The woman's purse was lost in the crisis, and the police were called in today to try to identify her. Officer Wade claims she is your wife."

And for an instant, gray became dark, black, but he fought through, and then Farr was facing him, grave and grim. "How bad is she?"

"Bad, sir, alive, but in serious condition."

He was going through the door. "Where is she?"

"Bellevue," Farr said.

CHAPTER
FIFTEEN

"SHE'S NOT UNCONSCIOUS, COMMISSIONER. She's asleep. She's been heavily dosed with laudanum for the pain."

Bragg stared at the small form sleeping on the hospital bed. Her face was turned toward him, and she looked unblemished and perfect, as if nothing had ever happened to her. He wanted to rush to her side, take her hand, stroke her hair. Aware of trembling, unable to control it, he forced himself to face Dr. Barnes. It was hard to breathe; he kept telling himself it would be all right, that he must not panic. "What happened?"

"She was brought into Emergency yesterday afternoon at three. A coach ran her down, sir. Apparently it was a runaway," the doctor, a tall, silver-haired man, said.

He could not think now about all of the accusations he had been making against her. *She hadn't left him. This entire time, Leigh Anne had been here in the hospital, hurt, suffering, alone.* "How badly is she injured?" he asked hoarsely, unable to look away from her.

"It's serious, sir."

He whirled—and there was so much fear. Briefly, there was also no air. He couldn't inhale; he was on the verge of choking.

"Commissioner, sit down. Let me get you some smelling salts."

He shook his head, somehow managed to breathe, hugely, deeply. "Is she dying?"

"No. She's currently stable—but her condition is very serious. She went into shock yesterday—we managed to bring her out of it. She's a bit better today than she was yesterday, sir. Her vital signs have improved slightly."

Relief made his knees buckle, his breath escape. *She wasn't going to die. She wasn't going to leave him.*

"Sir, I am optimistic—I am hoping to see a little improvement every day. We should be fairly certain of an outcome in the next few days."

Bragg couldn't smile, but he managed to nod instead. "Has she woken up?"

"Briefly, once. She is heavily drugged, Commissioner, against the pain from her injuries. She will undoubtedly wake up again, but I can't say when. However, feel free to talk to her. She may hear you." The doctor smiled at him.

Bragg managed a thank-you and hurried into the hospital room.

There were two other beds in the room, but both were empty. He knelt beside the hospital bed, noting now how unbelievably pale she was. She seemed as fragile as Katie, as small, as vulnerable and helpless. He reached for her hand, clasping it tightly, trembling even more. And it was then that he saw her left leg, slightly elevated by a pulley, three times its usual size, covered by a second sheet. *What had happened to her leg?*

Leigh Anne moaned softly.

His gaze flew to her face, but she remained asleep. Had he just heard her moan? Was she still in pain? He wasn't himself—he hadn't asked for all the details—she had been struck down by a carriage, but how? He was afraid, now, afraid to know every detail. He stroked her hair with his other hand and his heart broke.

What had he done to this woman? How could he have treated her so miserably? "Leigh Anne. It's me. Rick." He tried to smile, but if she heard him, she gave no sign. "Don't wake up; ssh, sleep; it's good for you," he said, thinking silently, *Darling.* "I'm sorry," he added thickly, and to his horror, his composure shattered then.

Tears fell. He could not stop them and he could not speak so he held her hand tightly. What a bastard he was.

All this time he had been accusing her of leaving him, and she had been in the hospital, gravely injured, in indescribable pain, alone. He hated himself. He would never forgive himself. And not just for thinking the worst—but for the past six weeks, for the terrible way he had treated her: for punishing her, day after day and night after night, for using her like a whore.

She wasn't a whore. Dear God, she was his wife.

He gained a semblance of control. He smiled through his tears. "I have been a complete bastard. I am so sorry. But I'm here now, and you are not alone." He touched her cheek with his knuckles then, and froze. Had her dark lashes just fluttered slightly? Had she heard him?

He swallowed hard and kissed her cheek. "I am sorry," he repeated firmly. "When you get well, when you come home, it will be different, I promise you."

And this time, he knew her lashes moved.

"Leigh Anne? It's me, Rick, I'm here, and I won't leave you. I promise." He hesitated and had to add, "You'll never be alone again." He smiled a little, facing his own vulnerability then, and the fear inside him was an ocean, deep and dark and vast, but if she heard, there was no indication. Her breathing remained deep and even, her face an expressionless mask of beauty and perfection.

He no longer understood himself. He only knew he wasn't noble at all; the world saw a thin surface layer, his

most superficial side. For if he were noble and good, he
would have never made that sordid deal with her, allowing
her to move in with him for six months in order to gain
her consent to a divorce. If he were truly noble, he would
not have taken her to bed each and every night, a prisoner
of his own lust. He should have given her the house, moved
out, and treated her with the consideration and courtesy she
deserved. How could he have been so rotten to her? How?
It was amazing that she had tolerated him at all. She had
been a loving mother to the girls and a good wife to him.
And every time he added the past twenty-four hours to the
terrible equation that was their married life, the guilt consumed him, overwhelming, black, and unbearable. She had
been lying here alone, all this time, and he had been in
their home, hating her.

*His wife had been gravely injured and he hadn't been
there for her.*

Never again.

He stroked her cheek, her forehead, her temples, her
hair.

And he cried some more.

Francesca was at her desk, going over her notes, hoping
she would find a clue she had somehow missed. And every
now and then she would think about Calder Hart, wondering if he would go out prowling that night, trying to find
someone who could lead him to the children. Perhaps tonight she should go with him. She could don a disguise.
Maybe she could even pose as a prostitute.

She sat up straight, dropping her pen. *She could pose as
a prostitute.*

The idea was a brilliant one. Why rely on Daisy and
Rose to find the children? She could find some terribly
revealing clothes, go down to the Jewel, meet Solange Marceaux, and try to gain employment there. It crossed her
mind that if she succeeded, she might find herself in a terrible position. She wished that she could dismiss that wor-

risome possibility, but she could not. She had to get into the club and begin asking questions, yet she also had to avoid winding up in some patron's bed.

Francesca grinned widely. She would drug any man she wound up with! In fact, as she had no idea where the Jewel was, she would have to ask Rose or Daisy. Perhaps she could convince Rose to refer her to Solange Marceaux. Surely she would help her in this instance! And surely Rose or Daisy would show her how to drug an unwanted customer. Francesca was triumphant. Her plan was a brilliant one. The only flaw was that it needed some preparation and she would have to wait until tomorrow evening to actually put it into effect, as she did need Rose and Daisy's help.

She stood and flung open her armoire. Hart had said that Solange Marceaux had been elegant. Still, she was a genuine madam, so it didn't matter. Francesca was a rather obvious intellectual—she would have to dress the part or Solange Marceaux would see right through her.

Francesca debated having her maid, Bette, alter one of her gowns. Then she smiled. The Countess Benevente had the most daring dresses. It was early; she was probably at the Channing home, where she was a guest, preparing for an evening out. Francesca decided she would telephone her and ask her if she could borrow a dress. She was thrilled. Her plan was a perfect one.

Francesca hurried to the door and bumped directly into her unsmiling sister. Connie grimaced at her. "Where are you off to?"

"I have a telephone call to make," Francesca announced cheerfully. She was beyond excitement. What if she found the children tomorrow? She could not liberate them herself; she'd have to get Bragg and the police.

"I see you haven't heard the news."

"What news?" Francesca asked, thinking about logistical details now. She would undoubtedly need to be interviewed. And how should she dress for that occasion?

Should she call on Madame Marceaux in the morning or the afternoon?

"Francesca, have you heard a word I said?" Connie demanded sharply, having seized her wrist and preventing her from sailing down the hall.

Francesca faced her, her smile fading, finally noticing that Connie looked extremely serious. And she had been trying to tell Francesca something, but Francesca had been too involved in her scheming to hear what she was saying. "I'm sorry; I was thinking. Con? Is something wrong? You look very grim."

"Please sit down."

Francesca went on alert. "Has something happened? Is it Neil? The girls?"

Connie took her hand. "Neil and I were to have dinner tonight with Rathe and Grace Bragg. We just received a telephone call from Rathe. There has been an accident."

In that moment, Francesca's world went dark. "Bragg?"

"No, Fran, it is Leigh Anne. She was hit by a runaway carriage yesterday and she is gravely injured."

Francesca cried out, "Where is she?"

"Bellevue," Connie said. "Fran? What are you doing?"

But Francesca was already running down the hall. "What do you think I am doing?" she flung over her shoulder, now madly and dangerously dashing down the stairs. "I am going to the hospital, Connie. Dear God, poor Leigh Anne. . . . Bragg needs me!"

When Francesca arrived on the second floor, a floor for seriously ill patients, she saw the Braggs standing at the far end of the hall in a hushed conversation. Francesca hesitated for a single moment, then started toward them.

Grace looked perilously close to weeping. Rathe had his arm around her. Even in middle age, they still made an outstanding couple. Nicholas D'Archand, a dark-haired eighteen-year-old who was Bragg's cousin, stood with them, as did Rourke. Hart was not present. But surely he had not yet learned of the tragedy, otherwise, surely, he would be there.

As Francesca approached, Rourke was speaking. She heard him saying, "Very serious, but stable. She is slightly improved today from yesterday. Dr. Barnes is hopeful there will be some improvement every day."

Francesca was relieved. "Stable" sounded good to her, and an improvement from yesterday, why, that was simply wonderful! But how badly hurt was Leigh Anne?

Grace seized his hand. "What are her chances of fully recovering?" Her voice was hoarse.

Rourke hesitated, excessively grim. "Mother, she will never fully recover. Her left leg is injured beyond recovery; she will never walk again."

Grace gasped.

Francesca stifled her own cry.

Grace turned and saw her. So did the three men.

Francesca said, "I am so sorry." And she looked past the Braggs, into the hospital room.

There were three beds in the room, but only one was occupied. Bragg sat by the bed closest to the corridor, slumped in a chair, holding his wife's hand. *Leigh Anne would never walk again.* "How is he holding up?" Francesca asked worriedly, not taking her gaze from Bragg.

At first, no one answered. Francesca looked up, suddenly realizing the family might consider her an intruder, but Grace smiled at her tearfully and said, "The best that can be expected. Thank you, Francesca, for coming."

"I had to come. Dear God, how terrible this is." So many images of Leigh Anne rolled through her mind now, and in each and every one the tiny woman was impossibly graceful as she moved. She would never walk again. It was more than a tragedy.

"They were going to amputate her leg," Rourke said, "but decided against it."

Rathe and Grace turned, about to go into the room. Rourke stopped them. "He doesn't know about her leg. Dr.

Barnes thought he would speak with him later, when he is not quite so shocked."

They nodded and went in.

Bragg looked up as his father clasped his shoulder and Francesca saw how emotionally ravaged he was. His face was lined—he had aged ten years in a day. There was no mistaking his grief, his anguish, his fear. She closed her eyes, hard. She so wanted to comfort him now, but how could she? And didn't this prove what she had always known, that he loved his wife before anyone else—including her? She wasn't sad, nor was she bitter; she only knew she had to comfort him, reassure him, soothe him. Then she looked at Rourke. "Has anyone told Calder yet?"

"I sent word; he wasn't home," Rourke said.

Nicholas, a dashing young man with silvery eyes, smiled grimly at her and went into the room as well. Francesca shifted, hesitating.

"Come on," Rourke said kindly, taking her arm.

"Thank you," Francesca whispered, going into the room with him. She grimaced, as Leigh Anne no longer looked like an angel; she was deathly pale, frighteningly so. Francesca wondered if, in her surgery, she had lost a lot of blood.

Rourke had touched Bragg's shoulder, letting him know that he was there. Bragg smiled up at him and his smile was so lost, so forlorn, so fragile, that it broke Francesca's heart. She had never seen him more anguished.

She smiled sadly. She ached for them both.

He saw her. He started, their gazes locking.

"I'm so sorry," she whispered. "Is there anything I can do?"

He stood up slowly. "Your being here is enough." And as if his family weren't present, he walked over to her— right into her arms.

She held him as if he were a child. She didn't speak, because the situation was too grave for platitudes, and she knew that what he wanted from her was comfort and nothing more. She felt him tremble in her arms as she stroked his back. Then she realized that his parents had walked out of the room and Rourke and Nicholas D'Archand were following. She was relieved; she wanted to be alone with him.

He looked up at her, agonized. "When I think of how I have treated her . . ." He could not continue.

"Don't," she said thickly. "Don't go back to that dark, ugly place. The present is what matters. She needs you and you are here."

"She was here for over twenty-four hours, hurt and alone," he whispered roughly. "I thought she had left me, Francesca. I thought she had left me and the girls."

She pulled him close again. "But she didn't. She didn't leave you because she loves you. Let go of the past, it's over now, Rick. Please." And realizing the many layers of meaning in her words, she felt tears rise in her own eyes as their gazes met again. He also understood, she realized. Maybe she had to let him go, too. Maybe he had to let her go. But could she, really? Could he? He might love Leigh Anne, but nothing would ever sever the odd bond that remained between them.

He reached out and tucked hair behind her ear, his hand unsteady. "I need you so, Francesca. I really do. Maybe I always will." He held her gently now.

"And I'm here." She hesitated, swallowed. "That's what friends are for." Her smile felt tenuous then. "Leigh Anne will be there for you, too, if you let her."

She saw his nose redden and he glanced at his wife, in real despair. She stroked his shoulders, his back, studying his perfect profile. Endings were here, but so were beginnings, if they both had the courage to go forward without looking back.

"Francesca." He turned to her and took her shoulders in his hands. And somehow, they moved into each other's embrace, cheek to cheek, breast to chest. And briefly, he held her hard.

Then he stepped back, but he cupped her face in his hands. "You are an amazing woman, the most selfless, kind, and compassionate human being I have ever met." Their gazes locked.

Fear rose. What if nothing had changed after all? "I am hardly as you make me out to be," she whispered, her heart beating hard.

He just stared at her, and murmured, "What am I to do?" And his gaze moved to his wife.

The question could have meant many things, but Francesca knew it meant one thing and one thing only: how to navigate a journey of the heart, with Francesca one berth, his wife another.

He pulled Francesca close, stroked her hair, and stepped away from her then. He returned to his wife's side, taking up her hand, holding it tightly, his knuckles white.

Then she had an inkling, a bad one, and Francesca turned to look at the door.

Hart stared coolly back at her.

How long had he been standing there? Francesca felt quite sure, from his dark expression, that it had been for some time. She tried to smile at him, about to ask him to come in, but he turned and left abruptly, without a word, his strides hard and angry.

He had misunderstood. He was angry and jealous; of that she had little doubt. Francesca could not cope with him now. She could not run after him and beg him to calm down as she always seemed to do. Leigh Anne was seriously hurt, and Bragg was a wreck—Bragg needed her. She would have to explain to Hart later.

"Alfred, dismiss everyone," Hart said, striding through the huge front hall of his home.

Alfred had greeted him at the door. Now the slim bald butler carefully closed it. "Shall I have Cook prepare and leave you supper, sir?" Worry was reflected in the flickering light in his gray eyes.

Hart was striding past the life-size nude sculpture of the

lovely Lady Brianna. "No. I want everyone out, immediately."

Alfred stared after him.

Hart felt the stare as he bounded up the sweeping gold-carpeted stairs two at a time, ripping off his tie. He did not like Alfred's obvious concern; once upon a time, his butler hadn't given a damn, and he preferred it that way. But those times had changed, hadn't they? And he knew damn well who had changed them. His clever and pretty little fiancée.

Francesca affected everyone whose life she entered, clearly, even his butler. Well, he didn't like seeing worry in Alfred's eyes. He wanted to see nothing in his eyes. He did not want a reaction when he gave an order. He wanted to be obeyed, instantly—he expected that and nothing more.

Images of Francesca and Bragg in each other's arms danced in his mind.

The wing of rooms that comprised the master suite was on the second floor. He strode violently down the hall, finally giving in to his blackest rage. His jealousy was blinding then. It was as if he could not stand it; the memory haunting him was beneath his skin, in his blood, boiling it, him. If he could peel off his own skin and the memory with it, he gladly would. But he could not, now could he?

There had been so much love in her eyes.

He didn't care.

"Fuck it." It was hard to breathe. He slammed into a salon with dark green walls and high ceilings trimmed in gold, through another private salon, his private den, and finally the master suite itself. The room was triple the size of every other bedroom in the house. The walls were upholstered in dark red paisley flecked with amber, brown, and gold, and two fireplaces were on its opposite sides, the marble mantels orange flecked with gold. Three lavish seating areas invited one to recline and relax, one by the bar, one by the wall of books, one in front of the far hearth. A massive bed that had once been in a duke's state bedroom was in the bedroom's center on a raised dais. This room had been intended to be the master of the house's ultimate sanctuary by the house's architect. In fact, Hart never used it except to sleep and dress. Until recently, that is.

Now he poured himself a stiff drink and walked over to the first fireplace, a new habit of his.

Above it, he had hung a portrait of a lady who looked terribly like Francesca. He had found the portrait several weeks ago in a small barely reputable gallery downtown when Francesca was out of town. The artist was Russian, the model French; it had been painted twenty years ago in Paris. He knew it wasn't Francesca, but he had fallen in love with the painting the moment he had seen it, and even as angry as he had been at her disappearance, he had purchased it on the spot, with no negotiation, and had hung it there on the wall, facing his royal bed.

He stared up at it now, simply furious.

Instead of the Frenchwoman in her corset and petticoats, he saw Francesca in Rick Bragg's arms, her face soft with caring, compassion, love.

He cried out, throwing the glass of scotch at the mantel, where it shattered.

Hart paced. He had to face it, didn't he? Francesca remained in love with Rick. She would always love him, because she was as stubborn as a woman could be—it was one of the things he found so endearing about her. She simply never gave up.

But when it came to his half brother it wasn't endearing; it was provoking, annoying, infuriating . . . enraging.

He reminded himself that for a woman in love with another man, she was terribly hot and passionate in his, Hart's, arms.

He was a man of the world. In this one way, she was no different from most men and women. Choosing the socially appropriate spouse—while choosing the sexually appropriate lover. She might have once wished to marry Bragg, but it was he, Hart, whom she wished to bed.

He slumped down on a ruby-red sofa. His head pounded now, the force terrible, painful, and the illicit images remained, of his worst rival and the woman he planned to wed.

He wrenched around to stare up at his new portrait. New images of Francesca danced in his head, replacing the seductive model, in that stunning red dress, her hair coming down, her eyes dewy and soft from his kisses. She was everything that was fine and good in this ugly, sordid theater called life. She was like the sun, warming everything she gazed upon—warming him. He had smiled more in the past two months since first meeting her than he had in his entire life. He knew they would be good for each other; he'd never doubted that their marriage would be an interesting one in every possible way.

He had been looking forward to it. He, Calder Hart, the most heartless of sworn bachelors, had been anticipating his marriage to Francesca Cahill, crime-solver extraordinaire.

Another image intruded, Francesca and Bragg in each other's arms, but instead of there being anguish, there were warm smiles. How many times had he seen them share an exclusive look? How many times had he watched them, instantly becoming the intruder, an outsider? But goddamn it, he was her fiancé; it was Bragg who was the outsider now! And he closed his eyes, hard.

He was an extremely smart man. He was not a man who made excuses, who conveniently fooled himself. He was the outsider, not Bragg, and it would always be that way, even after their marriage, because it had been that way his entire life. He had never once measured up to his older brother, and he never would be accepted by anyone, not even Francesca, in Bragg's place.

He opened his eyes, stared at the portrait, and cursed himself for being a fool.

He had to face the terrible truth. Leigh Anne was at death's door.

If everyone else wanted to be optimistic, let them be. He had spoken to Rourke and then Barnes before stopping by her room, and he knew the truth. She was by no means out of the woods, and they were sugar-coating just how seriously ill she was. She had suffered major surgery on her leg, had lost a tremendous amount of blood, and was now fighting an infection. She was currently stable; at any time she might go into shock, a coma; tomorrow she could even take such a turn for the worse that she would die.

He stood, inhaling sharply, temples throbbing. *Leigh Anne might die.* Dr. Barnes had refused to give him odds. Rourke had thought it about fifty-fifty. Who was he fooling? Francesca might want to be in his bed, between his legs, but the moment Leigh Anne was dead, she would be back in Rick's arms, and it would be his bed that she was warming.

If Leigh Anne died, Francesca and Rick would be free to marry after all.

And instead of a familiar and welcome rage, there came the first stirrings of panic. Hart did not know the feeling— and he did not want to know it. Firmly he told himself that he didn't care—and it was a monstrous lie. He did care, very much; he could not bear Francesca leaving him for his goddamned half brother. He could not bear losing her, not now. She had become as important to him as the air he breathed, as the sunlight on his face.

Hart looked up at his intricate ceiling. Not very long ago he had laughed at men who were smitten with a woman, who wanted to marry, who cared. Caring had changed him, and sometimes he liked the changes; now he hated them. The vulnerable, frightened, and needy orphan he had been as a child had been deeply buried a long time ago. A powerful, indifferent, and selfish man had replaced that boy. Now the boy felt perilously close, perilously near. Hart despised the boy.

He reminded himself that she was far too good for him. That she deserved his noble, civic-minded half brother. She deserved a white picket fence and dinners of state. She deserved the finest things life could offer; she deserved to have all of her dreams come true, every single damned one of them; she deserved true love.

In that instant, his future paraded itself before his very eyes, a future without the clever and ingenious Francesca Cahill. There would be more women than he cared to have, women whose faces would be forgotten before they had even left his bed; there would be business to conclude, deals and negotiations, new companies to form, build, steal, acquire. When he was sixty, he'd have a twenty-year-old mistress and more money than any man had a right to. He'd have a dozen fine homes scattered about the globe and a collection of art worthy of a European museum. And dear God, he'd have his portrait of Francesca, too, wouldn't he? Her good-bye gift to him.

He walked over to the mirror above the bar and smiled grimly at himself. And his blackest self reared up, taunting and insistent. He closed his eyes, bracing himself against the devil.

You don't have to give her up. But you already know that, don't you?

Hart fought against the ugly voice inside of his head.

So what if Leigh Anne dies? Take what Francesca has been offering, seduce her—ruin her—and she will have to marry you.

He opened his eyes and stared at himself in the mirror. And he saw the man who didn't just move mountains; he saw the man who commanded a mountain to come, and it came. It was the reason he had built a fortune from pennies; he simply did not know how to lose or give up.

But Francesca had the kindest and most selfless heart of anyone he knew. She deserved more than passion and friendship; she deserved love. And that he could not give to her.

She deserved Rick Bragg. And to make matters worse, he truly knew it.

Seduce her. Seduce her tonight. Make sure you are caught in the act—or close to it. You won't have to wait a year, my friend, and once her father knows you have compromised her, nothing will prevent your getting what you want. Nothing will come between you and Francesca, not even that bastard brother of yours, not even Rick.

He stared at himself in the mirror.

Then he thought he heard a knock on the bedroom door. But that was impossible, wasn't it? He walked across the huge bedroom and opened it.

Alfred smiled grimly. "Sir, Miss Cahill is downstairs. She has asked to see you. What shall I tell her?"

He stiffened. *Seduce her. Here is your chance.* He wet his lips and heard himself say, "Send her away. Tell her anything that you wish."

Alfred hesitated.

Hart was livid. "Do it, Alfred, do it *now.*"

"Yes, sir. And before I go, is there anything I can—"

"No." Hart shut the door rudely in his face, then leaned against it, sweating.

Fool. You had the perfect chance.

Hart quickly recrossed the room, as if he could really and truly outdistance the evil voice in his head. He poured another scotch and downed it in a single gulp.

He poured another scotch, calming now, this time sipping it. The liquor was doing what he wanted it to do; it was silencing the worst side of him.

"Calder?"

He whirled—and gazed at Francesca Cahill, smiling tentatively at him, standing on the threshold of his bedroom.

And here is golden opportunity, knocking at your door. He laughed.

Hart trembled. "Francesca, you should not be here. Not now, not tonight."

She smiled at him. "I'm not leaving," she said.

CHAPTER
SIXTEEN

SUNDAY, MARCH 30, 1902 — 7:00 P.M.

"YOU ARE VERY BOLD."

Francesca smiled firmly. "Yes, I am." She couldn't help glancing around, trying not to appear awestruck by his palatial bedroom. She refused to stare at the bed—not that she hadn't seen it the moment she'd stepped into the room or, rather, the moment after she'd seen Hart. As she had imagined, it was huge.

"I'm giving you one more chance to leave," Hart murmured.

Francesca started—his tone was soft and sexy, seductive. She had come to explain about that afternoon at the hospital, and she had been expecting jealousy and anger, not this. She took a breath. "We need to speak."

His brows lifted, his expression sardonic. "In my private rooms?"

"One day these will be my rooms, too, won't they?" she said, her heart racing at the notion. She gave up. She turned to stare at the bed. "I'm afraid to ask. Have kings slept there?"

"And princes and dukes—and undoubtedly their lovers, too."

Her gaze flew to his. He wasn't smiling. He was staring. "Calder. Are you all right?"

"Why wouldn't I be all right?" he returned smoothly.

A vast space separated them—the distance of two or three bedrooms. His behavior seemed—and felt—odd. It was almost as if he were playing a game—carefully, deliberately. Francesca approached, thinking about being at the hospital, about comforting Rick—and Hart having seen. "You're not angry with me?" she asked, realizing that her tone was unsteady. It was impossible, in spite of the room's dimensions, not to be acutely aware of being alone with Calder Hart in his bedroom. Now, as she came closer, she saw how disheveled he was. His dress shirt was unbuttoned well past his chest, revealing an interesting slab of muscle and some equally interesting black chest hair. His sleeves were rolled up to the elbows. His forearms were also dusted with hair, and sculpted with tendon, bone, and muscle. But then, she knew exactly how strong he was.

"Why would I be angry with you?" Hart drawled softly.

She halted, meeting his gaze. It was impossible to look away. She wet her lips. "I wanted to explain—but I see I don't have to."

He turned and walked away. Francesca watched him go to a bar built into the wall. As he poured two drinks, she saw his carefully neutral expression in the mirror above the countertop. His being so mild of manner and temperament was very odd. It wasn't right. She was vaguely alarmed.

But it was delicious, being alone with him in his bedroom. She smiled a little then, turning to really look around. She gazed upon a dozen museum-quality rugs, antique tables, exquisitely upholstered chairs, tufted ottomans, exotic mirrors. There were four sofas in the three different seating areas. She saw a large cast-iron box that appeared distinctly Spanish on one small table. A round red lacquer Chinese box was beside a different table. As she studied the room's contents, she knew exactly which items Hart had chosen and which had been purchased by his decorator. She smiled, pleased with herself.

When he spoke, she felt his breath teasing her nape. "I think you could use a drink."

She turned and he stood so close, staring at her with such watchful eyes, that her skirts brushed his thighs. She stepped back, accepting the drink. Why was he regarding her that way? As if she were a mouse in a laboratory experiment? "Thank you, Calder. Not for the drink. For not being in a jealous rage. I must admit, I am terribly surprised—and very relieved."

He said nothing, saluting her with his glass.

She had an idea that he was also thinking about their being alone in his bedroom, so she sipped quickly. As the incredibly smooth scotch floated over her tongue, she smiled. "My, this is good."

"Yes, it is, isn't it?"

Their gazes locked. Francesca couldn't hold his gaze—there remained something different about him that she could not identify—and she turned away, disturbed but frankly titillated. "It's terrible about Leigh Anne," she murmured.

"Yes, it is. A tragedy."

Francesca would have whirled to see if he was mocking, but instead, she stiffened. There was a portrait hanging over the fireplace, and the woman in it looked like her!

"Amazing, isn't it?" Hart whispered from behind.

She could only stare. "For one moment, I thought that was me!"

"It was painted twenty years ago, in Paris," he said softly, his breath teasing her neck.

Francesca could not move, as the implications of his having this portrait there in his room, facing his bed, tried to sort themselves out in her mind. "Why? Why did you put this here?" she asked roughly.

His hands cupped her shoulders. "Because," he said,

nuzzling her nape, "it seemed extremely appropriate."

She didn't move. She couldn't. He stood close enough that she felt a stiff hardness against the edge of her hip. She inhaled, trembling—it was his manhood, wasn't it?

His hands slid down her arms. "She kept me company while you were away," he breathed.

She swallowed. "What are you doing?"

She felt his smile against her skin. "Kissing you." And his lips brushed the side of her neck.

Her eyes closed. Red-hot desire paralyzed her. Hart wrapped her in his arms, still from behind, and she felt every inch of his arousal, straight up, against her. He crushed her even closer, his strong arms lifting her breasts. His mouth moved with increasing urgency on her neck and he breathed her name, a seductive sigh.

Francesca gasped, clinging to forearms.

"I missed you when you were gone," he whispered, covering her breasts with his hands.

"I missed you, too," she managed, surprised by his boldness. Her nipples hardened instantly.

"I hope so," he murmured, sliding his hands slowly down her belly.

Francesca tried to restrain herself, but she could not; she began shaking like a leaf, knowing where he would soon go.

His palms splayed low on her belly, just above the mound of her sex. "Darling," he whispered roughly.

"Please," she gasped, increasingly dazed.

He laughed and nipped her neck and pressed his arousal harder, between her buttocks, and moved his hands over her sex. Francesca's mind went nearly blank. She only knew that the desire raging in her veins had to be satisfied, and soon. "Calder."

And as if he understood, he lifted her skirt and underskirt slowly, inch by inch, up her shins, her knees, her thighs. It was hard to breathe. As the fabric slid up her silk-clad thighs, she gave up and collapsed in his arms. He laughed softly, kissing the corner of her mouth. She felt his tongue there.

And then his hands covered her, a thin layer of French silk the only thing between them. Francesca arced against him, whimpering, as he teased her flesh with his fingers, toying with each lip. She became dizzy with need. He held her up, stroking each plump mound through the silk. His fingers delved lower, tracing another intriguing outline. And from behind, he shifted himself, pushing between her legs, never mind her skirts, his trousers.

Francesca cried out, squeezing her thighs together, around him.

He said harshly, "Enough."

She was afraid he meant to stop. She protested, but too late—he lifted her abruptly in his arms and strode across the room toward the raised bed.

She stared at his face. His expression was ravaged by lust, and she was overcome by what she saw—and as overwhelmed by what was about to happen. "Calder," she managed, touching his cheek, something warm and wonderful blossoming in her chest.

He kissed her palm savagely, then laid her down on the bed, kneeling over her, one knee on each side of her hips. "Ssh," he murmured, unbuttoning her jacket, his smile brief and strained. He tossed the jacket aside and then quickly opened her shirtwaist. Francesca never looked away from his face, and when he had bared her breasts she saw his eyes widen and, as quickly, turn to midnight.

He liked what he saw and she was thrilled. She arched restlessly, murmuring, "Kiss me." She wanted him to suckle her breasts like a babe.

He met her gaze, bent, and kissed her nipples, one by one. "I have never wanted anyone more," he said huskily.

"I think I know," she returned, amazed, because she did.

He framed her breasts with his large hands, then lowered his face, touching his tongue to one nipple, and then another. Francesca gasped and begged.

He laughed a little. "Slow down. We have all night, darling."

They had all night. As he sucked her distended nipple into his mouth, a vague sense of alarm began. This was odd—a sudden about-face on his part—what was wrong? But then he began tugging with his teeth and pain mingled with the pleasure. She shot up; he held her down. He laved the tortured area, healing it.

She could not stand it, faint now with need to ricochet off that cliff. She gripped his shoulders, then slid her hands under his collar, his shirt a barrier she dismissed. His bare skin heightened her senses even more. "Calder. I am about to pass out."

He sat up, staring down at her, his gaze as brilliant as a black sun, unbuttoning his shirt. Francesca watched his chest appear, his rib cage, the taut muscles of his rock-hard abdomen. He was more magnificent than she remembered. She squirmed. He threw the shirt on the floor and he smiled at her.

She reached up and stroked his chest in awe. "You are so gorgeous."

"The feeling is mutual." He bent, nipped her breast, and briefly buried his face there. Then he was quickly divesting her of her skirt and petticoat.

His every touch enflamed her. For as he removed her clothing, he caressed her thighs, her knees, her feet. "Calder."

"Hush." He slid her drawers off and touched her naked flesh.

She closed her eyes, crying out, flying high.

He slid his hand between her thighs, hard, palming her as if he owned her, or as if he wished to. Then he began investigating every slick, throbbing inch. Francesca felt the universe beckon. She whimpered, thrashing, begging. "Hurry. Please. Come inside, Calder, please."

"You are so impatient," he murmured. "Spread your legs."

Francesca felt only exhilaration, and it was a moment

before she realized she had misunderstood. He did not impale her, instead, she felt a slick wet caress, and she looked down, gasping, as his tongue moved over her, exploring her, inch by delicious inch.

He swirled the tip of her sex and she shattered, hugely, impossibly, arcing through time and space. And when she floated back to earth and his bed, he remained there between her legs, staring up at her, an odd intense expression on his face.

"Oh, dear God," she said, swallowing. Her body was shaking like a leaf.

He laid his cheek on her belly, cupping her sex. His breathing was fast and harsh. She saw his eyes close, a crease of concentration—or pain—upon his brow.

"Calder," she whispered, still out of breath, "oh my."

He made no response except for the tightening of his hand.

Instantly her body swelled, still incredibly sensitive, incredibly ready. She stroked his hair. "Don't stop now."

She thought he smiled against her belly, briefly. His fingers combed through her hair. "Don't tell me you are ready for more, already?" His voice was rough—she had never heard it so raw before.

"Are you all right?" she asked.

"Hardly." He looked up. His eyes were hard, almost savage.

"What's wrong?" she whispered, suddenly frightened.

He made a sound. He moved over her, and in spite of his trousers, he stroked himself once, twice, hard, between her legs.

She wrapped her thighs around him, spiraling again. "Take off . . . take off the trousers . . . hurry," she gasped.

He caught her nipple with his teeth, so hard that she cried out, and then he caught her lips, as hard, forcing her mouth open, thrusting his tongue in. He moved against her sex one more time and he was so hard it hurt, but it was also electric, heaven, and Francesca begged, "Please. Please, I am going to die again, Calder, please!"

He didn't respond verbally. Instead, he reached down, stroked more gently over her several times; then, as a huge tidal wave crashed over her, he simply held her, hard.

This time, she landed back in his bed with a jolt. His entire weight was on her, and he was rigid with sexual tension. Something was wrong, terribly so. "Calder?"

"I am a damned fool," he muttered, and he leaped out of bed.

For one moment she remained still, and then she sat up. Hart was pacing restlessly, like a wild beast, his face drawn, the muscles in his back and shoulders rippling. She stared. "I thought you intended to make love to me." She realized how foolish her words were. She was stark naked, she had climaxed twice, she was in his bed, and the man had done the most naughty things to her with his tongue and his sex. Never mind that he hadn't consummated their affair. If that wasn't making love, what was?

He faced her, clearly still aroused. He ran one hand through his thick black hair, his stare intent. "I vaguely thought so, too."

Francesca stilled. Her instinct was to cover herself, but after what they had just done, that seemed absurd. Besides, she liked the way he was looking at her, his gaze moving over her breasts, her belly, her sex. She liked it very much, oh yes.

"Am I too thin?" she heard herself whisper. The air had caught on fire yet again.

"Hardly." His gaze slowly lifted to hers. It was smoking now, burning embers of ash.

"Too fat?"

He almost smiled. "No."

"Calder?"

"You should go," he said brusquely. "I think we've done quite enough tonight."

She was shocked; she slid to the edge of the bed. His gaze slammed over every inch of her again. She was aroused, and she knew he knew—her nipples were so tight they hurt. "Why?"

"You need to go. Now, before someone gets home."

He was right. Being caught like this would be terrible. Andrew would put Calder's head on a chopping block—or would he? "What about you?" she asked carefully.

His laughter was harsh. "I'll survive. But thank you for asking. Please get dressed, Francesca." He took one last look at her thighs—and the plump vee in between—and turned his back to her.

Francesca did not move. Hart was clearly in pain. She could guess why. Images of an interlude she should have never witnessed came to mind: once she had spied on him and his mistress. Then she had been somewhat guilty; now an idea began, and it was more than brilliant—she became breathless as she planned.

Why couldn't she be as bold and seductive as Daisy had been that day? After all, they were engaged.

Hart clearly needed her administrations, didn't he?

She was afraid of his rejecting her advances; still, if he hadn't rejected Daisy, why would he he reject her?

She stepped from the bed, trembling, undeniably excited. The dais it was on creaked. Hart had been pacing; now he froze, not turning. "Why aren't you getting dressed? My mood is foul. You need to leave, Francesca. I mean it."

Something else was torturing him and it wasn't just unrequited desire. Francesca summoned her courage and walked over to him. She could hardly wait to touch him—she had already waited so very long. "Calder."

He turned and looked at her. "Get dressed." His fists clenched at his sides.

She shook her head. "Sit down," she breathed, wide-eyed.

"I beg your pardon?" He was incredulous.

She dared to reach out and stroke her hand across one rock-hard chest muscle. His nipple became taut instantly and he froze, not even breathing. "Sit down," she said again, a soft, surprisingly seductive whisper.

He didn't move. He was rigid, staring at her with wide eyes.

She slid her hand lower, over his ribs. "I know you understand English," she breathed, smiling briefly. She could feel every one of his ribs, just barely, and his abdomen felt like a silk-sheathed rock.

"You little witch," he returned roughly. He gripped her wrists, immobilizing her.

She met his gaze, when she had so been enjoying mapping out the planes and angles of his body. "Let me go."

"And if I do not?" he asked softly, dangerously.

"Then you are only delaying what is inevitable," she returned quickly.

He looked heavenward and made a sound. Then he met her gaze and dropped her hand.

And she knew she had won. As he stared, she knew he knew, too. Finding it very hard to breathe, she slid her hand to his waist and into the waistband of his pants. He did not move a muscle, but he flinched. She no longer cared what he was doing, mesmerized by her own task. She slid her hand to the front of the waistband, knowing what she would find. Her fingertips brushed him.

"You are playing with fire," he warned.

She managed to look up; he burned her fingers. "You have more control than any man I know."

"Not tonight."

"Sit," she breathed, her heart racing, her knees weak from the excitement of what she intended—what she was really doing. And before he could obey, she unsnapped his trousers.

Hart was disbelieving. He looked down. Francesca inhaled as the tip of him was exposed, big and bulbous.

He slowly looked up. "Fire," he said.

"Just sit," she returned, a gasp. "Sit now, Hart!"

His mouth tightened and he dropped down in the closest chair.

Francesca laughed shakily and their gazes locked. "Forgive me if I'm giddy," she managed, dropping to her knees—between his thighs. She smiled a little at him.

Hart said not a word. But his chest was heaving as if he were running a marathon.

The power she had rippled over her, adding to the excitement. Francesca unzipped his trousers. He sprang erect, long and thick, huge.

Hart made a sound.

She glanced up. He was staring at her, but she had never seen such an expression before—it was beyond lust, and in that moment, she felt the extent of a vast and timeless power. It was her power, over him, and she began to understand it now. She smiled and gently took him in her hand. Hart clamped his hands on her head. "Damn it," he said.

She smiled as she lowered her face and tasted him with her tongue.

Hart fought a losing battle—he cried out.

She began exploring the tip with her tongue. He was salty and sweet. The experience was overwhelming—and why hadn't anyone ever mentioned this act before? It was too good to be true. It was better than licking any lollipop.

And Hart moaned.

She shook with excitement, tasting him, loving him, sucking him down as she had seen Daisy do. Hart gripped her head. Her hair finally spilled free. Francesca came up briefly for air. "Darling," she began in exhilaration, and she stopped.

Hart had his head thrown back, his eyes closed. He was in either pain or ecstasy or both. Another thrill swept over Francesca. She had tamed the beast, oh yes. She slid her hand around him, down him, reveling in the strength there, and she took him slowly in her mouth again, this time trying to suck his entire length down her throat.

Hart threw her aside.

On her hands and knees, Francesca turned. "Calder?"

"That's enough," he ground out, gripping himself.

Francesca almost asked him what he was doing but knew better. She bit her lip instead.

He turned aside, wrenching hard. His breathing was impossibly fast. He opened his eyes to glance at her and she saw the focus disappear. His eyes closed—thick black butterfly lashes on his dark skin. He grunted, once, twice, three times, and it was over.

Francesca sat staring, her heart racing, her body yearning. Calder Hart was more than magnificent—there were simply no words to describe him.

And she watched Hart recover.

His eyes slowly opened and his face, now drained of all tension, rearranged itself. He sat up and their gazes met. Francesca smiled a little, Hart did not. He stood up, swiftly closing his trousers, and then he met her gaze again.

A very long silence ensued.

He said, "I hope I did not offend you."

She was wide-eyed and had to bite back laughter. "Not at all." She got to her feet, feeling wanton and splendid in her nudity. "I would watch you do that happily anytime. You are fascinating, Calder." And oh, what an understatement that was.

He softened, his gaze slipping down her body. "Maybe you should get dressed?"

"I guess so," she said, suddenly not wanting to go. When they were married they would have all night to indulge themselves. She simply could not wait.

His gaze slid over her. "You are more than lovely, Francesca."

She smiled a little at him. One would think it hard to act normally when she was stark naked and still aroused, but she had a bit of the trollop in her, because it was as easy as baking cookies. "I hope you really think so." She preened a little, arching her back and squaring her shoulders and tossing her hair.

And he laughed, the sound as warm and rich as heated molasses, rippling over her. "How could you doubt it?" he asked, moving to her and taking her gently in his arms. His eyes were oddly, impossibly, tender and warm.

Gazing up into them, she felt faint, because it was as if

she saw real love shining there. "Oh, Calder," she began on a breath.

"No," he said firmly, and he bent and kissed the tip of her breast and then the tip of her nose. "I am getting you home—mostly in one piece."

She smiled teasingly then, absurdly warmed in her heart, where joy was growing like a hot air balloon. "You are honorable, you know. I mean, you had me naked in your bed and didn't do what most other men would do."

"You shouldn't have been naked in my bed at all, Francesca," he said, rather grimly. He released her, but as if he could not keep his hands to himself, he touched her breast, her waist, her hip. Then he began picking up her clothes.

She watched him. She should know better than to be surprised by this man. He never did what she expected. She smiled because he had said she kept him on his toes, but the opposite was true. She grinned, simply thrilled with what they had shared. Besides, he thought her lovely. And as beauty was in the eye of the beholder, she was going to accept the fact that he did.

"You could not be more seductive, grinning like a happy fool, and stop looking so pleased with yourself." He moved behind her and held the open corset over her chest, and she slid her arms through the two narrow shoulder straps. He quickly hooked it from behind. "I'll wait in the other room," he said flatly.

"Why?" she teased, eyeing him over her shoulder.

"Because you have learned just how tempting you are, Miss Cahill," he said, kissing her again, this time quickly on the lips. "And that is dangerous indeed."

Francesca stepped into her drawers, knowing he never took his gaze from her. "I don't mind if you stay while I dress."

"Don't tempt me," he warned, and he walked out.

She laughed happily to herself.

Five minutes later she found him in a huge green salon, staring out a window at the grounds and tennis courts, which were lit. She had managed to put her hair up, but she looked absolutely ravaged. Anyone who saw her would know she had been up to no good that night.

Now, watching him—he was so grim and appeared very disturbed—she recalled the fact that Alfred had told her Calder had dismissed the entire staff. What was wrong? What had caused him to behave so oddly? "Calder?"

He turned, his expression softening. "I'll take you home in a cab. I'm afraid Raoul is not able to take you home tonight."

"Because you dismissed the staff?" Francesca asked.

He was annoyed. "Alfred is treading upon thin ice."

"Don't blame him!" she cried. "He is rather worried about you, and now I can see that something is wrong."

He stared at her.

"Something is wrong. What is it?" she demanded. Panic began as she suspected the answer.

"This is wrong," he said abruptly, taking her arm.

"What—what do you mean?" she cried as he hurried her to the door.

"This should not have happened."

"We're engaged. This is hardly the end of the world," she protested.

"Be quiet," he said suddenly.

And Francesca heard the voices as well—in the corridor outside. She looked at him, afraid.

He was grim. He lowered his tone to a whisper. "Rathe and Grace, they must have just come home from the hospital."

The hospital. Images of Leigh Anne and Bragg filled her mind. For the past hour or so she had forgotten all about them, and it had been a terrible relief.

"We'll wait a moment and let them get to their rooms," Hart said. He was very serious now. "I don't want them seeing you leaving my suite, Francesca." Hart gave her an odd look—one she could not decipher.

And finally, for the first time since arriving at the house, Francesca began to blush. It would be embarrassing, and worse. "Neither do I," she said.

CHAPTER
SEVENTEEN

SUNDAY, MARCH 30, 1902 — 10:00 P.M.

THEY HURRIED THROUGH THE house like two thieves intent on escape after a lucrative heist. Francesca did not say a word as they hurried downstairs and down the corridor. Wall sconces lit the way.

The reception room was empty. So was the vast front hall. They paused before Caravaggio's controversial painting, *The Conversion of Saint Paul.* "We made it," Francesca breathed.

Hart's expression was strained. "Yes, we did. I'll get your coat."

Francesca was about to agree when from the shadows, a familiar voice said, "I didn't realize anyone was at home."

Her heart sank as Rathe Bragg stepped into the light in the entryway. He was smiling politely, but she felt her cheeks turn every possible shade of red. She forced an answering smile.

Hart had frozen with her coat in his hands; now he

turned slowly. "I let the staff off for the evening—an odd habit of mine," he said, coming forward. "Francesca called. I am taking her home."

Rathe nodded. "Hello, Francesca."

Relief then surged. He hadn't batted an eye and he clearly could not tell that she was terribly disheveled—he didn't suspect anything. "Have you just come from the hospital?" she asked.

"Actually, we picked the girls up. Calder, I hope you do not mind. We put them on the third floor. Mrs. Flowers is with them, and so is Peter."

"Of course I don't mind. It is late. I must get Francesca home."

"Yes, you should," Rathe agreed levelly.

Francesca so wanted to ask how Rick was, but she decided it wasn't a good idea. She said good night and stepped outside with Hart. He held her arm as they walked up the driveway. The night was cool, the breeze a touch sharp. Francesca could feel the tension in the man beside her.

She tried to study him in the darkness. "Calder? He didn't suspect a thing."

Hart said nothing.

"You don't have to worry about compromising my reputation," she added softly, wishing he would speak so she might comprehend what was on his mind.

He made a sound.

"What is it?" she asked with worry.

He faced her. "I think we should reconsider our hasty engagement."

The world disappeared from beneath her feet. Hart seized her elbow. *"What?"* she gasped.

"Before this goes any further, I think we should carefully reconsider our plans."

She could not breathe. She was going to faint. *He no longer wished to marry her.*

"There's a cab. Wait here." Hart broke into a run, letting loose a piercing whistle.

There was nothing to hold on to except a tree. Francesca leaned against the coarse bark, breathing so rapidly and shallowly that little bright white lights filled up her vision.

Hart was backing out. He no longer wanted to marry her.

He no longer wanted her.

She was strangling for lack of air. She felt as if she were choking, frantic, desperate.

Hart didn't want her anymore. One night in his bed—a few hours—and he was done with her.

The pain was unbearable.

He had just ripped open her heart.

"Francesca? Let's go," he said, taking her arm.

Like a mechanical creature she let him guide her to the street and into the cab. Instantly she faced away from him, staring unseeingly at Central Park. It was vaguely illuminated by gas lamplights.

"Number Eight-ten Fifth Avenue," Hart said.

He did not speak again.

Neither did Francesca.

MONDAY, MARCH 31, 1902 — 10:00 A.M.

"Promise to be a good girl."

"I promise, Mama," Bridget O'Neil said, flushing. They were standing on the sidewalk in front of the building that housed their ugly new home, and that odd boy, the one with the too-black hair and the red cheeks, was staring at them from the adjacent stoop where he sat.

"I should be back by suppertime—if they hire me, that is," Gwen said, laughing nervously.

"They'll hire you. You're the best housemaid there is," Bridget said earnestly.

Gwen's smile fell. "Darlin', I don't have any references."

Bridget closed her eyes, fighting fury. Then she gave in. "I hate the earl!" she cried. "It's because o' him we have to live in this horrid dirty city! It's because o' him Daddy

is in jail! It's because o' him you don't have a reference.
Damn him to hell!"

"Don't speak that way!" Gwen cried, tears slipping
down her face. "Never speak about him that way again!"
She bent and hugged her daughter hard.

Bridget despaired. It was so obvious to her that her
mother loved the dashing earl, but she simply could not
understand why. He had seduced her, causing her to break
her sacred wedding vows, and if that were not enough, he
had wrecked her marriage, too. Now they were alone in a
frightening new world, a place Bridget had never wanted
to be.

"He's a good man, darlin'," Gwen whispered. "I know
it's hard for you to understand, but he is. He never meant
for anything bad to happen to us."

Bridget stared sullenly.

Gwen kissed her cheek. "I'll get this job, darlin', and
we'll have beef tonight, I vow."

Bridget wished it were true. It had been so long since
she'd had a bite of beef or even mutton that the mere notion
made her mouth water and her stomach growl.

"Be good. Mrs. Kennedy left some lunch for you to take
with Matt, Paddy, and Lizzie. Her eldest son will watch
over you all until she or myself gets home."

Bridget cast a glance at the stoop where the boy sat,
hunched over now. "He don't speak. His cheeks are red.
He assists that lady. He's so odd, Mama."

"Really?" Gwen smiled. "He's a good boy, that's what
I think, and handsome, too."

Bridget flushed. "Ugly as a doorpost."

"Be pleasant to him and mind your manners," Gwen
advised, hugging her daughter one more time. And then
she hurried off to catch a trolley uptown.

Bridget walked to the corner and hung on to a dirty
lamppost, watching her mother until she could no longer
see her. Tears stained her cheeks. She hated it when her
mother left looking for a job, because then she was really
alone in this awful place they called New York City. Stiff

with tension now, she glanced warily around.

The boy, Joel, had disappeared, undoubtedly going up to his flat to look after his brothers and sister. In a way, she wished he were still sitting on the stoop. Some heavy women were walking down the block, carrying sacks of groceries, and several men were setting up their carts with merchandise they were selling that day on the street. One was roasting chestnuts. Bridget's tummy growled again. She had two pennies to spend, enough for a chestnut if she wished but also enough for two peppermint candies.

The grocer was sweeping the sidewalk in front of his store. The shoemaker was opening up. Several wagons, loaded up, the goods wrapped in canvas, were going by. A gentleman was walking on the opposite sidewalk, looking terribly out of place.

Bridget froze, her heart stopping, and she took another look. For God's sake, the gent looked like the earl!

For one moment she was terrified and in disbelief, certain it was the earl, but then he turned the corner and was gone. Only then did she begin to breathe.

She was looney, that's what she was, as the earl was in County Clare, at his country estate, or in Sussex, where his father lived. That hadn't been him.

Her spine, however, tingled.

Bridget turned.

Two men were ogling her. One was short and fat, the other bald and chewing tobacco. He spat a wad out, grinning at her.

The grin was lascivious.

Fear paralyzed her.

They started walking toward her.

From the corner of her eye she saw the boy coming out of the building they shared. Relief swamped her and she turned and smiled at him.

He halted in his tracks, his cheeks turning bright red, his eyes widening in comical disbelief.

"Yer name's Joel, right?" Bridget had begun when the sun abruptly disappeared.

The sack thrown over her head smelled of rotting potatoes. Terror overcame her. Hands grabbed her. She could not breathe. She fought wildly as she was lifted up and slung over a beefy shoulder. She tried to scream for help. She choked instead.

"Shut up and we won't hurt you," the man holding her growled. "Be a good girl and you won't get beat. You understand me?"

"Let me go! Let me go! Mama!" Bridget screamed, but no words came out, just hoarse, frantic choked-up sounds. She ripped at the hood over her head.

"Let her go!" the boy shouted ferociously.

"Hey! Ow! Hey! Get that fucking kid! Ow! He bit me!" the man howled.

"Let her go, you bastard!" the boy screamed.

"Owww!" the man shouted, enraged and in pain.

Bridget felt him release her. She landed hard on her shoulder and hip, tearing off the hood, blinking into the bright sunlight.

Joel was on the ground, wrestling with the fat man, whose ankle was bleeding. His pants were short, and Bridget could see he'd been bitten there. Now she crouched, cringing with fear, because the fat man had gotten Joel by a hank of his hair and flipped him onto his back, landing a mean blow to his face. Joel went still.

Was he dead? Bridget was horrified.

A hand seized her braid, jerking her to her feet, and she met steely brown eyes. "Little whore," he said, and he lifted her up and threw her into the back of a rickety wagon.

Terror adrenalized her. She shot up, gripping the backboard, in order to jump out.

He struck her across the face, sending her flying against the side railing, head first. Pain made her see stars.

Her wrists were seized and tied as Joel was thrown into the wagon beside her. He landed on his belly, unmoving, maybe dead. Bridget just glimpsed his awfully pale face before her ankles were seized and tied, and then she was jerked down onto her back. Her captor grinned at her and she could only stare back, mute now with terror. And then he shoved the sack back over her head. The wagon tilted as the two men climbed into the front seat, and it rolled off.

Alone in darkness, the boy dead beside her, Bridget prayed for help.

Francesca grimly faced the handsome mansion that housed the Jewel. She was sick inside, but she refused to think about the failure of her relationship with Calder Hart. Instead, she had a case to solve, children to save. Nevertheless, Calder loomed beside her like a dark and torturous shadow. Breaking up hurt beyond belief.

Still, she had just come from his house. Not that she had wanted to see him, as she had not; in fact, she hoped to never set eyes upon him again. She had gone to visit Dot and Katie. However, the children had been taken to the hospital to visit Leigh Anne at Bragg's request and she had discerned that he had yet to leave Leigh Anne's side. And fortunately, Hart had not been in the residence; he had left for his offices at the crack of dawn that day.

She almost hated him.

Francesca inhaled and started up the three wide front steps of the elegant brick house. It was on the corner of 19th Street and Fifth Avenue; once, it had been a gentleman's home. She had gotten the address from Daisy as well as a small vial of a sleeping potion that she could slip into a drink. And Rose had loaned her the dress she was wearing. It was the color of its mistress's name, with a revealing neckline and black lace-trimmed sleeves and a matching hemline. Francesca had heavily rouged her cheeks and lips and had used kohl on her eyes. She had become amazingly exotic—Francesca Cahill no longer seemed to exist.

The door was answered by a butler who took her card, showed her to an elegant salon, closed both doors, and told her to wait. Extremely curious, finally escaping her thoughts of Calder Hart and the viselike hold he seemed to have on her heart, Francesca gazed openly at her surroundings.

The salon was a pleasant shade of pale green with a huge crystal chandelier and several works of art upon the walls in gilded frames. They seemed French and late-eighteenth-century. The furniture was worn, but the upholstery had once been quite fine, and Francesca suspected that at night one would not notice how tired-looking the furnishings were. She wondered what this room was used for. Did the gentlemen await their escorts here? As she had first come into the house, she had noticed a dining room, as well as a piano in the reception hall. She was simply fascinated, imagining this salon at night, filled with gentlemen, prostitutes, laughter, and conversation.

The double doors swept open.

Francesca turned. A very elegant and very beautiful platinum blond woman stood between both doors, clad in a remarkably simple pale blue dress. Francesca knew it had been costly, that the silk was the finest made. Her heart began to sink. Francesca suspected that Solange Marceaux was only six or seven years older than herself, and she was incredibly elegant and very beautiful. Sick once again, Francesca dropped her gaze from Solange's fine, classic features to her hands. They were milk white. She wore only two rings, a small garnet flanked by two smaller diamonds and a large turquoise stone set in gold. She also wore small diamond earrings shaped like flowers and Francesca knew they were from Asprey.

There was so much dismay, and there was so much hurt. Last night she had experienced joy and ecstasy in Calder Hart's arms. Today he no longer wanted her. And the other night he had sparred with this regal woman, in this illicit and dangerous place, in the darkest hours of the night.

Francesca knew he had found Solange Marceaux attractive. Of that she had no doubt.

"Miss Baron?"

She smiled firmly. "Madame Marceaux?"

"Yes. I'm afraid that while you seem to know me, I do

not know you." She closed both doors, coming gracefully forward. She had the figure of a woman twenty years old.

"I am a friend of Rose. She knows I am currently unoccupied, and the other day she suggested that I call upon you, as she recommends your establishment highly." Francesca smiled more pleasantly now. She had work to do, a mission to accomplish.

Solange lifted both pale brows, as if not quite impressed, and she gestured to a seat. As Francesca sat, she asked, "Would you like some tea and sandwiches?"

"No, thank you." Francesca smiled.

Solange now studied Francesca frankly, looking at her hair—which she had tonged and waved and swept loosely up, beneath the rose felt hat she wore—and then gazing at her darkly shadowed eyes, her cheeks, her nose, her mouth. Francesca told herself not to blush, but she was thoroughly discomfited. Worse, Solange looked directly at her breasts and then at her waist. Finally, she sat down opposite Francesca. "You are quite beautiful," she said.

"Thank you," Francesca said, her cheeks feeling hot.

"Are you blushing?"

"Of course not. I am merely warm," Francesca lied, her hands clasped in her lap.

"I prefer far less cosmetics. The girls here are elegant and underdone."

Francesca was startled. Then she shrugged. "Whatever pleases you, madame."

"I never accept anyone without a written reference," she said calmly.

Francesca smiled, reaching into her bag. She was prepared for this, oh yes. "I have several references," she said, pleased with being so clever. She handed them to Solange.

The minutes now ticked slowly by as Solange read the three letters, clearly word for word. Francesca began to worry a bit and to fidget. The first was a brief note from Rose. The other two were fabrications written by Francesca herself. Surely Madame Marceaux could not tell that the last two were sheer lies. Francesca had made up two fictional madams and was claiming to have worked for the past four years in London. That was a reference that could not be easily checked.

Solange Marceaux finally looked up. "So you have been in London until last month," she said, studying her closely. "I adore London."

Francesca smiled, hoping she was not about to be outwitted. "So do I."

"Then why return to the United States? Clearly you are American," she added.

Francesca did not hesitate. "One of my clients fell in love with me—unfortunately."

"Really? Only one?"

"Oh, I have had dozens of men beg me to marry them," Francesca continued baldly, "but this was different. This man was very prominent in public affairs, and our liaison could only hurt him. You see, I liked him. He was a gentleman. I left so he could enjoy his reputation, unsullied and untarnished." And at that moment, she thought about Rick Bragg with a small, sad pang.

"How noble of you. And what was this gentleman's name?"

Francesca raised her eyebrows. "I beg your pardon. That is information I will not reveal."

"I see." Solange did not bat an eye—it was impossible to tell what she was thinking. Then she said, "I have spent several years in London. In fact, I believe we were there at the same time—in 1899. While I have never heard of Madame Tiffany, Mrs. Stanton was a good friend," she said.

Francesca had made up Mrs. Stanton, and she almost fainted. But she quickly recovered, smiling. She had not provided any details with her supposed reference—no address, no establishment name, nothing. "What a small world we are in."

"Yes. In '99 she was operating from a fine townhouse in Belgravia. Is her club still there?"

Francesca continued to smile, her mind racing. She decided to go for broke. "Actually, as you probably know, there was quite a stir in the neighborhood and a bit of police interference, so Mrs. Stanton decided to move to Knightsbridge."

"Really?" Her pale brows rose again.

Francesca wondered if her smile had turned to plaster. "The new establishment is actually nicer than the first."

"Knightsbridge is a pleasant suburb," was all that Solange Marceaux said.

Did she know? Did she know that Francesca was an impostor? Was there really a madam named Mrs. Stanton? Her brother traveled frequently—had he made an offhand reference that Francesca had somehow subconsciously retained? Or was this a game?

As Hart had said, this woman was undoubtedly a master poker player.

Solange broke the silence just as it became strained. "You seem very well educated, Miss Baron. May I ask if that is the case?"

Francesca did not hesitate. "Yes."

Solange looked questioningly at her.

Francesca shrugged. "My family was genteel. However, it is not my nature to marry, and I was disowned."

"I see. I have heard this story before. You are not bitter?"

Francesca smiled, looking away. "No. I like relations," she added. And images from the night before invaded her mind.

"How old are you?"

"Twenty-three," Francesca lied.

Solange stood. "You are an interesting woman. And your references are impeccable."

Francesca also rose to her feet. Clearly the interview was at an end. Was Solange Marceaux being sarcastic? One could not tell, as her face never changed expression.

"I am willing to try you. I warn you, however, that our customers are demanding."

Francesca also stood, breathless and giddy with delight. *She had won.* "How demanding?" she breathed.

Solange looked at her. "I see this excites you. That is very good." She smiled then, a smile that finally brightened her pale blue eyes.

"How demanding?" Francesca asked again.

"The gentlemen who come to this establishment are looking for pleasure denied them in more conservative brothels. We cater to every need. You will have to be very daring, Miss Baron. The only thing we do not allow is extreme physical punishment. I prefer my ladies alive," she added.

Francesca thought that a good idea. "What should I prepare myself for?"

She did not hesitate. "Costumes, whips and chains, several gentlemen at once, several ladies, orgies, lower-level brutality, bestiality, opium, heroin, cocaine."

Orgies, brutality, bestiality . . . Francesca nodded seriously, hoping she hadn't paled. Dear God, Hart had been right—this was a very sordid place.

And what if something happened tonight, something she could not get out of?

Francesca dismissed the thought, but for the first time, she was alarmed and anxious, even though she carried Daisy's potion in her purse.

"You will enjoy yourself, I think. Of course, some of our clients prefer straight sex or to merely watch their friends carry on wildly." Solange Marceaux shrugged, as if she could not comprehend it. "When can you start?"

"Tonight," Francesca said, hoping it did not sound like an eager question.

Solange nodded. "You receive ten percent of what I charge for you. I always charge exorbitant amounts for the new ladies. Very few retain that pricing. Right now I am pricing you at three hundred dollars an hour—or a thousand dollars for the entire evening. If you prove to me you are worth it, we will keep that price."

Francesca blinked. That was a fortune! But she said arrogantly, "I am worth it."

"I doubt it. Be here this afternoon at four. I will show

you to your room and you will have plenty of time to prepare yourself for the evening. We open at nine, but we do have some preferred customers who may arrive earlier."

Francesca followed her into the reception hall, tingling over her good fortune. "Thank you, Madame Marceaux," she said.

Solange nodded, amusement finally flickering in her eyes. "A word of advice," she said. "You are new. You can expect to be busy for most of the evening. The new ones are always eagerly gobbled up."

Her choice of words—and the look in her eyes—was odd. Francesca was suddenly afraid. But she shrugged, feigning nonchalance. "I am always in demand," she said.

"I hope that is the case," Solange Marceaux said. "Adieu, Miss Baron."

Francesca managed a bright smile. "A bientôt," she said.

CHAPTER
EIGHTEEN

"Sir? This came by messenger. The boy said it was urgent, but there is no name on the envelope."

Hart had just concluded four business meetings, back to back. He was very pleased with the results of two of them—one would enable him to expand his shipping operation to Singapore and Hong Kong. In the other, he had acquired his first van Gogh. He had just begun to smoke a cigar, his intention to enjoy it and the moment of triumph immensely. But it was impossible. For, his day almost done, his thoughts instantly veered to Francesca.

He had done his best to avoid any thought or memory of her all day. Last night he had locked himself in his private den, reviewing the facts he would need to conduct his business the following day. He'd stayed up until four, and then, exhausted, he'd found himself unable to sleep in his bedroom—in the bed they had shared. He'd slept on a sofa in the adjacent sitting room instead.

He'd slept a single hour, washed and shaved, skipped breakfast, and been at his office at half past six. His first meeting had been over breakfast at a private club at eight. He hadn't stopped to breathe—or think—all day.

He jumped to his feet. He did not want to think about her. He did not want to think about how ingenious and clever she was. He did not want to think about how sensual and sexy she was. He did not want to recall her eyes, her smile, her laughter, her touch. *Damn it.*

"Sir?"

He had forgotten his clerk was standing there on the threshold of his huge corner office. Beyond relief, Hart expelled the thick, rich Cuban smoke. "Did you get word from the hospital yet?" he heard himself ask. He'd sent a clerk over to Bellevue three times thus far that day. Leigh Anne had taken a turn for the worse.

Edward, a lanky young man with thin blond hair and a darker mustache, now entered the spacious room. He was holding a sealed envelope. "Rodney should be back at any moment, sir."

Hart nodded grimly, more images flashing in his mind. Leigh Anne, as still and pale as a corpse, with Bragg grimly hunched over her unmoving form.

"Let me see that," he said, putting down his cigar. Once, he would have been mildly interested and somewhat amused by an unsigned and hand-delivered note. It would have signified an unusual business deal or the beginning of an illicit affair. Not anymore. Now, he could not care less.

He slit the envelope with an ivory-handled knife and pulled out a costly sheet of creamy stationery. The script was flawless and floral. His eyes widened slightly as he read.

> *My dear Mr. Hart,*
> *I have been able to resolve the matter we recently discussed. Please stop by my place of*

business at your earliest convenience, tonight if you wish.

> *Sincerely,*
> *Solange Marceaux*

Hart carefully folded the letter, his mind racing, smiling a little now. Solange Marceaux had procured a child for him. He would go by the Jewel that evening and, he hoped, end this sordid case once and for all. How he wanted to tell Francesca.

But that was not a good idea. Not when she must be given a chance to follow her own heart. He stood. It was time he paid a visit to his brother anyway. "Edward, have Raoul ready my carriage. Cancel my last appointment. I am going to Bellevue myself."

She had stopped crying a long time ago. Bridget sat on the floor in a corner of a bare room, furnished only with one bureau and a big bed, hugging her knees to her chest. She continued to shake sporadically, convulsively, and even her teeth would chatter then. The two men who had captured her had deposited her on that bed at least two hours ago, while untying her and removing the hood. The moment she was free, she had scrambled off the bed and into the corner, where she had been sitting ever since. They had left immediately, locking the door behind them, but she remained frozen with fear.

The dead boy had been dropped on the floor, not far from the door.

Bridget looked at him and threw up, not for the first time. A tear crept down her cheek.

She was so scared. How would Mama find her and save her? She knew what those men wanted; she had seen it in their eyes. She wasn't a fool. She had seen Papa in bed with Mama, quite a few times, and even if she hadn't, she'd heard them often enough, because their cottage in County Clare had had one room, and their bed had been separated from hers by a thin curtain. She'd even seen Mama, once, by the brook, in the earl's arms. Mama had been smiling. Bridget had never seen her so happy. She'd been as beautiful as an angel.

The earl had been smiling and happy, too.

Bridget choked. She was never going back home, not to that horrid little flat, but to Ireland, and she'd never see Papa again, but even worse, she'd never see Mama, and Mama would die from the grief of it.

She screwed her eyes closed shut. How long did she have until those men came back? Mama wasn't going to save her. She had to think, but it was so hard because she was so scared. She had to think of a way to get free.

Something made a sound in the room, by the door.

The noise had been a slight scratch, and Bridget froze, looking around warily for a rat. She hated rats. Some were bigger than small dogs. If there was a rat in the room, it would eat the dead boy. She had to find something to kill it.

She heard a soft sigh.

Bridget climbed slowly, shakily, to her feet. She scanned the room but didn't see a rat. Her gaze slammed back to the boy. And this time, he moaned.

For one moment, she froze, disbelieving—first the two brutes, then a rat, and now a ghost? And then she saw his thick sooty lashes flutter.

The boy wasn't dead!

Bridget ran to him, gasping in relief. She sank to her knees, cradling his head. There was so much blood from where the fat man had punched him. "Boy? Boy?" she whispered urgently, and then she gave up. She knew his name—she'd only pretended not to because he was always ogling her. "Joel! Wake up! How badly are ye hurt?"

He groaned, long and low.

She held him in her lap, wanting to slap his face because he had to wake up before those two men came back, but hitting him seemed mean, even cruel. She shook his thin shoulders instead. "Joel, it's me, Bridget! Bridget O'Neil!

Please wake up! We got to get outta here!" she cried.

His eyes slowly opened and he gazed up at her, clearly unfocused.

Had the blow to his head made him daft? "Can ye see me? D' ye know who I am? Talk t' me, ye fool!"

And she saw the comprehension begin to fill his gaze. "Bridget?" he whispered in some confusion.

"Thank God yer alive—I thought they killed ye, I did!" And she hugged him hard, then realized what she was about and backed away, still on her knees beside him.

He sat up stiffly, wincing, his hand going to his head. The color was returning to his face, thank the good blessed Lord. He then took his hand from his head and looked at it as if he didn't know his own hand. It was bloody.

Instantly Bridget ripped off a piece of her skirt. The material was so thin from so many wearings and washings that it tore easily. "I thought ye were dead," she said, moving closer. She quickly wrapped the strip around his head. "D' ye remember what happened?"

"Oh, yeah," he said hoarsely, his eyes turning dark.

Their gazes met.

Bridget saw the fierce determination in his eyes and she shuddered.

"How long have we been here? Ouch!" He shoved her hand away.

"Let me knot it, brat," she said firmly, but inwardly she was thrilled. The boy wasn't dead, and from the look if it, she had a partner to help her—them—escape.

He shoved her hand away and stood, no longer appearing at all shaky. "You're younger than me an' that makes you the brat," he warned. He tied a knot in the bandage himself. "Well? How long have we been here? An' where are we?"

"I think it's been a few hours. It's hard to say," she said, also getting to her feet, the side of her skirt exposing her stocking-clad calf and the holes in it. "I don't know where we are. They put a smelly old sack on my head and I couldn't see a thing!"

Joel walked over to the door and tried it.

"It's locked," she said, aware she was stating the obvious.

He gave her a dismissive look. "Give me a hairpin," he said.

"I don't got any hairpins, me hair's in a braid," she said, hands on her hips.

He looked disgusted, but he went over to the bed, wrinkling up his nose as he tossed up the thin sheets.

She instantly understood. That bed had been used by a man and a woman—even she could smell the sex—and he was looking for missing hairpins. How clever he was!

He grinned at her, holding up a long but misshapen hairpin. "Look at that."

She began to smile, then frowned. "What use do you got for a hairpin?"

"I'm gonna pick me a lock," he said with another smug grin.

She was incredulous, and she watched him straighten the pin and then march over to the door. She hurried, following and standing so close behind him that her budding breasts brushed his back. He jerked a little and she stepped back, watching as he slid the pin into the lock, gently moving it about. The lock snapped open almost immediately.

"Oh, my God!" she gasped. "Are ye a burglar then?"

"Naw, I gave up them days when I met Miz Cahill," he said, giving her a look. "Stand back. I need to make sure no one's outside the door."

Bridget hurried to obey.

Joel slowly cracked open the door, inch by inch, until he could peer outside. And then he closed it as slowly—as soundlessly.

"What'd ye see?" she breathed.

"Ain't no one about," he said, "and there's a stairs at the end of the hall and a window to our left."

She nodded, uncertain. "But do ye want to simply march out? Surely those horrible men are downstairs?"

"We're going to jump out the window," he said.

Bridget swallowed nervously. "All right," she whispered.

"C'mon." He took her hand. "Maybe there's a tree outside."

She prayed they were on the second floor and that there was big fat oak tree outside the window. Even more, she prayed they would not be caught while escaping. Joel slowly opened the door again, still holding her hand. His grasp was warm and reassuring. He was so brave that she had to sneak a real glance at him.

"C'mon," he whispered.

They slipped into the empty hall and hurried past several closed doors and to the closed window. Joel released her hand to push it open, a task that took him a long moment, as it was stuck. Finally, the heavy glass slid upward. Bridget strained to look past him and cried out. They were very high up and the tree in the backyard was too far away to be of any use. "We'll break our necks!" she cried.

Joel hesitated before facing her. "You stay here. I'll climb down as if it's a cliff. Then I'll get help."

"Ye can't climb down the side of a building!" she gasped. "And I don't want to stay here!"

Joel had started to speak when they both heard footsteps on the stairs. "Ye don't got a choice!" he cried, pushing her aside.

"Wait," she began, terrified, but he was climbing through the window as she spoke.

"Hey! Hey! It's the new girl—and the boy's going out the window!" The fat thug was almost on the landing.

Joel paused astride the window ledge. "I'll be back," he promised.

"Hurry," Bridget breathed, glancing back toward the stairs.

Both men were racing toward her and she turned to bar their way.

"Get the boy!" the tall one shouted.

Joel smiled at her and disappeared from view.

Bridget stuck her foot out, tripping the fat man, who had

hit Joel so hard his head was a bloody mess. As he went down, she felt a savage satisfaction fill her.

"You little bitch!" The tall man grabbed her and threw her aside, leaping at the window.

Bridget reached out and grabbed his trousers.

He cursed, turning and trying to kick her off.

She clung with all of her might.

The fat man hit her, and as her world went black, she heard one say, "Shit! The kid made it to the street. C'mon! Before he gets away!"

The blackness was a relief.

It was a bit past four and she was late.

Francesca had expected to be greeted by Solange Marceaux herself, but instead, a stunning brunette who was about her own age appeared, clad in a flimsy satin wrapper and embroidered high-heeled shoes. "Emerald?"

Francesca was going by the name Emerald Baron. "Hello," she said with false cheer. She was now as nervous as she was exhilarated. She was also clutching the dress loaned to her by the countess, as it was carefully wrapped in paper.

"I'm Dawn." The brunette smiled. "Come. Let me show you to your room."

Francesca nodded and followed Dawn through the hall and past the piano, where the pianist was beginning to play. He was a young man close to their own age and he ogled Dawn as she passed, then smiled at Francesca. Dawn might as well have been naked in her flimsy robe, and she wiggled her behind a little as she passed the pianist. "Fred is a lovely boy," she said. She gave Francesca a wink.

Francesca assumed they were lovers. She managed a smile and had a bad feeling that the night might not turn out the way that she wanted it to.

"This is your room. Lovely, isn't it?" Dawn asked, allowing Francesca to precede her inside.

Francesca was surprised. The room was lovely, with pale

ivory walls and accents of pink and green. The bed was a big four-poster, which she refused to look at. There was a fireplace with a marble mantel, and a cheerful eating area in front of it. She laid her purse on the gilded bureau and turned.

"Here, let me hang that up," Dawn said, taking the dress from Francesca and unwrapping it. "Well, this will certainly gain you a few admirers," she said with a wicked grin.

"That is the plan," Francesca said, and then realized her choice of words was unfortunate.

Dawn laughed. "Tea?" She moved sinuously to the sofa, where a silver tray with a teapot, saucers and cups, and some petits fours was placed. She poured.

Francesca sat down and smoothed her rose-colored skirts. "How long have you been working here?" she asked.

Dawn slid onto the sofa, revealing her gartered thighs as she did so. "About a year. It's a nice place to work. Most of the women here are friendly, and it's not too competitive," she said.

Francesca almost echoed, "Competitive?" but managed to stop herself.

"Of course, one never knows how an evening will go. Some of the gentlemen here are quite odd in their requests," she said, sending Francesca a sly look. "You look so ladylike. You will be very popular, I think."

"I hope so," Francesca managed.

"We had a Spanish prince, recently," Dawn said, as if she hadn't heard Francesca. "He was so handsome. I prayed he would choose me—and he did! Me and five other women. He was simply insatiable, Emerald, but of course, he used a cock ring." She made a face.

Francesca somehow smiled. A cock ring?

"It was three days before he tired. Needless to say, we all made a fortune, as we were so exhausted and so sore that Madame Marceaux charged him ten thousand dollars for the orgy."

"That's a lot of money," Francesca whispered, afraid her cheeks were red. What was a cock ring? She would ask

Hart—except she wasn't speaking to him, so she could not. She reminded herself that she needed information, not titillation. "What is it like, working for Madame Marceaux?"

Dawn shrugged. "But my favorite client was this boy. It was his fifteenth birthday. His father brought him in. He chose me. No artifices, no devices, no aids. He was huge, too, and he went all night. I must say, I have never had so many orgasms." She glanced seductively at Francesca.

"I am very pleased that Madame Marceaux has given me this opportunity to work here," Francesca said, aware now that she was most definitely in over her head.

"She knows how to choose her ladies of the night," Dawn breathed. "You are so beautiful and you will be good for business."

"She seems a determined businesswoman," Francesca tried.

"Do not try to cheat her," Dawn laughed. "You won't last a minute if you do."

Francesca almost winced. Cheating undoubtedly included conning and lying, didn't it? "How long has she been the madam here?"

"I don't know." Dawn straightened from her indolent position beside Francesca. "Are you interested in Solange, Emerald?"

"What?" Francesca gaped.

"Oh." Dawn laughed then. "I thought maybe . . ." She trailed off and lightly touched Francesca's hand.

"I am interested in having a mutually productive relationship with her."

Dawn smiled. "Let's have a glass of wine." She stood, her robe gaping open again, this time revealing bare, plump breasts.

Francesca looked quickly away. "She seems very fair," she said unevenly.

Solange had pulled a chilled bottle of white burgundy from a wine cooler. She shrugged. "I adore Madame. Everyone does."

Francesca sensed the opposite was true. Clearly, Dawn

had no wish to discuss their employer. "Does she ever entertain?" Francesca had asked curiously, recalling how Hart had suggested she entertain him by sleeping with Rose.

Dawn faced her, a glass of white wine in each hand. "Very rarely," she said briskly.

Francesca decided to change topics before her questions became suspicious. "We are allowed to imbibe?"

"As long as we don't get drunk," Dawn said, handing Francesca a drink and sliding her hand over her shoulder. "Madame Marceaux prefers alcohol to drugs. And she does like us to be uninhibited."

The hand slid away, a soft caress. Francesca stiffened, alarmed. Was this woman making a sexual overture? She glanced across the room at her purse, now on the bureau. In it was the vial she had gotten from Daisy.

Dawn sank down on the sofa, somewhat close to Francesca. She smiled. "Yummy," she said.

Francesca took a hasty sip. "What can I expect tonight? A Spanish prince?" She laughed and it sounded nervous to her own ears.

Dawn eyed her. "Just about anything. But I am sure Madame told you if it gets too rough, you may call for help. Most of the men here, though, are not interested in violence. They prefer perversions."

"Perversions?" Francesca said with real worry.

"One man wished for me to perform for him with a dog," Dawn smiled.

Francesca's shock was acute. She quickly began sipping her wine. It was hard not to choke.

"He brought his Great Dane," she laughed then. "It was so odd."

Francesca swallowed and took a breath. Her fertile imagination rescuing her, Francesca said, "Yes, dogs were quite popular in London."

"Kittens are nice," Dawn now purred. She gave her a look. "We don't even need a man for that."

Her mind raced. What was Dawn talking about? And

this was off the track, oh yes. "Kittens are lovely," Francesca agreed.

Dawn smiled. "All those little tongues. I can get us some kittens if you wish."

Francesca stiffened. Her gaze locked with Dawn's. There was simply no mistaking her meaning.

Dawn stood. "I want to make love to you—for pure pleasure . . . for us. Not for some fat old bastard with rotten breath."

Francesca also stood. "Is that allowed?" she managed to ask.

Dawn shrugged. "Solange prefers us to make money with our bodies. She doesn't have to know. However, I do have a client coming tonight. He would love to watch us, Emerald. If you are afraid of Solange," she added slyly.

Was this really happening? "Yes, of course," she breathed. She quickly debated the best way to get out of the situation she was now in. Running out the front door seemed the wisest course.

Dawn seized her arm. "You've never done this before, have you?" she asked quietly, unsmiling, her dark eyes penetrating.

Francesca blinked. "Of course I have—"

"You're a virgin and a lady, aren't you?" Dawn asked as quietly. Her stare never wavered.

Francesca could only stare back in return. And then she looked at the door. It was solidly closed.

"Why are you here?" Dawn asked. But she didn't seem angry. She was wary and watchful, but not angry.

Francesca swallowed hard and took her hand. She could not believe her own audacity, but if Dawn was attracted to her, she would use that now, for the sake of the children. "I am a sleuth," she said, "and I am begging you for your help."

Dawn stared into her eyes and then down at their clasped hands. A frisson of fear swept over Francesca as Dawn looked up at her, now tightening her grasp on Francesca's palm. "Tell me what you want. And maybe, I can be convinced to help."

And Dawn smiled a little at her before letting her go.

CHAPTER NINETEEN

HIS HEAD WAS BLEEDIN' again. And it hurt like the dickens. Joel had left the deceptively pleasant brick house where he and Bridget had been imprisoned at a run—now he was limping and finding it impossible to breathe. He'd sprained his ankle in the fall, or worse. He had a hammer bangin' in his head. But Mulberry Bend was around the corner. *He had made it.*

But Bridget remained in that place with those two bad men. Joel's first instinct had been to rush uptown to find Miss Cahill, but that would take too long. Going downtown to Bridge Street to get help from Mr. Hart would also take too long. As much as Joel hated and feared the police, the brown six-story building that was police headquarters had just come into view. His limping gait increased. So did his fear.

What if no one believed him? What if they threw him in the cooler and hid the key? It might be days, weeks, months, years before anyone found him, before he could go home and be free! He'd heard stories like that, terrible stories, of the damned flies taking innocent boys and men away from their families, puttin' 'em in the Tombs, throwing away the key, and laughin' about it. He hated the flies more than he hated anyone.

But the boss of the flies wasn't as bad as the rest. Joel had to grudgingly admit that. He paused before the stone steps leading to the reception lobby, trembling. He'd never walked in alone, not of his own free will, before. But there'd been plenty of times when he'd been dragged in by his hair or his ear, caught in the act of snatchin' a purse or just after. Then he thought of Bridget.

What if they were hurting her even as he stood there, bein' a real jackass, a real coward?

He launched himself up the steps.

Two of the flies were coming out the front doors as he went in. They didn't look at him, not even once, as if he didn't even exist, as if he were invisible or something.

Joel froze, staring at the reception counter, in real dismay. He didn't recognize any of the officers on duty there.

He heard some arguing and saw two drunks in the holding pen. He looked back at the front desk, debating what to do. Maybe he should just go upstairs and find Bragg.

He turned and started running for the stairs.

"Hey! Hey! Hey, you! Kid, stop!"

Joel ran faster, reaching the stairs.

"Stop that kid!"

Joel bounded up the first flight and turned the corner as two men who were detectives were coming down.

"Stop him!"

The detectives realized what was happening and reached for him. Joel dodged one hand, then another, making it to the landing. He raced up the hall, footsteps sounding behind him with more cries.

The door to Commissioner Bragg's office was closed. There was no time to knock. Joel grabbed the knob, barging in. And he halted, incredulous and disbelieving, because the chair behind the desk was empty.

A beefy hand clamped down on his thin shoulder from behind. "Got you!" the man said.

Joel tried to turn but could not, as his hands were quickly twisted behind him and manacled. "I got to speak to the commissioner!" he screamed.

"Like hell you do, boy," a big, beefy detective sneered. "Looks like we got us a breakin' and enterin', now don't we!"

The other detective and an officer who had been at the front desk came into the room. "Crazy kid," the officer said, shaking his head.

"I ain't crazy!" Joel cried, and to his horror, he thought of Bridget, and tears filled his eyes. "Me friend's been abducted, her name is Bridget, but I escaped and she needs help before they hurt her!"

"Yeah, right," the big detective laughed. "Toss him in the pen with the drunks. I'll file the charges."

The officer seized Joel by the elbow and began to pull him from Bragg's office. "Kid's bleedin' in the head," he remarked. "Think we should look at it?"

"What is this, Bellevue?" The detective was mocking.

"Ye got to help me friend!" Joel cried. "Please! Or at least tell the commissioner. He'll help, I know he will!"

"Shut up," the detective said, slapping Joel across the face.

Joel cried out in response to the painful, brutal slap. Now he tasted blood from where he had bitten his lip. As he was dragged down the stairs, he found his voice. "Fuck you," he snarled. Hatred filled him.

The detective turned to strike him again.

Joel couldn't stand straight and tall; he flinched.

The officer grabbed the beefy detective's arm. "Don't beat on the kid," he said.

Joel's heart was pounding hurtfully in his chest. He smiled rudely at the fat detective.

The beefy man smiled as meanly back. "Guess we'll add

petty theft to those charges, boy," and he shoved some pencils and paper clips into Joel's pockets.

Joel stared in growing horror. Breaking and entering, petty theft—he was going to go to jail for real this time!

The detective laughed and walked past them.

Tears filled Joel's eyes. "They're going to hurt Bridget," he whispered forlornly. "I need to speak to Bragg, please." He knew he was begging and couldn't stop as he faced the somewhat kindly officer. "Tell him it's Joel Kennedy. He'll speak to me."

"The commissioner is not coming in today, boy," the officer said as he approached the cell holding two drunks. One was sleeping on the floor now, the other urinating in a corner. "Hey, you, Artie! Use the damn pot, okay?"

Artie nodded with a foolish grin, continuing what he was doing.

Joel was desperate. "Then I got to find Miz Cahill," he said. "Please, sir, I got to speak with Miz Cahill!"

The officer halted in amazement. "Francesca Cahill? The sleuth?"

He nodded eagerly. "She's my friend. An' I work with her. She's on a case right now, her and the commissioner, and I know where the missing girls are kept. I just come from there, sir. An' that's why I got to speak to Commissioner Bragg or Miz Cahill or both of them."

The officer stared. Then, reaching for the key ring hanging outside the cell, he said, "I'm not bothering the commissioner, not when his wife is in the hospital. But I'll try to get a message to Miss Cahill. Not that I think you're telling the truth, because I don't," he added. "But it can't hurt to send a man."

"Number eight-ten Fifth Avenue," Joel cried eagerly. "That's where she lives!"

The officer was opening the cell; he blinked, wide-eyed, taken aback. "Maybe you are telling the truth," he mused. "Go on, boy."

Joel entered the cell, gripping the bars. "Just find Miz Cahill," he said.

The door closed; a moment later it was locked.

. . .

They were all there, just as he had expected them to be. Hart stared from the threshold of the hospital room. Bragg sat slumped in the chair closest to Leigh Anne, and, although holding her hand, he appeared to be asleep. Grace sat beside him. Rathe stood by the window, staring out, and Rourke sat on a stool at the foot of the bed, thumbing through an issue of *Harper's Weekly.*

The toll appeared to be telling on them all, Hart thought. Grace was pale and appeared exhausted; Rathe looked strained and unshaven, as did Rourke. And as for his half brother, well, he looked more like a zombie than a living man.

Pity stirred. Hart pushed it away. He refused to feel sorry for the man who held Francesca's heart so carelessly in his own two hands.

"Refreshments, anyone?" Nicholas D'Archand appeared beside Calder, a tray containing mugs of coffee and pastries in his hands. "Hello, Calder." His smile turned into a grimace.

Everyone started, turning, except for Rick, who awoke and yawned, rubbing his face. Nick entered the room, setting the tray down on a cart and handing out coffee as if a soldier on duty in a battlefield. Hart still hadn't stepped into the room. He stared again at his brother's slumped shoulders. Rick now leaned forward, tucking some wisps of hair behind Leigh Anne's ear. She looked, Hart thought with pity he could no longer control, like death warmed over.

Rourke approached. "About time," he remarked dryly.

Hart met his gaze. "Is there any good news?"

Rourke hesitated, their gazes locked. "I'm afraid not."

So this was it, then. The moment of truth approached. For Francesca—and for himself.

And Rourke knew. He clasped Hart's arm. "I'm sorry. Thank you for coming, Calder," he said quietly.

Knowing the end was so near—not just for Leigh Anne, but for him and Francesca—made it hard to speak.

Rourke started.

Hart sensed a presence and turned.

Sarah Channing smiled nervously from behind him. Her big brown eyes were huge and filled with worry and compassion, and they were on Rourke, not him. She held flowers. There was an odd green color—paint—on her hand. "I just heard. I'm so sorry," she whispered.

Rourke recovered, coming forward. "It's good of you to come. You didn't have to." His gaze held hers.

Now it was Hart's turn to be surprised as he watched them. For the first time, he saw what Francesca had suggested, and he thought, *So that is how the wind blows; how odd.* He was even more surprised when Sarah slipped her hand into Rourke's, squeezing his palm. Rourke reacted instantly—he pulled Sarah close and embraced her hard, his eyes closed, his expression giving way to anguish and despair. Then he released her. "I am sorry," he said grimly.

"It's all right," Sarah whispered, her eyes filling with tears.

"Would you take a walk with me?" Rourke asked. "I need a bit of air."

Sarah nodded.

As they left, Hart entered the room. He went first to Grace, who smiled tearfully at him. He kissed her cheek and she took his hand and clung to it as if it were the line to a life preserver and she were adrift in stormy seas.

Rathe came over and slapped Hart's back, then tugged on his wife's arm. Grace stood, gestured to Nicholas, and the three of them left the room, leaving Hart alone with his half brother.

Bragg glanced at Hart. He was clearly agonized and he looked miserable. And in that instant, as their gazes locked, an image became so clear it was as if the past had become alive and he was ten years old again. They were no longer in a hospital room. They were in the sordid one-bedroom flat where they had lived for as long as Calder could remember. Lily lay on the bed, impossibly beautiful, with her ivory skin and raven black hair, dying. Rick held a glass of water to her lips, but she was so weak, she could not sip it. Calder watched from the foot of the bed, knowing the end was near, wishing desperately that his mother would wake up, one last time, and swearing to God that he would never ever speak to Him again if she died. But the fear was stronger than the anger, and tears slid in a silent stream down his face. He was afraid, afraid, so afraid to be left alone.

Don't die, he kept thinking. *Please don't die!* Panic laced his fear, choking him.

"Please drink, Mother," Rick whispered. He was sweating profusely, holding the chipped cup to her lips. Calder wondered if he was afraid, too. He didn't think so. Because his older brother was always so brave and so strong, always doing what was right—always berating Calder for doing what was wrong.

Which was why Lily loved him best.

Lily's lids fluttered and stilled.

Calder stiffened like a shot. "Is she . . . ?" He could not get the word *dead* out.

Rick turned to look at him, pale and wide-eyed with anguish. Then he put his ear to his mother's chest.

Calder couldn't stand it. He turned and ran out, out of the sour-smelling bedroom, a room that had smelled like death for weeks and weeks, out of the dirty, squalid flat, out of the rotting building. In the street, he continued to run. He dodged carts and wagons, horses and mules, people, running as fast and as hard as he could. How could she leave him? He was terrified now. Tears blinded his vision.

Someone shouted at him. He tripped in the street and fell on his hands and knees, but the cart veered around him, the driver cursing at him. Then he felt someone seize him by his shoulder, and he knew it was Rick before he turned and saw him.

"Let me go!" he shouted, twisting.

"Do you want to die, too?" Rick screamed at him, dragging him to his feet.

"Get off of me!" Then he stopped. His heart seemed to stop beating, too. "Is she . . . ?"

Rick met his gaze and shook his head. "No. Not . . . yet." And he seized his arm. "We have to go back. She needs us."

He tried to pull away and failed. Every day seemed to be the last one, yet somehow, it wasn't. He wanted her to live, but knew she wouldn't—and he didn't need a doctor to tell him that. But with the relief there was more fear and so much exhaustion. He couldn't bear seeing her that way anymore. It hurt too much. He couldn't bear the smell of death. "She needs you."

"C'mon." Rick spoke as if he hadn't heard him. "We need to get back. I got to see if Doc Cooper will come."

"Cooper won't come 'cause we can't pay him." Calder pulled his arm free. When he was a man, he was never going to be poor again. Being poor was for lackwits, for fools. One day, he would be so rich that he could buy anything he wanted—even life, for someone he loved. For someone like Lily.

Hart shook himself free of the vivid memory, one that still vaguely hurt. Lily had lingered on for another few days, hadn't she? It was hard to recall, when it was so easy to see himself as a young, dirty, skinny boy, his brother there beside him—older, bigger, braver. It was odd, but he couldn't recall the day she had died.

Hart shook his head, cleared his vision until the two boys had disappeared and only the adult Rick Bragg remained. He walked slowly over and Rick looked up. There was a question in his eyes as their gazes met.

Hart clasped his shoulder. "I'm very sorry," he said, meaning it.

Rick started slightly, then relaxed, nodding. "Thank you."

"Is there anything I can do?" And he realized that even his power and wealth could not save Leigh Anne's life.

Rick stared. After a pause, he said, "No."

Hart nodded and pulled up the chair Grace had vacated.

He sat down, determined not to squirm, and watched Leigh Anne dying.

The first customers were arriving and Francesca was filled with dread, standing on the landing above the main floor. If she had gotten into such a difficult situation with Dawn, what would happen once she went downstairs? She could barely imagine; she only prayed that Dawn would not expose her real identity. Dawn had listened to her account of the case she was working on, but if she cared at all about the missing girls, Francesca had not been able to tell. She had given Francesca an odd look and walked away without another word. Francesca had not seen her since.

And what did that mean? As Francesca listened to the soft rumble of male voices, mingled with Solange's graceful softer tones, as the pianist began to play a pleasant classical tune, she wondered if her charade were already over. Had Dawn spoken to Solange? And if so, why hadn't she been tossed out on her backside? Or was Dawn playing her own waiting game, hoping to lure Francesca into her bed? As shocking as that notion was, it was far better than Dawn telling Solange the truth.

Francesca dreaded going downstairs.

She was perspiring and her face felt flushed. She reminded herself that she was in the Jewel for one reason and one reason only—to find out if it trafficked in children and, if not, find out where a brothel that did was. She had yet to attain any useful information, and she had to play this out. After all, the one thing she was not was a coward.

Francesca looked down at her legs. She hated the Countess Benevente's dress. She felt naked in it. The layer of gold lace appeared to expose her flesh, but in fact, the chiffon underneath was a nude color. The dress also slithered down her every curve. Where could the countess have worn this dress? It would never be accepted in polite society, and Francesca was afraid it had only been worn to some bacchanal in Italy.

"Would you like me to accompany you downstairs?" Dawn asked from behind.

Francesca whirled and saw the brunette standing just behind her in a beautiful ruby-red gown. But while low-cut, the gown wasn't half as daring as Francesca's dress. "I seem to have lost my courage," Francesca said nervously.

"I don't blame you," Dawn said, glancing up and down.

Francesca winced.

"You should not be here, Emerald." She gave her a look, clearly indicating that she knew the false name was just that.

Francesca waited for a pretty redhead to pass them on the stairs before she spoke. "You know why I am here. I have no choice," she said in a low voice.

"This is not a place for ladies. I didn't lie about the prince or the dog or anything else," Dawn said. She seemed grim.

"Why do you care? If I get into trouble, it's my problem, isn't it? After all, you don't seem to care about the missing girls," Francesca said very quietly.

Dawn stared at her and a pause ensued. "Would you consider sleeping with me?"

Francesca stiffened, thought about the children, but said, "No."

"I didn't think so." Dawn sighed. "A child was brought here a few hours ago."

"What?" Francesca cried.

Dawn touched her mouth with her fingers. "Ssh. Her name is Rachael and a customer is coming for her tonight. I wanted to speak with her, but she is being guarded as if she is a royal treasure and I could not get into her room. Nor will anyone say where she came from," Dawn added.

Francesca was shaking with excitement. "That must be Rachael Wirkler!" She seized Dawn's hands. "Which room is she in?"

"The last one on our floor, on the right," Dawn said. "But Joseph is up there, outside her door."

Francesca nodded, thinking. She would need a diversion. Perhaps Dawn could provide it. But she had to get to Rachael and find out where she was being kept. For surely that was where all the girls were!

Dawn slid her fingers over her arm. "We should go downstairs. Before Solange sends someone for us."

Francesca balked. "I have to speak to Rachael."

"You cannot. Not now, anyway. We can find a time later."

"We?" Francesca stared.

Dawn shrugged. Their gazes locked.

"Thank you," Francesca whispered.

Dawn made a disparaging sound. "Once, a long time ago, I was somebody somewhat like you." She shrugged again, linked arms with Francesca, and they started downstairs. "I think you should slip out the back door and come back with the police. Rachael will be here for a few hours, at least."

Her plan made sense. Francesca smiled at her. "Is there a back door?" she asked.

"Straight down the hall, but unfortunately, you'll have to go past Solange's office and suite."

Francesca nodded as they stepped into the reception hall, scanning the gathering crowd. Six or seven gentlemen had already arrived and were sipping flutes of champagne, some of them accompanied by the ladies of the house. Francesca saw Solange by the front door, with the doorman—and Hart.

She cried out.

"What is it?" Dawn asked quickly.

She clamped her hand over her mouth in horror as Solange apparently greeted the newly arrived Hart. He handed his coat and gloves to a valet, smiling at the madam and greeting her in return.

"Someone you know?" Dawn asked.

"Yes," Francesca whispered fearfully. She no longer recalled that Hart wished to break off their engagement; she only knew that if he saw her now there would be hell to pay.

"Calder Hart," Dawn murmured, following her gaze.

"He was here the other night." She glanced curiously at Francesca.

"I have to hide!" Francesca cried. She stepped back, behind Dawn.

Dawn turned to gape at her. "I don't think you can hide in that dress."

"I don't think so, either," a blond young man said with a grin. His eyes were bright with appreciation as he bowed to both ladies. "Philip Seymour's the name. And the pleasure is all mine."

Francesca looked past Philip frantically and saw the moment Hart spotted her. He and Solange had begun to walk into the reception hall and he halted right in his tracks, stumbling. And briefly his gaze was riveted on her, wide with shock and sheer disbelief.

Had the situation been otherwise, his stunned expression would have been comical.

And instantly his surprise vanished, an expressionless mask slipping into place.

Francesca turned her back to him, praying, but God only knew for what.

"And your name is?" Philip was asking, reaching for her hand and taking it to his lips.

And he actually kissed her flesh. Francesca could only stare blankly at him.

"Her name is Emerald," Dawn said quickly, "and she is new here."

"I can see that." Philip grinned. "Damn, being new, you will be too pricey for me. I'll have to wait a week, at least!"

Francesca pulled her hand free, unable to even attempt to smile at him. She glanced back over her shoulder with more horror, more dread.

She was expecting to see Hart charging her like a bull seeing red. But he was chatting politely with Solange and another gentleman, someone he seemed to know. Relief flooded her then—he wasn't going to expose her, at least. And her mind began to race. If Hart was here—and Rachael had just arrived—then hopefully she had been brought for him. More relief made her weak in the knees. Hart could take care of Rachael and learn where she had come from while Francesca escaped and got the police.

"Bloody hell. Hart can pay your price."

Francesca jerked to look at Philip Seymour. "I'm sorry," she said. "This is all so new and I am very nervous tonight."

He took her hand again. "Honey, you don't have to be nervous, not in that dress." He smiled and raised her hand to his lips.

Her stomach turned and she tugged it away before he could kiss it again. "Until next week," she promised firmly.

He clearly liked that, never mind that she had lost any ability to be seductive or coy, as he grinned and turned away.

"You need to get out of here," Dawn advised. "Because you looked like a frightened fawn a moment ago and you seem to have forgotten how to flirt."

"Hart is working with me," Francesca said quickly. Dawn looked surprised. "If you need help—or if you learn anything—tell him. And I'm quite certain Rachael was brought here for him."

Dawn nodded. "I begin to see. We have to mingle. *You* have to mingle. And at some point, when Solange is not present, you need to leave."

Francesca nodded. Had the woman not wanted to sleep with her, she would have hugged her. "Thank you so much."

Dawn laughed softly. "Another time, Emerald."

"It's Francesca," she whispered.

Dawn started, smiled, and glided away.

Francesca was alone. She inhaled, turned, and came face-to-face with Solange Marceaux. She almost gasped.

"Is something wrong?" Solange asked.

"No." Francesca smiled.

"I see you have your first admirer," she said.

"Yes, Philip Seymour. He is looking forward to the day when he can afford me," Francesca said quickly. Hart was now with two women, both of whom were acting far too seductive. He was being far too pleasant to them in return. Was he enjoying himself? She realized she was staring and forced her gaze back to Solange.

"No. I meant Dawn," Solange said calmly.

Francesca started as her gaze locked with the other woman's. She did not miss a thing! What else had she seen?

Solange smiled and it did not reach her eyes. "You did not tell me you also worked in Paris."

Francesca froze and tried to think. Had Solange seen Hart's reaction to her? Had he said something to cover it up? He was so clever—no one could outwit him. "I also worked in Hong Kong for two months," Francesca said softly.

And perhaps, just perhaps, Solange was surprised. "Mr. Hart has his plans for the evening. However, he wishes to renew your acquaintance briefly first. He is your first customer, my dear. Unfortunately, he only paid for an hour." Then she smiled. "Fortunately, he paid triple what I was asking. You must be very good in bed."

Francesca smiled grimly. Hart had detached both women from his arms and was walking toward her and Solange. She knew him well. His stride was very purposeful. Inwardly she quaked.

Solange seemed to lift a brow as she shifted so she could watch their "reunion."

"My darling Emerald," he murmured, his lashes hooding his eyes. "How wonderful to find you here."

She tried not to wince. "Calder. It has been a long time."

"Such a long time." Both slashing black brows lifted and he finally looked up—directly at her. "I wish I had known you were here. I would have reserved my entire evening for you . . . darling."

His face was perfectly composed; however, his eyes were not; they glittered, hot and dangerously black. "Another time?" she managed, her pulse racing wildly. He was terribly angry with her.

"Oh, absolutely." He smiled without warmth and took

her arm possessively in his. In fact, she knew she would not be able to free herself unless he wished it. He nodded at Solange. "Thank you, Madame Marceaux. And hors d'oeuvres from Emerald and the entrée I previously requested—this is quite a feast, beyond my wildest expectations."

Solange smiled at him. "*Bon appétit,*" she said, drifting off.

His fingers dug into Francesca's arms and he was propelling her up the stairs, so forcefully her feet barely touched the ground.

"You're hurting me," she warned breathlessly.

"Good," he ground out. "Which room is yours—*Emerald*?"

Francesca nodded down the hall. At the door she indicated, he pushed it open, never releasing her. Francesca had the unhappy feeling that he wanted to kick it down.

Once inside, he released her, closing and locking the door. Francesca ran to the far side of the room, the big bed between them, operating on pure instinct. He turned. "What the hell are you doing?" he ground out in a low tone.

"You know what I am doing!" she cried.

His gaze slammed over her. "You are naked in that dress!"

"Not really. The chiffon below is nude and—"

"Like hell!" He exploded and before she knew it, he was in front of her, gripping her shoulders. "Do you wish to be raped?" he demanded.

"Calder . . ." she tried.

"No! I mean it! How do you think to survive an evening here? The next man to take you up here won't take 'no' for an answer and he won't jerk himself off to keep you innocent!"

She inhaled hard. "What do you care?" she whispered.

He froze. "What?"

She began to shake, with a different fear—with the sickness haunting her all day. "Obviously you don't care."

He stared at her as if she were insane. "Francesca, I want you out of this place, now."

"I don't understand." She was now furious herself. She struggled to break free of his grasp and failed. "Let me go!"

"No."

"You have no more rights!"

"Like hell I don't." He was dangerous now.

"Men who throw away their fiancées like a discarded half-eaten piece of chocolate have no rights!" She glared. To her dismay, she felt tears forming in her eyes.

His grip softened. *"What?"*

"You heard me." She glared again. Being upset now—being heartbroken—was the last thing she wished to be.

He released her but touched her face. "You're not a piece of candy, Francesca."

"You spent the night with me—well, a few hours or so of it—and have decided you are finished with me!" she accused.

He straightened, eyes wide. "Is that what you think?"

"Yes." She trembled.

"My clever, ingenious, eccentric little sleuth," he whispered, pulling her close and tilting up her chin. He kissed her deeply, opening her mouth, his tongue sliding over hers.

Everything that had happened in the past few hours swept through her mind with stunning force—Dawn's wish to seduce her, the Spanish prince's three-day orgy, kittens' tongues. Francesca moved closer, moaning, her body exploding with fire. Hart's hands, on her lower back, tightened. His arousal had formed between them, long and hard, infinitely enticing, electric. He broke the kiss, whispering, "This is not the time or the place."

"You're supposed to be making love to me," she whispered back. "Just do it, Hart."

His gaze held hers. "For a sleuth, you have missed many clues, darling, when it comes to me and you."

"What?" She trembled.

He reached up to touch her lips, her cheek, and her hair.

"I wanted to give you a chance to decide what it is that *you* really wish to do, as we both know I am not the man you love." He stared.

His words were like ice-cold water, and the raging fever died. She backed up a step. It was hard to comprehend his meaning. "Calder?" She became incredulous. "You don't want to break off our engagement?"

"You heard me," he said, shoving his hands into the pockets of his trousers. "Of course I don't."

She began to smile as a thrill rippled within her. Then she composed herself. "Well," she said briskly, "now that that misunderstanding has been laid to rest, we must visit Rachael and rescue the other girls."

"I am visiting Rachael, and the police will rescue the girls. You are getting out of here and do not think, for one moment, that you are off the hook."

She smiled sweetly at him. "Very well."

"I am very angry with you, Francesca."

"I know." She smiled sweetly again. "Rachael is just down the hall and I think we should both visit her. Solange thinks we are preoccupied. She won't think to look for me for another hour."

"No. Go downstairs and if she or anyone asks, I wanted quick pleasure, that is all. Mingle until Solange is in her apartments. Then hurry out, Francesca, and I do mean hurry."

Francesca so wanted to see Rachael and find out how she was. She sighed, thinking ahead. "All right. I'll notify the police. Is Bragg still at the hospital?"

Hart nodded, his gaze changing.

Francesca did not know what that meant. "I guess I will have to get Chief Farr," she said, hating the very notion.

"We don't want a raid here," Hart said firmly.

She gave him a look, annoyed. "Which might warn the brothel where the children are. I am no fool, Calder, and this is *my* case. The brothel where the children are needs to be raided first so we can rescue the girls."

He took her wrist and reeled her in and kissed her nose.

"We are on the same side, darling," he said, softening. Then his eyes hardened. "Now get going."

She nodded, aware of some fear rising. She hesitated, gave him a look, and went to her purse. She withdrew her small pistol.

Hart groaned. "Just where the hell are you hiding that?"

The question was a good one. Francesca knew her dress hugged every inch of her body and she was at a loss.

"Try your garter," he said.

She glanced at him.

Hart gave her half of an encouraging nod.

Francesca lifted her skirt, aware of him watching as her leg was exposed. She tucked the pistol in her garter on the inside of her thigh. "It won't stay," she said.

He strode over and knelt, adjusting the garter.

She stilled instantly, his hands precariously high on her thigh.

He lowered the garter and the pistol, positioning both above her knee, then retied the garter so tightly, Francesca wondered if her blood could possibly circulate. Then he glanced up. "Hopefully that won't be for too long."

Their gazes held. It was a moment before she could speak. "Hopefully my leg won't fall off."

He rose gracefully to his feet and she dropped the gown. The gun felt cold and bulky against her inner knee, but it didn't seem visible. Then she looked at him.

"You should go," he said grimly.

She nodded.

He walked her to the door. "Francesca, be careful."

She smiled at him, far more bravely than she felt. "It's a piece of cake."

He grimaced.

She slipped into the hallway.

Two lush women and one older man were walking past her, arm in arm, sipping champagne and smelling of an odd smoke. Francesca smiled at everyone and went to the stairs. The piano tune had changed. It was more lively, more festive, and no longer at all classical. The conversation level had changed, too. It was loud and raucous.

Her heart felt as if it were wedged in her upper chest somewhere. She started down the stairs.

As the reception hall came into view, she saw several men and women, including Philip Seymour, but no sign of Solange. Hart had told her to mingle until the coast was clear. She stepped into the hall, glancing into the dining room, and she saw several gentlemen dining there with several servants. Still no sign of the madam.

She turned and glanced into the salon, which was now quite filled with clients and the ladies of the house. Francesca met Dawn's gaze instantly. The woman gave her an urgent look. If Francesca understood, she was signaling to her. Francesca turned and glanced toward Solange's apartment. The door was solidly closed.

Her heart leaped with hope. She turned back to Dawn, wide-eyed, silently asking her if Solange Marceaux was closeted in her suite.

Dawn nodded urgently at her and seemed to say, *Go*.

Francesca turned quickly. The doorman was preoccupied with arriving clientele; she hurried past Solange's closed door and down the empty hall. Dear God, could it be any easier?

A small feeling of dread formed.

Ahead was a closed door, painted blue. This was too easy, in fact.

She reached the door, testing it. It was locked.

She realized it was locked from the inside, and as she unlocked the small lever, she reminded herself not to look a gift horse in the mouth. Francesca was greeted by a sky filled with stars and a half-moon. She stepped swiftly outside, closing the door behind her, filled with relief.

She had made it. She had escaped.

And from behind, Solange Marceaux said, "Seize her."

CHAPTER
TWENTY

THE CHILD WHO WAS waiting for him had silver-blond hair and silvery gray eyes. She had been dressed up in a gown more appropriate for a schoolgirl of eight or nine, all white cotton and frilly lace. Hart closed the door behind him and smiled at her. She stared at him through a drug-induced stupor. His stomach turned as if he had actually been poisoned, as if he were actually ill.

His reputation was not a groundless one. He had discovered the pleasures of the female body at thirteen and had been sexually active ever since. But in fact, at that age, his first few lovers had been several years older than himself. In his mid-adolescence, he had devoted a great deal of his time to hedonism, most of it sexual. But he was not a pedophile, thank God. Still, in the course of experiencing some of life's more illicit and sordid pleasures, he had, from time to time, met gentlemen known for their pedophilia. It was also a fact of life that children were abducted and sold into slavery all of the time, and not just for sex. But his own dark and lusty world had never before so openly collided with that other even darker world, and having now stepped so frankly into it, he was furious. Determination made him ruthless. He looked forward to exposing the men and women behind this latest effort at child prostitution; oh yes, he did. He would enjoy bringing each and every one single-handedly to his and her knees. Unlike his sainted half brother, he would prefer to lock them up and throw away the keys. However, as he was not a policeman, he would not have that opportunity. But a whisper in the right and most honorable ear would have the same effect.

Grim, he paused to glance around. There was a mirror on the wall. Was it a mirror or a window to a viewing room? He walked directly to it and took it down. He was prepared to be angry and call in the management, but it was just what it appeared to be, a mirror. They were alone.

He faced the bed where Rachael sat and put his finger to his lips. "Ssh," he breathed.

Rachael simply stared.

He walked slowly to her, but she did not flinch or appear afraid. He paused before her, kneeling. "Rachael? Is your name Rachael Wirkler?" he asked in a low voice, afraid they might be eavesdropped upon from the hall or the door that clearly opened to an adjoining room.

He finally got a reaction from her. She blinked, starting with surprise.

"I am not a customer. I am going to take you home," he whispered.

Rachael bit her lip, no longer appearing quite so inebriated, a light of comprehension in her eyes.

"My name is Calder Hart," he said, with a reassuring smile. "Can you tell me where your friends are being kept? Emily, Bonnie, and Deborah?" he asked.

She nodded, now wetting her lips. She did not speak.

He understood. He went to the nightstand and poured her a glass of water. He suspected she had been given a small dose of opium, just enough to sedate her and not enough to make her a rag doll. He brought it to her and helped her drink.

"Who are you?" she whispered after taking several thirsty sips.

"Calder Hart," he repeated patiently, and he smiled as kindly. "Now, do you know where you have been staying? It is very important that we free all of your friends."

She blinked, suddenly in tears, and nodded. "On Jane Street," she said huskily. "Just off Hudson."

"Where is that?"

"Near Fourteenth Street," she said, staring. "One of them is sick. She needs to go home, sir."

"Who is sick?" he asked quickly.

"Emily," she whispered.

He patted her back. "Don't worry, it will be over very soon." Hart suddenly realized that he could not go through with the plan he and Francesca had developed. The plan had been to get information from Rachael and leave her behind, allowing the police to rescue her later. But what if the raid on the Jane Street brothel alerted everyone at the Jewel, and Rachael was spirited off before she could be freed? There was simply no way he could leave her behind, and he saw no alternative but to walk out the front door with her. But then word would be sent to Jane Street, alerting them of his actions.

He had to get word to Bragg. And by now, Francesca should be on her way to Mulberry Street to rouse Farr—but only to have the police stand by.

The night had become a black one. Free Rachael—or free the other girls. Both options did not seem viable.

Suddenly a sharp knock sounded on the front door. Hart ripped the covers up. "Get under the covers and pretend to be asleep," he ordered.

Rachael obeyed, but slowly. When she was safely tucked in, he went to the door. Whoever was there was knocking again—insistently. He loosened his tie and cracked the door open a hair's breadth.

The brunette who had been with Francesca said, "Let me in."

He started and opened the door; she hurried in and closed it breathlessly. "Francesca is in trouble."

"What?" he asked, alarmed.

"She's been taken to Solange's office. Not willingly, I might add," the brunette said. Her gaze went to the bed.

Hart faced her. "How much will it cost me for you to help us?"

"Nothing," she said.

He shoved several hundred-dollar bills down her bodice. "Take Rachael out the front door. My brother is police commissioner and he is at Bellevue. Tell him the children are at Jane Street off Hudson. I will meet him there."

She nodded, already at the bed, encouraging Rachael to get up. "I'm Dawn," she said with a smile. "Come on. We're leaving this rotten place."

Hart opened the door and saw Joseph lying on the floor, unconscious. Blood was trickling from the back of his head and a bookend was on the floor. Hart quickly dragged the body inside and then gestured to Dawn and Rachael to follow him out. The hall had been empty—now a prostitute and a young, inebriated man exited one of the rooms. Hart smiled at them both—the whore smiled back and followed her customer downstairs. "Let's go," Hart said.

Solange sat behind her lovely desk, smiling at Francesca. Francesca sat in a chair, facing her, feeling like a student in the dean's office, except for the two thugs standing behind her. "So, what is your real name and why are you here?"

Francesca was wide-eyed with innocence. "Madame Marceaux, my real name is insignificant. I have used 'Emerald Baron' for many years. I am afraid we have a terrible misunderstanding," Francesca said with a smile.

"Really?" How pleasant Solange was.

"I was taking some air. Mr. Hart was quite, er, vigorous,

and I wanted to refresh myself before my next customer."
Francesca smiled again.

Solange looked at one of the thugs behind Francesca and
nodded.

Francesca tensed, turning to see what was happening.
He struck her hard across the face, so much so that she
cried out, the pain in her cheek making her wonder if he
had cracked or broken her cheekbone.

"I despise liars," Solange said calmly.

Fear almost paralyzed Francesca, fear and pain. She
slowly straightened and met the other woman's pale gray
unblinking eyes. "My name is Francesca Cahill," she began, and she saw a light of triumph in the madam's eyes,
"and I am a sleuth. You are trafficking in children, Madame
Marceaux, and I intend to see you appropriately charged,
tried, and convicted for your disgustingly self-serving and
unabashedly shameless crimes."

Solange stood.

Francesca told herself not to be afraid—Solange was just
another woman, and a whore at that.

Solange walked around her desk.

Francesca grimaced, preparing herself for a very unpleasant encounter.

Solange struck her again, across the same cheek, and her
turquoise-and-diamond ring cut through the skin there.
"Bitch," she said, staring, her eyes as hard as the diamonds
that had abraded Francesca's cheek. "I knew you were a
fraud the moment I interviewed you."

Francesca blinked back stinging tears. "At least I am not
a whore."

Solange didn't hit her again, but Francesca did cringe,
expecting another blow. Instead, Solange smiled and looked
at the thugs behind Francesca. "Take her, use her as if she
were the cheapest whore imaginable, and then, when you
are through, get rid of her. Dump her body in the river,
please. I do not want it found, not ever."

Francesca felt real fear. What should she do? Before she
could think and formulate a plan, her arm was seized. Fran-

cesca did not hesitate. As she leaped to her feet, she reached for the gun between her legs and pointed it at Solange. "I don't think so," she said.

Solange froze. Then, calmly, coolly, "Get that gun from her, George."

Francesca turned. George hurled himself at her. As his body collided with hers, she fired. He grunted as they both went down, Francesca on her back, George on top of her. God, he weighed a ton!

Their gazes met. "You little whore," he rasped, pain in his eyes. His hands closed around her throat.

Francesca whimpered, pressed the gun into his chest, and fired it again.

His eyes widened and he collapsed.

She shoved him off as the locked door flew in off its hinges. Relief soared. It had to be Hart. "Calder!" she shouted.

Something in the office crashed to the floor as Francesca struggled out from under the huge thug. Hart said, "Are you all right?"

Francesca paused on her knees, glancing up. He was a most welcome sight. A bookcase had collapsed from the wall near where he stood and the other thug was on the floor, staggering to his feet. "Fine," she whispered, glimpsing Rachael and Dawn, hand in hand, in the doorway. Then they ran off, just as she saw and heard Solange moving behind her.

She turned as the thug launched himself at Hart. Solange was at the desk, digging in a drawer. Did she have a gun? Francesca still gripped her own gun and she leaped to her feet, raising it. "Freeze, Solange," she warned.

Solange paused, slowly looking up.

More wood splintered and broke, behind them.

Francesca half-turned. Her eyes widened as she saw Hart kicking the thug in the chest, whirling away, and then kicking him in the jaw. As the thug collapsed, Hart came back, lifting him up and chopping him once with the side of his hand on the back of the man's neck.

The man's eyes rolled back in his head and he slid unconscious to the floor.

"Oh my," Francesca said. "Where did you learn to fight like that?"

"Thailand," he grunted, straightening himself and his tie. "I spent six months there when I was seventeen."

Francesca was impressed. "Shall we go?" she asked, turning to Solange. Francesca passed her, checked the drawer, took out two guns, and tucked them both under one arm.

"We need to hurry," Hart said. As they left Solange in her office, he said, "Jane Street off Hudson."

"Where is that?" Francesca asked. They entered the foyer, which was filled with both the guests and their escorts, the pianist now pounding out a ragtime tune.

"Near Fourteenth Street," Hart began.

"Do not let them out," Solange ordered from behind them.

Francesca turned and saw her standing by the stairs, livid. She turned to face forward and saw two very big doormen coming toward them. One of the men had to be 300 pounds; another, six-foot-seven. Wincing, she handed Hart a gun.

He declined. "No thank you," he said.

"Calder," she began in protest.

He walked up to the obese man and smiled. "Can I help you?" he asked.

The man sneered and reached out, as if to grab Hart by the collar or some such thing. He was as slow as a tortoise.

Hart struck him in his jugular and, as he gasped and bowed, simultaneously on each temple. He followed with a kick to the kidneys; Francesca winced. The fat man hit the floor like a rock.

Hart smiled at her.

The club had become very quiet.

"Uh, Calder?" Francesca said, as the giant was approaching from behind him now.

Hart turned as the giant struck at him. He blocked the

blow, ducking beneath the man's outstretched arm, spun around and kicked him in the back, spun forward, and kicked him there again. The giant wobbled but did not fall, and turned to face Hart, grinning.

"Fight," someone said with avid interest. A crowd was gathering now.

The giant grinned at Hart and reached for his neck.

"Calder!" Francesca shouted, alarmed, as the man grabbed him around the throat.

Hart somehow slid his arms into the vise of forearms, and before Francesca could blink, he was free and striking the man on the underside of his jaw, with first one foot, then the next.

"Fight!" someone shouted.

"Fight!" another man answered excitedly.

Something crashed in the salon, glass shattering.

The giant refused to go down. He stood there, staggering, but also grinning at Hart.

"Goddamn it," Hart said with annoyance.

There were more crashes; Francesca dared not look away from Hart, but she was vaguely aware of several fights breaking out among the various gentlemen in the club. Hart smiled. "I do beg your pardon," he said, and he kicked the man right in the testicles.

The giant gasped and slowly but surely sank down to the floor, turning white.

Hart held out his hand. "Now I'll take that gun," he said.

Francesca glanced around, wide-eyed, and saw that a riot had broken out—even several women were throwing things at and on their customers, for lamps, glasses, ashtrays were all flying about the rooms. Some very serious fisticuffs were also taking place. Francesca glimpsed Solange, pale now with alarm, and turned back to Hart, handing him a gun.

He turned it around and hit the giant with its butt right on the crest of his head. The man's eyes finally closed. "Let's get out of here," Hart said.

Francesca blinked once more at the melee now in progress—the glorious Jewel was turning into a pile of broken furniture and adornments; even some magnificent paintings were being torn from the walls and stomped upon. Bodies were everywhere. Philip Seymour suddenly smiled at her, appearing at her side, his nose bloody, his eyes bright. "Now this is fun." He grinned.

Francesca blinked at him.

A woman hit him over the head with a champagne bottle, and he grinned again at her, just before his eyes rolled back and he sank to the floor. She raised the bottle threateningly at Francesca.

Francesca ducked and ran by her, meeting Hart on the other side of the reception hall. He took her hand and they hurried out the front door. Hart let loose a piercing whistle. Across the street, Francesca saw Raoul leap into the driver's seat of Hart's brougham.

"We made it!" she cried, smiling at him.

He did not smile back. "God, I abhor violence," he said.

Even though Raoul drove the team at a near gallop, running interfering vehicles off the road, by the time they arrived at Jane Street, the police were already there. A police wagon and Bragg's Daimler motorcar were parked in front of a decrepit-looking building; a number of policemen in uniform were hustling two roughs and a well-dressed middle-aged woman in a navy blue suit who had to be the madame down the brownstone's steps. Several gentlemen who had undoubtedly been there as customers were also being handcuffed. Hart said, "I sent Dawn to Bellevue to get him. It's odd that he managed to bring the police so quickly."

His tone was suddenly strange and Francesca glanced at him. He smiled grimly at her and walked past her, toward the crowd that had gathered in front of the brothel.

Francesca suddenly saw Bragg coming out of the building, a child in his arms. Joel was following, and so was a familiar girl. But surely her eyes were deceiving her and that wasn't Bridget O'Neil? And then she took a second look, because her brother was with both children!

And then she saw Rourke Bragg behind them, with two more girls.

Francesca ran forward. Bragg was coming off the front step when she reached him. "Is everyone all right?" she cried. She was wearing Hart's jacket over the countess's dress and clutched it closed.

His gaze flew to her cheek. "Yes. What happened?"

She gripped his arm, gazing at a flushed child in his arms. She had dark hair and pale skin. Was it Emily O'Hare? "Is she hurt?"

"No, she's ill. It's Emily O'Hare. Apparently she's been ill for some time."

Francesca smothered a cry as Rourke said, "Put her in the Daimler. She looks feverish. We should get her to a hospital immediately."

Bragg transferred the child to his half brother's arms. "You take her. I'll meet you there later."

Rourke nodded and hurried off.

"What happened?" Bragg asked again, taking her arm.

"It's nothing," she said, meeting his dark gaze. "But the Jewel, a club on Fifth Avenue, is also trafficking in children, Rick. The madam is Solange Marceaux." She hesitated and decided not to tell him what had happened to her just yet.

"I'll send some men down to raid it immediately and pick her up," he said. "I'm afraid to ask what you were doing there tonight." His gaze slid over her legs, obviously visible in the revealing dress.

Francesca winced a little. "Don't ask." She turned to Joel and Bridget. "What are you both doing here?" she cried. "Are you all right?" And then she looked at Evan. "How are you involved?"

"A police officer found me at my hotel," he began, flushing and avoiding looking at her legs. "I am afraid to ask you what you are doing in a garment like that."

"I can explain," Francesca began quickly.

He waved at her. "Another time." He patted Joel's shoulder. "Your assistant is a hero, Fran."

Francesca swelled with pride. "Whatever happened?"

Joel grinned at her. "The police threw me in the cooler when I tried to git help fer Bridget," he said. "A fly went up to Mr. Cahill an' he come down to tell 'em I was on the up-'n'-up."

"What?" Francesca cried. She remarked now that Bridget appeared somewhat distraught, but she was also casting wide, worshipful glances at Joel. He grinned baldly at everyone. "She got caught by them thugs and I got caught trying to save her."

"Joel!" Francesca cried one more time, now aghast. "When did this happen?"

"This mornin'," he said. "But ye don't got to worry. I escaped an' went to the police. They didn't believe me, not at first, that's why I sent 'em to your house, an' why your brother came and witnessed me," he said proudly.

Francesca put her arms around both children. "Thank God you are both all right," she managed, glancing now at Bragg. He and Hart were having a hushed conversation, neither one of them smiling. Then both men glanced at her.

Francesca knew they were speaking about her, undoubtedly about her part in the events at the Jewel. She turned back to the children, not liking both brothers' talking together about her behind her back. In fact, it worried her no end. "We have to get you both home, and Deborah and Bonnie as well." She glanced at the two beautiful girls. They were both wide-eyed and holding hands tightly.

And both children had been listening, because one said, "I don't want to go home. He'll just sell me off again."

Francesca started, her heart breaking. She glanced at Evan. He said, "I'll take Joel and Bridget home."

"Thank you," she whispered, rushing over to the girls. "Are you Bonnie?" she asked the honey-blonde who had just spoken.

"I'm not going home," the girl breathed. She had bright green eyes and thick, dark lashes. "Yes, I'm Bonnie."

"All right," Francesca said. After all, Bonnie's father had claimed she was dead and someone had filled her coffin with stones. She faced Deborah Smith. "Your mother misses you terribly."

Deborah's eyes filled with tears. "I miss her, too. But if I go home, my papa will beat me, or worse."

Francesca pulled her close. "No, he won't. Your father isn't at home, Deborah, and he's not coming back."

Deborah stiffened and looked up, hope in her eyes. "Are you sure?"

Francesca wasn't about to tell her that her father was dead. "I'm sure," she said.

Bragg walked over to them. "We'll take everyone to headquarters and find them a comfortable place to sleep. We'll have Eliza Smith and Mrs. Cooper brought to the girls." He gave Francesca a look and she understood. John Cooper was going to be arrested for his part in selling his daughter into slavery, whatever part that was. He had also lied about her death, and that was an obstruction of justice. "I'm also having an officer notify the O'Hares that Emily is at Bellevue," he said. "Rachael will also stay in police custody until we can rest assured it's safe for her to return home."

Francesca nodded. "Good. And is she the one behind all this?" She glanced toward the middle-aged woman in the navy blue suit.

"We don't know yet," he said. "But her name is Elspeth Browne—or so she claims." For a moment he was silent. "The bald thug cannot stop talking. He's already confessed to killing Tom Smith, but said he was only following orders."

"Whose orders?" Francesca asked quickly.

"We don't know yet."

Francesca hesitated, searching his gaze. He appeared exhausted and was both unshaven and unkempt. He also looked haggard, drawn, and too thin. "How are you?" she asked softly, reaching for his hand.

For one moment he let her hold it before he pulled it back. "I'm fine," he said, looking away from her.

She tensed, knowing he lied and wishing he would not

put another wall between them. "Is there anything I can do to help?"

He faced her, softening. "You have helped by solving this crime," he said.

Francesca didn't hesitate. "This time, it was a team effort. I couldn't have done it without Joel and Calder."

Bragg's jaw hardened, but he nodded. "I'll need full statements from you both," he said, turning away.

Briefly she was aghast. It was as if she was now losing his friendship, too. Or was he too raw to be able to speak with her intimately and personally?

Suddenly he turned back and took both of her hands in his. "The girls are at Calder's with my parents," he said. "I took them to see Leigh Anne." He stopped, clearly fighting for composure. He cleared his throat. "Katie is dismal, Francesca. And even Dot seemed to understand that Leigh Anne is ill."

"I'll see them tomorrow, first thing," she said, her heart hurting her now for the two little girls. "In fact, maybe I can take them to the zoo and distract them from what is happening."

"I'd appreciate that," he said. Their gazes met. "I'd appreciate that a lot."

Suddenly a familiar voice came from above. "Look at what I have found."

Francesca glanced at the brownstone. Standing on the porch was the very rakish youth Nicholas D'Archand, and he was holding the collar of a very familiar man. Her eyes widened as she met a pair of terribly pale eyes.

"Well, well." Hart moved to stand beside her. "If it isn't a Tammany lapdog."

Recognition came then. "Is that Tim Murphy?" He was the man she had met while having lunch with Grace!

"Yes, it is. He was commissioner of education in Van Wyck's administration. I guess he enjoyed his tours of our city's wonderful public schools," Hart drawled.

Francesca felt ill. "What a crook," she breathed.

Nick pushed Murphy down the stairs. "I found him attempting to burn a big ledger book in a back office, Rick," he said. He shoved Murphy at Bragg. "Why bother to arrest this scumbag? I vote we take him for a little jaunt in the countryside—a one-way tour, so to speak." His smile was distinctly unpleasant and his own silvery gray eyes flashed.

Murphy straightened. "You will suffer for your maltreatment of me, young man. And you, Commissioner? I warn you, do not toy with me or you shall pay a heavy price indeed. My friends are in high places and terribly loyal."

"Shut up," Bragg said, seizing his arm. "Sergeant, gag him, shackle him, and put him where he belongs. In a cell in the Tombs."

Murphy cried out, "I demand to speak with my lawyer and you cannot imprison me without a trial!"

Bragg smiled at him. "Imprison you? Who said anything about imprisoning you? The holding pen is full at headquarters; we are merely placing you in the next most convenient location, and can I help it if the prison is filled with murderers and cutthroats? You shall stay there until you are formally charged. That shouldn't take too long, I think. Maybe a week . . . or two . . . or three."

Murphy flushed, crying, "You are twisting the law, Bragg! You will pay for this!"

"Get him out of my sight," Bragg said, turning his back on him.

Francesca watched as shackles were snapped on his wrists and he was shoved forcefully into the police wagon. As the back door was bolted and locked, the other prisoners were herded into a second wagon. The crowd on the sidewalk began to disperse. One of the horse-drawn wagons trotted away.

Bragg glanced at them. "I'll need to see you both downtown. We can do it now or we can do it tomorrow," he said without inflection.

"Tomorrow," Hart returned firmly. "It's time for me to take Francesca home."

"I don't mind," she began, her gaze seeking but not finding Bragg's. He stood staring into the night, looking terribly lonely and terribly sad. She plucked Hart's sleeve. She lowered her voice so Bragg wouldn't hear and said, "If he is going back to the hospital we should go with him."

"I am taking you home," Hart said flatly. "It's late and we've both had a hellish day."

She hesitated; Bragg was now speaking to another policeman and she wanted to stay with him, at least for a while.

"I want to talk to you," Hart said.

She started, meeting his eyes. The expression there remained different, disturbing. So much had happened and so quickly that it was only then that she became aware of a new anxiety. "Is something wrong?" she asked cautiously.

He took her arm, steering her toward his brougham. By now, the last police wagon was also leaving and most of the gawkers had dispersed. Bragg and Nicholas were walking back toward the brownstone, probably to go search Murphy's office. Francesca took one last look over her shoulder and allowed Hart to help her up into the coach. He settled down beside her, ordered Raoul to drive them to her home, and turned to gaze directly at her.

She became uneasy. "You're worrying me. This isn't about tonight, is it?"

"No."

"Then what is it?" She couldn't help recalling how sure she had been that he wished to break off their engagement.

He smiled a little, grimly, not at her, but at himself. "I have something to ask you," he said.

Her alarm grew. "Very well," she said with even more caution.

He didn't look at her. "I have been thinking," he said. "And my conclusion is that we should elope."

She gaped.

CHAPTER TWENTY-ONE

HART SEEMED INCREDIBLY GRIM and now he gazed out at the passing buildings as his brougham rolled by.

"What did you say?" Francesca whispered, her ears ringing as if she'd been the victim of a blow.

He faced her. Shadows flickered over his face. "I've been thinking and you are right. A year is far too long to wait."

Images of the few hours they had shared on Sunday in his bed assaulted her then. They were followed by an image of her in a white wedding dress with Hart behind her, undoing her gown. She could barely breathe. "Did you just suggest that we *elope?*"

He smiled slightly—and it was strained. "Yes, I did." Now he watched her carefully, unblinkingly.

She sat up impossibly straighter. He wanted to *elope?*

But he was right. Wasn't he? Waiting a year to be together was absurd. It was that simple. *But elope?*

Why not?

She stared excitedly at him. He stared back, intent and intense. She began to frown. But Calder Hart was the most patient and controlled man that she knew. What was going on?

In fact, his behavior had been odd recently. First his lovemaking on Sunday, then his suggestion that she reconsider their engagement, and now this stunning proposal. Was something going on that she did not know about?

Francesca tried to think clearly, rationally, logically. It felt impossible. "Calder, Mama would kill me. She'd kill you. She'd kill us! She is planning some kind of ridiculous event, I overheard Papa ordering her to make certain her guest list is under six hundred, and I know she is booking the Waldorf Astoria for the wedding and the reception." She stared at him with huge eyes, trembling. Would this man ever be predictable?

"We won't tell her."

She was speechless.

"No one has to know that we are married," he said.

She simply stared as her mind raced once more. They would elope—and keep the fact secret. So Mama could have her grand affair and never mind when their public wedding day came; they would already be married. *Oh, my God. Did she dare do such a thing?*

He reached for her hand and said nothing.

She tried to study his face, but it was hard to make out his expression in the dim light of the carriage. What was going on? Why this sudden about-face? Why the urgency? Hadn't he told her to reconsider their engagement yesterday? Because he wished for her to follow her heart?

A terrible pang followed and she thought about Bragg, wrapped up in his grief, unable to leave his wife's side. She still wished she had remained behind with him at the brownstone, looking for more evidence with which to convict Elspeth Browne and Tim Murphy and their lackeys. Bragg had never needed her more—as a friend. Because clearly, when his wife recovered, things would be very different for them. If not, Francesca intended to hit him over the head several times with a solid object, as it was so terribly clear that he was in love with Leigh Anne.

Francesca smiled a little at Hart. "Yesterday you wanted me to reconsider our engagement."

"I changed my mind." His smile was as brief as before. His grip on her hand tightened.

She moved closer to him, felt his body tighten in response, and laid her palm on his shoulder. Oddly, he seemed to flinch. "Calder? Is this because of the other night?"

He hesitated. "No."

"I don't understand."

"You don't have to." He took her shoulders in his palms. "I have a good friend who is a judge. I happen to know he is in town. We can be wed by noon tomorrow, Francesca," he said.

"Tomorrow!" she cried, stunned.

"Francesca," he suddenly said, his tone turning rough, and he pulled her close and kissed her mouth once, hard. "Think about it. We'll speak first thing in the morning."

TUESDAY, APRIL 1, 1902 — 10:00 A.M.

Francesca paused in the doorway of Bragg's office. She hadn't slept all night, but she was too nervous to be tired. She had gone directly to Hart's upon arising that morning, but Hart had already been gone—apparently he had left for his downtown offices at six. She had had breakfast with Katie and Dot, and they had been joined by Rathe and Grace. As much as she needed to finish her discussion with Hart—she found it almost impossible to believe that last night's suggestion had even happened—she had yet to give her statement to the police. She would continue on downtown after doing so. Sanity had returned—somewhat—and she did wish to know the latest developments on the case.

So now she knocked gently on the open door. Bragg was with the chief of police, Brendan Farr, and as Farr turned, he looked up.

Francesca instantly sobered. Seeing Bragg reminded her of how precarious, unpredictable, and fragile life could be, and every time she thought about Leigh Anne, who would never walk again, she was unbearably saddened. Still, some good would come of this, and she was certain once Leigh Anne was out of the hospital, Bragg would be a proper and devoted husband to her. Maybe he had to come close to losing her in order to realize his real feelings. She smiled briefly, noting how pale and haggard he was. "Good morning. I hope I am not interrupting."

"Not at all," Bragg said. "Chief and I were just finishing. Thanks, Chief."

"No problem." Farr walked out, nodding at Francesca as he did so.

"I came to give my statement," she said. She held her coat over her arm. She could not help herself, as seeing him in his grief hurt her so, and she said softly, "Are you sleeping at all, Rick?"

He walked back behind his desk, putting it between them. "We have the brothel's ledger, and Murphy was apparently the man behind the operation. According to our bald friend, who is Eddie Flynn, by the way, Murphy ordered Tom Smith's murder and the assault upon you. Murphy is in the Tombs, apparently demanding a lawyer and his release." He looked up grimly. "Boss Croker is going to buy whichever judge we wind up with, Francesca. I expect Murphy to be back on the street after his pre-trial hearing."

The fact that he did not wish to be at all personal with her hurt, but his following words shocked her. "That's terrible! Can't we do something about it?"

"Most of the judges in this city are Tammany men. It's a huge problem," he said. Then, sitting, he added, "We did not find Solange Marceaux. She has, for the moment, disappeared, but I have issued a warrant for her arrest. Calder told me she intended to kill you," he added, finally looking her in the eye.

She winced a bit. "She did, er, intend to dump my body in the river." She sat down in a cane-backed chair, facing him. "How will you ever find her?"

"I don't know if we will. Elspeth Browne worked for Murphy, and she has started to talk. It sounds as if Murphy began searching out these girls late last year just before Van Wyck's term as mayor was over."

"That is disgusting," she said, appalled. Thank God her mother was not related to the previous mayor! "As commissioner of education he could walk into any school he wished whenever he wished."

"I'm having Principal Matthews brought in as well. However, I don't think he was involved—I suspect apathy, not criminal intent."

"And Bonnie Cooper's father?"

Bragg sighed, sitting back in his chair. "He and his wife sold Bonnie to Murphy, and Elspeth Browne has confirmed it. We are looking for some kind of receipt in the ledger, but Newman found two hundred dollars in gold hidden beneath a floorboard in their flat."

Francesca could not speak. She had expected this, but the reality was nauseating.

Now he smiled a little. "Emily's fever broke this morning. Her parents are with her, and Rourke expects her to go home tomorrow."

"That is wonderful!" Francesca cried. Then she leaned forward, delight vanishing. "How is she—other than that?"

"She was never violated, because she fell ill instantly." He stared. "The other girls have suffered a terrible ordeal. Deborah and Rachael are at their homes, and the doctors here have recommended psychiatric treatment for them. Bonnie has been placed in the care of the state, but Eliza told me she wished to help and is applying to foster her until she reaches her majority. I have asked the mayor to pull some strings, Francesca, and he said he would, so Bonnie should be able to go to her new home shortly."

She simply stared at him, in that moment reminded of why she had fallen in love with him in the first place.

He began to flush and avoided her gaze.

She didn't care. She reached over his desk and took his hand. "You are such a good man."

He glanced down at their hands and removed his from hers. "If something like that ever happened to Katie or Dot . . ." He could not finish.

"It won't," she said firmly. Then, "Bragg? Katie needs to see Leigh Anne again, it is terribly important even if she is still ill, and—"

"No." He stood abruptly. "I will have Sergeant O'Malley take your statement."

She realized he wished for her to leave and she could hardly believe it. "Bragg—Rick—I had breakfast with the girls. Dot is a bit confused, but Katie misses Leigh Anne desperately!"

"When is Hart coming in to give his statement?" Bragg asked, walking past her to the door.

She stared at him. He was shutting her out and she was in disbelief. It also hurt.

"I need Hart's statement," he said impatiently.

"I don't know when he is coming in," she returned. She stared at Bragg, who refused to meet her gaze.

"If you see him, tell him to come in immediately," he said. Then, glancing at her, "I am sorry to be in such a rush, but I do have to go."

Francesca bit her lip and nodded. "Actually, I, er, have some plans to attend to as well."

He was so preoccupied it was as if he hadn't heard her. Francesca watched him donning his hat and coat, realizing he was off to Bellevue. She hesitated, wanting to go with him but knowing that would compromise her plan to go downtown to Hart.

Bragg paused. "O'Malley can take your statement."

She smiled grimly and watched him go.

· · ·

Francesca felt flushed as she was shown to the doorway of Hart's large corner office. He was standing, staring out one of the large windows, gazing out over the harbor, filled with masts. His back was to her. The clerk, someone she did not know, murmured, "Miss Cahill, sir."

Francesca gripped her reticule tightly. Slowly, Hart turned.

He still remained darkly seductive and equally disturbing, not to mention enigmatic. Francesca noted that Hart wasn't smiling—he was as solemn as he had been last night. Her insides tightened with dread. Was she reading something into him that wasn't there? He also looked as if he had passed the same sleepless night that she had. She had a bad feeling that he had been conflicted with doubt. Why was he doing this?

"I was preparing to come to you," he said politely. Too politely—as if they were strangers, as if she had not spent several hours mostly unclothed in his bed. "You did not have to make such a trip downtown."

Now she was very alarmed. "I am such an early riser. In fact, I just gave my statement to the police." Dread churned in her belly.

"I will have to find some time to make a statement as well."

That was it—something was terribly, dreadfully wrong with Calder Hart. He did not seem pleased—or thrilled—to see her. He was not behaving like a man who wanted to elope with his bride. And if he had so recently wished for her to reconsider their engagement, did he mean that he wanted her to be certain of her decision—or had that been a platitude, a way for him to be polite? He had always insisted that he would never hurt her. What if he was really the one unsure of their engagement? For goodness' sake, this man had been a confirmed bachelor, sworn against the very notion of marriage, for at least ten years.

Francesca knew she was a fool. Clearly he was torn;

clearly a part of him did not want to ever marry, not her and not anyone else.

She blinked back a sudden tear and looked out the window. She had decided she could not elope, because it was not the right thing to do. She could not elope because she wanted her parents and Connie, not to mention Evan and Sarah, at her wedding. She wanted Maggie and Joel there, too. And Alfred. And eloping would be a terrible lie, one she simply could not live with.

And being newly wed now, with Rick fighting the tragedy and crisis of his wife's accident, that, too, did not seem right.

But Francesca was afraid to tell him now that she had decided to wait for as long as her parents wanted her to wait for a proper wedding.

Hart suddenly said, "I cannot go through with this."

Francesca failed to breathe. She stared, her worst nightmare finally coming true. *Hart was ending it with her.*

Francesca was ill. Fortunately, she hadn't been able to eat and had only taken a sip or two of tea that morning; otherwise she would have surely ruined the lovely dress she was wearing.

"Francesca," he said grimly, taking her arm. "Please, sit down."

Francesca wanted to fling him away, but she was too sick at heart to do so. *He had said he would never hurt her—he had lied.* Francesca pulled away from Hart, turning her back to him, hugging herself.

"I cannot go through with this," he said to her back.

She knew she could not get a word out, so she didn't even try.

He took her arm and turned her about to face him. "There's something I have to tell you," he said grimly.

She closed her eyes with dread. Maybe she would retch after all.

"Leigh Anne is dying."

It was a moment before she digested his words. She opened her eyes and saw Hart's expression—grim, resigned, and even, possibly, agonized. *"What did you say?"*

"She went into a coma yesterday afternoon. She is expected to hang on for a few days, maybe a week or so."

She finally comprehended him. "Leigh Anne is in a coma?" And now she understood Rick's anguish. Why hadn't Rick told her? "Oh, dear God." How terrible she felt for Rick and his wife. "When did you find out?"

His expression odd, almost pained, he said, "Yesterday. Yesterday afternoon."

Her mind sped. So he had known about Leigh Anne's terrible turn for the worse last night, when he had suggested they elope. "Are they certain she will die? Perhaps she will regain consciousness—"

"They feel very certain," he said flatly.

She met his dark eyes. It was a long moment before she could speak, as her racing thoughts were so jumbled. "She simply cannot die!"

He shrugged.

"We had better go to the hospital," she said quickly.

"Yes, you had better go."

His tone was extremely odd. She had been about to rush across his office and out the door; she paused, facing him. "Calder, what is it that you are not saying? I am confused. Is this what you wish to discuss with me? Leigh Anne? Or is there something else you wish to say? And we must go to the hospital together." It didn't seem right, to even utter the word "elope" now.

His hazel eyes darkened, like a coming storm. "Leigh Anne is dying, Francesca. I wasn't going to tell you. But I am not such a ruthless cad after all. Now you know. Do you have a driver? If not, I will send you to Bellevue, as that is where you wish to go."

Comprehension began. "I beg your pardon. I do wish to go to the hospital, of course I do, but . . ." and she paused, taking a huge breath. "Are you breaking off our engagement?" she asked cautiously.

He started, his gaze wide. "Francesca, I have no wish to break our engagement."

And she finally understood. And her heart began to

pound differently now. "You thought to marry me—to elope—before Leigh Anne died."

"I have never claimed to be noble. I do want to marry you—but in the end I could not go through with such a deception—one that would make you so unhappy."

For a moment she stood there, unmoving and staring at him. He stared back unblinkingly, frighteningly. She understood it all, then. The battle he had waged—to do the right thing.

And as she stood there, thinking, something slowly unfurled in her breast.

"I have never lied to you before—I lied to you last night," he said grimly.

It was joyful and relieved. "Calder, you are noble, can't you see?" And she felt tears rising rapidly.

He was harsh. "I almost seduced you the other night, with ill intent, and today we could have eloped, with equally foul play. I am not Rick, Francesca. I am nothing like him, and I will never be."

"I disagree," she whispered, meaning it. "You are a good man, Calder Hart." And the emotions swirling in her chest became more identifiable then. *Am I falling in love with this man?* she wondered, suddenly dazed by the notion.

"The love of your life—the man of your dreams—will soon be available." He made a harsh sound. "The two of you can have that white picket fence after all. God knows you deserve it." His expression was so hard and tight his face appeared in danger of cracking. "I . . ." He stopped, clearly unable to continue.

And she realized what was happening.

"I want you to be happy. I wish you both the best," he said, and abruptly, he turned away.

For one moment, she stared at his rigid back, shocked. Leigh Anne was in a coma and the doctors said she would soon die. It was terrible, terrible news. They must both gather around Rick now. And she simply knew what she must do. "Calder, come back."

He stiffened impossibly more.

"Please."

He turned. Five or six feet separated them now—the gulf felt as vast as an ocean.

"I feel terrible for Leigh Anne, and even more so for Rick. But you are the man I am engaged to, and I have no intention of ending our engagement."

His face began to change. "What are you saying?" he asked in disbelief.

She dared to reach out and touch his stubbled jaw. "I am saying, my dear, that we have an understanding and a commitment, and I have no intention of so easily letting you off the hook." She trembled violently. She was finally falling in love with a man with the worst reputation, but then, others did not know him as she did. Her entire life she had known that one day she would fall in love with a man like her father, reliable, respectable, and a reformer. But she was becoming dangerously fond of a man known to be a ruthless businessman and an unrepentant womanizer. She was scared—she would be a fool not to be—but she was oddly thrilled. "We all fight the devil, Calder."

He stared, incredulous. Then, "I don't think you understand. You have always wanted Rick. In a few months, you can marry him, Francesca. Don't you see that?"

She was aghast and horrified. "On the altar of Leigh Anne's grave?" Her feelings for Rick remained strong—he was everything she admired in a man, and everything she had once believed was right for her—but she could never marry him that way. She would always care about him, far too much, she supposed, but in a way, she was glad—she wanted him in her life. But not the way Hart was suggesting. Never the way Hart was suggesting.

he took her hands. "What are you saying to me, Francesca?" he demanded harshly. "What, exactly, does this mean?"

She bit her lip, hard. Her mind sped, spun, gyrated, raced. There was only one coherent thought, one coherent feeling. But Julia's face appeared there in her mind's eye, and she could hear her mother as clearly as if she were in the room.

Do not tell him that you love him, Francesca. Do not say a word until after the wedding, if then!

"I am saying," she said softly, her heart beating with explosive force, "that everything has changed since we first met, Calder. Our friendship has become as important to me as it is to you. I also agree: we will have a very interesting union—one in which neither of us shall ever be bored." She smiled up at him. "But eloping is out of the question."

His grip tightened upon her hands. And Hart, for once, seemed speechless.

"Well?" She managed, smiling tremulously. "Do you not have something cynical and caustic to say?"

He pulled her close, tilted up her chin. "I do not want you to *ever* have regrets."

She hesitated. "I won't."

He studied her closely and slowly began to smile. "Actually, in that department, I might be able to help."

And she gave in to the giddy delight, the bubbling anticipation. "Help," she said. "Help all that you want." She moved into his welcoming arms.

His smile softened and he whispered, pulling her close, "You have become the sunshine in my life, Francesca."

She jerked back, meeting his gaze, stunned. *"What did you say?"*

He pulled her close again and feathered her mouth with soft, heated kisses.

She pushed him away. "Did you just say what I think you said?" she cried, breathless with surprise, and now, delight. In fact, she was thrilled!

He smiled tenderly at her. "I'm afraid I did—and that I may soon live to regret it."

She laughed. The sound was exultant even to her own ears. Calder Hart had said, quite off the cuff and from the heart, she was certain, that she had become the sunshine in his life. How romantic was that?

He reeled her closer. "Darling, do not gloat."

"Ha," she chuckled in glee. "Ha! I am the sunshine in your life!"

He rolled his navy blue and gold-flecked eyes. "Ladies do not gloat."

"This lady does," she said, seizing the lapels of his jacket. She was ready for his lovemaking now. "Kiss me, Hart. Kiss me while I am gloating."

He smiled and did just that.

*Experience love at its most dangerous,
and pleasure at its deadliest.*

The FRANCESCA CAHILL Novels

DEADLY LOVE

DEADLY PLEASURE

DEADLY AFFAIRS

DEADLY DESIRE

New York Times Bestselling Author
BRENDA JOYCE

Brenda Joyce has enthralled millions of readers with her *New York Times* bestselling novels. Now, join us in the next chapter of her unforgettable storytelling: the Francesca Cahill novels. Travel back in time to turn-of-the-century New York City, where a metropolis booming with life also masks a dark world of danger, death, and daring desire...

"Joyce excels at creating twists and turns in her characters' personal lives." — *Publishers Weekly*

"Joyce carefully crafted a wonderful mystery with twists and turns and red herrings galore, then added two marvelous, witty protagonists who will appeal to romance readers...Add to this a charming cast of secondary characters and a meticulously researched picture of society life in the early 1900s. I can hardly wait to see what Francesca and Rick will be up to next." — *Romantic Times*

"A delight!" — *Reader to Reader*

DEAD 2/02

THE
CHASE

—

BRENDA JOYCE

NEW YORK TIMES BESTSELLING AUTHOR

CLAIRE HAYDEN has no idea that her world is about to be shattered: at the conclusion of her husband's fortieth birthday party, he is found murdered, his throat cut with a WWII thumb knife. He has no enemies, no one seeking revenge, no one who would want him dead. But the mysterious Ian Marshall, an acquaintance of her husband's, seems to know something. Because someone has been killing this way for decades. Someone whose crimes go back to WWII. Someone who has been a hunter . . . and the hunted. As Claire and Ian team up to find the killer, they can no longer deny the powerful feelings they have for one another. Then Ian makes a shocking revelation: the murderer may be someone close to her . . .

"Joyce excels at creating twists and turns in her characters' personal lives."
—*Publishers Weekly*

ON SALE JULY 2002
FROM ST. MARTIN'S PRESS

CHASE 10/01